WINTER WORK

DAN FESPERMAN, a former reporter for the *Baltimore Sun*, is an award-winning author whose thriller novels have won the John Creasey and the Ian Fleming Steel Daggers as well as the Hammett Prize. His plots were inspired by his own international assignments in Germany, Bosnia, Afghanistan, Pakistan and the Middle East. He is a graduate of the University of North Carolina and lives in Baltimore, Maryland with his wife and their two children.

DAN FESPERMAN

WINTER WORK

HEAD
of ZEUS

An Aries Book

First published in the UK in 2022 by Head of Zeus Ltd,
part of Bloomsbury Publishing Plc

9 7 5 3 1 2 4 6 8

A CIP catalogue record for this book is available from the British Library.

ISBN (HB): 9781804540558
ISBN (XTPB): 9781804540565
ISBN (E): 9781804540541

Typeset by Scribe,
Philadelphia, Pennsylvania

Printed and bound in Great Britain by
CPI Group (UK) Ltd, Croydon, CR0 4YY

Head of Zeus Ltd
5–8 Hardwick St
First Floor East
London EC1R 4RG
WWW.HEADOFZEUS.COM

WINTER WORK

1

In winter, the forest bares its secrets. Hill and vale are revealed through disrobing trees. Mud and bone arise from dying weeds. Woodpeckers, taking notice, pry deeper on leafless limbs and rotting logs. Their drumbeat goes out like a warning.

Emil Grimm, out for a morning walk, exulted in all of it. Being a German of a certain age, he loved getting into the woods, and as a professional keeper of secrets he was impressed by any display of full disclosure.

The trouble was that this year's unveiling hadn't confined itself to the trees. His employer—indeed, his country—was being stripped as bare of its cloaking as the oaks and beeches. All because a concrete wall in Berlin had been knocked to the ground a few months earlier, a shocking act of defiance that had set people loose in ways forbidden for nearly thirty years.

Freedom of movement was fine by Emil. Long overdue, in fact. But the attendant bustle and bother were letting light and air into places not built to withstand scrutiny. Inquisitive people had begun unlocking cabinets and closets that, for good reason, had long remained undisturbed.

Soon enough, Emil, too, would be flushed from cover. In a few weeks he would receive his last paycheck from the HVA, the foreign intelligence service of the Ministry of State Security, or Stasi, as everyone now seemed to be calling it. Weeks earlier, the ministry's headquarters complex—five city blocks of hulking gray buildings—had been emptied of its seven thousand employees, Emil among them. He wasn't even allowed back in to clean out his desk.

Protesters had already ransacked one building, tossing documents out the window like ticker tape for a capitalist parade until police finally intervened. Foreign intelligence services, friendly and hostile, were eagerly lining up for a look at the leftovers. Some were offering money for the slightest glimpse.

Just thinking about it made Emil queasy. Certain secrets had always been toxic in the German Democratic Republic. Turn them loose now, with the two Germanies preparing to reunite, and there was no telling what might climb off the pages. Figuratively speaking, a plague was at hand, with no cure available. Although Emil was working on that.

He had other worries, too. In the West German capital of Bonn there was talk of prosecuting the East German spymasters who had outwitted them for years. Treason, they were calling it, as if East Germany had never existed as a separate nation. Emil's name was said to be high on the list of targets, and at the age of fifty-seven prison was an especially daunting prospect. As borders were opening for his countrymen, his were closing. Should he flee? Hire a lawyer? Go into hiding?

In the meantime, he had taken refuge with his wife at their woodland dacha north of Berlin, near the rural village of Prenden, where an hour ago he had set out on his favorite trail. It looped uphill along a mossy path before descending through beeches to a loamy circuit of a small, pretty lake, the Bauersee. His plan was the same as on every other morning: Clear his head by listening to the birds as they reported in from their dawn patrols; keep an eye out for fox, deer, and boar. Breathe deeply, stretch his legs, find out what had happened overnight. Nature was the only realm still offering free rein to his curiosity.

But as Emil began his descent he realized that even this frontier was now at risk of closure. The voices were the first sign—a grim mutter of officious males, punctuated by bursts of static from a walkie-talkie. He paused on the hillside to listen, breath misting, nose running, right knee aching from an old injury best left unexplained.

Peering through the branches toward the lakeshore, forty yards downhill, he saw a cordon of yellow plastic tape. Near it were three men in dark greatcoats—no, four—moving to and fro like foraging ravens. The overcast lighting of a forty-watt sun turned them into silhouettes, but the gloomiest sight was the body that lay among them at the water's edge, a man's, sprawled facedown across tree roots glassy with ice.

Beside the body was a bright orange watch cap. Emil knew this cap, and knew its owner. The man's name rose to his lips on a gush of nausea and then died before he could utter it. He swallowed with difficulty, tasting bile, and tried to regain control of his emotions. Perhaps the hat belonged to someone else—a thread of hope that began to unravel the moment he grasped it.

He held still, hoping no one had seen him. Then he sighed, because they had. One of the four men—the one in charge, a tall fellow in his early forties—began tramping up the hill toward him.

"Grimm. I was thinking you might turn up."

"How did you know that was even possible?"

Dieter Krauss shrugged, a gesture freighted with meaning: *We are state security and so are you, so of course we are familiar with your usual movements.*

"Your dacha is near here, yes? Not far from Wolf's?"

"Near enough, but Wolf is gone."

"So I've heard."

Markus Wolf, they meant—Emil's former boss, now retired. Wolf's reputation as the Stasi's most renowned spymaster ranked him higher on the Bonn hit list than Emil, so he had recently fled to Moscow. From Emil's vantage point you could see the chimney of Wolf's A-frame poking just above the treetops. There had been no smoke from it for weeks. Maybe he was gone for good.

"What have you found down there? What's happened?"

"Come see."

Krauss led him down the path as the three other men stepped aside to reveal more of the scene. The victim had tousled silver hair. He wore loden wool pants and one of those British waxed cotton jackets with a corduroy collar. Nearby, tossed aside with the orange cap, was an old-fashioned hiking cane covered with tin badges of all the places its owner had been. For Emil there was no longer any doubt.

Krauss halted on the hillside and spoke again.

"I regret to say that we believe it is your neighbor and colleague, Lothar Fischer. You will assist us in making a positive ID."

Emil knew it would be best to react with shock and sorrow, and nothing more. But by pausing to collect himself he squandered the opportunity, so he simply nodded, poker-faced.

"I'll do what I can."

Krauss held out a hand to help steady him on the muddy path. Emil waved away the gesture and surged forward as Krauss fell into step behind him.

"I've always thought it was odd the way so many of you HVA people ended up here in Prenden."

"Odd? You talk like we're a coven of witches. We just happened to work together."

But Krauss wasn't the first person to have noted the unlikely concentration of spies in this patch of woods, twenty-five miles north of central Berlin. As with Wolf and Fischer, Emil's main residence was an apartment in the city, even though he hadn't been there in weeks. There was an HVA safe house nearby as well—roomy and well furnished, the nicest dwelling on the lake if you didn't mind the concealed microphones and surveillance cameras.

"Who found him? And why did they call you first?"

Krauss, ignoring the questions, flipped open a notebook and began scribbling. Emil stooped beneath the tape without asking permission and moved closer to the body. Where was Lothar's dog? The man almost never went walking without his shepherd, Gretel. Unless, of course, he had gone out on a woodland chore that even an animal couldn't be trusted to witness.

Lothar's hair was matted with blood around a black hole near his right temple. His right arm was outstretched with a gun loosely in hand, the forefinger poking through the trigger guard. It was a Makarov, or Pistol-M, the compact service weapon they'd all been issued on their first day as Stasi officers. A suppressor was screwed onto the end of the barrel.

"Well?" Krauss sounded impatient.

"It's him. It's Lothar. A suicide?"

"Is that what you think?"

Emil shrugged. Two other high-ranking members of the Stasi had killed themselves in the past month. Witnessing the collapse of everything you've devoted your life to could have that effect. Even Markus Wolf's son-in-law had tried to take his own life, shortly after turning down a West German offer of half a million deutschmarks for telling them everything he knew.

"Anything's possible, I suppose."

"That's one way of avoiding an answer."

Krauss smirked. Maybe he had picked up on the same detail Emil had already noticed, although Emil doubted it. More likely was that Krauss was trying to project an air of threat, of superiority. Emil outranked him, a colonel to his major, but Krauss's Stasi unit, the Spezialkommission, had long ago carved out a powerful role in all investigations involving "political sensitivity," and he had never hesitated to press this advantage. But now that the entire ministry was going out of business, why was Krauss even here?

Emil scanned the ground around the body, trying to make sense of all the footprints. Krauss's men had made quite a mess. Emil wasn't helping either, he supposed. He turned and carefully made his way back beneath the tape.

"Have you determined which direction Lothar was coming from?"

Krauss eyed him carefully, as if deciding whether Emil merited an answer. He nodded to one of his men, who supplied it.

"That way, from up there. That's what we're putting in our report."

The man pointed toward a hillside path diagonal to the one Emil had just descended. Emil knew where it led. Now he had a pretty good idea of why Gretel wasn't here.

"Is that his usual walking route?" Krauss asked.

"Lothar was not a man of rigid habits."

"No? Hardly the impression I had. Well, you can come away from there now. My men have work to do. Schalk! Check the coat pockets."

The fellow who had pointed uphill moved back inside the tape and stooped toward the body. He reached into a pocket of Lothar's jacket and withdrew a small plastic pouch.

"Here's something, sir!"

"A bag of dog treats," Emil said. "Yes, a major breakthrough."

Krauss frowned in irritation.

"Keep looking. Check the lining!"

They were interrupted by the sound of voices from the other end of the lake. Three men were approaching. Two wore the peaked caps and belted, gray-green overcoats of the Volkspolizei—cops, not secret police, the fellows who probably should've handled this matter from the beginning. Leading them was a young plainclothesman, late twenties, with windblown hair. Emil recognized him as Lieutenant Marius Dorn, a detective inspector from the district headquarters in Bernau. They had met a few years earlier through another, lesser matter.

"Gentlemen," Dorn called out. "We meet again. Hopefully this time our affairs will end in better order."

Emil lowered his voice and turned to Krauss.

"You two have also worked together before?"

"That's one way of putting it. I'll set this right."

Dorn preempted him with a shout.

"You will clear your men from the premises, Major Krauss. This is our case now."

Krauss stepped up the path to block his way.

"You don't seem to understand, Herr Dorn."

"*Lieutenant* Dorn."

"The victim is a high-ranking officer of the HVA. I am countermanding your jurisdiction for reasons of national security."

"The only relevant security issue is where you'll be working a month from now. A major issue for you, certainly, but quite private in nature, yes? Whereas my men and I will be keeping our jobs, maybe even long enough to close this matter. Clear your people from the perimeter."

Krauss drew up his chest. He looked ready to throw a punch. Then some of the air began to squeeze out of him as the reality of Dorn's words sank in.

Emil could barely suppress a smile.

The standoff might have lasted longer if Emil hadn't decided to move things along. He lifted the yellow tape and motioned for Krauss's men to leave. They glanced at one other and then at Krauss, who nodded forlornly.

Emil turned toward Dorn and bowed like a maître d'.

"Your case, Lieutenant."

Krauss belatedly fired back.

"We'll see if you're still smiling when I've finished interrogating you, Grimm."

"Colonel Grimm will answer my questions first, Major Krauss. I'll need to question you as well, of course, since you seem to have been among the first on the scene."

"Don't be an ass!"

"Oh, I plan to be the biggest possible ass. Or a major pain in yours, anyway. You and your men will wait until we've processed the scene. You will then accompany me to headquarters."

But Dorn's new authority had its limits. Krauss whistled, and his men fell into step behind him as he shouldered past the policemen and set off down the path. Dorn, trying to save face, called out after them.

"I will meet you in Bernau."

Krauss answered over his shoulder without breaking stride.

"If you wish to see me, come to my office on Normanenstrasse."

It would have been a fine parting shot if all of them hadn't known the building was padlocked, which raised the question as to where Krauss and his men had come from to begin with. Who had summoned them, and where were they going now? Emil marveled at the strangeness of it all. Not even as a young boy during the horrible years of the war and its bleak aftermath had he ever felt as disoriented as he had in these past few months. Up was down, down was up, and the future was a ledge staring off into fog.

Then he glanced again at poor Lothar, and his sense of baffled wonder gave way to despair. So many years of working together, of sharing drinks and meals, here and in Berlin. Lothar had never exactly been a close friend, but professionally they had trusted each other with their deepest secrets, right to the end. And it was their final collaboration that now gave Emil his greatest cause for worry. Perhaps that, too, was dead.

Dorn's voice jolted him from his reverie.

"What do you know about this, Colonel Grimm? How long have you been here?"

Emil bristled at the peremptory tone. Four months ago, he might have dismissed the question with a haughty wave and let his rank do the talking. But given the evolving dynamics of power, maybe this was an opportune moment to curry favor with the young policeman. Krauss had burned his bridge, Emil would build one.

"As you correctly observed, Lieutenant, Krauss and his men must have been among the first on the scene. Then I came along. I was out for a walk. I'm happy to help you any way I can."

Dorn smiled in gratitude, or maybe relief. One of his men began snapping photos. The other, a sergeant, paced the perimeter while scanning the ground, notebook in hand.

"Should we put up our own tape?" the sergeant asked.

"Theirs will do."

"But, sir, it's not set at the regulation distance from the body, and if—"

"*Theirs* will do," Dorn repeated.

Emil turned aside to hide a smile. Germans and their precious *Ordnung*.

Dorn again addressed Emil.

"Is it true what Krauss said, that the victim is a ranking officer of the Stasi?"

"Yes. Lothar Fischer, a colonel from the HVA. He was a friend. His dacha is not far from here."

Dorn couldn't hide his surprise. Nor could his men, who paused to exchange glances. The one with the camera rose up on his toes as if he'd suddenly realized he was on poisoned ground. Emil wondered how many years it would take before a mention of the Stasi no longer increased pulse rates and produced feelings of dread.

"Perhaps it would be more convenient if you and I continued our conversation at your dacha."

Certainly more convenient for you, Emil thought. *You'll be able to snoop around my house without an invitation or a written order.* But to refuse him would only arouse suspicion.

"As you wish. But there's something that you and your men should know first."

"Yes?"

The other policemen paused, attentive. Obsolete or not, a colonel was still a colonel. Emil nodded toward the corpse.

"Lothar was left-handed."

All three policemen looked down at the gun in his right hand. The sergeant began writing in his notebook at a furious pace.

"Does Major Krauss know that?"

"Good question. You should ask him before he has a chance to find out on his own."

Emil stepped past Dorn as casually as he could manage to head uphill. Dorn, momentarily distracted, belatedly set off after him.

Emil's muscles and his bad knee needed a stretch after all of the standing around, and he eased into a comfortable stride as he ascended. But the damp morning air felt different now, carrying a hint of something new—a cozy scent of woodsmoke.

He paused and glanced toward the rooftops peeking above the trees. Smoke was now rising from Markus Wolf's chimney.

Sometime during the night, or perhaps earlier that morning, Emil's enigmatic old boss had returned from Moscow.

2

Berlin was not her city, so Claire Saylor moved with extra caution—alert to surveillance, listening for any false note in the music of the streets. Just because the Cold War was suddenly over in this part of the world didn't mean there weren't still enemies to worry about. Or even friends.

Yet to anyone watching from, say, a café table or a shop window, Claire looked as if she absolutely belonged on this gray February evening. Her stride was easy, her features calm. Her unremarkable wardrobe—tapered cotton blouse, trim wool slacks, dun overcoat, and shoes so sensible they made her frown—might have come from the closet of a midthirties office worker in Steglitz. She spoke the language.

After fifteen years as a spy, going native on short notice was all in a day's work. So was keeping her feelings under wraps, because at the moment she had good reason to be on edge.

Two days earlier she'd been summoned here from Paris along with a dozen other colleagues from across Europe: reinforcements in a CIA mop-up action against their recently defeated adversaries in the Stasi. Their weapons of choice? Pay phones. Like scam salesmen in a Florida boiler room, they had begun dialing up the homes of Stasi foreign intelligence officers to make a hot new pitch: Trade in your secrets for a few bucks and a safe place to land. Cash and carry for the minions, but a new identity and maybe even a California condo for the more exalted. Act now to put those prosecution worries and gloomy German winters behind you forever. But hurry, offer expires soon! Operators are standing by!

Okay, so maybe it wasn't quite that crass, but it was close, and by the end of her first day of cold calling Claire was almost feeling sorry for them as one after another of her targets either slammed down the phone or lashed back with a lecture.

You Americans always think everyone's for sale. Our life's work for the price of a washing machine? Fuck off!

Then, earlier today, just before lunch, West Berlin base chief Bill Gentry had pulled her aside to launch her in a different direction, one with bigger stakes, and starring a willing participant from the other side. The sudden change of mission was flattering, but its details—or lack of them—immediately made her wary. That's when Claire decided it was time for a little field research, even if it ran afoul of office rules.

So now, instead of resting in her hotel room before dinner as Gentry believed she was doing, Claire was out on the streets, dodging ghosts through the shadows of spying's most storied theme park as she made her way to an unauthorized meeting with an off-limits source. And when a bicycle courier swerved a little too closely on her left, and then a fellow up ahead knelt to tie his shoes, she braced for evasive action even as she strolled onward without a hitch.

The bicyclist wobbled, found his line, and pedaled away. The kneeling man rose and rounded the corner. To her rear, nothing. All clear, then, with only a block to go. Claire checked her watch. Six minutes early. Ample time for a deep breath and, then, a brief reflection on her upcoming meetup.

The contact was Clark Baucom. Claire had last seen him ages ago on her home ground of Paris, when they had teamed up to help a colleague on the run, a mutual friend named Helen. Baucom, recently retired, was an old hand of the old school, which made him a trove of knowledge with regard to Eastern Europe's murkiest corners. He had spent years on hostile ground, sometimes going months without letting his guard down. Lately, or so she'd heard, he had developed a tendency to drink too much and tell too many stories, although he was careful to play the raconteur only among former colleagues.

Claire's recollection of their first meeting was of an easy rapport that had served them well. Not surprising, given their similar outlooks. Both were meticulous about tradecraft, yet open to improvisation when circumstances allowed, and they expected no less from colleagues.

Baucom had cut his teeth as a spy in the late '40s, when freewheeling excess came with the territory. Claire, hired in the '70s, had won her freedom of action partly by default. Station chiefs unaccustomed to supervising women had tended to overlook her, which gave her leeway to expand smaller roles into bigger ones—at least until someone noticed. Whenever an op confined her to the dark, she sought her own path toward the light. It kept the job interesting even as it tended to thwart professional advancement. And that's what she was doing now by meeting Baucom—seeking knowledge above her clearance and her pay grade.

Baucom lived in Charlottenburg, one of the few West Berlin neighborhoods that still looked a lot like it had before American bombers and Soviet artillery pounded the city to rubble in the Second World War. He had a grand old apartment with high ceilings, tall windows, and built-in bookcases, up on the third floor of a brownstone with a marble foyer. Helen had once described it to her, and Claire was hoping he would invite her upstairs to see it.

Streetlamps flickered to life as she made her way up the cobbled walkway, lending a sepia wash to the scene, like in a tintype of Old Berlin. She could have pinpointed her location by smell alone—the bracing *Berliner Luft*, with its wintry bite of coal smoke, the raw dampness that stole into your clothes like a pickpocket.

She reached the building. Next to the massive oak doorway was a panel with six buttons, one for each floor. She glanced up at the windows. There was no flick of the curtains—Baucom would never be so obvious—but when she pressed the buzzer he answered right away.

"Ja?"

Even through the static of the squawk box she recognized the rumbling baritone.

"It's me."

A pause, followed by the hiss of a deep exhalation.

"Zwiebelfisch. Ten minutes."

"Onion fish?" If this was code, she didn't know it.

"It's a bar. Savignyplatz."

So much for the idea of being invited up. She supposed that with no office anymore he had become even more protective of his lair. Maybe he regretted having invited her at all.

"Okay. See you there."

Zwiebelfisch turned out to be one of those joints that looked like it had been around forever, but without seeming tired or run-down. Plate glass windows threw a welcoming glow onto empty trestle tables on the chilly sidewalk. Above the doorway was an inscription in Latin from Dante, *Lasciate ogni speranza voi ch'entrate*. Abandon hope, all ye who enter. An in-joke for regulars, no doubt, because the place instantly felt like a cheerful getaway, somewhere you'd be allowed to get comfortable for a few hours without having to drink yourself into a stupor. The shallow main room had a cozy bar along the opposite side. Off to the left was a second room with more tables, most of them small. The walls were covered by old posters and moody black-and-white photos.

Helen had once told her about a bar where she and Baucom used to meet, long ago, but that place had sounded darker, mustier, and it supposedly had an inscrutable old proprietor who flipped a towel over his shoulder as he descended into the cellar for rare and wondrous vintages. The barman here was young, no towel, but seemed affable enough. She nodded to him and headed for the far room, where she took a table in the most remote corner, but with a seat facing the windows. All the rest of the early arrivals were in the other room, keeping their voices down. That was one of the things Claire liked best about Berliners. They knew how to keep quiet.

A waiter approached, a wiry man in his twenties with a wry expression that said he knew she was a first-timer. The others were drinking beer, so she ordered one, and he soon returned with a foamy glass of Schultheiss.

When half of it was gone, she began to wonder if Baucom had stood her up, even though that had never been his style. When only foam remained, she began to fear for his safety.

3

It was now thirty-four minutes past their scheduled rendezvous.

Claire tried to be rational about it. Maybe in retirement Baucom had grown timid, and had concluded he'd be putting his pension at risk. It happened, even to the boldest of old field men. She knew about the forms they made you sign on your way out the door, the promises they extracted, especially when you were planning on staying overseas. A memoir? Don't even think about it, unless you had the best of connections and were prepared for page after page of redactions. She had contacted him by phone, which in retrospect felt careless.

But there were other, more disturbing possibilities. Perhaps someone had waylaid him, or even bundled him into a van, and by now he was either answering questions in a windowless room or knocked cold on a sidewalk, with blood coming out his ears.

She decided to give it another fifteen minutes before setting off to look for him, by retracing her steps to his apartment.

Then she looked out the window and there he was, staring back with an expression of frank curiosity, like she was an oddity in a museum. Jarring, but Claire checked herself from flinching. His eyes narrowed, like he was deciding whether to come in. Maybe it was the lighting from the streetlamp, but the years hadn't been kind to him. More bulk in the middle, a greater sag to the jowls. Creases around his eyes looked careworn, and his color was off.

Claire tried out a smile and gestured toward the empty chair. Baucom's face lit up with a grin, and ten years fell away. He set out for the door with a stride that was surprisingly brisk, although by the time he got to the table he was out of breath and reaching for his cigarettes. Gitanes, she noticed, then remembered they had always been his brand. He was a classic long-term expat, adopting European clothes and customs, yet, in his case, with a leathery face as American as a baseball glove.

"I was beginning to think you were a lost cause."

"I took a rather roundabout way."

"Do you think that was necessary?"

"Hard to say. Maybe that depends on why you're in town and what you want to know. And, well . . ." He shrugged and glanced toward the window.

"What?"

"Little things, the past week or so. Probably nothing. Maybe I'm just out of practice."

Baucom rested his cigarette on an ashtray. The waiter brought a beer without taking an order. Baucom nodded in appreciation, took a long, deep swallow, then licked the foam from his lips and settled into his chair.

"This isn't where you used to bring her, is it?"

"Who?"

"Oh, c'mon. You know who I mean."

He dipped his head as if to hide a blush.

"She probably told you about Lehmann's."

"That's the name. With some sort of wonderful cognac?"

He smiled again, and this time his eyes wandered off to a distant locale, far beyond Claire's reach.

"That stuff was older than she was. But not older than me, of course."

The age difference had been a subject of Agency gossip, although Claire had never faulted Helen for it. Then, as now, Baucom projected a raffish charm, a man with valuable lore at his disposal, the very reason she'd sought him out. As if to drive home the point, he immediately offered a story.

"I met Lehmann in the winter of '46. Coldest on record. Not enough grub to even keep the dogs fed. Any friend you made then tended to be forever. Gone now. So is his bar. They turned it into a *Friseur*, a place with pink walls where the *Hausfrauen* sit in their curlers. Wish he could have been around to see all the fun last November. He would have picked up a sledgehammer and joined in."

"Must have been pretty great for you as well."

Baucom shrugged.

"It's always nice to win, even by default. So, yeah, I went down there like everybody else, hugging and cheering and popping corks while we watched the Trabis roll through the breach. But now the Trabis are still here, blowing all that bilge out their tailpipes while the *Ossis* squander the last of their 'welcome money' on currywurst and refrigerators. And what I'm starting to realize is that I kind of *liked* being stranded on a free capitalist island in the middle of their goddamn Red Sea. Because now the developers and architects have come ashore, and next it'll be that whole goddamn crowd of paper pushers from Bonn. By the time they're done fucking up the place I won't be able to afford the rent. Or do I sound ungrateful?"

"You sound like an old spy who liked feeling needed."

"Yeah, that too. Not that we ever did anything in this city but get our asses kicked. Well, mostly."

He looked Claire in the eye, and for a second she thought he was about to get down to business. Then he clasped his hands on the table and leaned a little closer.

"Are you ever in touch with her?"

"Now and then. Christmas cards, mostly. Some years she's newsy, some she's not. She's married."

"Hardly unexpected." He gazed at his beer glass and steepled his fingers.

"A farmer's wife."

His hands unclasped. He picked up his cigarette and erupted with a smoky laugh. "Our Helen? Stranded in a goddamn cow pasture?"

"I couldn't believe it, either. Chickens, crops, a barn."

"Children?"

"One. And she was pregnant at Christmas, so by now there may already be another one. I forget the due date."

"I don't suppose she's ever, well . . ."

"Asked about you?"

He nodded.

"Afraid not."

"Just as well."

"For both of you, probably."

He inhaled deeply from his cigarette, then swallowed more beer as he scanned the customers in the other room. She could sense him shifting back into an operational posture, a heightened sense of his surroundings. Old habits, never far from reach.

"Obviously you didn't seek me out to talk about the good old days."

"Not those good old days, anyway. I need advice. On personnel."

"Ours or theirs?"

"Both."

He looked around again, fiddled with his lighter.

"Are you part of this goddamn phone bank Diggs and Gentry have put together?"

"So you know about that?"

He chuckled, venting more smoke.

"It's the biggest running gag in town. In our circles, anyway. You know how all this got started, don't you?"

"Enlighten me."

"Middle of January, the night the protesters broke into Stasi head-quarters. You catch any of that on the tube?"

"Who didn't?"

"Our president did, that's for sure. And when the longhairs started tossing boxes out the window, everything falling to the ground like candy from a fucking piñata, Bush turned to his aides and said, 'I hope we're getting some of that.' Completely offhand, but, hey, when the president's your former director . . ."

"So people jumped."

"Like lemmings from a cliff. First thing they did was put Lindsey Ward on a plane to Berlin. Now there's a woman on her way up in a hurry, so she was the perfect choice to come light a fire under their slack asses. By noon the next day she's sitting in a bad Italian restaurant on Mexikoplatz with Diggs and Gentry, asking why their people weren't out on the cobbles, scooping up the goodies. A month later and here you are, part of the big push, even though we're still playing catch-up. So who's running this shit show?"

"Diggs. In name, at least, although Gentry seems to give most of the orders."

Lester Diggs ran the Agency's small station in East Berlin, and still reported to a different boss than his West Berlin counterpart, Bill Gentry. Both of their bosses reported to Lindsey Ward, the new deputy director for operations.

"From everything I've heard, Diggs still can't get used to the idea that the game is over, and that he's suddenly free to move around as he chooses," Baucom said, shaking his head. "For years the poor bastard couldn't even walk down to the corner *Tante-Emma-Laden* to buy his milk without the Stasi snapping his picture. Every agent he recruited was either blown or turned out to be working for the bad guys. You know what he told Lindsey Ward while they were twirling their noodles?"

Claire shook her head. She knew better than to interrupt when Baucom was on a roll.

"That it was still too dangerous to make a move. Poke your head above the trench, he said, and they just might blow it off. Hell, no one is even *in* their trenches anymore, much less armed and dangerous."

"Then why are you still being so careful?"

"Because our other old pals from the KGB are still in business, of course. Glasnost or not, their station down in Karlshorst is business as usual."

"Do you think the Stasi's not even listening to the phones anymore?"

"Even if they are, who cares? Now, the KGB, that's another matter. They're as preoccupied as we are with trying to scoop up the loose marbles rolling out of Normanenstrasse. Too worried some of them might have their fingerprints. Reach for the same marble and maybe they'll step on your fingers. Or chop 'em off."

"I knew there was a good reason I wanted to see you."

Baucom shrugged.

"I haven't told you anything you couldn't pick up around the office."

"Not yet, maybe. We'll get there in a second." Baucom raised an eyebrow. "If it makes you feel any better, Diggs made an executive decision a couple days ago to ditch the phone calls. From now on it's going to be strictly a door-to-door operation."

Baucom's mouth dropped open. Then he laughed loudly enough to draw a disapproving stare from a young man in the next room, who shook open the pages of his newspaper as if to block any further intrusion.

"Like the goddamn Fuller Brush man? Wonderful. Will you be carrying sample kits? Maybe some greenbacks from the petty cash fund to show 'em what's waiting for every lucky winner behind door number three?"

"I agree. It's clumsy, all of it. But how would you do it?"

His eyes narrowed in thought.

"I'd use cutouts, not our own people. And I'd approach their people on the fly while they're out and about—shopping at the market or walking their dogs. Use a little goddamn discretion. Slip them a message in a park, or on a crowded street, then clear the hell out of there to wait for a response."

"And if they're willing to bite, how are they supposed to get back in touch?"

"By fax. We'd put a number in the message."

"*Fax?*"

"The East Germans and Russians never figured out how to intercept those. Or not in any way that they could make heads or tails of the signal."

"You sound like you're speaking from experience."

He shrugged.

"Anybody operational in Berlin base has a fax machine at home. Or used to."

"Do they take it away when you retire?"

"Not if you bought it with your own money, and used a private number."

"Was this an authorized means of communication?"

"No comment."

She smiled appreciatively and nodded.

"If I was still going to be part of this sideshow, I'd be tempted to ask for your fax number."

"Wait. You're *off* this job now?"

"Off the sales force, anyway, as of noon today. Gentry put me on another piece of it. He claims it's mine and mine alone."

"I see."

Baucom slid his chair a little closer and took another drag from his cigarette. Claire glanced toward the other room. The fellow who'd looked over was still walled off behind his paper. The waiter was gone.

"A hot lead, he called it. A single source, from high in the food chain."

"HVA?"

"Yes."

"Surprised we even had his phone number."

"We didn't. Or not at first. Apparently, *he* reached out to us."

"I hope he's offering more than just his memories."

"Meaning what? Documents?"

"It's the most valuable item they still have, and apparently even those are disappearing fast. They've been running shredders nonstop for so many hours that they've burned out every machine. Take a nice new model over there and you could probably sell it for a bundle. The rest of the records they're either burning or shipping off to Moscow. Unless this fellow says otherwise."

"All that Gentry will say is that it's bigger than anything else we've got going. There's an asset, and I've been assigned to handle him."

She expected Baucom to be impressed. Instead he frowned.

"What? You look skeptical."

"The right name might bring me around. But I suppose this is where you tell me it's beyond my clearance."

"I might've, except I don't know yet, either."

"Well, how high in the food chain, then? Top ten? Top twenty?"

"A colonel. That's all I know."

Baucom sat up straighter. He swallowed more beer as he thought it over.

"That probably means at least top ten. What's he asking for?"

"Gentry says his biggest concern is safe harbor."

"Makes sense. If the West Germans prosecute, anyone at that rank is bound to be vulnerable, and most of his colleagues would rather see him in the grave than in the dock, where he might implicate all of them. But, at the risk of being rude, there's one thing I don't get."

"Why me?"

"Exactly. Nothing personal, but . . ."

"No. I agree. I don't know the territory, the players, or much of anything else about the way business is done here."

"Did you ask Gentry that question?"

"A fresh face, he said. He told me the asset wants to deal with someone who won't be easily recognized."

Baucom frowned.

"Depends on who they pair you with from Berlin base, I guess."

"No one. I'm on my own. The fewer moving parts, the better, Gentry says."

Baucom's frown deepened. He wiped away a ring of condensation.

"If I'm the asset—and I'm not, although I *am* a careful old bastard who grew up playing by the same set of rules—then I'd insist on someone who, if need be, could walk every street and alley on his side of the fence in complete darkness, and still find his way home. And it wouldn't be a woman, no offense."

"None taken, but why?"

"Because that's how those bastards have always operated. They love honey traps and Romeos and using women in all the wrong ways as much as any intelligence service, and they've placed a few of them in the West. But in terms of advancement and trust and sensitive matters of their own survival? No girls allowed. It's just not in their DNA. And that's almost certainly how this guy is wired. He'd also want his contact to come equipped with plenty of support. Or I would, anyway. You said he reached out first? Who was his initial contact?"

"Gentry didn't say, and I asked him three different ways. Nothing."

Baucom shook his head.

"Christ almighty, Claire. What *have* they told you?"

"Only that the whole thing goes operational tomorrow. With a meetup, a *Treff*, sometime in the afternoon or evening. All I have is an address, at some greasy spoon over on their side. They'll brief me on the rest tomorrow morning."

"So this meetup, is it to give him a look at you, or for him to proffer a sample of the goods?"

"That's up to him. All we know is that someone's supposed to come to my table, take a seat, and ask if I think Andreas Thom is good enough to make it with Bayer Leverkusen."

"East Germany's best footballer. The first one to sign a contract with the West German Bundesliga."

"I know. I looked it up. I'm supposed to answer, 'He can't miss.'"

"And after that?"

"I've been instructed to follow his lead. Or the lead of whoever he sends."

"Who's your backup?"

"None. Solo, coming and going. No spotters, either, far as I know. And no route security."

"Is there an emergency signal? An extraction plan? I mean, I know Gentry wants to move as quickly as possible, but still."

"He says things are fast and loose enough now that I won't need any of that."

"Christ on a donkey. He's probably right, but he's paid to think like NASA. On something this big you'd better have backups for your backups. All I can figure is that you'll have them, but he's not telling you who they are, or where they'll be deployed. Which, to me, is a dumb fucking way to run an op, but maybe that's the style now."

"I doubt that's the case. Gentry seems to mean what he's saying."

Baucom drained the last of his beer. Claire had nothing to add, because he was echoing her own doubts and anxieties.

"Well, I hate to say this, kiddo, but if I didn't know any better, I'd suspect that someone was, well . . ."

"Setting me up to fail?"

He frowned and waggled his right hand. "That's one possibility. Or setting up the asset to fail, which is just as bad. It could also mean they don't want to look overeager. Maybe this is our way of telling him there are other offers on the table. Or, hell, maybe it's like Gentry says, that this is the way the asset wants it. Could be any of those."

"But if it's one of the former, why?"

He pondered that a moment, then shook his head.

"Sorry. I've still got a few friends inside, but for what you need? I'm probably wasting your time."

He sagged in his chair. For all his supposed reluctance to get involved, it was clear that he had hoped to be more useful.

But Claire still had a surprise for him.

"Hold that apology. There's another favor I need, and this one's operational."

"Operational?"

Baucom perked up like a hungry old dog that has just heard the rustle of a food bag. By the time she was finished telling him, he again looked ten years younger.

4

It was only a five-minute walk from the crime scene to Emil's dacha, if you stayed along the lakeshore before cutting uphill to his back gate. But Lieutenant Dorn didn't know that, so Emil took the long way instead, circling uphill to a gravel road that ran along a ridge to his front gate. He needed extra time to think about what to say—about Lothar, their relationship, the man's recent movements. He also wanted to impart some information about Krauss without seeming too eager or obvious. And, frankly, he needed a few moments to deal with his grief, and an extra five minutes of brisk walking proved to be just the tonic.

"Here we are," he said, stepping forward to unlatch the gate.

Surrounding the small wooded lot was a high fence with an unsightly coil of barbed wire along the top. Dorn stared in apparent surprise.

"That's not very neighborly."

"It was the security committee's doing, after Wolf built his place. They didn't want to make it easy for some foreign invader to scoop up all three of us in one fell swoop."

"With Lothar Fischer being the third?"

Emil nodded.

"And that big birdhouse, looking down at us from that post over there. A surveillance camera?"

"They said it was necessary for my security, although an enterprising wren didn't think so. She built a nest last spring that blocked the lens for two months. I wouldn't let anyone clear it away until the fledglings were gone. I'll confess, it was liberating to not have them know who was visiting my house all that time."

"So someone besides you also received the signal?"

"That's how all of those cameras work."

"Interesting. Even the Stasi has to hide from the Stasi."

"Had to, Lieutenant. *Had* to."

A mere four months ago they wouldn't have had this conversation, or not without each of them worrying that the other might report it. Dorn was silent a few seconds, as if still adjusting to these new freedoms. And even they didn't come without risks, Emil supposed, or else why would Lothar Fischer be lying dead at the bottom of the hill?

The path to the door was covered by wet leaves. Emil really needed to do some weeding and raking. He'd become such a slacker. He wondered if he'd have the energy to plant vegetables this May. Maybe instead he'd still be looking for a job. He should have already started some seedlings indoors.

The scent of smoke from Wolf's A-frame was even stronger now. Should he mention that to Dorn, or let the cop figure it out for himself? Maybe it was only Wolf's wife, Andrea, who had come back, or the ill-fated son-in-law, recovering from his breakdown. There were only a half dozen houses at this end of the lake, and none was really suited for cold weather. Their isolated little community had never before been this crowded in the dead of winter.

"We won't be alone," Emil said as he opened the door.

"I assumed as much. You're married, right?"

"Yes, but my wife won't reveal anything. She's, well . . . you'll see."

They stepped into a cramped hallway with a kitchenette to the right. Looming just ahead was a rustic great room with a vaulted ceiling spanned by timber beams. Big, drafty windows at the far end looked out toward the lake. Another large window on the right had a view of the woods and a row of bird feeders. There was also a rumpled couch, a matching easy chair, and an end table piled with paperback novels, a nature guidebook, and a pair of binoculars. A braided oval rug and a woodstove sat in the middle of the floor. There was no television. The doorways to two bedrooms opened from the wall on the left.

A woman's voice called out.

"Emil, is that you?"

She emerged from the doorway of the second bedroom, an attractive woman in her early fifties, trim and a bit flushed, with hair clipped short enough to show off delicate ears and a graceful neck. Dorn doffed his cap in a courtly gesture.

"Sorry to disturb you, Frau Grimm. I'm Lieutenant Dorn from Bernau station. I won't be long."

She reddened slightly and looked to Grimm with a pleading expression.

"This is Frau Weber, Lieutenant. Karola Weber. She is a caretaker for my wife, Bettina."

"My apologies."

Dorn's gaffe appeared to have thrown him off balance. Emil was fine with that, even if he wasn't particularly proud of how he had managed it.

"Everything all right with Bettina?" Emil asked, hoping to at least set things right with Karola.

"Yes. She's sleeping at the moment, but she's had a good morning. I fed her, and we watched a little television."

"Good."

He turned to Dorn.

"Mind if I look in on her?"

"Please."

"Can I take your coat?" he asked.

"I think I'll keep it on for now."

"Sorry about the chill. We run a space heater in Bettina's room, but otherwise there's only the woodstove. Excuse me a moment."

He stepped through the doorway. His wife was indeed sleeping, on an angled hospital bed, or otherwise he would have leaned down to give her a peck on the cheek. Her skin always seemed powdery these days. Emil could taste it without even kissing her. He slipped through a side door into a shared bathroom that led to the other bedroom, a smaller, colder chamber where he slept every night.

Emil removed his overcoat as quietly as possible and placed it on the end of his bed. He could have gone directly from there back into the great room, but instead retraced his steps through Bettina's room. He reemerged to find Dorn facing Karola in awkward silence.

"May I ask why a policeman is here?" Karola said, with characteristic frankness.

Now Emil was off balance. He looked to Dorn for help, but the policeman obviously expected him to deliver the news.

"Our neighbor, Lothar Fischer, was found dead this morning down by the lake. Perhaps a suicide, perhaps not."

She put a hand to her mouth.

"I will make a fresh pot of coffee," she whispered.

"I'll do that. Go and sit with Bettina. And, if you don't mind, could you please shut the door?"

She nodded and practically tiptoed away.

"I'm fine without coffee, as long as you are," Dorn said.

"Very well. Please, then." He gestured toward the couch. Dorn took a seat while Emil settled into the easy chair.

"So your wife is not well?" the policeman asked in a lowered voice.

"ALS. It's a wasting disease. She has had it for nearly five years. A miracle she has survived this long, although the doctors say she may live for another three or four, so we try to keep her as comfortable as possible."

"Well, that is lucky, at least."

"Perhaps. It's not much of a life, but she does understand everything that's said to her. The doctors say her mind remains quite active, which is both a curse and a blessing. I read to her when I can. Play music. Tell her about my day. There's a small television in there that we watch sometimes. But I do lean on Karola, her and another caretaker. Their presence allows me to work, and to make some time for myself. Of course, I don't need as much of that as I used to, now that I no longer go into the office."

"Do you still have an apartment in Berlin?"

"We do, in a tower block on Frankfurter Allee, only a few blocks from Normanenstrasse. I used to walk to work. But we haven't stayed there in weeks. What would be the point anymore?"

Especially when your neighbors were now shunning you, and people on the sidewalk stared with open hostility. Not that he blamed them, at least not when he was thinking clearly and frankly about what had become of his country during the past decade or so. Or maybe the rot had set in even sooner, while he, like so many others, had still been pretending not to notice. Relocating to Prenden had been an easy choice, even with the difficulties involved in moving Bettina.

"So this is your home now?"

"I suppose it is."

And how humbling was that, he wondered, to admit that he could no longer face life in the city where he had grown up and had worked for decades. This dacha had once been their oasis for spring and summer weekends, when the dappled sunlight of lengthy days could make it feel enchanted. But at this time of year, beneath drooping pines and a lowering sky, it often felt gloomy and marooned, a hideout more than a home.

Dorn took out his notebook.

Emil sat up straighter. The tricky part was about to begin.

5

"Tell me how you came to be at the scene of the shooting this morning," Dorn asked.

"I went out for my morning walk. Up the hill first, then down toward the lake. That's when I saw the crime scene tape. Krauss and his people were already there."

"At what time did you leave your house?"

"Around 7:30. It was barely light."

"Is that your daily routine?"

"You can check all of this with Karola, by the way, after we're done."

"I plan to."

Emil nodded.

"I go for a walk first thing every morning. I try to vary the routes, but this morning I set out on my favorite one, which is about three miles long. It stays away from the lake for a mile or two, going off in that direction." He gestured toward the side window. "Then it comes downhill to the upper end of the lake. I knew it must be Lothar the moment I saw the cap."

"The orange one that was lying beside him?"

"He's the only person up here with a cap that bright. You can always tell it's him from clear across the water. Or could."

"Had you passed by that spot earlier?"

"I hadn't. I'd been up higher, in the trees."

"And what time was it, do you think, when you reached the body?"

Emil checked his watch and thought about it for a second.

"Close to 8:30, probably."

Dorn took down every word, in neat but slow shorthand.

"Oh, by the way, we'll need to get a photo of the bottom of your shoes. To try and make sense of who went where in all of this mud."

"Of course."

An interesting idea, if they could pull it off. He wondered what they would learn about Lothar's movements that morning. Or Krauss's, for that matter.

"When did you last see him alive?"

Here was where things got complicated.

"Two, three days ago? And only in passing. He was out in his garden when I was walking by."

"Doing what?"

Emil pretended to think about it for a moment.

"Putting away some tools, maybe? Chores."

"Did you speak?"

"Only to say hello. He might have said something about the weather."

"Did he seem overly depressed or despondent?"

"No more so than all of us have been from our department."

"Did he have any particular enemies that you know of?"

"Do you really need to ask that under our current circumstances? He was a high official with the Ministry of State Security. I can think of a few million people who would have been happy to see him dead."

"Then I take it you're feeling similarly threatened?"

"Not actually. No."

"Then maybe you should stop making speeches."

Emil flushed at the rebuke, another reminder of his sudden fall in rank and privilege. But he held his tongue. Let the policeman vent.

"My question was more specific, as I'm sure you understood, but let me rephrase it for you. To your knowledge, was Lothar Fischer doing anything recently that might have made him a target, either in his work, or personally?"

"If he was, then I'm not aware of it."

Dorn held his gaze. Emil, from his own experience in interrogation, knew better than to look away.

"You're certain?"

"Only of my own knowledge, or lack of it. And that's merely from my casual observation, as a neighbor and a colleague. Lothar only seemed to be doing the things that we have all been doing. Worrying about his future, trying to get his affairs in order for whatever might come next."

"And what does 'getting your affairs in order' mean, for someone in your position?"

"Figuring out how long your savings will last. Wondering if the new state will accept you, or try to put you in jail. Lining up the names of a few lawyers in case the latter comes to pass. Thinking about possible employment. Making arrangements for my wife's care, even if I'm no longer here to help with it."

"You have no children to help with that?"

"No. We tried for many years, but . . ."

Emil's voice drifted off. If Bettina was awake, he hoped she hadn't heard that answer. It was still a source of pain to both of them.

"What about Lothar? What was he saying about all this?"

"Pretty much the same. Except that he lives alone. He and his wife split up several years ago."

"And you say he was left-handed? You're sure of that?"

"Yes. It will be in his personnel file, if there's still anyone around to let you see it."

"I am curious as to why you didn't point that out to Krauss."

Emil shrugged. He was back on delicate ground.

"The charitable view would be to assume Krauss knew. Maybe he was waiting to see if I did as well."

"And is that your view?"

"The word 'charitable' would not apply to any of my views with regard to Dieter Krauss."

"Do you believe he's capable of having placed the gun in Lothar Fischer's hand?"

"That would mean believing he was capable of killing him."

"And?"

"Personally?" He paused to choose his words. "Killing is not his style. Or not with a gun. Krauss isn't one to dirty his hands. His method has always been more in the nature of making sure others are available to do things on his behalf."

"Like those men who were with him?"

Emil shook his head.

"No. The messier the job, the further removed he likes to stay. That's one reason it's called the Spezialkommission. They have always had a, well, unorthodox way of going about their business."

"I am aware of that through my own previous contact with Dieter Krauss. He meddles quite a bit when he feels like it. But do you think he's capable of having placed the gun there for the benefit of someone else?"

Emil shrugged again. He wasn't going to venture any further out on that limb, but he was pleased that Dorn had gone there. All the same, it was a disturbing possibility.

"I wouldn't want to venture a guess, not without knowing for sure. Even now he probably has . . . *allies* who could make things difficult for me."

"He certainly seems to act as if he does. And who are some of these allies?"

"Other government figures, a few who still hold some leverage. I'm not sure I could even name them."

"I think you're underestimating your ability on that count, but let's stay with the facts from this morning. How do you think Krauss was able to reach the scene before I did? Who told him about the body?"

"More worthy questions that I don't have answers for. When did you first receive the call?"

"At least twenty minutes before I arrived. Fifteen for the drive from Bernau, plus another five for our walk down the lake. A neighbor phoned it in. A Frau Kunstler?"

"Yes, I know her. She lives maybe a quarter mile from here, further down the lake. She's quite dependable."

"She'd seen the body on a walk, and telephoned as soon as she got back to her house. So that's at least five more minutes from the time of discovery. But she hadn't seen anyone else. Krauss must have gotten there not long after she phoned me, and if he was coming from Berlin that's at least a half-hour drive."

Useful information. Emil filed it away.

"And you only saw Krauss when you were on your walk, and came upon the body? Not sooner?"

"Not sooner."

"Do you also have a Makarov pistol?"

"Of course. It was issued to me the day I was commissioned as an officer of the Ministry of State Security."

"Is a silencer part of the kit?"

"It is. Along with a holster and, of course, ammunition."

"Do you keep it with you?"

"It's here at this house, if that's what you're asking."

"I am. I'd like to see it."

"Certainly. It's in my bedroom."

Emil rose from his chair. Dorn stirred, and for a worrisome moment Emil thought the policeman would follow him. It's certainly what he would have done. Instead, Dorn flipped a page to take more notes, and by then Emil was stepping through the bedroom door. He didn't shut it behind him—that would have invited suspicion—but to his relief the door swung back far enough to shield what he needed to do next.

He picked up his overcoat, which was still lying across the foot of the bed and still smelled like the outdoors. As quietly as possible, he reached into a baggy interior pocket and withdrew the pistol. He then stepped over to his dresser, where he noisily opened the top drawer and rooted around for several seconds, to provide suitable sound effects. Then he shut the drawer, went back out the door, and handed the gun to Dorn, who by then had put on a pair of surgical gloves.

The policeman took the gun without comment and raised it to his nose. He sniffed the end of the barrel, checked the chamber for ammunition, and slid his fingers along the gun's various parts, as if probing for residual heat.

"It's loaded," he said.

"It wouldn't be much good to me unloaded."

"You might want to clean it sometime soon."

"I'll take note of that."

Emil remained on his feet. Dorn handed back the gun. Emil placed it on the end table by his binoculars, which now drew Dorn's attention as the policeman peeled off his gloves.

"Do you ever use those from up here, first thing in the morning?"

"Only if there's something interesting at the bird feeder."

"And was that the case today?"

"Not as I recall."

"How's the view of the lake from here?"

"See for yourself."

Dorn picked up the binoculars and stepped over to the big windows at the back of the house. He peered down toward the water, scanning from side to side as he adjusted the focus.

"Anything interesting?" Emil asked.

"I can see one of my men, but only because he has come up the path from the scene. Mostly it's a lot of tree branches."

"That's why I keep them by the other window."

Dorn returned the binoculars to their spot by the gun.

"How long since you last fired that?"

"Three months, maybe more? On the ministry's practice range in Berlin."

"There will be records of that, I suppose."

"Of course. But . . ." Emil threw up his hands in a gesture of helplessness.

"Yes. I suppose retrieving any sort of paperwork from Normanen-strasse is going to be a problem."

"Unless you can get this new interior minister, Herr Diestel, to do you a favor."

"I gather he's rather busy with other things, like deciding what to do with all of you people."

"That shouldn't take long."

"Tell me about your workplace, especially with regard to Lothar Fischer's duties. I am of course aware that the HVA's main job is, or was, foreign intelligence. But, if I may ask a delicate question, what precisely was his area of responsibility?"

"Don't be shy, Lieutenant. None of those kinds of secrets counts for much anymore. Lothar was in charge of our operations in all the Western countries beyond Bonn and the Federal Republic. The UK, France, the United States."

"Did those duties overlap with yours?"

"To a degree. My focus was mostly NATO, and their headquarters in Brussels. So I was also interested in the Americans and the British, but strictly from the aspect of their military alliance in Europe, and anything they might be up to on that front."

"One makes plenty of enemies in that sort of work as well."

"Yes, except all of those enemies no longer have much of a reason to want us dead. They've been quite happy to accept our surrender."

Dorn let the remark settle. Then he shut his notebook and looked up with an expression of earnest interest.

"I'd like some advice."

The request took Emil by surprise.

"All right. If I'm able."

"What approach should I take with regard to getting a statement from Dieter Krauss?"

"Well, I gather from what you've already said that you have a history with him."

"He horned in on one of my investigations, a few years back. Took it over completely. They gave us a copy of the final report, but it was missing a few key details, and that's putting it charitably. So I complained to the ministry."

"And?"

"No one ever replied, other than a perfunctory 'Thanks for your interest.'"

"That sounds about right. They treated us the same, if it's any comfort. The Spezialkommission is its own little empire, reporting straight to the top. Or used to be."

"Do you think he would agree to be questioned at a neutral site?"

"Not a chance. He only answers to people who do things his way, with a show of force. Take those two men of yours, and maybe one more, and catch him out when he's alone and off his home ground. Even then, he probably won't say much, but you'll at least have his answers on record."

"With the ministry closed I wouldn't even know where to find him. Even his home address is probably still a state secret. Unless you have it."

"I don't. But those goons of his didn't materialize from nowhere. He must have set up a new base of operations, off site and unofficial, and even Krauss wouldn't be able to do that without other people knowing. Would you like me to ask around?"

"Yes, I'd appreciate that."

On that front, Emil was glad to help. Making an ally out of a police lieutenant could be quite helpful going forward, and he had his own reasons for wanting to know Krauss's current whereabouts.

"Anything more?"

"I'll speak to your caretaker now, if you don't mind."

"Certainly."

Emil went to fetch Karola. He had little doubt she'd been listening the entire time from behind the closed door, and he was confident she would back up his account—so much so that he excused himself to wait outdoors to put them both at ease. Might as well make Dorn think he had nothing to hide.

The sky was clearing, or trying to. Emil walked to the lake side of the dacha and peered through the trees toward the other houses—Wolf's, Lothar's, Frau Kunstler's, plus a few others that were deserted for the season. Lothar's death meant he now had some extra chores to do, but he couldn't attend to them until Dorn and even Karola were no longer around.

It was chilly, and he hadn't put on his coat, partly because he hadn't wanted to remind Dorn that he'd stashed it in the bedroom. He pulled an old pack of Juwel cigarettes from a pants pocket, along with a lighter he hadn't used in weeks. He had been trying to quit since November, but he kept these items with him as an ongoing test of his willpower. Very Germanic, he supposed. But for the moment the temptation was too great.

The lighter chirped three times before providing a flame. The tobacco smelled stale and tasted worse, but the rush of nicotine was warming and welcome. His brain felt the charge of it, and he was grateful for any assist to his powers of reasoning.

He looked downhill. One of Dorn's men was visible through the branches, pacing as if measuring the distance from the murder scene.

Emil thought back over his chat, reexamining it for possible missteps. He was painfully conscious of having referred to Lothar mostly as a neighbor and colleague, but not as a friend. It felt like a betrayal, a craven act of self-preservation. Although it was also true that the two men had always maintained a certain distance, never quite crossing the final boundary to a deeper trust, even during their recent cooperation.

He wondered if he should have mentioned to Dorn the possibility of Markus Wolf's return. Emil had no interest per se in protecting his old boss. Maybe he was hoarding that line of inquiry for himself—for now, anyway.

He took another drag from the cigarette, only to discover that it had gone out, a common fault of the dense Bulgarian tobacco. He decided to take it as a sign and dropped the cigarette to the ground, smashing it with the toe of his shoe. He looked up toward a patch of blue where the sun had broken through, and then watched with a dismayed sense of inevitability as the clouds sealed it back up.

What happened to you this morning, Lothar? Where did you go wrong? Or had someone else's mistake led to this? His own, perhaps. Emil began making a list in his head of everything he needed to do—some of it easy, some of it risky. Night chores would be involved, another walk through the trees. The moon was new, so he would be working mostly by starlight.

Reflexively, he shook loose another cigarette from the pack, then stared at it as if wondering how it had gotten into his hand. His mind was running on its old tracks, as if he were back on the job. He examined the cigarette longingly before dropping it into his pocket, beating temptation for the moment. No more distractions, not until current matters were under better control. He resolved to begin thinking of this as his last op, even though the state would no longer be paying him.

Then he grinned at his own folly. His last op? More like his first, since he'd always worked at a desk. Supposedly he was a spymaster, a Wolf acolyte who had learned all his tricks from the master himself, tricks that he had then passed along to the men and women he'd sent into the field.

So, yes, he had run agents and operatives from afar. He had trained them, paid them, provided cover for them, and, when necessary, helped them elude capture. Yet Emil himself had never once made a brush pass, chalked a mark onto a tree, cleared a dead drop, or called for a crash meeting. He'd never once had to exfiltrate because he had never once had to infiltrate. The greatest personal hazards of his job had been paper cuts, indigestion, official reprimands, and lost sleep.

The closest he had ever come to doing actual field work had been five years ago, when Wolf had decided to dispatch him into the wider world to run his own agents at ground level, not just across the Wall but across the water—in America. At the time the HVA had only a handful of assets there, mostly because they'd been running operations out of their embassy, which was carefully monitored. Wolf wanted Emil to run things from outside the embassy walls, in an undercover role, mostly with an eye toward stealing technological secrets. To prepare for the posting, Emil had begun running the USA desk, which had ruffled the feathers of Lothar, of all people, since that was part of his duties.

But a few months before the posting, doctors diagnosed Bettina with ALS. She was already suffering early symptoms, and to Emil it had felt like fate telling him the option was closed. So he backed away from the offer, told Wolf to find a replacement, and returned to his old job.

Here he was now, then, a virgin operative finally preparing to enter active duty. A two-man venture had become a one-man job, meaning he would have to do all the legwork, a handler to himself, self-taught and self-run. Impossible, perhaps, and certainly risky. Just ask Lothar.

The rear door of the dacha opened. Dorn stepped outside with Karola behind him, her face unreadable in the shadow of the threshold.

"I will be in touch as the investigation demands," the policeman said. "If you learn anything about Krauss's whereabouts . . ."

"Of course. I will cooperate fully."

Dorn nodded and headed toward the lake. Emil watched until he was out of sight. He got out his pack of cigarettes yet again, lit one, watched it sputter out, then relit it and inhaled deeply. For today, at least, old habits were officially still in play.

Emil was back on the clock, except now he was his own boss, fighting for his own cause, a patriot of his own private republic—an isolated spy, quite alone, with winter upon him. He gazed disdainfully at the burning cigarette, and then tossed it to the ground.

6

Bettina's eyes were the first thing Emil had noticed about her on the night they met, thirty-three years earlier in a Berlin café. Now they were the only way she could speak to him. One blink for yes, two for no, with a wide range of emotions forever swimming deeper in those pools of blue. They were his last available portal to her thoughts, his best remaining refuge from his own.

Sometimes he believed he could translate everything she was trying to tell him, just from the shimmer of her cornea, the quiver of her iris, the dilation of a pupil. Other times he was equally certain these powers were illusory.

Now, with Lieutenant Dorn having just departed, Emil believed he was detecting fear, or at least apprehension. He leaned closer and spoke softly.

"Did you hear any of what the policeman and I were talking about?"

Bettina blinked once.

"All of it?"

Two blinks.

"Would you like to know more about what has happened this morning, my love?"

One blink—but slowly, perhaps reluctantly.

He checked over his shoulder for Karola, who was straightening up in the kitchen as she prepared to go off duty. He took Bettina's hand and whispered, watching intently to make sure she was comprehending every word.

"Lothar Fischer has been shot to death. It happened down by the lake. I don't know who did it, but I intend to find out. I am not in any danger, nor are you and Karola, but I will be keeping some odd hours for the next few days, and I may have to be away from you more than I'd like. So do not worry about me if my routines change, all right?"

She waited a few seconds and blinked once. Her breathing was a little quicker, her gaze unwavering. Then she blinked again, slowly, as if to affirm her readiness for whatever came next.

He squeezed her hand, nodded, and bent down to kiss her lightly on the lips. A smell of soap, meaning Karola had bathed her. His eyes watered at the thought of her helpless body, naked and wet, the slack muscles that no longer worked. He sighed and was angry with himself for having to blink back a tear. This was a moment to offer a brave face, a resolute smile. He placed her hand back at her side and released it. She exhaled slowly.

"Whatever I do from here on out, it is for our future. Maybe that is how I should have always acted, but that is how I will act now. Not for the state. For us."

Her eyes watched him as he stood.

Bettina had entered the "locked in" phase of her illness nearly a year ago—a vibrant mind shut inside an unresponsive body. At the onset of her symptoms, five years earlier, she had begun to stumble, drop things, feel fatigued. Her mouth would suddenly refuse to function, unable to form a certain word. Then came the tests, the consultations, and the agony of learning what was ahead. She had last been able to speak eleven months ago.

Emil now found himself confiding in her more than ever about his deeper feelings, a phenomenon that troubled him. Why hadn't he done more of that before? He supposed his job was to blame, his bosses with their insistence on professional secrecy. A ministry where everyone was always looking over everyone else's shoulder. The irony now was that his wife had become an unassailably secure source. No one on the planet was better equipped to keep his secrets. Yet for all that, he would not—*could* not—tell her everything about what he was up to now.

When the events of November 9 had occurred—the crowds, the sledgehammers, the breach in the Wall, the TV lights illuminating everything for an astonished world—they had watched together as it unfolded on television, although some of it they could watch and hear through their windows. Upon returning from his own sorties into the streets of Berlin he had related to her in vivid detail everything he'd witnessed, as if it were the latest chapter in a radio serial. Even as he spoke, he was never quite sure how he was supposed to be feeling. Apprehension certainly, and repudiation. But there was also a sense of excitement, and even of vindication. Both took him by surprise.

They shouldn't have, he decided later. Emil had long since grown skeptical of the ideals that officially guided his work, his daily activities. Even with their privileged status, the state had become an overbearing presence in their lives. It had begun to rankle years earlier, during their futile visits to fertility clinics—so many forms to fill out, so many intrusive questions, all of those people who forever needed to know more. Buy a book and someone always had to know which one, and then made a note of it. Make a phone call and you assumed it was overheard. Say something critical, even in passing or in jest, and perhaps someone would get the wrong idea. If you heard nothing about it later, was that good or was that worrisome?

Surely others, even in leadership, must have reacted this way? Emil hadn't foreseen the system's collapse—who could have?—but the widening gap between the party's slogans and the reality on the street had been evident for anyone who wasn't either blind or a fool.

So if Emil had experienced relief in watching those sledgehammers do their work, then so be it, and he had imparted some of that excitement to Bettina in his account of the night's events.

The return messages from her eyes had been equally complex— pupils that widened in surprise; a little shock, a little uncertainty, but mostly a sense of wonder that also was evident in her pulse. Everything that they had depended on for decades had crumbled in a single night, but they couldn't help but notice that even the light looked different now, and the shadows were not quite as dark.

The other surprise was Emil's sense of detachment as he watched the structures of the state collapse. All the battles he had fought for his country had in effect been on foreign soil, even though he had always worked from Berlin. Their operatives and agents had worked in Bonn, in Munich, the Ruhr, or scattered across Western Europe and the United States, and by focusing on them perhaps he had always averted his eyes from many events closer to home. That sense of distance had protected him, he supposed. Maybe it had also blinded him. Perhaps that was true for Bettina as well.

Karola's voice called to him from the great room.

"Are you ready?"

Bettina's pupils dilated. She liked and trusted Karola. And why not? The two women had become close friends well before Bettina's illness. They'd met on a lakeshore walk many summers ago, just after Karola had lost her husband, a farmer, to a heart attack. He'd been digging post holes on a far corner of the state's acreage.

To Emil's shame—or maybe that was too strong of a word—there were additional reasons he was grateful to have Karola close at hand, ones more directly beneficial to him. And, yes, he and his wife had discussed even that topic in their own halting manner, with Emil fumbling for words while she blinked along, dry-eyed and rational and supportive.

"I'll be back as soon as I can."

Bettina blinked once, then shut her eyes.

.   .   .

Emil opened the gate to his driveway and started his boxy, mustard-colored Wartburg for the short ride to Karola's house. She asked her first question before he had even backed into the rutted dirt lane.

"How serious is this for you?"

He looked over to read her face and was relieved to detect concern but not suspicion.

"One could take that question in a lot of different ways."

The vehemence of her reply took him by surprise.

"I'm not a damn policeman, Emil. He was your friend, so I'm worried for you, whether you had anything to do with it or not."

"Well, I didn't, so you can stop worrying on that count."

"Good. I'm glad. But if someone wanted to kill Lothar . . ."

Her words trailed off. The car bounced through a pothole that made the springs wheeze. A startled deer took off through the trees to their left. Emil braked to a halt, put the car in neutral, and took her hand. She started to pull away, then relented and squeezed his fingers.

"Well?" she said.

"I suppose that everyone in my line of work is vulnerable in some way now, although I'll confess this shocked me."

"Do you think it was foreigners? Westerners maybe?"

He shook his head.

"All their interest now is in keeping us alive for our information. Even Dorn knows that."

"Well, I didn't. For years I've been hearing how everyone on the other side—the CIA, MI6, NATO, all of them—were the sworn enemies of people like you."

He released her hand, put the car back into gear, and slowly accelerated.

"They always said the same things about us, you know. Talking about what a threat we were to their way of life. It was a narrative that suited both sides, especially whenever budgets were being discussed."

"Are you saying it wasn't true?"

"Certainly we were always in competition. But would we have shot one of them, or them one of us? No. The only poor souls who ever got killed were the ones caught in the middle. The messengers and the cutouts. The bystanders. And those kinds of rules never change."

He glanced over to see her staring coldly.

"Were you always this cynical about your work?"

He sighed and looked straight ahead.

"I've been learning all sorts of new things about myself, it seems."

"Then maybe he did kill himself. Because if *you* feel this way . . ."

"Yes. I suppose it's possible."

He didn't really, not in the least, and not with that gun in the wrong hand. But if the idea eased her worries, then fine.

They reached the end of the dirt lane and pulled onto a narrow paved road that ran past open fields and more forest. Nearby was a sad little golf course surrounded by chain-link fencing. A mile farther on was a small military barracks with an underground bunker that had been built years before as a shelter for the state's top leaders, in case of nuclear war. From all the remote quietness, you never would've guessed that Berlin was only a half hour's drive away. Hardly any traffic ever passed down this highway.

Emil had bought their lot and paid for construction of the dacha in the 1970s, but he supposed that just about everything else around here—the farms, the golf course, the HVA safe house, even the bunker—would become part of a huge liquidation sale of state assets, a matter already being discussed in Bonn and Berlin.

"Have you started thinking yet about what all of this might mean for us?" Karola asked.

Emil was about to say something about the real estate market before he realized she was still talking about the murder, and their status as a couple—or, as a man and a woman in some sort of complex relationship, however ill-defined.

"I don't think that anything happening in the country right now, here or elsewhere, will change our . . . our situation. You know my thoughts on that, Karola. Whenever I think of you, what I mostly feel, after the pleasure and gratitude, is guilt."

"It's what she wants for you."

"I know. You've told me. So has Bettina, in her way. To my eternal embarrassment."

Karola smiled. She was always amused by his discomfort with these conversations. Emil supposed he was in love with both of them, although he was still uneasy about how it had all come about—more a result of discussions between the two women than anything he had ever asked for. Perhaps he should stop questioning it.

"When will you need me next?"

She always made it sound like such a loaded question. Or maybe he was imagining it.

"I think we'll need you for some extra hours in the coming week, if you can arrange it. Maybe some overnights. So while you're home you should pack a bag and get your affairs in order for that."

"My affairs, yes."

"You know that's not how I meant it."

She was smiling again, so he smiled back, even though his heart wasn't in it. They were approaching the turnoff to her house.

Prenden was a cluster of a few dozen farmhouses and barns at a picturesque bend in the road. Some of them had been built centuries ago, with plastered walls and timber beams. Shaggy goats and sheep kept watch over its narrow lanes, the rams with full sets of curled horns. Karola's one-story house had a small lawn with a plum tree and berry bushes. It sat at the end of a cobblestone alley opposite a timbered medieval shed that leaned three ways at once. Bright green moss covered its wood shingle roof.

Emil, a solid proponent of rational thought, had nonetheless always sensed that the little village was enchanted. Sometimes at dusk he would not have been at all surprised to see elves and dwarves come strolling down the lane. But this morning the usual view was ruined by the sight of Dieter Krauss's car, a black sedan, parked on the verge just after the turnoff, only thirty yards from Karola's house.

"Whose car is that?" she asked. The smoked windows made it hard to see in, although she turned in her seat as they passed. "A Volvo. Must be someone important."

"Krauss. He must have guessed I'd be coming here next."

"The Stasi man you and the lieutenant were talking about?"

"Yes."

"Will he make trouble for you?"

"The better question is whether he was making trouble for Lothar."

"Oh." Her voice sounded small. "I see."

Emil rolled to a stop just downhill as they pulled alongside Karola's house.

"I probably shouldn't walk you to your door. The less important he thinks you are to me, the better."

"Yes. I can see that. Although it's all right with me if you tell him about us. Unless of course he's one of those ministry prudes who still thinks like an old schoolmarm, like that bastard Mielke."

"That bastard Mielke is now locked up in solitary confinement, so you can stop worrying about him, at least."

She climbed out, then turned and spoke before shutting the door.

"Be careful, Emil. There are two of us counting on you."

"I'll come by for you in the morning. Early. Six-thirty."

She nodded and turned up the walkway, glancing uphill toward the Volvo before reaching her door. Emil waited until she was inside before getting out of his car. He walked briskly, making a beeline toward the Volvo before Krauss could react.

It was time to test the new dynamics of power. Time for a confrontation that would get a few things out in the open. Time also to put a little fear into Dieter Krauss, because the man had certainly earned it.

Emil opened the Volvo's passenger door and climbed in.

7

The move was so sudden and unexpected that Krauss didn't have time
to turn off his radio, which was blaring an American rock tune from a
station in West Berlin. Emil glanced at the dial like it was something
subversive, and Krauss switched it off. There was a moment of awkward silence before Emil spoke.

"Well?"

"I wanted a word with you, someplace where we wouldn't be interrupted by that officious ass Dorn."

"He speaks well of you, too, Krauss. Make it quick, my wife shouldn't
be alone for long."

"What was Lothar up to? What's been keeping him so busy?"

Emil made a show of checking his watch.

"Less than three hours since our colleague was killed. A little early
to begin reassessing his career, even for you."

"Don't be a moralist. This is an investigation."

"Not yours, apparently. And if Lothar was 'busy,' as you put it, then
that's news to me."

"You two were close. You must have noticed something."

"Not nearly as close as we used to be. I saw him far more at the office
than I ever saw him up here."

"But you must have heard the whispers."

"And how would I do that up here? The only whispers in my dacha
come from the wind in the trees, the swallows in the chimney."

"Well, in Berlin there was plenty to hear. All sorts of chatter about him scurrying back and forth among the wrong sorts of people. Out to that storage bunker near Leipzig. Or over to Marzahn, to see that fellow who's running the task force in Sub-Department 7."

"Plotz?"

"Andreas Plotz, yes. And whenever anyone like me got too curious he'd run back up here to hide in the woods."

This was disturbing news indeed. Surprising, too. Lothar had always been one of the most careful people he'd known, and an inveterate planner. Everything by the book, nothing done in a rush or on the spur of the moment—not if he could help it. If anything, he'd been meticulous to a fault. Had he really become this sloppy without Emil noticing? Or maybe other people were the ones who'd become careless—Andreas Plotz, for starters—which would be just as disturbing.

"All of us have too many secrets, Krauss. It's what we were paid for. Maybe you'd like to tell me yours."

"You HVA people." Krauss shook his head. "All of you always pretended to be above the fray, cleaner than the rest of us because your work was abroad. It's like that pose of yours in choosing that stupid car. A piece-of-shit Wartburg, when you could have had a Peugeot. Or even a Volvo, like mine."

"Maybe I was never comfortable with the idea of advertising my status every time I went for a drive."

"Yes, because you're such a man of the people. Like Wolf, with his driver and his nice duplex in Berlin, and his fat pension. Yet look at what happened to all of you at the first sign of trouble. Wolf runs to Moscow like a crying boy to his nanny. You and Lothar go to ground in your dachas, leaving the rest of us to defend what little of the ministry remains."

"The ministry's gone, Krauss. You're fighting for a ghost."

"No, I'm fighting for our *legacy*. Our future. With the right use of what's left, we might even have one. But not if everyone gives up, or destroys the remnants. And he was helping them. Or that was the word."

"Lothar? Helping who?"

"All those asses like Plotz, working their shredders nonstop, then tearing up the paper by hand when the machines broke down, or burning big piles of it in trash bins. Some of that is still worthy information, Grimm. Some of it is still worth protecting."

"And some of it *has* been protected. I have heard that much. Even Andreas Plotz would tell you that. He's an archivist, one of our best. Why don't you ask him?"

"I asked one of his people. He told me to fuck off, then threatened to report me to that new interior minister, Diestel, the one who wants us all to disappear."

"Another good reason not to get involved."

"Is that what you and Lothar decided, huddled around your woodstoves at night? What else were the two of you talking about?"

"It's not like you think. We came up here to keep to ourselves, each to his own. Even before November, Lothar and I were drifting apart. It started a few years ago, after . . . well, you remember."

Krauss nodded, as if finally conceding a point. The affair, Emil meant, an indiscretion that had reverberated in the corridors of Normanenstrasse. Lothar Fischer had been the HVA's brightest rising star at the time. He was even mentioned as a possible successor to Stasi chief Erich Mielke. Then he threw away his marriage in pursuit of an actress thirty years his junior.

Initially he had planned out this affair with as much care and energy as if it were a matter of state security. But as matters progressed, and then deteriorated, he had acted more like a blundering stalker, and he had done so openly, sometimes drunkenly. It was Lothar's lone bout of recklessness—until now, anyway—and it had cost him dearly.

It hadn't helped that their big boss, Mielke, was quite old-fashioned about such things. Like a schoolmarm, as Karola had put it only moments before. For all that, Lothar might have weathered the episode without sanction if it hadn't damaged the one aspect of his reputation he was most valued for—his rigid insistence on playing everything as carefully as possible.

Mielke had confronted Lothar with a dossier of the most lurid evidence—some of it probably gathered by Krauss. Lothar had avoided demotion, but his professional ascent ended, and his wife, Käthe, left him. He went into seclusion for a while, brooding and resentful. For a year or so, he had seemed drunk almost every time Emil saw him on weekends. At the office he had looked haggard and expendable.

"Okay, so you two were no longer close. But you have eyes and ears. You couldn't have missed *everything*."

"Not in normal times. But now? And with my wife needing extra care? This hasn't been an easy time for any of us, Krauss, you should know that as well as anyone. But how about this—how about I ask around for you? Prod a few old sources—Andreas Plotz, some others. Knock on a few doors. Maybe, between the two of us, we can find out what Lothar was up to."

Krauss narrowed his eyes as if trying to figure out an ulterior motive. Then he sighed and nodded appreciatively.

"Yes. That would be helpful. Contacts, that's mostly what I'm looking for. People he's been in touch with in recent weeks. On both sides of the Wall."

"The Wall's gone, Krauss. Or will be soon enough."

"Physically, yes. But it still exists in our minds, and in theirs. Our enemies are still our enemies."

"Even if the fight is over?"

"For you, maybe."

"Fine. How will I reach you with any results? Surely you don't still have access to your office?"

"My office!" Krauss said, freshly outraged. "Do you know that I was barely able to recover my own personal possessions before they shut it for good?"

"You're lucky. Last time I went I had to bribe a guard to let me in the main door, and when I got upstairs there were six people from the Citizens Committee, going from desk to desk."

"The Citizens Committee! A bullshit name for a bunch of fucking anarchists. We should have locked them up years ago as enemies of the state."

"With a few of them I believe we did. But do you know what they were doing up in our office?"

"Stealing state property, no doubt. And state secrets as well."

"No. They were watering the plants and flowers."

"*What?*"

"Apparently it occurred to one of them that all of us must have rushed home without rescuing our office plants, so there they were with watering cans, sprinkling every plant. It was kind of sweet, and I told them so. As a peace offering, they let me take home the African violet Bettina gave me years ago."

Emil told the story mostly because he figured it would enrage Krauss. He was right.

"Peace offering! There's no making peace with that crowd. It's outrageous the way they treat us. Have you heard what they've done to Mielke? Solitary confinement, it's intolerable."

"You sound as if you actually feel sorry for him."

"It's the symbolism I detest. If they can do that to Mielke, what does that say for the rest of us?"

"What we think doesn't matter anymore, Krauss. But you still haven't told me how to reach you."

"Ah, yes." Krauss smiled. "A few of us from the Spezialkommission have set up our own new digs. Off site, of course, but rent free for the moment. We do still have friends out there, Emil, our secret patrons, and this place is not far from your old apartment."

He offered a street address, which Emil committed to memory.

"I wouldn't mind meeting some of these 'secret patrons' you speak of, especially once the paychecks stop."

Krauss winced, as if he wished he hadn't made that little boast. Then he moved on.

"It's quite convenient, our new base of operations, and there is a wonderful little sausage stand right next door with the best currywurst in the district. That's one thing that has improved since November, I'll give them that. You don't have to go to one of the party's special stores to get something decent to eat. But we're not accepting the new order without a fight, Emil. You should fight back, too."

"That's not so easy for someone like me, as you saw this morning. Now even the Volkspolizei feel that they can push us around."

"That goddamned Dorn. What did he want from you?"

"About what you'd expect. My whereabouts and movements. Anything that I might have known about Lothar's recent doings."

"And what did you tell him?"

"Exactly what I just told you. Nothing more, nothing less."

Krauss seemed taken aback by the idea that a mere cop could extract as much information as he could. Another slap in the face by the new order. Emil spoke again before Krauss could register his disapproval.

"Actually, he seemed more interested in learning everything I knew about you."

"And what did you tell him?"

Emil opened the car door and swung his feet onto the ground. He stood, turned, and leaned in to deliver his parting answer.

"You should properly direct that question to Lieutenant Dorn."

Emil slammed the door as Krauss's mouth fell open in surprise. Then he offered a jaunty wave through the smoked window and set out for his car, slapping the Volvo's hood in passing.

8

Karola, watching from her kitchen window, exhaled in relief. From the moment Emil had climbed into the Volvo she had worried that the car would take him away forever, and that no one would ever find his body.

But there he was now, safe for the moment, with a forced smile and a stilted jolliness, like a man trying to convince himself that he had gained the upper hand. Karola wasn't so sure. She worried about Emil's growing tendency toward recklessness now that he was at loose ends. She also knew that he had been in touch with Lothar Fischer far more often than he had admitted to Lieutenant Dorn, which made her wonder what else he was hiding, and why.

In the past few days she had heard him talking on the phone to Lothar several times. The first time he'd left the house afterward, setting out on foot in the direction of the man's dacha. He was gone more than an hour, and he'd seemed preoccupied afterward. The second time he'd returned well after dark, tracking mud and twigs into the house without pausing to put on his house slippers, which wasn't like him at all. She surmised that the two men must have gone off into the woods. Or maybe Emil had taken the long way home. Then she overheard a third conversation, and arrived at a different conclusion.

The irony was that, until recently, Emil had always been a little too careful, too much of a planner. Loosen up, she had always chided him. Stop fretting over every detail. The moment the ministry shut down, she began encouraging him to remake himself, to relax his routines.

Now, here he was, finally making it up as he went along, Mr. Spontaneous, and her first impulse was to rein him in.

If these changes had occurred while Bettina was still able to speak—say, a year ago—then the two women would have shared a good laugh as they discussed him in private. Emil had been one of their favorite topics of conversation whenever Karola pushed Bettina's wheelchair around the lake. They were as much like sisters as friends in the way they shared secrets, a closeness that had come to their relationship almost the moment they'd met. It was one reason why she had helped take care of Bettina not only at the dacha, but also when Bettina and Emil had been living in Berlin, even though she had to drive half an hour to reach their apartment. And, yes, it was also the reason she and Bettina had decided so readily on their current, well, *arrangement*, for lack of a better word.

The whole thing had been Bettina's idea, a parting gift to her husband as she slipped into the final stage of muscular failure, with its inevitable retreat into the silent world of her thoughts.

"I know he finds you attractive," Bettina had said, speaking slowly by then. "He almost always averts his eyes when you come into the room, like he doesn't want me to know it."

"You're imagining things."

"I'm not. Nor am I imagining it when I see you do the same thing."

For a moment, Karola had been too embarrassed to answer.

"Okay, maybe so. But none of that matters, because he clearly still loves you."

"I know that. This isn't about love, Karola. It's about loneliness, for both of you. It's about the feel of a warm body next to you in bed. And in another few months, when I can no longer even move my little finger, or open my mouth to speak, he won't even have that. I won't, either. And you won't. Unless . . ."

"Stop, Bettina."

"Why? Do you find him unattractive? Am I wrong about that?"

"Well, no. You're not."

"Is there someone else, then?"

"No, no. There has been no one since Jürgen. I would have told you. But Emil? He's *yours*."

"Do you think there is nothing selfish in this for me? If he's happy, he'll take better care of me. So will you. If he's happy, he won't feel like he's such a prisoner of what has happened to me. And what better person for him to be happy with than someone I know and trust and love? Someone who I will still see almost every day."

Karola needed a bit more convincing, but within a few days they were in agreement, and began to discuss how to bring it about. They sometimes laughed over the way their plans aligned so easily with the political lessons the state had taught them. It was almost like arranging a teen event for the Young Pioneers, based on the teachings of Karl Marx—*From each according to his ability, to each according to his needs*. Only the silly uniforms were missing, the perky little songs, as they cooked up their experiment in collective love and affection. And it *was* love, Karola decided, even if not the kind that made you swoon when you were younger.

She continued to sense Bettina's approval of the arrangement in her eyes. During the past few months the two women had kept communicating in a way that even Emil hadn't mastered, and perhaps never would. Where he saw blinks and a narrow range of emotions, Karola believed she could detect entire thoughts and sentences. They shared a wavelength, and the signal remained strong. And on the subject of Emil, Karola had become Bettina's eyes and ears, even as Bettina, in her own way, continued to offer knowledge about Emil from the earlier years before Karola had known them. Thus had Karola built up an emotional dossier on this man in their lives—his worries, his hang-ups, and, now, the vulnerability of his deeper secrets.

She backed away from the kitchen window as Emil walked to his Wartburg. Now that the two men were no longer focused on each other, she didn't want them to see her watching.

Emil started his car. The engine coughed blue smoke out of the tailpipe as he made a U-turn, passed the Volvo, and turned right onto the highway—in the opposite direction from his dacha. He could be headed to Berlin, or anywhere else you might want to go in their suddenly wider world. And he was doing so even though Bettina was waiting alone at home, which worried Karola.

Seconds later, the Volvo crept away and followed, accelerating smoothly with no trace of smoke. She crossed to another window and saw the Volvo tuck in behind the Wartburg and easily close the gap. She watched, holding her breath, until both cars were out of sight.

9

Bill Gentry locked in on Claire the moment she arrived at Berlin base.

"Where'd you go last night? I called your room and there was no answer."

"Went for a walk, over toward the zoo. Needed to stretch my legs."

"Eventful?"

This was not idle curiosity. Gentry was checking up on her. Claire had no way of knowing what he knew of her movements, so she answered carefully.

"Not particularly. Stopped in a neighborhood bar for a beer along the way. A few of them, in fact."

"Beers or bars?"

"Beers."

"Meet anyone special?"

The path ahead narrowed. She picked her way forward.

"I'm not involved with anyone here, Bill, if that's what you're asking."

"Oh, well, that's nice to know. Glad to hear it."

She was pleased to have diverted him from any track that might have led to Baucom, but annoyed that he seemed so pleased by her response, and was now stepping closer. Gentry had recently left his wife, and was said to be a man on the prowl, and not particularly choosy. He was one of those fellows who liked to casually touch, squeeze, or even pat you on the rump if you gave him half a chance.

"Sorry I didn't reach you, then. It would have been nice to have had a drink before this op gets rolling."

Now she detected a hint of a leer in his tone. Claire knew all about men like Gentry, and while they were a damned nuisance, their eagerness sometimes also made them an easy mark for cultivation as a source, as long as you could hold them at bay.

"We could have lunch today," she suggested. "If you're free."

"I am, but I doubt you'll be. Someone's waiting to see you, and will probably be keeping you tied up well past noon. I promised to deliver you first thing. This way."

He smiled a bit wickedly, took her by the arm, and led her toward the conference room. She resisted the urge to shake him off, only because of her worries about who might be awaiting her arrival. Maybe it was a security officer, a grim-faced fellow who would display surveillance photos of her and Clark Baucom and then hand her a plane ticket home.

Gentry opened the door to a view of a long table with a woman in a navy blue business suit seated at the far end. Her head was lowered, face obscured by a curtain of light brown hair as she examined some papers.

"Claire Saylor, as requested," Gentry said.

The woman nodded but didn't look up. Gentry left and shut the door. So much for a proper introduction. Claire resisted the temptation to clear her throat, but decided to remain standing until her presence was acknowledged. The only sound was the whisper of pages as the woman set aside one to read another. There was a coffee maker at the opposite end of the room, so Claire walked over and poured a cup, even though she'd already had plenty.

"Get one for me," the woman said, bossing her like Claire was a secretary. "With milk, unless it's the fake stuff."

Claire poured a second cup. There were little plastic tubs of milk, but the customer hadn't earned that level of service, so she walked the cup across the room, set it down just out of reach, and watched with amusement as the woman groped for it without success. When she finally looked up to locate her coffee, Claire recognized her face from newspaper photos—Lindsey Ward, the new deputy director of operations.

Ward frowned when she saw the coffee was black.

"Sorry, didn't see anything but powder," Claire said. "I heard you'd gone back to Langley."

"I did. Then the issue of this new asset came up, so I flew back. Didn't even have time to unpack."

"It's that important?"

"And I'm here to personally tell you why, because a lot of it is beyond Bill Gentry's need to know."

It was almost enough to make Claire wish she'd added milk. High-priority ops were rare occurrences for her. It's one reason Paris station had made her available when Berlin called for reinforcements. Expendable. Although she supposed her fluency in German had also played a role.

Ward gestured toward a chair to her right. Claire angled for a peek at the pages, but Ward gathered them up, popped the edges against the tabletop, and slid the pile into a folder stamped "Top Secret."

"Will I be getting a look at that?"

"I'll brief you on the contents."

"That sounds like a no."

"Gentry said you weren't easy. He also said you're good at your work. I guess that will have to be enough."

Some managers softened backhanded compliments with a smile. Not Ward. Claire was fine with that as long as the same rules applied to her. She had some tough questions, and didn't want to have to disguise them as admiring ones.

"What do you know about the hierarchy of the HVA?" Ward asked.

"Not much."

Not entirely true. Baucom had given her a decent briefing the night before, covering half a dozen names and titles, but admitting to that much knowledge might have invited unwanted curiosity as to its source.

"Apparently none of us knew all that much until the last month or so. Here's a flow chart and a few bios from the upper echelons that we've managed to assemble. Study it after we're done, but it's not to leave the room."

"Is the asset on the chart?"

"We'll get to that. How much do you know about their record keeping, particularly their agent files?"

"Practically nothing." Which was true. She and Baucom had covered a wide range of topics while lingering at Zwiebelfisch a few hours longer, but this wasn't one of them.

"From what we've managed to determine, there's no central registry. It's more like a puzzle, with different pieces in three separate card files. The first and largest covers around three hundred thousand 'persons of interest' to the Stasi. Buried among those are two thousand or so HVA agents serving abroad, but to ID them you need the cards from the second file, which summarize their ops and actions, plus the third set, the 'agent' cards, which give you their cover names only, plus some biographical detail. All of them are apparently on microfilm. Our concern is that anyone offering this material might really only have one or two of the pieces, especially since the East Germans have been destroying most of them, and have supposedly shipped surviving copies to Moscow."

"So this could be a con job?"

"Or disinformation, perhaps in cooperation with the main enemy." Meaning the Russians. "Or he could be the real thing."

"Is he at least someone who could potentially deliver the goods?"

"His rank gives him the right access, and he has offered enough authentication to at least verify his identity. It's the product that's in question."

"So what will I be doing? Accepting delivery of a sample?"

"He hasn't said. But I have a rendezvous time for you. Four-thirty this afternoon. Early this morning we confirmed that the meeting is still a go."

"Confirmed how?"

"Direct contact with the asset."

"Impressive."

"As for what you can expect, you know as much as I do. We're leaving it to the contact to set the tone. The vagueness is one reason I chose you for this job."

"You personally?"

Ward nodded.

"For your demonstrated ability to . . . *improvise*, if necessary."

"My superiors have at times characterized that talent as insubordination."

"I reserve the right to do the same, if you abuse it."

"Hard to see how I'd manage that this afternoon, if the contact is setting all the rules."

"We're counting on increasing our leverage as events transition forward. You'll be our instrument for that."

"How so?"

"Since he first got in touch, other developments have changed the equation more in our favor. Let's just say that it's no longer strictly a seller's market."

"He has a competitor?"

"It's not that simple. If it was, I'd be happy to have you tell him so."

"Then what *do* I tell him, assuming he's even the one who makes contact?"

"As little as possible. We want to see his play, and, hopefully, get a clearer idea of what's on offer. Then we'll plan our next move."

"If this is so important, why am I going it alone?"

"Because he insisted. It's his strictest rule."

"How would he even know if we were breaking it?"

"He probably wouldn't, but the meetup is in his territory. And, based on the track record of our station over there, well, our operational security has never exactly been airtight in East Berlin." Her polite way of saying they might still have a few leaks. "We did look at the possibility of supplying you with a portable communication device."

"One of those new mobile phones?"

"Yes, but apparently they're completely unreliable here. Can't even get a signal, here or anywhere else in East Germany. But you won't be totally isolated. You'll be taking this with you."

Ward opened a stainless steel attaché case and withdrew a black metal square four inches per side and about an inch thick. She handed it to Claire.

"A tracking beacon?"

"Yes."

"What's the range?"

That would at least tell her how closely any sort of support might be lurking as she moved toward the rendezvous point.

"It's state of the art, the latest model from our technical people."

A non-answer, which told her not to ask again.

"You're to activate it the moment you leave Berlin station, whether that happens to be an hour from now or later. You'll leave it on until you've returned."

Meaning that Ward wanted to know her whereabouts before, during, and after the op. Did they already suspect she'd made an unauthorized contact? If so, why would they even keep her on this job?

"Whose protection is this for, exactly? Mine or yours?"

"Why can't it be for both? In the meantime, here are some further briefing materials to help you prepare, mostly to do with the location, the best routes in and out, the current status of different crossing points, that sort of thing."

She slid over a pile of maps and photographs.

"Those items will also remain in the room, but take your time studying them. We'll have your lunch sent in."

"Do I at least get a name?"

"You have it in your hand. He's the number five man on that flow chart."

News to quicken the pulse. Based on the ranking, she was pretty sure she already knew who it was, thanks to what Baucom told her the night before, but she consulted the chart to make sure. All the while, Ward watched with interest.

"Lothar Fischer," Claire said.

"Age sixty-one. Deputy chief of the directorate for foreign operations. Potentially the most important asset we've had here for quite awhile. Your own little cameo in the final act of the Cold War."

Claire nodded, pleased yet wary, mostly due to the one big question that continued to chafe at her, like a blister on her heel: Why her?

10

Back in the prime of his career, Clark Baucom had never much liked playing a backup role—watching from the weeds, for example, while someone else took care of the main event. This was partly because in many of the places he'd worked—Hungary, Czechoslovakia, and Poland, to name a few—the Agency's resources had been so thin on the ground that you were lucky if you could scare up a couple of local agents to help with logistics or serve as extra sets of eyes and ears. So he had generally taken the starring role for himself.

But at the moment, seated at a dreary tram stop on Frankfurter Allee in what was still known as East Berlin, the role suited him fine. He was happy to be needed, even if this job was unpaid and off the books. He hadn't felt quite this alive since, well, six months earlier, when Bill Gentry had gently but firmly nudged him into the ranks of the retired.

Baucom had known exactly where to set up shop almost from the moment Claire had told him where her rendezvous would take place. As soon as she'd opened the map on the table at Zwiebelfisch, he had jabbed this very spot with his index finger.

"There. That's the optimal vantage point for observing your approach. It's a tram stop shelter, with plexiglass sides and a roof in case it rains. Enough different lines stop there that it won't look suspicious if I let a few trams pass without boarding."

"Great. And then?"

"Well, let's see . . ."

He ran his finger along the yellow lines of the busier streets, able to envision from memory exactly how everything looked. Some of the names—Karl-Marx-Allee, Lenin Allee—would almost certainly be purged in the coming months, just as previous names honoring kaisers and imperial heroes had been purged in the aftermath of the Second World War, and, before that, the names of Jews and leftists when the Nazis had taken power. With every block came a memory of smells, sights, noises—sensations so vivid that he wouldn't have been surprised to find his fingertip covered in grit by the time he lifted it from the map.

"Here's the café where you end up. It's a *Café-Imbiss*, actually, a fast-food joint that sells coffee and crap sausages. Half a block away, on the same side of the street, there's a news kiosk, right here." He tapped the spot twice. "It sells cigarettes and coffee, with a couple of tables out front. I can walk over there from the tram stop. Buying a coffee will give me an excuse to hang around for another ten or fifteen minutes, longer if he's got other customers to keep him busy. Then I'll make my way back up the street slow enough to keep the doorway of your café in sight for another ten or fifteen. I'll watch for you. If you don't like the feel of things when you're leaving, button up your overcoat as you come outside. Otherwise, leave the coat unbuttoned."

"Okay."

"And if you're not out of there in twenty, I'm coming in for a look."

"Make it thirty."

"You sure?"

"Yes. But what if they take me out the back?"

"The café is in a standalone building. I'll watch both sides for anyone passing to the rear, and for any arriving vehicles in the back alley. I'll scout the alley before I set up shop."

"Sounds good. If I'm already feeling threatened on arrival, I'll pause at the door to check inside my purse before going in."

"Got it. Oh, and I'm following you back afterward, whether you button up your overcoat or not. That's mandatory. But if you do button up, I'll tighten the distance."

"I'll want plenty of notes afterward on anyone who comes onto your radar. I guess that means I'll need to debrief you after Ward has debriefed me."

"I'll find us a nice, neutral location with more privacy."

"Not that I mind this place."

"Nobody minds Zwiebelfisch. Or not after their second beer."

Claire smiled, folded up the map, and signaled for the waiter.

"In that case, let's have another. If you're up for it."

Baucom was more of a whiskey and cognac man when he was having more than one. All this beer would keep him up half the night, peeing and gassy, but he sensed in her offer a need to keep talking, so he nodded, and she called for another round, which arrived at its usual efficient speed.

"It's a good thing for me you decided to stick around Berlin," she said. "Will you ever go back to the States?"

"To visit? Sure. To live?" He shook his head. "I don't even know the place anymore. The politics, the popular culture. Maybe I was never really at home there, a Foreign Service brat from age five. Warped me for life."

"Any family there?"

"My younger brother and his big brood. Four kids. They came over for a visit back in the late '70s. Fun enough while they were around, but mostly it made me glad I didn't have kids of my own. They wore me out."

She smiled.

"My sister has three, and it always makes me claustrophobic. They're sweet and precious, and they're not brats. But whenever I see my sister with them, barely keeping track, I can't help but think of her as this once magnificent ship that's now dragging three anchors through shallow water. Family stabilizes you, but you can never go far from the home port. Not for long."

"Still."

"Still?"

"I dunno."

He held his tongue, mostly because he knew she wouldn't have wanted to hear what he had to say. This was no time for a gloomy lecture on finding yourself alone late in life, not right before a sensitive op.

But Baucom knew the symptoms firsthand, and in Claire Saylor he saw someone for whom the job, the *life*, had taken hold deeply enough to pull her free from all other attachments. Exhilarating while it was happening—a life rich in experience that left you with plenty of stories and memories, but perhaps no one to share them with. It's why he tended to talk too much whenever companionship did come along, if only to feel the blood move again, not so much from the company of an attractive woman as from the kinship of a colleague still on the chase— possibly the last great chase that the Cold War would offer in this city.

Claire asked again about the logistics of crossing in and out of East Berlin now that the Wall was breached. He filled her in on the latest. But as they neared the bottom of their glasses he decided to at least take a stab at articulating his thoughts on where his life had led him. Maybe he was feeling fatherly. Or maybe he was just curious, because Claire had always struck him as someone worth knowing better.

"So, any men in your life?"

"Why's that always the question every guy eventually asks?"

"Is it? Well it's not some sort of ham-handed pass, if that's what you're thinking."

"I wasn't. But would you be asking a male colleague that kind of question?"

"Five years ago? No way. Now? I kind of wish someone had asked me back when it might have made a difference."

Her expression softened.

"I don't go begging for company, if that's your worry. I lead quite the full life in Paris. In fact, there's one man in particular who I am sure is missing me as we speak."

"And are you missing him?"

"I will be in an hour or so."

Baucom laughed along with her, even as he couldn't help but picture her later in her hotel room, undressing for bed as she thought of her lover in Paris. He pushed away that image and swallowed more beer.

"You're right. I shouldn't have asked."

"Oh, I don't mind. Or not that much. And they do tend to come and go. Men, I mean."

"Your doing or theirs?"

"They seem to think it's mine."

"This work will do that. The travel, the isolation. And the trust issues alone, well . . ."

She nodded in sympathy.

"You spend entire months building a personal façade and concealing the real you, then in your downtime you're supposed to open up to somebody you've just met? How's that supposed to work? Your glass is empty, want another round?"

"No. But go ahead."

"God, no. Haven't had this much beer since college. I'll be peeing till two in the morning."

He laughed and reached for the tab, but she grabbed it first and motioned for the waiter.

"Let Paris station pick this up. Besides, you'll be earning it tomorrow."

"And beyond then?"

"Good question. Let's see how it goes."

And now he was watching from the tram stop as dusk approached, with today's *Berliner Zeitung* unfolded in his lap. He wore a fraying wool overcoat, black wool pants, clunky brown shoes, and a gray flat cap, which made him look like one of those old men who sold hot chestnuts from dented chrome carts.

Taking stock of his surroundings, he noticed that flourishes of color and Westernized glitz were already sprouting on the wider boulevards like this one. The bench opposite him was plastered with a red ad for West cigarettes. The slogan read like a cheeky taunt: "Taste the West!"

Baucom supposed it wouldn't be much longer before discarded burger wrappers from McDonald's would be blowing around his ankles. The signs of rapid change had been even more prevalent at Potsdamer Platz, where he'd crossed over without even being stopped.

That had felt strange, and other crossings were reopening every week. Long-shuttered "ghost stations" on the U-Bahn and S-Bahn lines were stirring to life after years of disuse, as city transit workers began restitching the wounds of division. The station at Anhalter Bahnhof still looked like a time capsule from the end of the Nazi era, an echoing vault of white tiles and Gothic lettering, still smudged with the grime of the 1940s.

After walking through the Brandenburg Gate an hour earlier he had passed Soviet soldiers selling watches, uniforms, mess kits, rifle scopes, and other military items recently stripped from their barracks. Word on the street was that, with minimal discretion, you could bargain with some of these fellows for more lethal items stashed in more secure locations a few blocks away, like AK-47s, or even grenade launchers.

He had taken a roundabout path to the observation post, partly to check for surveillance, partly to see how things looked on the narrower, drearier streets where change would be slower in coming. He still found it hard to imagine how people had lived here, year after year, without going a bit crazy from the drab sameness of it all. Stucco buildings coated in soot, a monochrome gray world where the curbs were lined bumper to bumper by boxy Trabis, the same scene replicated on every block, grim little tunnels that led deeper into dystopia. It even smelled different over here, especially at this time of year—a sour bouquet of coal smoke and boiled vegetables that would cling to his overcoat for days.

Baucom checked his watch, trying to look like a bored passenger awaiting his tram. Claire was due almost any second. They had agreed the night before that it would be better if he didn't follow her here.

"If you acquire an entourage along the way, I'll have a far better chance of spotting it if I'm not a part of it," he'd said.

"And there's no sense in giving them an easy look at you this early in the game," Claire said.

"True for our side as much as for theirs. I'm not too keen on losing my pension over an unauthorized involvement in a sensitive op."

They had agreed that at the first sign of any CIA personnel, Baucom would quietly depart the playing field and melt into the background. If Ward had secretly provided for backups, then his role would not only be superfluous, but potentially disruptive. He was seeing no sign of that, however, as he watched from the tram stop, waiting for Claire.

And there she was now, emerging from around the corner at the spot where he had expected to see her, striding at an unhurried pace up Karl-Marx-Allee, with three blocks to go.

She was good at this. Baucom felt that instinctively as he watched her stride, her face, the way she carried herself—alert, but not glancing around like someone who felt hunted; a spy in her natural state, meaning watched yet essentially alone. No pursuers yet from either side, or none that he'd been able to spot. It brought his own alertness to the fore, and the old excitement as well.

Claire reached the block of the café. And that's when he first saw them, maybe forty yards farther back—two men who had just moved out of hiding. Then a third man stepped into view a block beyond the café. Like Baucom, all three must have been lying in wait, and they were now converging like iron filings drawn to a magnet. Each man was dressed in dark warm-up pants and a black leather coat, plus shiny leather shoes, probably Italian. It was the signature wardrobe of a new breed of Russian mobster that had arisen as the effects of Perestroika began opening the Soviet economy. That, plus the collapse of the Wall, had inevitably drawn these sorts of fellows to East Berlin. But why here, for this meeting? Had the HVA contact hired them as cheap labor, now that his own agency was being dismantled?

Two of them were younger, late twenties. One had a tattoo on his neck. The third fellow, hanging farther back, looked closer to forty, and was probably the team leader.

Christ, they were so obvious. It was like they *wanted* to be noticed, thugs staking a claim to this newly abandoned turf, and to this woman who had dared to enter it. Either they'd known in advance she was coming alone, or they simply didn't care who spotted them.

Claire reached the café and disappeared inside. She did not pause to check her purse, meaning she apparently didn't feel threatened by the recent arrivals—not yet, anyway—because she certainly would have noticed them.

One of the men behind her continued toward the door. The one in the opposite direction took up an observation post at the news kiosk, the spot where Baucom had planned to go next. The older fellow, the apparent leader, hung back a block away, still not making any effort to blend in.

His face was vaguely familiar, and Baucom wondered if that was because he was one of the regulars from the big KGB complex down in the suburb of Karlshorst, where the Russians had been based since the end of the war. In 1945 they had shared their barracks with the Red Army and its victorious leader, Field Marshal Zhukov, who became such a celebrated hero that a jealous Stalin got rid of him.

Baucom checked his watch and began his countdown. Half an hour. If he didn't see her by then, he was going in. He yawned and stretched, wanting to look as bored as possible, and in doing so allowed himself a look at the apartment buildings behind him, Soviet-style drabness at its worst, yet also an achievement of a sort. The East Germans had managed to construct hundreds of these buildings almost overnight back in the late 1970s.

On a gloomy day like this the residents tended to keep their blinds drawn to prevent the warmth from bleeding out their poorly insulated windows. Maybe that's why his eyes were so easily drawn to one particular window in the middle of the sixth floor, where a solitary figure stood in the fading light as if he, too, were watching this scene unfold.

A passing bus diverted Baucom's attention. He turned his gaze back toward the café, where the first of Claire's pursuers was now stepping inside. The second one was still lingering at the newsstand, although he hadn't bothered to buy anything as a pretext. Yes, they were making a statement. It was a show of force. For his benefit, or someone else's?

He shook open his newspaper and watched the doorway of the café from above the pages. No vehicle had yet entered the alley behind the building.

A creeping sensation of being observed overcame him, but neither of the two Russians was looking his way, nor was their boss down the block. He glanced over his shoulder, up toward the apartment window in the middle of the sixth floor. The shade was now drawn, but not completely.

Baucom didn't like being this outnumbered, but there wasn't a damn thing he could do about it. If someone was able to whisk Claire away from here, she'd have only him and the tracking beacon to help her.

He decided that wasn't good enough, which meant he needed to start planning some contingencies. Two blocks down, on the opposite side of Frankfurter Allee, he watched a taxi stop at the curb to let out a fare.

Baucom again checked his watch. Twenty-five minutes to go. He stood, folded his newspaper, and set out across the boulevard.

11

Several hours after Claire and Baucom had finished their last beers at Zwiebelfisch, Emil Grimm had headed up a woodland trail near his dacha on the first of two nocturnal errands. It was bitterly cold. A doughnut glaze of ice already coated the shallow end of the lake.

Night animals stirred as he ascended. A massive owl passed overhead with a gentle throb of wingbeats, which Emil felt more than heard. The underbrush crackled as something on four legs moved off to a safer distance. On the horizon, a new moon came to rest atop the tree line like a clipped thumbnail. Stay out here long enough and he would almost certainly hear the shriek of a fox searching for a mate.

Emil's business was just as urgent as that of the fox, he supposed, so he took care to move as quietly as possible as he continued uphill. Earlier scouting had revealed a car parked on the dirt lane about forty yards down from his front gate, a dark Citroën, no doubt manned by one of Krauss's goons. By now the driver was probably chain-smoking to stay awake as he kept an eye out for Emil's Wartburg. Emil doubted the fellow would have the initiative to come tramping after him through the woods at this cold and lonely hour, but he assumed nothing.

A thump to his rear made him stop and switch on his flashlight. The sound repeated itself as the beam settled on a pair of glowing white eyes in the underbrush, shoulder high. Probably a buck, stamping a hoof to warn him off.

Years of practice had made Emil pretty good at decoding these eerie orbs of light. Pale red eyes lower to the ground usually belonged to a rabbit. Yellow, a raccoon. Green was a housecat, greenish white a fox. Boar eyes didn't glow at all, which was disconcerting because their poor night vision meant they—and their tusks—were more likely to blunder into you.

That was how he now thought of Dieter Krauss—as a dangerously equipped creature blundering about in the dark. After their chat near Karola's house, Emil had watched Krauss's Volvo loom up in his rearview mirror in a clumsy show of intimidation on his way out of Prenden. He had tested Krauss's resolve by pulling into a gas station just beyond town. The Volvo had braked, paused, then accelerated onward. Emil watched it turn onto the ramp for the Autobahn as he rolled to a stop by the gas pumps.

As soon as Krauss was out of sight, Emil went inside the gas station and asked to use the telephone. When the clerk hesitated, Emil showed his Stasi ID. In Berlin the gesture might well have provoked a defiant insult, a snort of derision. Out here it still carried some weight. The clerk put the phone on the counter without a word, and then disappeared into the back as if to wash his hands of the matter. Fine by Emil. It was a call he hadn't wanted Bettina to overhear, and any additional privacy was a bonus.

He dialed the number for the police station in Bernau. Dorn wasn't in, so he left a message.

"Tell him that his friend from Prenden called and left an address. He'll know what it means. Ready?"

"Go ahead."

Emil read out the address Krauss had given him for his new base of operations.

"Tell him that the best time to go is probably around noon, just before lunch, when his target usually heads over to an *Imbiss* next door. Oh, and one other thing."

"Yes?"

"He should make sure his evidence technician carefully checks the lining of Lothar Fischer's jacket."

"Noted. Your name and number, sir?"

"The lieutenant has it."

He hung up, pleased by the idea of letting Krauss and Dorn keep each other occupied. He then returned to his dacha, where he fried a leathery schnitzel and made a salad for his own dinner, and then carefully fed Bettina before reading her a short story by Stefan Heym, from a new collection that probably would have been banned only four months earlier. Not everything was worse than before.

Afterward, he attended to his usual nightly chores for keeping Bettina clean and sanitary, which by now came as naturally to him as doing the dishes. He decided to make an early night of it, turning in at 9:30. It was an easy adjustment out here in the quiet woods. He cranked open his bedroom window a few inches because he liked to sleep in the cold beneath heavy blankets.

There was a light thump on the roof overhead, and then a skittering sound, like tiny feet. Mice, perhaps, or a squirrel, always a problem in these old wooden dachas, but he was accustomed to it by now.

After a few hours that felt like only seconds he jolted awake to the chirping of the alarm on his plastic Casio watch. He had set it for 3 a.m., because that was when his Stasi training told him these sorts of errands were most likely to be successful. The Hour of Opportunity, the instructors called it. So here he was, then, out on the prowl.

Emil switched off the flashlight and listened as the buck sauntered off. Thinking of Krauss made him worry again about two-legged creatures, so he slowly backtracked twenty yards to check for pursuers. Then he stopped to flex his right knee, which had stiffened after the climb. He sniffed the air for cigarettes but detected only the smokiness of his own coat—another reason he never should have lit up earlier that day. Otherwise, the air was sharp and clean, like on a night in the Arctic.

The big owl called out, four hoots with a rising note at the end. Emil took it as a good omen, the town crier saying all was well. The trail forked at the top of the hill, and he turned left onto a wider path favored by mountain bikers.

Just ahead, lit dimly by starlight, was the spindly outline of a twenty-foot-high structure built of planks and two-by-fours. It looked like a scale model of a watchtower, a security outpost you'd find at the border. In the night it gleamed black, although it was painted forest green. It was a hunter's stand, with a ladder leading up to a rough hut with firing slits and a sloped plywood roof.

Emil and Lothar Fischer had built it seven years ago after securing permission from the local hunting collective. As with all such activities, this one had been strictly regulated. They had filed their design plans with the district forest ranger, who had locked them away at the lodge next to his house, where the collective's members stored their rifles and ammunition. Technically, any member could use the stand by registering in advance. But once word got around that two Stasi colonels had built it, Emil and Lothar tended to have exclusive use, which was fine with them. Of the two, Lothar was the more frequent and enthusiastic hunter. Emil tended to enjoy the waiting and watching more than the shooting.

He slowed his pace as he passed to the right of the stand, not daring to stop in case he was being observed. He flicked his flashlight a few times, ostensibly to check the path ahead, and those flickering moments offered just enough light to see that the ground beneath the tower was undisturbed, still covered by pine straw and windblown leaves. The framing around the base was sturdy enough to keep out any boars, and it seemed clear that no human had been poking around.

So that was one chore done.

Emil continued to the next trail junction, where he turned left and headed back downhill toward the lake. It was the route Lothar must have taken on his final walk, and within seven or eight minutes Emil reached the yellow crime scene tape. The body was gone, the scene searched and combed. He shivered, probably from the cold, and then checked over his shoulder before resuming his walk. At his rear gate he punched in a security code to enter, and then walked around the house to the nearest bedroom window, where he cupped his hands on the pane to peer inside.

It was like looking in on a child in a winter slumber. He envied her the warmth of the bed and hoped that she was dreaming of a scene in which her health was restored, her legs strong as she bounded along, laughing, at his side. Emil looked down at the ground to collect himself. His toes were numb, so he stamped his feet twice on the hard ground and set out for his next stop.

He took the back way in case the watcher in the Citroën had his eyes on the lane, and within a few minutes had reached the narrow path that led to Lothar Fischer's dacha.

Earlier that day, Dorn's men had taken custody of Lothar's dog,

Gretel. Emil had watched out his window as they led her down a path on a leash. The poor dog had looked bewildered, repeatedly checking over her shoulder for any sign of her master. She was a sweet dog, with a weakness for treats. He hoped they found her a good home, but for the moment the most important fact of her removal was that Lothar's place was now empty and unguarded.

The first thing he checked was Lothar's vegetable garden. He was displeased but not at all surprised to see that someone had recently been digging there. The earth was turned and gouged, with clumps of brown weeds cast to the side. A shovel was propped against the nearby wall of the dacha. Whoever had used it hadn't even bothered to clean off the blade. Footprints of various sizes crisscrossed the raw ground. He turned away with a shudder.

Emil bypassed the front door and went around to the back. In his overcoat pocket was a small kit with an array of lock-picking tools, which the ministry had given him the same week as his Pistol-M. He took off his gloves, chose a slender steel tool, and within seconds sprung the lock. He stepped inside, shut the door behind him, and switched on his flashlight just long enough to refamiliarize himself with the lay of the land. Then he switched the light back off and waited for his eyes to readjust.

Lothar's dacha was a little bigger than his, with an extra bedroom and a second bathroom. It was also better appointed—electric baseboard heating, newer appliances. The great room was furnished like a typical living room of almost every tower block in the German Democratic Republic, with a massive wood-grain console that took up most of the main wall. Its shelves and compartments housed a TV, a hi-fi with a turntable, plenty of books, and a framed glossy photo of Erich Honecker, the East German premier who'd been forced from his job the month before the Wall came down. Honecker was now holed up only a few miles away, taking refuge at an Episcopal vicarage in Bernau.

"Hello, Erich," Emil couldn't help but whisper. "Started packing for South America yet?"

The curtains, the carpet, and the upholstery were dominated by brown and gold tones in bold, modernist patterns that had looked out of date almost the moment they were installed. Everything smelled like cigarette smoke.

Emil slipped off his shoes, partly to keep his movements quieter, but also to avoid tracking mud and twigs across the floor. He scanned the room as his eyes adjusted to the gloom. Dorn's men had already been here, and had left obvious traces of their search—disturbed shelves, open drawers.

The carpet had been rolled up in a corner where they had removed a floorboard. Just like a cop to think that's where Lothar would have hidden something. Any well-trained spy would consider such a location to be beneath him, a cliché. Emil took a look anyway, flicking on his flashlight to peer into the opening. Nothing but a few mouse droppings, unless of course Dorn's men had taken something with them, which he doubted.

From previous visits, Emil knew that Lothar had turned one of his bedrooms into a hobbyist workshop, where he had spent hours building those quaintly kitschy little matchbox rooms that the tourists liked to buy at Christmas shops. He decided to start there.

The ashtray smell gave way to that of wood shavings and varnish as he entered the doorway. There was a long workbench, impeccably neat, with a wall of hand tools stored just so—screwdrivers and chisels in rows by ascending size, three kinds of spirit level, hammers, pliers, wrenches, awls, and so on. Off to one side, a few recently finished matchboxes, freshly painted, had been set out to dry. One looked like a tiny living room, with a Christmas tree in the middle and a boy on a stepladder, placing an ornament. The other matchbox had an outdoor scene of a father and son fishing from a rowboat. The father smoked a tiny pipe.

Like so many spies Emil had known, Lothar was a miniaturist at heart, a trait that knew no borders. He had read with fascination of their formidable American adversary, counterspy James Angleton, whose hobbies were fly tying and cultivating orchids. Little wonder that such people sometimes tied themselves into knots by pondering the details of files and agent reports. And what good had that done any of them?

How, then, had Lothar become sloppy enough in his work habits for Krauss to have heard so easily about his most recent movements? Disturbing.

Emil was looking for a specific item. In recent years, with his memory slipping, Lothar had taken to scribbling notes to remind himself of upcoming meetings and appointments. Such notations might be as simple as a number or two on a scrap of paper, or even a block of wood, along with a set of initials. That's what Emil hoped to find.

It seemed like such a trivial goal, but without that information Emil might soon be facing the prospect of a long and fruitless day, and perhaps the end of everything he'd been working toward. But where would Lothar put such a reminder? His pocket, perhaps? If so, then it had long since been confiscated by either Dorn's men or Krauss's.

There was nothing like it on the workbench, or pinned to any wall, or folded on the small table where Lothar kept sketches of the designs for his little matchboxes. Emil supposed it might be elsewhere—on a bedside table, maybe, or stuck to the refrigerator.

He was about to open a drawer beneath the workbench when he heard footsteps approaching outdoors. He held still, listening. The steps halted near the front of the house. A key rattled in the knob of the front door.

Emil slid into a corner on stockinged feet until he was hidden behind a huge drill press. He heard the front door open with a click and a creak. Then a light came on in the great room. Footsteps crossed the floor—one person, probably male, moving with the assurance of either ownership or authority. Lothar had a son who lived in Jena and an older brother in poor health in Leipzig. Emil watched the lighted opening to the great room for any movement or shadow.

A tall, well-groomed man crossed the opening. It was his old boss, Markus "Mischa" Wolf, and it was all Emil could do to keep from gasping in surprise.

Wolf disappeared as he moved off toward the big console. The next thing Emil heard was the sound of books being pulled from shelves, and of pages being flipped—in one volume after another. He wondered how long he could remain undetected. If Wolf next went into the kitchen, or a bathroom, he might be able to slip back into the great room and out the back door.

Then he remembered that he had left his muddy shoes by the back door, near the console. Wolf, one of the most careful observers Emil had ever known, surely would have spotted them by now.

The house went silent. Perhaps Wolf had sensed that he wasn't alone.

Emil sighed, came out of the corner, and announced his presence as he stepped through the lighted doorway.

"Mischa?"

Wolf did not flinch, or even widen his eyes. He had always been difficult to surprise, and Emil saw now that he was holding one of his muddy shoes.

"Well, that explains these, at least," Wolf said, speaking as casually as if they had just bumped into each other at the market. "Did you take them off to avoid leaving tracks, or because it was quieter?"

"Both."

"And during the Hour of Opportunity, no less. How predictable that we would both choose it. But what enticed you to come here, Emil?"

It was vintage Mischa Wolf—the seemingly offhand question, offered affably even as it implied that a confession was now in order.

"I suppose I'm here for the same reason as you. To try and make some sense of what happened to Lothar."

"Well, that's the beginning of an explanation, anyway. How 'bout if we have a drink while we discuss it further. Lothar keeps—*kept*—a very nice supply here."

"At this hour?"

"Unless you have somewhere more urgent to be." Wolf smiled slyly. "Besides, you look like you could use one. Make yourself comfortable over there on the couch. I'll do the honors."

Emil had little choice but to accept. The problem now would be in coming up with a plausible explanation for why he was here. And who knew? Maybe Wolf had suggested a drink because he, too, needed to come up with a cover story.

Wolf turned away from him and reached toward the top row of cabinets. He seemed to know exactly where to look. Emil glanced at his watch and settled onto the couch. The night was shaping up to be more complicated than he had bargained for.

12

Lothar's liquor cabinet was a revelation. Inside were French cognacs, Russian vodkas, scotch whisky, British gin, American bourbon. Every brand was top of the line, including some you couldn't find even in the exclusive stores for party officials.

On Emil's many previous visits, Lothar had always grabbed a few beers for them from the fridge, or, if he was feeling more expansive, maybe a chilled bottle of Riesling. Wolf, obviously, was accustomed to a higher level of hospitality, which made Emil wonder what else Lothar had held out on him.

Wolf sorted through the offerings with the eye of a connoisseur, and didn't ask for Emil's preference. He was a decade older than Emil, but his posture was still upright, his movements vigorous, his brown eyes probing and active. He had built a towering professional reputation that probably exceeded his abilities. The disparity had inspired some jealousy in the ranks, although mostly among those who'd been passed over for promotions.

Even at this ungodly hour, Wolf was impeccably dressed in creased charcoal slacks and a pressed white shirt. He exuded competence; a gray eminence eager to take charge. The only time Emil had ever seen him look out of his element was at a public appearance in the week before the Wall came down, when Wolf had gone to Alexanderplatz to address a restive crowd of half a million protesters.

Emil and Bettina had watched the rally on television at their apartment in Berlin, although they could hear the distant roar of the crowd through their walls. For three hours, dissidents and reformers climbed onto a rough wooden platform mounted on the bed of a truck to exhort the masses. Whenever a representative of the government spoke, the crowd jeered defiantly. It was extraordinary.

Then Wolf stepped to the microphone, holding a folded sheaf of remarks in his right hand. His other hand was stuffed in his pocket, as if for ballast, and his face radiated the confidence of a man accustomed to taking charge in difficult circumstances. Surely they would be won over by his calming voice of reform, the very sort of man to reunify the people with their estranged and discredited leaders.

But within only a minute the boos and whistles began, and at times they were loud enough to make him stop altogether. Wolf looked bewildered.

"My God, are his hands trembling?" Emil had asked aloud. Bettina blinked once, meaning she certainly thought so. The man seemed to shrink in stature before their eyes, and for Emil and many others watching that day, that was the moment when change felt not only inevitable but irreversible, even if no one would have yet predicted that the entire edifice would crumble five days later, virtually overnight.

Now Wolf looked more like the man who had always patrolled the corridors of Normanenstrasse, calm and resolute, a planner who surrounded himself with other careful planners. He poured them two fingers apiece of single-malt scotch, handed Emil a glass, and raised his own for a toast as he settled into an easy chair on the opposite side of a modernist coffee table.

"Prost!"

"Prost," Emil replied.

Each man sipped. Neither took his eyes off the other. Wolf reached into a pocket for a lighter and a pack of Kabinett cigarettes, his long-time brand. Then, after looking around the room, he seemed to think better of it and pocketed the items.

"No sense drawing attention to our visit, I suppose. Unless you'd like to light up as well."

"I've been trying to quit."

"Ah, well. To your health, then." He nodded, took another sip of whisky, then zeroed in on Emil.

"I hope it is not inappropriate of me to ask how Bettina is faring. I have been away, so if anything has, well, *happened* recently . . ."

"She is still living, if that's what you mean. But her condition continues to deteriorate. We do what we can."

"I am sorry. Christa was always fond of her."

Christa was Wolf's second wife, although he had split up with her four years ago to marry his current wife, Andrea. Both women were more than twenty years younger than him. Christa was tall, Andrea was short, and they were longtime friends. Or had been until Wolf's affair with Andrea, which had supposedly begun right here on the Bauersee, at Wolf's dacha. Emil had heard all the gossip then, partly because the prudish Mielke had made such a fuss about everything. Wolf had been on the verge of retirement at the time.

"Tell me, Emil. What do you know about that Citroën parked further up the lane?"

"It belongs to one of Dieter Krauss's people."

"Krauss has been here?"

"He was one of the first on the scene of the shooting, with three of his men. He claims he's still in business, working out of some satellite office he set up on his own. Then Lieutenant Dorn arrived, a cop from Bernau. He's investigating Lothar's case. Dorn and his men chased Krauss away."

Wolf laughed with what sounded like genuine amusement.

"I would have enjoyed seeing that." Then he frowned. "I did hear that it was done with his own pistol."

"Who told you that?"

Wolf shrugged.

"Well, is it true? You saw his body, yes?"

Emil found it odd that Wolf knew these details but hadn't known about Krauss. What sort of source would have told him the first item but not the other? Or had he perhaps watched some of the events firsthand, from a vantage point in the trees? Emil supposed it was even possible that Wolf had quietly walked down for a look at the scene while Emil was talking to Dorn in his dacha. Or he could have acquired his knowledge another way—by being there when the shooting happened—a thought jarring enough to make Emil take another sip of scotch.

"Yes, I saw it. Saw *him*. Lothar was holding a Pistol-M in his right hand."

Wolf showed no immediate reaction to the latter forensic detail, which was a bit surprising. The man knew the tics and habits of his agents down to the tiniest detail, but maybe he'd been less assiduous about learning those of his fellow managers.

"Do you really think it's possible he took his own life?" Wolf asked.

"Well, he was out of a job. Living alone, with an uncertain future."

"Oh, it's so much larger than that, don't you think? This is an existential crisis, Emil. We gave the greatest efforts and passions of our lives to a cause that has been deemed useless. It's as if our work never existed. And as spies, what are we to make of all those secrets that were once matters of life and death? How do we even assign them a value now? What are we even to make of *ourselves*?"

This, too, was vintage Mischa Wolf—turning a discussion of bleak practicalities into a philosophical meditation. Maybe at some level he was still tending to his image, that of the deep thinker among ministry knuckle-draggers; the Sage of the Spree, ruminating aloud to show that he hadn't lost a step.

"Knowing Lothar, I think he was most worried about where his next paycheck was coming from," Emil said. "And it's a valid question. Who could possibly want to hire us now?"

"I suppose you're right. Did you hear Bachmann is working as a doorman at some big hotel near the Ku-Damm?"

It was news to Emil, and a bit shocking. Bachmann had helped Lothar run their operations against the Americans.

"You're serious?"

"Quite. He wears a ridiculous uniform, like a nineteenth-century Balkan hussar. He bows and scrapes for everyone who comes through the door, surviving on tips from the bankers who pull up in their Mercedes. And, well, you heard about my son-in-law, I suppose."

"Yes. I'm sorry. I hope he's recovering."

"My daughter seems to think so, but we'll see. Half a million D-marks! Whoever would have believed it?"

Then, an interlude of silence, as each of them took a contemplative sip.

The whisky was already working its magic. Emil felt himself sag with weariness as the shock of their initial encounter wore off. The lateness of the hour lent an air of unreality to the scene. Were they really doing this, two intruders who happened to be old colleagues, chatting sensibly at half past four in the morning in their dead comrade's dacha? And if that were possible, had the Wall really fallen? For that matter, had it ever even existed, except in their minds?

The house creaked in a sudden gust of wind, and at that moment Emil would not have been at all surprised to see Lothar's former wife, Käthe, enter from the kitchen, followed by a younger, healthier Bettina, the two of them carrying trays of snacks, laughing and chatting, with the prospect of a pleasantly sociable evening ahead. He hoped that Bettina was sleeping comfortably.

Wolf broke the spell.

"Now the Americans have entered the bidding war."

"So I've heard. Dialing for dollars, I heard someone call it."

They shared an uneasy laugh.

"Apparently one of our people sold them an office directory which even has some of our home numbers. Have they reached you, Emil?"

"No. Any number listed for me would be for the apartment in Berlin. I haven't been there in weeks."

"Yes, well, I heard today they've started approaching people face-to-face. Bachmann, for one. They went up to him right there in the hotel. Took him aside in the lobby, didn't care at all who was watching. He blew them off, of course. Quite angrily."

"Incredible. I doubt they'll come tramping through the woods up here anytime soon."

"No? Give them time."

"Well, if they do, you could certainly command top dollar."

"The West Germans already tried. I said no."

"Of course, but who knows what the Americans might offer. Not just money. A house in a sunny climate. Asylum. You could name your price."

Wolf scowled and shook his head.

"Except the thing they'd want most from me is names, don't you think? Names of everyone who ever worked for us on their side. Everyone I ever recruited, nurtured, protected. And I just can't do that, Emil. Those people risked their lives for me, and they've remained loyal. I won't sell them out."

"Maybe in a way you'd be setting them free."

"*Free*? How do you figure that?"

"Don't you think our friends in Moscow will want to employ them now? Surely the KGB must have a pretty good idea of who's available. Or will soon, if they've carted off copies of our records like everyone says."

He paused, to give Wolf time to either confirm or deny that rumor. Wolf did neither, so Emil continued.

"Our old agents are a perfect fit for them. What's the term I heard one of our tech geeks use about some gadget of theirs? 'Plug and play'? That kind of sums it up, don't you think?"

"Possibly."

"And do you think that's what any East German abroad will want to do with his life? Trade one master for another, except now by working for a foreign country?"

Wolf dismissed the idea with a halfhearted wave, but his eyes looked troubled. "Fortunately, I decided years ago to divide up those agent records into so many different pieces that I doubt any of our old adversaries can possibly obtain them all. As for Moscow, they can't even make up their mind what to do with their own people, much less ours. A year from now even the KGB may no longer exist."

"So I take it that your trip did not go well."

Wolf raised his glass, this time taking more of a swig than a sip.

"For fifty-five years Russia has been a second home for me, and for others, too. We've worked with them like brothers. We wear their medals on our chest. Yet what good is any of that to us now?"

Emil knew the man's story well enough, because it was an integral part of the Wolf legend. In 1934, after the Nazis took power, the eleven-year-old Wolf had fled with his family to Moscow. They were communists seeking political asylum, and having a Jewish father had doubled the stakes. They remained in the Soviet Union throughout the war, surviving not only the German invasion but also Stalin's purges.

By the time the fighting stopped in May 1945, Wolf was twenty-two and spoke Russian with a Moscow accent. He returned to Germany with a cadre of like-minded expats, dispatched by Stalin to establish a political beachhead upon the ruins of Soviet-occupied Berlin. Their hope was to build an anti-fascist utopia based on the ideals of Lenin,

Marx, and Engels. The KGB, of course, was right there with them, watching over their shoulders, ready to assist in any crackdowns needed to get things under way.

Emil had been twelve when the war ended. Two years older and he might have had a rifle in his hands instead of sheltering with his mother and sisters in the cellar beneath their bombed-out apartment. Not until years later, at university, did he learn any Russian. By then his father had walked home from the war and gone to work for the Stasi's domestic security directorate. Later, his father was promoted to district officer, a prominence that made Emil a natural target for recruitment, and he joined the ministry in 1956. Five years after that, shortly after the Wall went up, Emil moved to the directorate for foreign intelligence, or HVA, which by that time was under Wolf's leadership.

Wolf, who had taken command of the HVA just before his thirtieth birthday, was already working wonders. His achievement in building up the agency had been a bit like taking a crystal radio kit and turning it into a massive signal tower, like the one the Americans used in Teufelsberg.

From Emil's first days as a spy he had sensed a cultural and professional gulf between "the Russians," as Wolf's founding cadre was sometimes known, and the later hires like him. Now, four years after Wolf's retirement, pretty much all of the old Russian crowd was out of the picture.

"So, you don't think Gorbachev will raise a finger to help us?" Emil asked.

"I couldn't even get an audience. He's too preoccupied with making the Americans fall in love with his new Perestroika. They don't all feel that way, of course. The KGB station chief in Dresden, that Putin fellow, is as outraged as we are. But I suppose we're on our own now. Isn't that why we're both here, poking around in Lothar's things? C'mon, Emil, you must have heard what people have been saying about him."

There it was again, the floating notion that the meticulous Lothar had recently turned reckless and indiscreet. Where was it coming from, and how had Wolf heard it?

"You think Lothar was going to sell us out?"

"It was certainly a possibility. Tell me, do you know that fellow running the documents task force for Sub-Department 7, Andreas Plotz?"

Plotz again. Also disturbing.

"I am familiar with him, of course. Why?"

"He's been saying some things. About Lothar, apparently. That's why I came over here, to see what Lothar might have left behind."

"And you entered with a key."

Wolf shrugged.

"We once had to use Lothar's dacha as a safe house, for debriefing a defector. One of the few who crossed over in our direction. It was before we built the *Waldhaus*, further down the lake. He gave me a key then, and I suppose I never gave it back. But, Emil, you still haven't really explained why you're here. By breaking in, no less, so I gather it must be for something important."

Emil sighed and stared at his feet for a few awkward seconds, gathering himself to deliver the answer that he had come up with after his second sip of whisky. Wolf, well trained in spotting fakes and lies, would be watching carefully for any telltale sign of stress or deception. But Emil was also trained in such matters, a thought that calmed him enough to look Wolf in the eye with complete confidence.

"I am looking for a file," he said. Then he shook his head in feigned embarrassment. "Lothar brought it here quite some time ago. Or *told* me he had, anyway. And, well . . ."

He let his voice trail off.

Wolf leaned closer and narrowed his eyes.

"This file, it concerns you?"

"Only in the sense that its subject was someone I'd once helped train and run, along with Lothar. An agent in the Federal Republic's foreign ministry. One of the Romeos."

The Romeos were among Wolf's most celebrated success stories—dashing young males inserted into West Germany to attract lonely females who were well placed in the federal bureaucracy. It was a new twist on an old tactic, the male Mata Hari. The Romeos had offered not only sex but also empathy and compassion as they preyed upon their targets. By mentioning them, Emil was playing on Wolf's vanity.

"This fellow was one of your top people," Emil said. "Code name Hermann."

"Ah, yes. Quite the looker, like an American surfer. Smart, too. And an excellent listener. You were his trainer, I seem to recall."

"And for a brief while, his main contact, before I moved on to the NATO job. So, you see, if Lothar *did* bring the file here, and never returned it . . . Well, it will certainly never reach the shredders, and you can see how that might become a problem for me, especially with all the talk of possible prosecutions. So . . ."

"Of course. Another item of 'evidence' on some cooked-up charge of treason."

"Exactly. And with Bettina in her current condition, we can't afford for me to wind up in jail, so I thought I had better come have a look."

"I understand. It wouldn't serve my interests, either, for it to remain on the loose. Or Hermann's. He's still living there, you know. He's done quite well for himself. And you're sure Lothar brought the file here?"

"That's what he told me, anyway. Back in September. He mentioned reading it out on his deck."

"Completely irresponsible, but it is what it is."

"Of course, Dorn's men must have already searched the place."

"But surely they wouldn't have just scooped up all his papers, willy-nilly?"

"I suppose we'll find out soon enough."

"Yes. Let's have a look around, then." Both men stood. Wolf scanned the room, as if pondering where to begin. "Why don't you start in the main bedroom, Emil. I'll look in here." Then, after a pause, "On second thought, maybe we should search in tandem."

Obviously, Wolf didn't trust him to share his findings. Fine, because he didn't trust Wolf, if only because Wolf hadn't really said what *he* was looking for. It wasn't as if a joint search would cramp Emil's style. The item he sought would seem meaningless to anyone but him, assuming it even existed.

"Sounds like a good plan," Emil said.

"Then let's begin."

13

They proceeded room by room, in the methodical way they had both been taught. The only sounds were the shuffling of papers, the opening and shutting of drawers, their steady breathing. Wolf stopped once to go outside for a cigarette. Emil accompanied him without being asked, saying he needed a break. No sense giving Wolf grounds for further mistrust.

But an hour later they had still come up with nothing. Emil began to lose hope that he would ever find what he was looking for, and it weighed heavily on him. His future was slipping away.

They were finishing in the final room—the second bathroom—when Wolf sighed in exasperation and retreated to the great room. Emil sorted despondently through the last two drawers, finding only a wilted supply of bandages and ointments, before rejoining his old boss, who by then had poured himself another whisky.

"I suppose we should be encouraged by our lack of findings," Wolf said, sounding anything but. "Perhaps Lothar remained loyal right to the end."

"Perhaps."

"Or perhaps that conclusion is premature. The police might have found something. And there are still other lines of inquiry to be pursued. Maybe you and I should pursue them as a team."

Emil doubted that was a good idea.

"Yes, that makes sense."

"Could you remain in touch with Krauss and Dorn for us? To see whatever it is they might be discovering?"

"I can try. And you?"

"I've decided to take aim at a slightly bigger target. The Americans."

Emil couldn't hide his surprise.

"Don't worry, Emil. I won't sell us out. But I might as well use my leverage while I can. I'd like to know what they're thinking, and what they're up to. And maybe by stringing them along for a while I can find out."

"Who will you contact?"

Wolf hesitated.

"Well, they've already reached out to me, of course. Through an intermediary. So that's one channel. But I may try another one first. An older one."

It was the most interesting thing Wolf had said all night.

"Who?"

Wolf smiled and swirled his whisky.

"Leave that to me."

Emil nodded, intrigued. The idea that any sort of back channel to the Americans had ever existed was the sort of revelation that would have buzzed through the corridors of Normanenstrasse in about five minutes. But for now it was a secret shared only by the two of them.

They stood in silence, as if neither was certain what to do next. Emil wondered if he would be able to sleep once he got back to his dacha, although he was exhausted, his mind overloaded. The windows of the great room were rectangles of darkness, with no sign of movement beyond. Even the night animals had all gone to bed.

Lothar's telephone rang.

They jolted to attention as if a fire alarm had sounded, looking first at each other and then at the clock on the wall. It was precisely 5 a.m. That detail, and the unlikeliness of a routine call at this hour, told anyone with their training that this was not a random communication. It could only be a prearranged contact.

The phone rang a second time, jarring and insistent. It was a blocky Bakelite model, avocado green, sitting on an end table by the couch. Wolf strolled over, beckoning Emil closer as he reached for the receiver. He picked it up in the middle of the third ring and angled it so that both of them could hear.

"Hallo?"

The line hissed and crackled until a woman's voice broke through the static, speaking German in an unmistakably American accent.

"As requested, this is your confirmation."

Her words were muffled, murky, like they were bubbling up from the bottom of the lake.

"All set for sixteen hundred and thirty. Preferred location. Ja?"

Wolf looked to Emil for guidance. He nodded.

"Ja," Wolf said.

They again exchanged glances, wondering if there was something more they should say or do. Then the line clicked and went dead. The dial tone resumed as Wolf gently replaced the receiver. He exhaled with a sigh and rubbed his eyes.

"Just when I was beginning to hope that I might be wrong. Our old friend let us down, Emil."

"Yes. That's certainly what it sounds like."

"The question now is, what damage has he already done, and is there still time for us to repair it?"

Emil nodded glumly in commiseration with his old boss.

But inside his heart was light, his mood hopeful. He finally had the information he had come looking for.

14

Claire, arriving right on schedule for the appointed rendezvous, took a seat facing the door, and wondered yet again about the strange dynamics of this assignment.

Maybe it would be a walk in the park—routine to the point of boring, the espionage equivalent of grabbing a takeout pizza. It might also be a fiasco, a disaster, a lost evening that would cascade into a lost week, or worse.

On its face, it was a simple chore with clear but limited instructions and open-ended possibilities. She was no stranger to work like that. At times, her job in Paris seemed to offer nothing but: Take this parcel and leave it there. Meet Man A and deliver his message to Woman B. Sit on that bench until 3 p.m., while noting every coming and going from the opposite doorway. And so on. Simple orders with complex possibilities.

Yet none of those errands had ever been pitched to her as the most vitally important work the station might ever do. None had been personally supervised by the deputy director for operations, and none had involved an asset as lofty as the local opposition's number five man. An HVA colonel, no less.

A young curly-haired waiter in a smock, who looked barely old enough to drive, approached her table. If he asked about the East German footballer Andreas Thom, she had her answer ready—*He can't miss*—and they would take it from there.

Instead, he said, "Menu?"

"Yes, please."

It was a dreary little joint, smelling of greasy sausage and of coffee that had been stewing for hours. On the opposite wall from the register was a discolored empty rectangle where Claire guessed that a framed photo of East German premier Erich Honecker had once hung in its requisite place of honor. Atop the serving counter was a plexiglass display case with a few sad pastries that seemed to have been abandoned the previous week. In Paris this place would have been out of business in a fortnight. Here, with change coming at the velocity of a Mercedes on the Autobahn, she gave it three months. At the moment she was the only customer.

The waiter returned with a plastic menu and a yellowed dishtowel, which he swiped across the laminate tabletop, deftly removing a coffee stain and a dead fly, but also leaving a streaky wet residue, onto which he plopped the menu.

As she peeled it off the table, the door opened. A man in his late twenties, beefy and tattooed, and dressed in warm-up pants and a black leather coat, pushed through as if annoyed the door were there at all, and from the moment of entry his eyes were on Claire. He was definitely not the right age for Lothar Fischer, nor did he look like the sort of emissary that a Stasi colonel would choose to represent him. He was one of the men she had noticed converging on the place just before she entered, but she had assumed they were for security or backup, not for making contact.

But what did she really know of the Stasi's taste in cutouts and couriers, other than what Baucom and Lindsey Ward had told her? Based on their advice she'd been expecting someone wiry and reserved, a technocrat in gray with pale, steady eyes, clunky shoes, and a deliberate manner. This fellow looked more like a thug, someone who might try to block her way if she decided to leave. His shoes caught her eye. Shiny leather, well polished, probably Italian.

He took a seat facing her from two tables away—there were only six tables in all—and he kept staring at her, making a show of his insolence. Snapping his fingers, he called out for a menu in German, his accent decidedly Russian. His presence had the feel of a challenge. *I dare you to meet your contact now, I dare you to even speak.*

Events were taking a turn toward fiasco, but she decided to ignore him, or at least to pretend to ignore him. She scanned the menu.

The young waiter reappeared at her side. He didn't seem to be handling the beefy man's presence particularly well, and he glanced nervously over his shoulder as he asked for her order. Maybe the two of them had a history, and she had walked into the middle of some other situation. A protection racket, with a payoff overdue. If so, that was more comic than tragic, although she doubted her contact would be amused.

"Coffee, black. That's all."

He nodded and scurried away.

The big fellow scraped his chair backwards to position himself closer to the door, although at least now he was scanning the menu instead of her. She was beginning to worry about how easily he'd be able to block any exit, but if push came to shove there was still a rear door, at the end of a back corridor that led past the restrooms. She trusted that Baucom had scouted the alley for her, and she had been pleased to see her old colleague seated as planned at the tram stop, peeping above his newspaper. His experience and competence were reassuring. At least she wasn't completely on her own. The tracking beacon in her purse had never seemed more useless.

The waiter took a bottle of vodka to the beefy fellow's table and poured a double shot into a glass. He downed it in a single massive swallow, set down the glass with a hammer blow, and wiped his mouth with the sleeve of his leather coat, watching her all the while. What a hammy performance. Puzzling, too. Claire had certainly detected unwanted watchers before at meetups like this, but never with such boldness, as if advertising their willingness to disrupt.

Or maybe he *was* the contact, which would be stranger still. She stole a glance at her watch. Twelve minutes past the scheduled time, and only eighteen before Baucom would come through the door. She was now wishing they had gone with his first instinct to enter ten minutes earlier.

The man's chair scraped again, and he stood. He was still staring, so she stared back as he stepped toward her table. He stopped on the opposite side and leaned forward until the knuckles of both hands were resting on the surface. His face moved to within a foot of hers, close enough for a burning whiff of alcohol. He spoke in English, again with a Russian accent.

"We know why you are here."

"Yes. For coffee."

She raised her cup, but the bluff was unconvincing even to her.

"No, not for coffee."

"And who are you?"

"Someone who can help you get what you came for."

And someone who hadn't yet offered the required question to trigger her required response, which meant that there was no way she was taking his bait. This whole meeting was blown, and so was she, that's all she knew for sure. Even if her contact were to enter now, he'd never approach under these circumstances. Time to abort. Self-preservation was now her top priority.

"I have nothing more to say to you," she said.

She stood. He lifted his knuckles from the table and straightened. He was at least eight inches taller than her. The corridor to the back door was right behind her, but even as she contemplated turning in that direction, she heard a creak of hinges from behind. Heavy footsteps came up the corridor and a second man, similarly attired, hoved up on her right.

"Sit back down. Speak with us." Another Russian, goading her in English. The waiter had disappeared into the kitchen.

She darted between them with a sudden move, catching them off guard just enough to elude the grasp of the second man. The first man reached for her. She spun like a dancer, placing a foot behind his and then ramming his chest with her left shoulder so that he tripped on her foot, losing balance just long enough for her to reach the front door and slip outside.

He caught the door as it closed and bounded heavily after her as she jumped to the sidewalk, ready to bolt, to run as fast and as far as she needed, or, if it came to that, to turn and confront him—unless, of course, he had a weapon, and was willing to use it on a public street.

Instead, as if summoned, a taxi quickly rolled forward, braking hard at the curb, with the back door almost opening into her face as Clark Baucom's voice called out from inside.

"Get in!"

The arrival of reinforcements seemed to bring her pursuer up short—did he fear a weapon?—and she heard the soles of his shoes skid on the gritty walkway as she lunged into the back of the taxi, which began accelerating away before the door was even shut.

She took a second to catch her breath as she looked over at Baucom, whose rakish smile told her he was enjoying this far too much.

"Moscow hoods," he said. "So much for Plan A. Oh, and there's their fearless leader."

Claire turned in the direction he was pointing and saw a third, older man, also in a black leather overcoat, standing on the sidewalk. He stared at their cab as it passed, his dark eyes as cold as January. Yet again, there was no attempt to hide his interest. They were sending a message, although she wasn't yet sure what it was, apart from, "We know your game, and we play it better."

"Ought to be one hell of a debriefing," she said.

Baucom barked with laughter, but Claire shook her head, disgusted with the whole affair. Her only small pleasure came from wondering what Ward must be thinking right now as she watched the signal from the tracking beacon receding from the rendezvous point at alarming speed.

Baucom turned to look out the rear of the taxi.

"Well, no one's following us, so there's that. And, unlike in the old days, we won't have any trouble making the crossing back into West Berlin."

Meanwhile, back on the opposite side of the wide boulevard, up on the sixth floor of the apartment building that faced Frankfurter Allee, the curtain flicked shut on the window in the middle.

15

Emil stood in the darkness of his empty apartment, assessing the strange and unsettling events he had just watched out the window. Lothar had chosen the rendezvous point on Frankfurter Allee specifically to give him this vantage point.

"You'll be my backup, with a comfortable front-row seat while I do all the work," he'd said only two nights before, as they sat in the great room of Lothar's dacha, drinking beer from his fridge. "It'll be like watching one of those stupid Hollywood thrillers you like so much. Pop some popcorn if you want. Just stay alert to all you see. Maybe shoot a few photos if you can get hold of a long lens. Although good luck with that, I guess, with the whole shop locked up tight."

"What if you need my help?"

"All I'll need is your eyes, Emil, so you can tell me afterward who all the players were. They've promised to send just one, but since when do the Americans ever send just one? I don't trust them, so you're going to stand witness to how badly they cheat."

"Of course. Understood. But, seriously, *what if you need my help?*"

"Emil. Stop."

Lothar had laid a reassuring hand on his shoulder.

"If you see them trying to haul me off in a car, then come running, or even call a policeman. Although, let's face it, you'll be too late. But that's not going to happen. They want what we're offering far too much to do me any harm. With any luck, they'll even honor my request to do this in a daylight hour. All the better for you. We'll know for sure tomorrow, when they set the time. I'll let you know as soon as I hear. Then, as they say in all those shit movies, we'll synchronize our watches."

"Fine, then. But tell me the operational details. Who are you meeting, and what are the protocols?"

"Please, old comrade, you know how these things work! I only tell you what you need to know, and you do the same with me. Better for both of us that way."

And now Lothar, their front man, was dead, and three Russians had shown up in his place, right on schedule, with the most alarming aspect being that Emil was pretty sure he'd recognized their leader.

Emil shook his head and sipped some cheap red wine that was just beginning to turn. Earlier he'd found the bottle on the dusty kitchen counter and had poured some into a glass, leveling the dose at the black 0,1 liter mark. The wineglass was a souvenir from fourteen years ago, when Bettina and he had attended the opening night gala of the Palast der Republik, East Germany's parliament building and performance center.

Erich Honecker himself had handed them out, party favors for the chosen few, the leader beaming with pride as he showed everyone around his cavernous creation, a long modernist block of glass and marble. The reception had been held in the lobby, everyone's voices echoing as they drank beneath a profusion of bright globular lights linked by chrome bars—"Erich's lamp shop," as the space would come to be known. Emil had thought the whole look was immodestly hideous, but he had smiled and kept his mouth shut.

Now the wineglass seemed like a relic from a vanished time, a touchstone from a life that would never return. It was one of several unwanted reminders of his past that Emil had encountered since reentering their old apartment after a two-month absence, although so far he had at least avoided bumping into any of their neighbors.

On the drive into the city from Prenden, he had been surprised to see how fast the city was changing. Not just the new billboards for goods of the West, but also the homemade banners of squatters who'd taken possession of several empty buildings. Already there was a new protest to replace the old one, with landlords replacing the party as public enemy number one.

After parking his Wartburg at a safe distance, he had strolled here on an indirect route, keeping a wary eye out for familiar faces as his Pistol-M sagged in the right pocket of his overcoat, banging against his side. He'd noted a spring in the step of many younger people, still flush from their victory over the regime. People closer to his age, on the other hand, seemed to proceed with a hooded caution. Like him, they had seen sweeping change come before—twice, in the case of the oldest people—and each time the utopian promises had led only to ruin.

Emil had considered showing up at the café as Lothar's stand-in, but due to Lothar's rigid restrictions of "need to know," he had no idea what Lothar had promised to give the Americans, or show them, or even what his introductory words were supposed to be. Lothar had only mentioned something vague about handing over a few "proofs" of their offered product. But he hadn't described those proofs, and Emil didn't even know if they still existed. Perhaps Krauss had them. Or Dorn. Maybe even Wolf.

Emil had slipped into the door of the apartment twenty minutes before the appointed hour. It was then that he'd spotted the wine bottle on the kitchen counter, so he had poured a glass to calm himself. He'd then opened the curtain in the living room to begin observing the state of play down on Frankfurter Allee.

From the left pocket of his overcoat he had withdrawn a miniature Zeiss monocular spotting scope that had belonged to him for years. At less than half an inch in diameter, it was slightly bigger than a fountain pen, yet it offered sharp images at up to three hundred yards.

Like Lothar, Emil had expected the Americans to cheat. They were firm believers in the doctrine of strength in numbers. But in his initial scan, the only anomaly Emil spotted among the pedestrians and passersby was an older fellow who sidled up the street and seated himself at a tram stop just across the boulevard from the café. He was dressed like a local, right down to his shoes, but upon further inspection he, too, had seemed to be in a watchful posture, and was only paying cursory attention to his newspaper.

Emil had noted a shift in the man's posture as he glanced left, so Emil had looked that way as well, and in doing so spotted an approaching woman, walking briskly. She was a shade too stylish for any *Hausfrau* from this part of the city, early thirties, a blonde, either American or French if he had to guess. Emil then immediately noticed a beefy fellow in black about thirty yards in her wake. His neck was tattooed, and he was making no secret of his pursuit. Russian, perhaps. Definitely not American.

The woman confirmed her importance by entering the café. Emil checked his watch. It was exactly 4:30, the appointed time. Sunset wasn't for another hour, so there should still be good visibility by the time she left. He wondered if she was the woman whose voice he'd heard over Lothar's phone. Her face wasn't familiar.

The man in black paused outside, then he entered as well. No one was being very careful or trying to go unnoticed, which puzzled him. He then spotted a second young man in black, heading toward the café from the right. Then, farther down the block, in the direction the woman had come from, a third man, also in black. They might as well have been wearing uniforms, a contrivance that struck him as silly until he turned the focus knob for a closer look at the third fellow.

The face was familiar. Emil then recalled the name, which came as an unwelcome shock.

Yuri Volkov.

That changed everything.

Volkov was a contract hire for the local KGB headquarters in Karlshorst. He was a known purveyor of "wet jobs"—chores of violence or physical persuasion that no competent intelligence service would ever admit being a party to.

An incident several years ago had first brought Volkov to Emil's attention. It began with news of a grisly murder in Leipzig, a killing that drew the HVA's interest when Volkspolizei investigators reported their suspicion of possible involvement by a foreign intelligence service.

A small group of his colleagues had met on Normanenstrasse to discuss the matter on a gloomy January afternoon. They had filled the room with cigarette smoke while passing around gruesome photos of the murder scene. The victim was Boyan Barkov, a male in his forties, a Bulgarian with forged papers. In the luridly colorful photos his naked body was tied to a chair with electrical wire. Deep knife wounds were slashed across his thighs and chest. The attached report said that all the wounds had probably been administered before he died. His head was slumped unnaturally forward, due to a broken neck. The scene was a bloodbath, horrid to behold.

The next day, word came down from the KGB in Karlshorst that the matter should be dropped. At that point, the case was turned over to the Stasi's Spezialkommission, which issued its final report only three days later, ostensibly in cooperation with the Leipzig Volkspolizei. It concluded that Boyan Barkov had been meddling with an arms smuggling operation that had been sanctioned by the KGB. Thus the Soviets had assigned one of their enforcement people to "tidy up," before the matter became an embarrassment not only to them, but to their East German comrades as well.

The Spezialkommission's final report had been brief, which made Emil and his HVA colleagues wonder what had been deleted from the Volkspolizei's findings. A phone call to the Leipzig police could have probably answered that question, but that would have attracted unwanted attention. The only notable item was a mention of the manager of the KGB operation, Yuri Volkov, whose photo was attached. It was his eyes that Emil remembered best—black orbs of anthracite, radiating a cold intelligence and, even more unnerving, a spark of amusement, perhaps enjoyment. The Spezialkommission report concluded that no further action was necessary on the part of the Stasi or any other East German authorities. It was signed by Dieter Krauss.

In the events this afternoon down on Frankfurter Allee, Emil had been relieved to see Volkov keep his distance from the café after the American woman went inside. But Emil had taken another close look at the man through his spotting scope, focusing carefully.

Those eyes still made him catch his breath.

He had put down the scope and scanned the wider area. The old fellow on the bench had still seemed to be the only other American involved. That, too, was a puzzle. Since when had they ever let themselves be outnumbered in this way?

Then, while Emil watched, the man had suddenly looked back over his shoulder in his direction, a glance probing enough to make Emil lower the spotting scope, so the lens wouldn't reflect the filtered sunlight. As soon as the fellow had turned back around, Emil shut the curtains until only a slit was open.

That one look at the American's face had been revealing. He, too, was familiar, and if it had been a normal workday Emil would have headed to the office and stepped aboard the paternoster—the creaky, open-doored elevator that was forever on the move, like a vertical conveyer belt—for a ride to the fifth floor, where he would've consulted the photo file of their American adversaries, a gallery they'd amassed from Berlin and the entire East Bloc. Surely this man's face would've been among the pictures. But those records were beyond reach now, locked away or destroyed.

After a few more minutes, the older fellow on the bench had stood and shambled across Frankfurter Allee. Would he, too, enter the café? He was walking fast enough to betray a sense of urgency.

Instead he had veered right, toward a taxi parked at the curb. Maybe one of his colleagues was at the wheel, or seated in the back. Emil had kept watching until the dramatic final scene played out. Lothar, after all his cracks about bad movies, would have gotten a chuckle out of how closely the climactic moment of the woman's escape resembled a scene from one of those films, even if the choreography was a bit lacking in style or grace, except on the part of the woman. He supposed Hollywood would have at least allowed Volkov's man to grab her by the arm, forcing her to shake him off with a deft bit of jujitsu or karate before jumping into the speeding taxi. Then, of course, a car chase would have followed, perhaps ending with a crash at the Brandenburg Gate.

Instead, Volkov watched her flee with no visible reaction, as did the other two Russians. None of them tried to block the taxi, or scramble toward a vehicle of their own. While they had obviously hoped to corner the woman, Emil sensed that they hadn't wanted to kill or even harm her. Maybe they had only sought further information. Their biggest error, as far as he could see, was that they had miscalculated by applying their usual rough edges to a maneuver that had called for finesse.

Emil had then shut the curtain completely before taking his final sip of wine. Now he returned to the kitchen and poured the remainder down the sink.

There was a thump on the wall, followed by the sound of laughter. The muffled voices of children filtered to him from the apartment next door, which meant that their mother must be home as well. Of all their former neighbors, Magda Holbein was the one he least wanted to see. The mere thought of her made his knee ache. How old would Magda's youngest be now? Seven? Eight? No longer in a stroller, certainly.

To escape the noise, Emil stepped quietly into the bedroom, where he was stopped in his tracks by the barest whiff of French perfume from a long-ago spill. He'd bought it for Bettina at one of the party's special stores. It wafted from the floor near her empty closet, and nostalgia seized him by the throat, making it difficult to breathe. The sensation was so powerful that he had to sit on the end of the stripped mattress, where he was overcome by thoughts of earlier years when Bettina had been healthy and strong. Closing his eyes, he saw her stepping to the oven to check a roast. Opening them, he saw her moving through the shadows on the opposite side of the bed, slipping on her nightgown. And then slipping it off.

He swallowed hard and then stood, exhaling loudly before he reminded himself of the task at hand. His overcoat shifted as he stepped back into the living room, and he again felt the nagging weight of his pocketed Pistol-M.

Clearing his head, he tried to reassess all that he had just witnessed, and what it might mean. One thing was now clear: At some point, even if only during his last desperate moments, Lothar Fischer must have revealed something that had endangered their entire plan. Endangered, yes, but not destroyed—Emil supposed he was living proof of the latter.

The question now was whether Emil should continue on his own, and if so, how to proceed. He moved to the doorway of the apartment and listened to make sure no one was out in the hall. He would take the stairs instead of the elevator, and upon reaching the street he would make sure all the Russians were gone. Yuri Volkov was not someone he wished to encounter, now or ever.

There were other nearby dangers, too, he supposed. Old colleagues might be out and about, or a cop who might have taken notice of the brief commotion outside the café and would now be paying closer attention. After more than forty years of training their citizens to keep their eyes on each other, one could never take lightly the idea of having your movements go unnoticed in the German Democratic Republic.

All he knew of Lothar's initial contact with the Americans was that it had occurred at some unspecified higher level. But from everything Emil had just seen, maybe that had been an unwise choice. Perhaps he should open a new channel of communications, preferably with someone in a less exalted position. The easiest way to do that was obvious, but it would require immediate action.

So, for only the second time since the night the Wall came down, Emil set out for West Berlin.

16

The biggest problem with supervisors, Claire thought, was that they always believed they knew better—especially in hindsight, when you were describing how their best-laid plans had just gone terribly wrong.

"Well, shouldn't you have at least tried to talk to him? He looked a little rough around the edges, so you just ran away?"

That was Lindsey Ward's initial assessment of Claire's after-action report. They were seated in the same conference room as before. Ward was still wearing her navy suit, but her hair was now pinned up in a tight bun. Bill Gentry, who had been brought into the loop, was pacing the floor behind Ward as she held forth from the seat at the end of the table. Claire sat catty-corner, facing her.

"I mean, who knows? He might have actually come there to tell you something important. Did you ever consider that?"

Claire's first instinct was to lash back—*You weren't there, so you can't possibly know*—but Gentry warned her off by shaking his head out of Ward's line of sight.

"He wasn't that kind of a contact. I've been to a few of these meetings over the years, and this was a show of intimidation, period. He had nothing for me. His only message was that they were on to us, so I wasn't going to stick around for more, or wait for them to stuff me into the trunk of a Lada."

Ward considered this for a moment and then frowned.

"Still. You overreacted. I brought you into this because Bill here said you were good at improvising, quick on your feet, but that's not what I saw this evening."

Gentry again shook his head, but Claire's tolerance had reached its limit.

"You didn't *see* anything, except the signal from the beacon. That's my whole point. You weren't there, but you won't trust my assessment, when it's the only assessment you're going to get. So, yes, you probably will be better off with someone else on this job. But I can assure you that, nine times out of ten, you'd get the same performance, and in the tenth one you'd probably still be looking for me, and that beacon would have gone dead by now at the bottom of the river Spree."

Okay, so that was an exaggeration, but when you were fighting an unreasonable judgment, hyperbole was sometimes the best option.

"A taxi, though? If your exit was so rushed and urgent, how did you manage to flag one down so fast?"

It was Ward's first perceptive question, and an awkward one for Claire. Fortunately she had anticipated that it might come up, a contingency she had discussed with Baucom on their trip back into West Berlin.

"I'd spotted it outside as I approached the café. Like I said, the Russians weren't exactly hiding in the woodwork. They'd made themselves known, so before I went in, I hailed the cab from up the street and asked him to wait out front."

"Smart move," Gentry said, then regretted it immediately when Ward shot him a caustic look.

"Did it occur to you that if they'd really wanted to do you harm, they would've shooed the cab away while you were inside?"

The correct answer, of course, was that they couldn't shoo it away because Baucom had commandeered it, but that wasn't an option, so she made another quick sidestep.

"It occurred to me later. I put it down to either sloppiness or another part of their message, with them telling me they were only prepared to go so far. For now, anyway."

"Sloppiness? By our friends in Karlshorst? Since when has that been a KGB trademark? And how can you be so sure this was even the Russians? Maybe that's just what they wanted you to believe. It might even be why they made themselves so obvious. But in your panic, you misread it."

Gentry stepped forward, holding up his palms like a traffic cop trying to prevent a head-on collision.

"How 'bout we look at the question of what we think happened to our asset? Why do we think he was a no-show?"

Ward stared him down, as if deciding whether he was being helpful or insolent. Then she turned back to Claire.

"You want to give that a shot?"

"Well, the obvious answer would be that he's dead. Maybe because of something you hinted at this morning, about how he was no longer operating in a seller's market. The competition took him out."

Ward frowned and scribbled something on a notepad. Behind her, Gentry looked down at his shoes.

"Did I say something wrong?"

"For the moment, let's file that theory under worst-case scenarios and operate under the assumption he got cold feet."

"Okay. Maybe on approach he saw what I saw, so he backed off."

"Or maybe he never had any intention of showing, and those fellows you blew off were his cutouts."

"If so, then they botched the intro, and that was the single most important part of the setup. They were supposed to ask about the soccer player. Instead, the first guy got right in my face and the second one came in to block any exit to the rear. Did they want something from me? Yes, probably whatever I could tell them about the setup, or the asset. But they weren't working for him, I think you can bank on that. And they were Russian, you can bank on that, too."

"For the sake of argument let's assume you're right. The third one, out on the sidewalk, the possible team leader. Describe him again. Everything you remember."

Claire did so. She had plenty of detail thanks to what Baucom had told her during the cab ride. Ward mulled it over for a second and turned to Gentry.

"What do you think, Bill? One of Leonid's people?"

"Possibly."

"Who's Leonid?"

Gentry looked to Ward as if seeking guidance, but she had already moved on. "Probably too early to speculate on his role."

"Never too early to speculate," Claire said. "That's why it's called speculation. And I'm assuming Leonid is a code name, but for who?"

"I might be willing to tell you if your description was a little more convincing."

"Well, the cab was going a little fast by the time I passed him. But you could always show me some photos."

"We'll keep that option in mind. In the meantime, Bill, why don't you follow up through other channels."

Gentry nodded, followed by an awkward pause. Claire decided that he must have been in the loop all along. Ward had only barred him from their earlier chat for show, to make Claire feel like she was privy to something special. It made her impatient for this to be over.

"What's next for me, then?"

"For now, we're dead in the water."

An unfortunate choice of words, because it reminded Claire of her own remark about winding up facedown in the murk of the river Spree. Yes, she'd hyped the danger to Ward, but at the very least the Russians had wanted to take her elsewhere to sweat her for more information. They were either Lothar Fischer's competition—working for this Leonid fellow?—or a team of enforcers for a Stasi-KGB effort to seal up leaks of sensitive information.

Ward probably suspected the same, but at this point was unable to do anything other than second-guess and assign blame. Understandable. Somewhere in her immediate future there was probably a humbling phone call to the Agency director, who would be awaiting news of success. It was early afternoon in Langley, meaning he'd probably just finished a nice lunch in the executive dining room on the seventh floor. Claire had been there once, with its sweeping view across the treetops of northern Virginia, off toward the Capitol. No chance now she'd be invited back anytime soon, she supposed. Or not by Lindsey Ward. Thwarted ambition left a bitter aftertaste.

Claire decided to offer her at least the possibility of optimism.

"If this was all it took to scare off our asset, then maybe he was never going to deliver the goods. But if he still wants to close the deal, he'll be back in touch."

"You really think so?" A note of hope had crept into Ward's voice.

"I do. Unless, of course, someone has already put a stop to it. Or to him. Which brings us back to our worst-case scenario."

Everyone was quiet for a few seconds. The prospect of a dead asset tended to have that effect.

Ward broke the silence.

"If they *did* kill Lothar Fischer . . . Well."

Claire looked her in the eye. She knew where that thought had been headed, and she wasn't going to let Ward stop short of giving it voice.

"Yes?"

"Then maybe it was a good idea you had that taxi waiting."

17

Emil crossed over without even showing his passport, a once unthinkable act that drew only a cursory glance from a bored official reading a newspaper inside a cubicle. He joined a steady stream of people on the move, none of whom seemed the least bit worried about being stopped or searched.

It all felt a little giddy, a lightness that put a skip in his step. He was like a child entering a meadow on the first day of spring. If only Bettina were with him. He wanted to push her wheelchair along these walkways, to let her see it for herself, let her lungs breathe in the air of this daring new world.

Then the gun bumped against his hip, reminding him of the business at hand. He lowered his head to trudge onward, pausing only for an occasional rearward glance for any sign of Volkov's contingent, or anyone else who might recognize him—colleague, neighbor, cop.

Emil had only been to West Berlin once since the night the Wall came down, and that had been back in December, on a humiliating errand to collect the "welcome money" of two hundred deutschmarks that he and Bettina were entitled to as East German visitors.

All their neighbors had already rushed over to collect. His first reaction had been to turn up his nose. Was everyone really this susceptible to a West German bribe? He'd rather not debase himself for their money.

He began to reconsider as soon as it became clear that he would lose his job. They didn't have much saved up, and he wondered how he would be able to keep paying for Bettina's care. The government provided for most of it, and presumably West Germany's system of free health care would do the same after reunification. But what about the interim period, when there would be forms to fill out, and possible delays? Would they run out of money? And would their coverage be endangered if he were convicted of treason?

He swallowed his pride and asked a neighbor how everything worked. Then he journeyed to a bank only a few blocks beyond the Wall. It was too cumbersome to take Bettina along, so instead he took her passport, a doctor's note, and other documentation of her medical condition, hoping that would be enough.

Although he'd waited weeks to cash in, he still had to stand in line with another twenty East Germans, which made him wonder if some of them were the double-dippers he'd been reading about—people who collected a second time by tearing out the stamped page in their passport that showed they'd already been paid.

The teller had flipped through his passport with undisguised curiosity, seemingly intrigued by all the countries he had visited—Cuba, Vietnam, Hungary, the Soviet Union, and so on—some of them due to his attendance every few years at the multilateral conferences for East Bloc intelligence services. When she was done, she looked at him with an expression of frank disapproval, probably because she assumed—correctly—that all those visa stamps meant he was a government official. He half expected her to refuse payment, but she counted out the banknotes without a word. She sighed irritably when he then slid forward Bettina's paperwork. Surely, she would find some way to refuse it.

Instead, she cut him to the bone in a way he hadn't anticipated. Flipping through the mostly blank pages in his wife's passport, she frowned and said, with a note of disapproval, "Your wife hasn't traveled nearly as much."

He drummed a forefinger on the doctor's note.

"That's because she's been in no condition to travel. As you can see."

The teller reddened in embarrassment.

"Of course. I did not mean to suggest that . . ." She fumbled for the right words.

"It's all right."

She paid out the cash without further comment, but it was not a victory worth gloating over, mostly because until the past few years Bettina had indeed been healthy enough to travel. The real reason she'd gone virtually nowhere was that the government hadn't allowed it, mostly because she had so many relatives living in West Germany, including her parents and grandparents in Munich. All of that had turned up in the Stasi's intensive background check just before Emil was sworn in as an officer. The ministry had ordered her to sever all ties—even by mail—with her relatives in the West.

Emil had offered to decline his promotion, but she begged him not to, mostly because they both knew the consequences of that would be bleaker still. So she had stoically written to her relatives a final time to inform them of the decision, and she had done it without a hint of recrimination, although for days she was silent with grief.

He would never live that down. Nor would he forget the way that, up to then, she had always reacted with such joy whenever mailed parcels had arrived from Munich—gifts of chocolate, coffee, or hand-me-down clothes, items she particularly cherished for their nostalgic scent of Persil, a West German laundry detergent. She would sigh as she held them to her face, and wouldn't wash them until the scent was gone. Now, with the whole world finally reopened to them both, her parents and grandparents were dead, and Bettina was unable to travel.

Emil's destination today was only to the south end of Dahlem, deep into what he still thought of as the American zone of occupation. He used some of his West German cash to buy a transit ticket that would be good for the whole day. It had been so long since he'd taken a train of any kind on this side of the Wall that he had to consult the big map at the U-Bahn station to plan his route.

What would happen if the cars were crowded? He worried that someone would bump up against him and feel the firearm in his pocket. He imagined they might even detect its potent smell of metal and gun oil.

But the cars were not that full, and Emil was able to find a seat where he could keep the gun pocket pressed against the side of the car. A little more than half an hour later he hopped off an U-Bahn train at the Oskar-Helene-Heim stop and headed up the stairs to the street.

It was dark by then, with a biting, damp cold that made you pull your coat closer and tighten your scarf. Emil tugged his wool cap lower on his forehead, partly for warmth, partly to shield his face from the revealing glow of the streetlamps. He walked north on Clayallee, a tree-lined six-lane boulevard with a grassy median, wide sidewalks, and, at this hour, light traffic.

The street was named for U.S. Army general Lucius Clay, who'd been military governor of Germany just after the war, and this stretch of the road was distinctly American. Off to Emil's left was Truman Plaza, a gated compound catering to the families of the U.S. soldiers still billeted here. It had a PX where you could buy Oreos, VCRs, and other goodies from home. There was also a U.S. Post Office, a Burger King, and, farther on, a movie theater that showed first-run Hollywood films in English, with no German subtitles to clutter your enjoyment. The current offering was *Born on the Fourth of July* with Tom Cruise. Not at all Emil's kind of movie. He supposed Lothar would have found that amusing.

On the opposite side of the street was a walled complex of blocky tan buildings. The biggest one housed the American consulate. Since the U.S. embassy was in the West German capital of Bonn, the consulate was where local Germans went to get visas for travel to the United States, and where Americans went for diplomatic assistance.

Tucked toward the back of those buildings was a low-slung wing that housed the local CIA base. Emil figured that's where the American woman he'd seen fleeing the Russians was now located, probably seated in some windowless room as she offered her version of how things had gone so terribly wrong. Maybe the older guy who had hailed the cab was there, too, lending his own descriptions and a little moral support.

Emil knew from personal experience how the aftermath tended to work for ops that fell apart. The routine was the same no matter whose side you worked for, especially in cities where your service had a sizable presence. The operative returned straightaway to headquarters to regroup, and to face the mandatory grilling of skeptical—and possibly hostile—overlords.

It was now nearly 6 p.m., or about an hour since the two Americans had fled in the taxi. He supposed it was possible the debriefing was already over, and that the woman had departed, but he doubted it. Spymasters never reacted well when things didn't go as planned.

They tended to go over and over the same ground until they were certain they'd considered every possible flaw—or every possible flaw that didn't involve their own planning. It would have taken her about half an hour to get here, and the debriefing would last at least an hour, maybe longer, meaning she wasn't likely to emerge for another thirty to sixty minutes.

Emil crossed in front of the main gate, which was well lit and had a guardhouse to one side. The visa office was closed for the day, so the gate was shut. He'd expected that. He also knew from HVA surveillance reports that the local CIA crowd tended to enter and exit from a smaller gate around the corner from here, on Saargemünder Strasse, and he'd have to backtrack to get there. So, after reaching the corner of Hüttenweg, a busy road that led to the Autobahn, Emil doubled back past the main gate and turned left up Saargemünder Strasse. The entrance was about a hundred yards down on the left.

There were few good places for him to wait. The ideal observation post would have been in one of the apartment buildings across the street, but most of those units were rented by U.S. military families. He knew because the HVA had tried without success to place a tenant there.

Fortunately, the Americans never seemed to patrol any of these streets, either with sentries or undercover people. They relied on the wall around the compound, the soldiers manning the gates, and their security people inside. The CIA contingent also enjoyed the sense of safety offered by the unwritten compact that had long been in force between Berlin's rival spy agencies: Don't harm our people, and we won't harm yours.

That's one reason Emil had been mildly surprised by the note of menace in the confrontation at the café. Would the Russians have actually abducted the woman? He doubted it, although since November the old rules no longer seemed to apply. Just ask Lothar.

Emil adjusted his scarf against a gust of wind as he walked by the gate. It, too, was well lit, which was a plus. He'd be able to clearly see anyone exiting without having to use his monocular scope. He walked another sixty yards until he reached a bus bench. It was an obvious spot—too obvious, especially if he had to wait more than half an hour—but it was the only realistic choice apart from pacing back and forth, which would be even more likely to draw unwanted attention.

He sat, feeling the chill of the hard plastic against the seat of his pants. As he settled in, he experienced an odd professional kinship with the older American he'd spotted earlier at the tram stop. He, too, had stood out, for similar reasons. Sometimes in this business you had to take what was offered, even if it made you an easy mark.

Much of what Emil knew about the Americans had come in the context of supervising his spies who worked at the Brussels headquarters of the NATO military alliance. He'd grown accustomed to reports of generals and staff officers who drank too much, had a weakness for flesh, and were surprisingly willing to dish dirt about their counterparts at the State Department. Lothar had been their resident expert on America, and by listening to him Emil had learned of the CIA's preferred ways of doing business, the prevalent personality types of its station chiefs, and the Agency's constant need to fight rearguard actions against Washington budget-cutters.

Lothar's stable of operatives in the United States had been relatively small, and on that front their most worrisome adversary had been the FBI, the law enforcement agency in charge of domestic counterintelligence. Lothar had described the Bureau's people as thorough but unimaginative plodders in dark suits and short haircuts—a prevalence of midwesterners and Irish Catholics who tended to be prudish about sex and mistrusted all things European. To Lothar's amusement, the FBI men had disliked the CIA almost as much as the Stasi. Similar, Emil supposed, to the way he and Lothar felt about Krauss's Spezialkommission.

The sound of American voices made Emil glance down the street, but it was only two young men coming out the gate, their breaths vaporing in the lamplight as they laughed and talked, their tone collegial. They headed off in the other direction.

He sat back and peered into the darkness around the apartment buildings across the street. A few windows glinted back at him, reflecting the glow of the streetlamps. It reminded him of Yuri Volkov's flinty eyes, which now seemed to be watching him from the shadows. Emil thought again of the whitewash report of the murder in Leipzig, signed by Dieter Krauss. He imagined how the two men, Krauss and Volkov, must have cooperated at the time, putting all their lies into neat rows of perfect agreement.

Men like that, once they discovered the utility of a new partnership, tended to exploit it again whenever necessary. Relationships like theirs were as symbiotic as that of a shark and a remora. And these were certainly times when useful contacts were more valuable than ever.

The wind gusted. Emil shivered and glanced back toward the gate. Still no sign of his target. He hadn't yet decided exactly how to make his approach once she came into view. The most important thing was to get close enough to pass a message. A brush pass—bumping into her on the street, for example, or while riding the U-Bahn—was one option, although that seemed especially tricky when only one party was in on the plan, because the other party might try to avoid contact. It had another drawback as well: He might not get a good look at her. Emil needed to engineer a way to see her face and, equally important, hear her speak, so he'd know whether she was the woman who had phoned Lothar's dacha early that morning.

Counterintuitively, he also wanted *her* to get a good look at *him*, as part of his plan to begin establishing mutual trust in a business where trust was often nonexistent. Yes, the rules of the game were indeed changing.

An idea occurred to him, a possible stratagem, and he took out the small notebook he always carried with him, along with a stubby pencil. Ink pens were often unreliable in the damp winters of Berlin, as he had discovered to his misfortune early in his career.

Emil considered what he wanted to say and began to write. He was done in only a minute or so. Another man exited the gate. Emil shut his notebook and waited until the man was out of sight before opening it back up.

He looked at the words he'd written in German, crossed them out, then flipped to the next page and began writing in English. He then paused to reconsider the timing. By writing this note, he was committing himself to taking the next step forward. Unless he wanted to end up like Lothar, he'd better allow enough time to plan it out carefully.

He came up with a time and date, and added them to what he had already written. After double-checking his grammar and spelling, he tore out the page. Then he took out his wallet to remove a banknote— not one of his precious new deutschmarks, but a wrinkled bill of East German money, a five-mark note in blueprint blue, with the image of Thomas Müntzer, who'd led a sixteenth-century peasant revolt. It already looked sadly obsolete.

Emil folded the bill around the sheet of notepaper and stuck it in his pocket. He put away the notebook and pencil and sat back against the cold bench. He was ready.

Four more people exited the gate during the next half hour. None was the woman or the older man. Two buses came and went. The doors levered open, and he waved them away. He was certainly pressing his luck, and his buttocks felt like blocks of frozen wood.

Then, four minutes later, there she was, the blonde woman, unaccompanied as she passed through the gate onto the sidewalk, the light shining on her hair as she headed away from him, toward Clayallee.

Emil stood and set off. His thighs were stiff and his knee ached for the first few strides, although he soon eased into an easier gait. Those long walks in the woods were paying their dividends.

Up ahead, the blonde was already checking her flanks, alert to her surroundings. Emil was quite certain she had already noted his presence, but he was fine with that. Being noticed was part of his plan.

Soon enough, it would be time to make his move.

18

Claire realized she was being tailed before she even reached the corner of Clayallee. As with the muscle-bound Russians, her pursuer's interest was all too obvious, although this fellow seemed to be alone, and was neither young nor menacing. He also looked local. Instead of a shorn head and a slick leather jacket, he had disheveled gray hair that poked from beneath a drooping flat cap. He wore a long wool overcoat that was downright shabby, as was the pale scarf that fluttered from his neck like a flag of surrender. His utter lack of guile told her he was either woefully undertrained or simply didn't care.

She decided it was the latter after crossing the boulevard to the entrance of the U-Bahn station, where she stopped in front of the doors to the stairwell, turned, put her hands on her hips, and stared at him. He reacted by also stopping, twenty yards back, and then took a half-hearted glance at his watch. No sign that he was worried or flustered, and when she moved on so did he. It was like turning on the lights in a bug-infested kitchen only to have all the roaches hold their ground, as if daring you to smush them.

Was this how it was going to be in Berlin from here on out, now that the Wall was down—all of the spies announcing their intentions out in the open? It would certainly change the nature of their business, rendering much of their training useless.

But after descending to the platform and walking to the end, she noticed that he at least seemed to be checking his own flanks as well.

His presence was annoying nonetheless, and she knew better than to underestimate the threat based on his obviousness.

After catching a train toward the city center and watching him board the car behind hers, she resolved to either lose or confront him unless he forced the issue first with some sort of approach. She certainly couldn't let him follow her all the way to her next destination, which was a meeting with Baucom. Fortunately, she had also ditched the tracking beacon, probably because Ward figured her mission was over.

The location was the apartment of Konrad Lehmann, eldest son of the barkeep and friend who had served Baucom all those wondrous drinks for so many years. Baucom had met him at Lehmann's funeral, and they had remained in touch. He sold insurance and lived in Wilmersdorf, only a few stops along the S-Bahn from Baucom's place, and he had readily agreed to let his father's old pal use his place as an impromptu safe house.

They had set the appointment so that she could share Ward's reaction to the failed rendezvous. Claire figured she owed Baucom at least that much, after he had saved her from an abduction, or worse. She had a sagging sense that the meeting would be their swan song, partly because with each passing minute she had begun wondering if maybe Ward was right. What if the Russians, in their ham-handed and overly aggressive way, really had only been trying to offer her something?

Whatever the case, she had lost Ward's confidence, and probably Gentry's as well. After debriefing Baucom she would bid him farewell and return to her hotel room to await the final verdict. The likelihood was a quick trip back to Paris. Life could be worse, but she was disappointed. The final act in the drama of Cold War Berlin would proceed without her.

She took some solace from knowing that if the Russians *had* been trying to offer something, they would certainly know how to contact the Agency for a second try. The traffic of espionage "walk-ins" at Berlin base since the Wall had come down had picked up to a brisk average of nearly three new arrivals per week, even though most of them had little of value to offer. Buyer's market, indeed.

If Lothar Fischer had been scared off from today's appointment, she supposed that he would probably get back in touch as well, although it was doubtful he would accept Claire as his contact, now that she had been so thoroughly compromised.

A few stops later, Claire switched to an S-Bahn line for the trip up to Wilmersdorf. The disheveled man dutifully followed, and this time boarded the same car. With a closer look at his scuffed and muddy shoes, she decided he was probably East German, and at that point she began wondering if he might even be Lothar Fischer. Then she noted the bulge in his overcoat pocket. Was he armed? All the more reason to lose him.

He certainly didn't match the description of Fischer that they had on file—too tall, too thin. Fischer also supposedly favored British-style outerwear and was generally "impeccably groomed." The wardrobe could be a disguise, but he couldn't have remade his body. Besides, why go to the trouble of a disguise only to make himself so obvious? Claire decided to ride to a stop beyond the one nearest the safe house. She would then shake him before boarding another train back.

She descended the stairs from the platform to the street as he dutifully shuffled along twenty yards in her wake. Two blocks farther on she bought a *Tagesspiegel* at a news kiosk. A block after that she went into a bar and seated herself at a table near the front. He took one to the side. She ordered a beer from a waiter, put down her paper as if to hold her place, then stepped into a rear hallway that led to the restroom.

A glance behind her showed that he couldn't see the corridor from his current vantage point, so she kept walking past the women's room to a fire exit at the rear. Fortunately the door did not sound an alarm when she pushed through it into a rear alley.

From there she made her way back toward the S-Bahn station from the opposite side of the rail line. No one was following. Her last turn before reaching the stairs was into a darkened tunnel for a street that crossed beneath the tracks. She rounded the corner onto the cobbles and . . . there he was, standing at the end of the tunnel, as patiently as if he'd been waiting for hours.

For the first time since she'd noticed him following her, they were now alone. The only sounds were the drip of water in a downspout, the rumble of an approaching train.

His expression was as bland as ever. His hands were out of his pockets, as if to show that he was not armed. She stood, waiting, fifteen yards away. Then he spoke. In English, no less, as if to make the point that he knew exactly what she was and who she worked for. His accent was German.

"Excuse me, miss, but I believe you must have dropped this a little while back, and I wanted to return it."

He put a hand into his right pocket, and Claire tensed, ready for anything. But he pulled out only a folded wad of paper and held it forward. She stepped closer for a better look. His hand remained outstretched, as if to give her every opportunity to inspect it. *Don't take candy from strangers*, she thought.

Unless, of course, it's really interesting candy.

Claire moved to within six feet of him, just beyond range of a lunging grasp, and saw that he was holding a folded five-mark note of East German currency. She studied his face and his build. Definitely not Lothar Fischer, and he wouldn't look her in the eye. He instead kept his gaze on the folded money in his right hand.

She was on the verge of saying it couldn't possibly be hers, if only to test his reaction. But something about his demeanor told her he wasn't accustomed to playing roles in clandestine transactions, and she felt an unexpected stab of pity, or maybe it was professional embarrassment. The man was desperate.

So, instead of refusing, or testing him further, she said, "Thank you, sir. That's kind of you," and boldly stepped forward to take the money from his palm.

Their eyes met as she did so. The folded bill was damp from his sweat. It was also a little thicker than she'd expected, a promising sign that the money was concealing something more. Could this be Lothar's cutout? His emissary? Such an unlikely choice.

Their gaze lingered for a second as she dropped the item into her purse. She sensed they were both assessing each other. There was wisdom in those brown eyes, and more experience than she had initially guessed.

Then, with a tilt of his head, he turned and strolled off through the end of the tunnel and around the corner, quickly moving out of sight.

The clatter of an arriving train drowned out the sound of his departing footsteps as it pulled into the station overhead. Claire headed for the stairs, breaking into a run so she wouldn't miss it, but also to get away from this suddenly vulnerable position. She half expected someone to leap from the shadows, having just witnessed the entire exchange, maybe even photographing it.

But no one else was on the stairs, and hardly anyone was up on the platform as she hopped through the open doors of a red car of the S-Bahn only a moment before they slid shut with a heavy bang.

She didn't dare take out the little parcel for inspection, not in the full light of a train car. A dozen other passengers were reading newspapers or idly observing their surroundings. She resisted this urge all the way to the entrance of the younger Lehmann's apartment building, where, ten minutes later, she entered the main doorway and then paused by the mailboxes in the chilly alcove.

Catching her breath and calming herself, she unfolded the bill. There was a note inside, handwritten in pencil, in English. The grammar was perfect. As she read it, the five-mark note fluttered to the floor.

Lothar is dead. Our offer is not. Details to follow are for you alone. 12:00 Monday, Gaststätte Zum Goldbroiler, Kanzowstrasse.

Claire refolded the note, then stooped to pick up the fallen money. She smiled, excited, as she pressed the button for Lehmann's apartment and announced herself to the squawk box. The instant the buzzer sounded she shoved open the door.

Then she bounded up the stairs, taking them two at a time all the way to the fourth floor.

19

They began speaking simultaneously, their words colliding like runaway trains.

"I just—"

"You won't—"

Claire, breathless from the climb, still managed to beat Baucom to the punch on the second try.

"I just heard from our contact. Our new one, anyway. Not far from here, face-to-face. He made an approach, gave me this note wrapped inside an ostmark, and took off."

She handed it to Baucom. His eyebrows arched as he read.

"Shit. And I thought *my* news was big."

"Your news?"

"It'll keep. Who knows, it might even be related. What did he look like?"

"Older guy, German. Midfifties, gray hair, alert. Played it like an amateur for a while, but knew what he was doing when I tried to lose him."

"So he followed you?"

"From the moment I left Berlin base, and he let me know it."

"You think he wanted you to feel threatened?"

"No. Totally different vibe from the Russians."

"So we're back in the game, then. Or you are."

"Only if Ward says so. I should phone it in, even if all I get is the night duty officer."

"Absolutely. But if this guy has decided you're the preferred contact, she'll *have* to keep you on this, especially if Lothar Fischer's really dead. Any possibility Ward already knows that?"

"Only if she's a better liar than I think."

"Could this guy have killed him?"

That stopped her cold.

"I hadn't even thought of that, not with those Russians out there. That would certainly complicate things."

"I doubt he's working with those three or he would've just showed up with them."

"I guess I'd feel better about him if he'd at least offered the line about the footballer."

"Sure. But Lothar Fischer might've kept that to himself. The higher the rank, the more obsessed you get about need to know, and he was way up the ladder. What next, then?"

"That'll be Ward's call, and Gentry's. She did mention a Russian who might be a competitor. Leonid, probably a code name. But, yeah, I'm betting they'll want me to follow up."

"Maybe this time they'll give you some support. If so, you won't be needing my services any longer."

"Well, look at it this way. Without you I might be in the back of a van right now."

"And without me, you wouldn't be privy to this other bit of news."

Baucom grinned a bit wickedly and handed her a curled sheet of glossy paper, a fax. The printed time signature was from earlier that afternoon.

"Stopped at my apartment on the way over and it was down on the floor below the machine. Been so long since the last one I'm surprised the goddamn paper didn't jam."

Claire uncurled it to read the brief message:

Your Czech friend Otto wishes to meet on a matter of urgency concerning the mutual interests of your former employers. I can arrange.
Roman

"Who are Otto and Roman?"

"Roman is Rudolf Kolaschnik, a Pole with contacts on both sides of the fence. Sells East Bloc military uniforms to Western collectors. I once used him as a go-between for a contact in Dresden. He enjoyed it so much he turned it into a side business. Sort of a back-channel UPS man for the spook world."

"And Otto, the Czech?"

Baucom smiled again.

"A German. You may have heard of him. Markus Wolf."

Claire was speechless. Everyone at CIA had heard of Markus Wolf. Of all their Cold War adversaries, he may have been the most imposing. His spies had thoroughly penetrated NATO and the West German government, yet no one at the Agency had even known what he looked like until 1978, when he was secretly photographed during a visit to Sweden.

"You're *friends* with Markus Wolf?"

"Not exactly. But we met once, way off the beaten path. It was only a month after that famous photo of him came in over the transom, or I never would've recognized him." She could tell by the look in his eye that a story was coming. "But first you better phone in this contact. While you're doing that, I'll find us something to wet our whistles."

She used the phone in the bedroom. The night duty officer patched her through to Bill Gentry, who sounded pleased to hear from her, more so once she told him the news.

"This is major, don't you think?"

"Yes. Although I'm less than thrilled he was waiting for me right outside the gate in Dahlem."

"Not the first time we've had lurkers from their side. Work here long enough and you get used to it. You in a safe place now?"

"Quite."

"Well, I better kick this upstairs to Lindsey. She'll want to start planning the next move first thing tomorrow. But, hey, any chance I could interest you in an informal debriefing tonight, while everything's still fresh? We could meet at your hotel bar?"

A loaded invitation, Gentry back on the prowl. Then again, Gentry knew things that Ward would never be willing to tell her. If Claire hadn't had work left to do here, she might have said yes.

"I'm pretty worn out from the whole day, Bill. But could I take a rain check on that offer? Tomorrow evening, maybe?"

"Absolutely. See you first thing tomorrow, then."

"Yes, bright and early."

When she returned to the other room, a frowning Baucom stood before a tall oak cabinet stocked top to bottom with wine.

"You'd think the son of Berlin's best barkeep would have a better selection. Every goddamn one of these is from California. Must've been what killed his dad. Here, uncork this one."

He handed her a Cabernet from Sonoma County. She did the honors, poured them both a glass, and sipped from hers. Perfectly acceptable. Baucom tried it and grimaced.

"I can already tell that working with you is going to mean one substandard tipple after another. Christ, I might as well be in Warsaw."

He took another generous swallow and settled onto the couch.

"So, you actually met Markus Wolf. This was, what, twelve years ago?"

"Nearly. October of '78. I got invited over to Prague for a weekend with our defense attaché, Tom Cofer. We were hoping to scope out a big Warsaw Pact military exercise they were running in the wilds of Czechoslovakia."

"Surprised they'd let you."

"They didn't. But it was easy enough to pull off, if you had the right papers and didn't wind up on the same road with a Soviet tank column. A little trickery didn't hurt, either. All the Western attachés had Land Rovers that looked like Czech military staff cars. They were even painted with the same camouflage."

"Cheeky."

"Very. The Italian attaché came along for the ride. He sat up front while I called out directions from the back. So there we were, a few klicks north of some village with a castle out in the hops fields of Bohemia, trying to make heads or tails of the units we'd spotted, when we pulled over to plot our next move. Five seconds later this car pulls up on our left and swerves in front of us to block us in. Riding up front is a Soviet colonel with a ski-slope hat and a whole lot of ribbons."

"Oh, shit."

"Our words exactly. The Italian was a little excitable. He was sure they'd haul us off to some dungeon, so I hopped out to smooth things over. By the time I got to the passenger side, the colonel already had his window down. I saluted smartly and was about to introduce myself as an assistant to the attaché, but before I could get a word out, he starts griping like a lost tourist.

" 'You goddamn Czechs can't mark your roads worth a shit! Maybe one of you could tell me where the hell we actually are.' "

"In Russian?"

"Oh yeah. He never would've stooped to the local language with an inferior. So I played along, the good Czech offering to help. My Russian must've sounded as bad as a local's, so he hopped out with a big-ass map and spread it on the hood of his car. And damned if it wasn't marked off with the whole plan of attack. Units, arrows, the works. So I said, 'You know, sir, my colleague can clear this up,' because Tom also spoke Russian, and I wanted him to see this. So I signaled for him to come join us.

"By then, of course, I'm studying the map like a kid cramming for exams, trying to memorize every item. It was like being handed your opponent's playbook the night before the Super Bowl, and I had five minutes to get it down."

Claire laughed. Even for Baucom, this was quite a tale.

"Well, Tom's eyes got really big, and he gives me a look. He makes a show of puzzling over which roads are which, drawing it out as long as he can until, finally, he jabs his finger down and says, 'Here, sir. This is where we are.' By then I had pretty much stored away everything I could, and that might have been the happy ending if this other guy hadn't climbed out to join us. 'Cause I could tell right away from the look on his face that he knew we weren't Czech. Tom pokes me in the ribs to get moving, but by then I knew we weren't leaving anytime soon, because, well, it was Markus Wolf, right there in the flesh."

"Traveling with the colonel?"

"Probably as his honored guest. Which explains why the colonel was so pissed off, getting lost in front of the Great Spymaster from Berlin."

"Jesus. Did they throw you in jail?"

"Wolf never blew the whistle on us. Maybe he figured it would only humiliate his host and fuck up the whole day. But he did fold up the map, quick as you please."

"Did Tom recognize him?"

"No, no. The photo was still classified, and I was the only one of us who'd seen it. It would be another five months before the thing would end up on the cover of *Der Spiegel*, so Wolf didn't know about it yet, either. And even I was starting to wonder if it was really him, until the Russian colonel helped me out. He said, 'Time to go, Mischa,' which clinched it, because Mischa was Wolf's old nickname from his Moscow days. Of course, Tom didn't know that, either, and by then he's wondering why the hell I wasn't getting back in the car, so we could make our escape.

"But, hey, for me this was a bigger deal than the map. Markus Wolf, live and in color. The big game animal we'd been stalking for twenty years, and he had just walked right into my clearing."

"Did Wolf say anything?"

"Oh, yeah. In fact, he knew my fucking *name*."

"Holy—!"

"Yeah. That certainly sent a message. He sidles up to me, smiles, and says, in perfect Russian, but in a real low voice so the colonel wouldn't hear, 'You're a long way from home, aren't you, Mr. Baucom?' Which was a shock, of course, but I was fine with that, 'cause I was about to give him a bigger one. 'Cause I'm sure he didn't know yet that I'd rumbled him."

"What did you do?"

"Well, first I needed a second or two to recover my composure. He's smiling the whole time, of course. Or was until I answered, in German, 'And it's a long way from Normanenstrasse, too, ja, Herr Wolf?'"

"That must have wiped the smile off his face."

"Not really. His eyebrows went up. Then he put out his hand, and before you know it we're shaking on it, like old pals who'd just finished a game of chess. He didn't say another word, but he winked as he climbed back into the car."

"What a moment."

"And that wasn't the last of it. A few weeks later I'm at home, sipping a whisky on one of those godawful Berliner nights with the rain sheeting against the windows, when my fax machine hums into action. Out rolls a message from a blocked number. In English, just like this one. All it said was, 'Pleasure meeting you in Bohemia. Looking forward to the next time under more favorable circumstances. Otto.'"

"To show you he knew exactly where and how to reach you?"

"Probably. I didn't know whether to laugh or go into hiding, but now I'm wondering if he wasn't already planning for the possibility of some future rainy day."

"And then, last November ninth, the skies opened up."

"Exactly. And now he wants to meet."

"You think it's related to Lothar Fischer?"

"It certainly crossed my mind. Especially if Fischer's dead."

"Maybe I should go with you."

"That crossed my mind, too."

Baucom opened his mouth to say more, then frowned and looked toward the window. A car was passing in the street below, the engine sputtering with a noise that only Trabis made. He stepped to the window and peered out the side of the shuttered blinds. Then he stepped to the other side, tracking the car's progress as it drove slowly away.

"Remember when I said the other night that I've noticed a few things lately? Well, I'm beginning to wonder if we've stirred up something in the zeitgeist."

"What kind of things?"

"Some guy on the S-Bahn, same day you first got in touch, stalking me from train to train before he took off. And last night on my block, late, there was someone in the shadow of a doorway, still as can be. Then a day later this message from Wolf rolls in."

"You think he sent someone to scout you out?"

"Or maybe Gentry did. Or Ward. Or maybe I'm just a paranoid old spook who's lost his touch."

"What's your next move with Wolf, then? Can I really come along for the ride?"

"You'd be up for that?"

"Only if it happens soon. I have a feeling things are about to get pretty busy, and if that happens my leash will only get tighter."

"I'm guessing he wants to meet as quickly as possible, but Roman will know for sure. I'll plead old age, say you're my academic assistant, helping with my memoirs or some bullshit. Being from Paris there's a decent chance Wolf won't make you."

"Unless he's working with the guy I just met."

"In that case it won't matter."

All of it was risky, but Baucom needed only a few seconds to make up his mind.

"On one condition. That you keep me in the loop on this business with your contact. Even if Ward and Gentry decide to give you some backup."

"That was already my plan. Within reason, of course."

He smiled as she drained the last of her wine. She held out her glass for a refill. He spoke as he poured.

"This is all getting pretty complicated."

"It is, isn't it? And how lovely is that?"

All in all, not a bad evening. Not only did Claire still have her part in the final act of whatever drama she'd first entered, but her role was expanding, and now it was time to start writing her next lines.

They tapped their glasses, sipped, and settled down to work.

20

Karola came out the door of the dacha before Emil could even switch off the ignition. She folded her arms as she waited for him to climb out of the Wartburg. He could barely see her face in the darkness. He wanted to get indoors to warm up and relax, but Karola blocked his path, her breath misting in the glow from the front window.

"You went to Berlin, didn't you? To do what?"

"Yes, I went to Berlin, but that's all I can tell you."

"I've been worried sick. We both have. You can't keep doing things in secret like this, Emil. It isn't safe."

He stepped forward to offer a reassuring hug, but she took a step back, so instead he placed his hands on her shoulders and looked her in the eye. A chill wind gusted through the space between them. The moon had yet to rise, but a frost pattern of stars coated the night sky.

"Secret work is what I've always done. Both of you know that. It isn't something I have ever approached carelessly, or without caution."

She held her ground.

If she had been a colleague on Normanenstrasse, or even a superior, he would have asserted himself and barked at her to step aside. But in any sort of standoff with Karola, Emil always felt a little humbled, lacking in authority. There was love to consider as well, he supposed.

"Can we please just go inside?"

She relented.

"Yes. You look cold."

She turned toward the dacha. Emil followed, and Karola kept talking.

"What worries me is that now you're doing this secret work on your own, without help or support from the ministry. I can help, you know."

"You're already helping, just by being here when I need you. When *she* needs you."

"I mean with your work. I can help with whatever it is that you're up to."

She turned to face him again as they reached the door, pausing on the threshold.

"Who says that I'm *up to* anything, Karola?"

"That policeman, for one."

"Lieutenant Dorn? Was he here again?" A shiver ran through him, head to toe.

"He's been calling. Three times, as recently as half an hour ago. Said it was urgent. He wanted to know where you were, what you were doing."

"What did you tell him?"

"The truth. That I didn't know. He wants you to call back, no matter how late. Look, Emil, my offer to help was serious. Because . . ." She faltered, looked down at her feet.

"Yes?"

"Nothing. Just call him. Maybe there's been a break in the case."

He smiled at her wording.

"And maybe you've watched too many detective films. A break in the case? C'mon, it's too cold to be standing out here."

He followed her into the dacha. The TV was on in Bettina's room, so he peeked through the door to check on her and was alarmed by what he saw. She was asleep, but her skin was even paler than normal, her breathing labored and shallow.

"See?" Karola whispered behind him. "She's worried, I told you." Then, as he bent to kiss her, "Don't! She needs rest."

He crept back into the living room, then signaled with his hands that he had to use the phone in the kitchen. She nodded and sat on the couch. Emil shut the kitchen door behind him, as much to keep Karola from listening as to keep from waking Bettina. He expected the call to ring through to a duty officer, but Dorn picked up on the first ring.

"It's Grimm. I'm back, and I heard you'd called."

"Where have you been?"

"Running errands."

"I know it's late, but I have something important to show you. Come to the station."

"Now? Can you be more specific?"

"Not on the phone. How soon can you be here?"

"Fifteen minutes."

"Hurry, then. I'll meet you downstairs."

Karola followed him back out to the car.

"Is it serious?"

"I won't know until I see him. Maybe it's even a 'break in the case.'"

"But you don't know."

"No. I don't know."

Even in the dark he could see that her eyes were troubled. She again folded her arms.

"I tell you what. Maybe tomorrow, or in the next day or two, I'll ask Frau Adler if she can go on duty for a while with Bettina. Then maybe we can spend a quiet evening together. At your house, if you'd like."

"Of course I would. But that's not my biggest worry. Not after everything that's happened. I'm shaken up. We both are."

Sometimes he believed Karola was trying to live her life for Bettina as well. It was as if every experience, mental and physical, was transmitted between them at some level he wasn't privy to. It was touching, but a little unsettling.

"I understand," he said. "And I *am* being careful. Very careful."

"We hope so. Will you be in Bernau for long?"

"I doubt it, but I'll call if that changes."

He climbed into the Wartburg, relieved to be away from them, and guilty for feeling that way, especially after having to tell Karola so many lies. He wasn't being careful at all, he supposed. Not in the way they'd want, or in the way that his job had once demanded.

Deception had always been a key part of Emil's work, but he had tried never to carry over those habits to his home life, an occupational hazard that had afflicted many of his colleagues. Some had become so addicted to trickery and false fronts that it guided their every action, even among family and friends. This led to infidelity and shameful secrets, hidden lives in which any sort of behavior became excusable.

Lothar, for example, with his carefully planned affair that had then become so reckless, a fall from grace that had made him resentful of Mielke, and perhaps of the entire ministry.

Emil sighed, put the car in reverse, and backed out of the driveway. At least Krauss's minion was no longer at his post. The Citroën had been gone in the morning, leaving only a pile of cigarette butts to mark its presence.

He set off down the lane. Glancing in the mirror he saw Karola, still with her arms folded as she watched his departure.

For all the unorthodox nature of the triangular arrangement between him, her, and Bettina, Emil seemed to be the only one who was still awkward about it from time to time. He remembered with embarrassment—and some fondness—how the two women had chosen to break the news to him of their plans for their joint future.

They had all been gathered at the dacha at the time, on a beautiful summer evening. Bettina was barely able to speak by then, and, because it had been a warm day, Karola had told him she was going to clip a few flowers from the garden before he drove her back home. She asked him to meet her outside in a few minutes.

Unaware that his life was about to change, Emil had said briskly to Bettina, "I'll be right back."

Instead of nodding, she'd smiled and said, "Come here."

He took her hand. With the strain of the effort showing in her face, Bettina had managed to squeeze back. A smile raised a corner of her mouth, and then tears welled in her eyes, but did not spill.

"What's wrong, love? Are you in pain?"

Her reply came slowly.

"I am happy. She. Will. Tell you. With. My blessing."

She had then sunk back in the chair, her face radiating the sort of bliss he hadn't seen since they were newlyweds dreamily discussing the sort of house they would have once there were a couple of children running around, laughing and playing.

"What do you mean?" He squeezed her hand.

"Just. Listen. To her."

She released his hand.

He asked Karola about it the moment they were in the Wartburg, but she told him it would have to wait until they got to her house. She invited him inside and poured each of them a drink from a bottle of brandy that her husband had made years before. She told him she'd been saving it for a special occasion.

"And what is the occasion?"

Emil was so overwhelmed by her explanation that he needed a second glass of brandy. He then told Karola he had to talk to Bettina before agreeing to anything.

"Of course," Karola said. "That is the only proper way."

She then took his hand, her grip warm and strong and full of passion, which stirred him enough to tell her that he would be happy, if a bit bewildered, to go along with everything as long as Bettina affirmed it.

The only other awkward moment had come when Karola had asked how the ministry might react if anyone—especially Mielke—ever found out.

"They won't. I'll see to it. Although I guess we'll have to be a little more careful about some of our neighbors up here. Wolf, and Lothar."

The whole idea of having to keep everything secret from them had irritated him greatly, and Emil had to shove it aside to avoid ruining the mood.

Bettina had been asleep by the time he got back to the dacha, so they had discussed it in the morning, after a night in which Emil had dreamed vividly of an attractive woman whose appearance kept changing, almost from frame to frame, her face never clearly recognizable as either Karola's or Bettina's. It was perhaps the only moment in his marriage when he was glad that they didn't have children, because how could he have possibly explained this complicated arrangement, this triad of mutual need, to a son or daughter? Much less the delicate emotional engineering that had brought it about.

Karola had two grown sons, and she still hadn't fully explained it to either of them, although one, Stefan, had arrived at her house early one Saturday morning to find Emil and Karola in their bathrobes, sipping coffee at the kitchen table. Stefan wisely never asked for more details, and Karola never offered them.

On that pivotal morning at their dacha, Bettina had asked Emil one final question. "Are. You. All right? With it?"

It had taken every bit of his willpower to look her in the eye when he answered. "Yes. I suppose that I am. But only if you are."

She offered him a crooked smile, one of the last she would ever manage.

Emil was still haunted by that moment. He had gone over it in his mind again and again, until finally convincing himself there had been a hint of regret in her eyes as she smiled.

He thought of that once more as he turned the Wartburg onto the paved lane leading to Bernau. Then he checked both mirrors. For the moment, at least, he had the road to himself.

21

Lieutenant Dorn glanced out his office window for the third time in less than a minute as he waited for Emil Grimm to arrive. It was late, and most of the building was dark and silent. No sign yet of the yellow Wartburg, a thought that made him wonder, not for the first time, how long before he and his wife could afford a new car. Preferably an Opel or a VW now that choices were unlimited. Certainly something peppier and more dependable than the Trabi they'd bought five years ago after eight months on a waiting list. Goodbye to shabby merchandise, he thought. Farewell to standing in line for bread, meat, and coffee.

All sorts of good changes were coming, Dorn believed. Cops in East Germany had always enjoyed a fairly solid status, but never the sort of authority that got you a better car or bigger apartment. That had been the reserve of party officials and the Stasi.

But the job's minuses had now turned into pluses, because they meant Dorn hadn't been irredeemably tainted by the system—in the eyes of the West, anyway. Being only twenty-seven, he also wasn't old enough to have been fully contaminated by the informant culture of the DDR workplace, one in which supervisors and subordinates alike had been expected to report any questionable political behavior by their peers.

The episode yesterday morning down by the Bauersee had helped clarify for Dorn the liberating possibilities of this new era. He'd been able to evict the powerful Dieter Krauss from a murder scene simply by ordering him gone. It was like magic. Heady stuff.

The previous weekend, Dorn and his wife, Frieda, had taken a lei-surely drive through the outer neighborhoods of West Berlin, just to see what their future might look like. Frieda was five months pregnant with their first child, so they were already dreaming big. They bought a map, rolled effortlessly through the checkpoint, and spent a pleasant afternoon motoring by tidy homes and brightly lit shops on tree-lined boulevards. They'd ventured as far as the shoreline of the Wannsee, where they braved the bitter winds of a tourist cruise before warming up with frothy coffee and some perfectly wonderful pastry at a nearby *Konditorei*.

The only dark cloud—apart from the shocking prices—was the con-descending smile of the waitress when Frieda ordered a coffee with cream and sugar by calling it a "Kaffee komplett," a dead giveaway that they were interlopers from the East, or *Ossis*. It was a valuable lesson. *Wessi* culture would have to be learned. It had its own words and customs. The people wore different clothes with a different smell, and their smugness could quickly get under your skin.

But in time, he supposed, those differences would become less evi-dent, especially if he was able to raise his status in the police depart-ment. The case of the dead Stasi colonel seemed to offer just such an opportunity, which was why he was working it around the clock.

Unfortunately, the case had also revealed a few pitfalls of this new era. Dorn's longtime boss, Rainer Bilke, had begun pressuring him not just to solve it, but to make sure its results reflected as poorly as possible on the old regime.

"Don't let *any* of those people come out of this clean or vindicated, even the dead one," Bilke had told him only a few hours earlier. "If we're to survive, we have to show our independence."

Speak for yourself, Dorn had wanted to say. Everyone in the sta-tion house knew Bilke was obsolete, a once nimble political animal as deeply stained as any Stasi man. *He* was the one who needed to show his distance, not Dorn.

Nonetheless, it probably wasn't a good idea to be seen cooperating with a Stasi holdover like Emil Grimm, so Dorn's plan was to whisk the man upstairs to the privacy of the evidence room before any colleagues spotted them. Fortunately, nearly everyone had gone home. But a small night staff was still on duty, so he kept looking out the window. And on his fourth glance, there it was—the ungainly Wartburg, passing beneath a streetlight, the same color as a blob of mustard spilled from a wurst. It eased to a stop in a shadow in front of the building. Then the door opened and a dark figure emerged.

Dorn rushed out the door of his office and headed for the elevator.

22

Emil generally enjoyed his little side trips into Bernau, even though its charming town center had been defaced by government housing planners back in the '70s, when they'd replaced many of its old timbered-beam buildings with drab low-rise *Plattenbau* apartments. But many older buildings had survived, and so had the moated stone wall that had surrounded the town since medieval times. Plus, Emil had a weakness for the *Bratkartoffeln* platter served by a local café—perfectly browned potatoes topped by a pair of shimmering fried eggs.

The police station, however, was an ugly modern aberration banished to the periphery beyond the wall, a giant translucent egg crate, three stories high. Presumably the architect included lots of windows to show the openness of the resident authority, but the occupants tended to ruin the effect by shutting their blinds. At this hour, only a few lights were on. Dorn was waiting in the lobby, which Emil took as a sign of eagerness until Dorn rushed them toward a back stairwell, which made him realize the lieutenant was simply embarrassed. Emil had become a pariah.

Dorn began asking questions as they climbed the stairs.

"What can you tell me about Lothar Fischer's vegetable garden?"

"His garden? What do you mean? Why do you ask?"

Dorn stopped on the landing between floors and turned to face him.

"You said it was the last place you saw him alive, two or three days ago. Was he digging when you saw him?"

"This time of year? There would be nothing for him to dig, unless he forgot about his potatoes."

"I'm thinking of something more like the size of a watermelon, or bigger. You're saying you didn't notice any holes of that size?"

"As I told you. I thought maybe he'd been putting away some tools."

"Yes, so you said."

Dorn narrowed his eyes before continuing up the stairs. Emil's lie about last seeing Lothar in his garden had been a throwaway remark, but he had realized even then that he should have mentioned a different location. Fortunately, Dorn had no further questions on the matter.

They went straight to a locked, windowless room on the third floor, where Dorn switched on a flickering pair of fluorescent tubes and quickly shut the door behind them. Spread out on a long table was Lothar Fischer's waxed cotton overcoat. There were dried bloodstains on the right shoulder.

"First off, thank you for your phone message from yesterday. But how did you know to check the lining of the coat?"

So they must have found something. Emil didn't know whether to be worried or excited.

"Krauss gave me the idea. It was the last thing he asked his men to check before you showed up, and they never got the chance."

"So do you think Krauss might have known, then?"

"Known what?"

"Here. I'll show you."

Dorn smiled and with a flourish flicked back the right side of the coat to reveal a long, surgical incision in the lining. He reached inside to pull out a clear plastic bag the size of a sandwich, which he handed to Emil.

"Take a look."

Inside were three dark strips of film. Each was about half an inch wide and a few inches long. Emil was reluctant to touch anything.

"Go ahead, everything's been checked for prints. I'd like for you to examine them. Use this."

He opened a drawer beneath the table and handed Emil a large magnifying glass. Emil put the strips on the table and stooped for a closer look.

"It's microfilm."

"Yes. Sixteen millimeters. Each piece has probably been clipped from a reel. But what do you make of the images?"

Emil looked again.

"Not much to see, is there? 'Reel 1,' it says on this one. 'Reel 76' on the second one. If I had to guess, I'd say they're the first and last frames from a set, maybe. And that third one has a lot of writing on it, although even with the magnifying glass it's not easy to read."

"But do you see those initials and numbers, in the upper right corner of the first one?"

Emil had seen them, all right, but had hoped to avoid discussing them. He went through the motions of taking another look.

"Gobbledygook. As you said, it's a bunch of letters and numbers."

"That's the best you can do? Read them aloud."

Emil obliged him, proceeding letter by letter, mark by mark, number by number. "MfS-F16,F22,SB-14/09/82."

"The M-F-S notation, that's pretty obvious."

"Well, yes. The Ministry for Security. Hardly surprising, since that was Lothar's employer. And the last numbers are almost certainly the date the microfilm was made, on the fourteenth of September, 1982."

"The rest?"

Emil shrugged.

"But most likely it's from Stasi archives, yes?"

"That would be the logical assumption. Find someone from Department Twelve and you might be able to decipher the rest."

"Department Twelve?"

"Records and archives."

"Do you know anyone who could help?"

"Offhand? No. Those are among the few people still allowed into the building, but . . ."

"What?"

"Most of those materials have either been destroyed or handed over to that new task force for Sub-Department 7, which is handling their final disposition."

"Sub-Department 7?"

"Of Department Twelve. The task force is run by a fellow named Plotz."

"Do you know his first name?"

Emil pretended to rack his brain for an answer.

"Ludwig, maybe? No. Andreas, that's it. Andreas Plotz. But anyone trying to get close to him now is probably going to draw a lot of unwanted attention."

"From who?"

"Just about anyone and everyone. On all sides."

"What do you mean, 'all sides'? People like Krauss?"

"Plus the Russians, the Americans."

"The *Americans*? They have an interest in these things?"

"Haven't they always?"

"Of course, but, well, they've just *won*, haven't they? I mean, not to express an improper political attitude, but why would they even care any longer?"

"Trust me. As far as ministry records are concerned, they care more than ever. Does it make sense? No. But when has sense ever had anything to do with our struggle against the West?"

"You're sounding almost as incorrect as me."

"There's no longer any such thing as an incorrect opinion, Lieutenant Dorn, or else we would both be racing to report one another as soon as this meeting was over, yes?"

"I certainly can't say that would have been my reaction, but, well . . ." He hemmed and hawed, then began to redden as Grimm smiled. "Okay. Perhaps for my own protection I might have said something to someone. These records, then. These archives. If they still retain such value, do you believe that's what Krauss was looking for?"

"You'll have to ask Krauss."

"I plan to. We're going over there tomorrow."

"I'd appreciate if you didn't tell him how you found him."

"Of course."

"You might also ask who is providing him and his men with their new workspace. Although you may need to check the building's records, to see which cooperative runs and manages the property. And keep me apprised of what he says."

Dorn nodded uncertainly.

"I'd be more inclined to do so if you could help me figure out the source of this microfilm. Surely you must know *someone* who could help, especially if you believe this fellow Plotz is off-limits."

Emil frowned and picked up one of the strips, as if to study it further.

"He might at least take a phone call from me."

"Plotz, you mean?"

"Yes."

"So you'll try to reach him? And ask him about the possible source of these items?"

"If you insist. I'll do what I can."

Emil then put all three strips of film back into the plastic bag and pocketed the bag.

"What the hell are you doing?"

"You want them identified, yes?"

"But that's evidence! I can't possibly allow it to leave the building!"

In the old days, of course, Emil could have just ordered Dorn to yield the microfilm, the way Krauss would have done it. But that had never been his preferred style, and it wouldn't have worked now anyway. Besides, guile was more enjoyable.

"Very well. Then I guess there's no way I can show it to any of the few people who might know. Plotz and some others. I could give you their names, of course, but . . ."

"What?"

"Under current circumstances? There's no way they'd ever feel safe enough to speak to a stranger. And certainly not a policeman. Even for me it will be a stretch, but you won't stand a chance. These are the kinds of items no one wants to be connected to any longer, not with all the talk of trials and prosecutions. In fact, I'll be better off not having them in my possession. So, here. Take them."

He tossed the bag back onto Lothar's coat and turned toward the door.

"Wait!"

Emil stopped with his hand on the knob.

"How long would it take you?"

"A few days, maybe? Certainly no longer than a week."

"A *week*! That's far too long!"

"Fine, then. Give me a deadline."

"Two days."

"Four. Tomorrow's Friday, and it's always harder reaching these people over the weekend. You said yourself they've already been dusted for prints, right?"

Dorn nodded.

"And I'm guessing Lothar Fischer's were the only ones."

Dorn looked him in the eye for a second before nodding again. Emil pressed his point.

"Meaning there's no forensic reason you'll need them to establish the identity of his killer, in case you come up with a suspect in the next four days."

Dorn picked up the bag and gazed at it longingly for a few seconds.

"How about if I made some enlarged copies for you?"

"You don't understand these archival people. They're hopelessly consumed by little details, like the type of film, or special coatings. They'll insist on the genuine article."

Dorn sighed. Then he handed over the bag.

"You'll be fully responsible for any loss or damage."

"Of course."

"And you'll have to sign for it. There's a form to fill out."

"There always is, but your name will also be on it. Do you really want to establish that kind of a paper trail?"

Dorn sighed again as he weighed how far he was willing to go. It was fairly amazing to Emil how quickly he had been able to steer the young policeman back to the old way of doing things. But he supposed ambition was a useful tool under any system.

"Very well, then. But guard it with your life."

Oh, he planned to. That aspect was unavoidable.

There was a noise from the hallway—approaching footsteps—and Dorn raised a hand for silence. He waited until they had passed beyond earshot before speaking again.

"Let's continue this discussion in my office, where we're less likely to be interrupted."

Emil again felt like a pariah, but he understood. He didn't particularly want to be spotted here, either. He nodded, and they proceeded stealthily to Dorn's office on the second floor.

23

Emil tried to get a better read on Dorn by scanning the landscape of his tiny office. There was a framed photo of a pretty young woman who must be his wife, but no shots of any children. Hanging from the back of his chair was a new-looking sport coat—made of fine wool, not polyester. Dorn and his wife had probably been splurging with their welcome money. His recent change of fortunes must have come at just the right moment for them. An up-and-comer with his eye on advancement.

But anyone that intent on getting ahead might yet change his mind about letting someone leave the building with a key piece of evidence, so Emil came up with a question to distract him, something he needed to ask anyway.

"What do you make of the use of the suppressor on Lothar's gun? That was odd, don't you think?"

"How so?"

"Well, if it was a suicide, why the need to keep the shot quiet, especially in such a remote location?"

"Oh, I've ruled out the possibility of a suicide."

"Have you, now? So you were able to verify he was left-handed?"

"It was evident from the fingerprint pattern on the everyday objects in his house. His toothbrush, pens and pencils, items in his kitchen."

"Smart. Very good. And when you dusted the gun, I'll bet that not only were Lothar's prints the only ones, but the gun was clean otherwise. As if someone had wiped it down before putting it in his hand."

"You're correct. But the more interesting story was told by the footprints."

"I'm surprised there was any story at all in that muddy mess."

"It was the trails leading to and from the body that told a story."

"Yes?"

Emil worried where this might be headed, especially if Lothar's path had come from the hunting stand. But Dorn's explanation took him by surprise.

"Lothar Fischer's footprints weren't on any of the approaching trails. None."

"Meaning his body was carried there."

"That's the most logical explanation. And apart from your footprints, and those of my men, all the other ones nearby were for that woman, Frau Kunstler, who first phoned us after seeing the body. Plus those of Krauss and his men from the Spezialkommission." He then raised a finger to the air, as if to heighten the drama. "Plus, *three other* sets of footprints."

"Belonging to . . . ?"

"Three males, most likely. We haven't yet identified the make of their shoes."

Probably because the shoes had been made in another country. East or West? American? British? Russian? If Dorn knew, he wasn't saying.

"I see."

"Well, I don't."

"What do you mean?"

"I suppose I don't understand why everything would have been done so . . ."

"Sloppily? Obvious?"

"Yes, don't you think?"

Emil shrugged.

"That was the old way of doing things, for people like Krauss. Unlimited authority has that effect. You grow accustomed to never having to explain yourself, especially when everyone else is always having to explain themselves to you, and you're the one who always writes the final report. The last thing he was expecting that morning was to see you coming up the path with your men. Even then, I'm sure he figured he would simply brush you aside. Until you reminded him that the old ways no longer applied."

"Maybe you're right. Or maybe those other footprints are something that even he would be unable to explain."

"Also possible."

Emil now had more questions.

"What about Lothar's body? Any sign that he had been beaten or tortured?"

"There were no obvious blows or bruises. No cuts."

Emil was relieved to hear it—for his friend but also for himself.

"But there was one item, less obvious. Having to do with, well, his scrotum. His balls."

Emil swallowed hard and waited for the rest.

"There was a red mark on them. A blood blister, in a narrow seam, with a sign of some burning. Not from an incision, but probably from a clip. The examiner wasn't positive, but he surmised that an electrode had been attached. Probably to administer a shock. Perhaps several."

"I see."

"Yes."

The whole hideous idea of it hung between them for a moment. Deeply disturbing, but it helped Emil steel himself for the maneuvers he needed to make next.

"Is there anything more you need from me?" he asked.

"Yes. Anything that you might have heard since yesterday morning from neighbors or old colleagues. Your wife's caretaker said you were out and about earlier today. Did your travels take you into Berlin?"

"They did."

"For errands, I believe you said. What sort?"

"Groceries. Gas for the car. Pharmaceuticals for my wife."

Dorn smiled knowingly.

"Nothing more?"

"It may surprise you, but the everyday details of life can become all-consuming when you're down to your last paycheck."

"Surely you'll have a severance package coming to you as well, yes? And at the rank of colonel, I can imagine it's likely to be generous."

Spoken like a budding careerist, Emil thought. But Dorn was right, and now he was the one who was a little off balance, so he decided to play his final cards, a couple of items he'd come up with during the drive into Bernau.

"You're right, of course. There will be a severance payment. And as to your earlier point about my neighbors, I'll admit that I've been wondering what some of them might know. Frau Kunstler, for one, the first person who called you. And Wolf, of course. Don't forget to check with him."

"*Markus* Wolf? I'd heard he was gone."

"To Moscow, yes. But he has returned."

"When?"

"You'll have to ask him for the exact time. But it must have been early yesterday morning, or the night before. I saw smoke coming from his chimney as we were climbing the path back to my dacha."

Dorn looked astounded, and maybe a little upset with himself for having failed to notice this earlier. It took him several seconds to absorb the news. Emil was fascinated that the name could still cast such a powerful spell.

"Do you think he'll speak with me?"

"He'll have to, won't he?"

"Well, yes, of course, but . . ."

"Would you like me to ask him for you? Maybe tell him to give you a call, so you can set up an interview?"

Dorn flushed with gratitude.

"That would be an immense help."

"I'll see to it tomorrow."

"Thank you."

Emil turned and opened the door, hoping to reach his car before Dorn changed his mind about the microfilm. But he had one last item to leave behind, figuratively speaking—a final seed to plant in the soil of Dorn's imagination. Because if thirty-four years of working for the Stasi had taught Emil anything, it was that it never paid to go poking around in sensitive places if you could get someone else to do it for you. So he paused on the threshold and turned back toward the young policeman.

"Oh. And a word of advice about Dieter Krauss, if you're open to that sort of thing."

"I'm all ears."

"If you're interested in seeing how he tends to operate in investigations like this, I can refer you to one he took off the hands of the Volkspolizei down in Leipzig a few years ago."

"I'm already quite familiar with how Krauss likes to throw his weight around. I have firsthand knowledge of that, remember?"

"Yes, of course. But I was thinking more in terms of matters that got a bit dirtier, and more brutal, and then needed to be erased. Although who's to say that will be the case with Lothar Fischer's death? So maybe this information wouldn't be relevant to you."

"No. It's a valid point. This was in Leipzig, you said?"

"Yes. Krauss was working with a Russian, if memory serves."

"A Russian? In the same line of work as you and Krauss?"

"Very much so. Based in Karlshorst."

"Do you remember his name?"

"I don't. But I'm betting the police in Leipzig would still have it in their file, since Krauss closed the case for them. And I do remember the victim's name, which is probably how it's filed."

Dorn took out a pen and a pad.

"Go ahead."

"Barkov. Boyan Barkov. A Bulgarian."

"I'll follow it up first thing tomorrow." Then, with a gleam in his eye, he checked his watch and said, "Actually, I'll call them now. Records never closes, not in a department as big as Leipzig's."

His zeal was mildly disturbing.

"And mum's the word on how you heard about that Barkov file, if you don't mind."

"Not a problem."

Emil backed into the corridor and shut the door. He tucked the bag with the microfilm deeper into his coat pocket. By sometime tomorrow, or maybe even late tonight if all went well, Dorn would have come up with Yuri Volkov's name. That might lead the policeman in an intriguing new direction, although Emil was even more interested in learning the identities of any other Russians whose names turned up. Because Volkov was essentially a KGB errand boy, and in tidying up the matter Dieter Krauss would have eventually dealt with Volkov's boss. That's the name Emil wanted.

He stepped briskly down the stairs, and by the time he reached his car he was feeling a bit smug about how deftly he'd handled the young detective.

The satisfaction was short-lived, mostly because he also couldn't stop thinking about the idea of Lothar with an electrode clipped to his balls. The images were vivid enough to make him shift uncomfortably on the car seat. A few miles later, as a crescent moon rose across a stubbled field during the lonely ride home, he began to reconsider the wisdom of his recent moves.

Yes, he had succeeded in putting Dorn onto Volkov's trail, and onto Krauss's as well. Yes, he had opened a conduit for new and perhaps vital information. For the moment, he had also fended off Krauss's probing curiosity. Wolf's as well. But in doing these things he had obligated himself to help all three of them on several fronts, and in each instance it would be difficult for him to fake it. All three men would demand further information in return for what he still needed from them. It would take some juggling, and dropping even a single ball might be dangerous, even fatal.

Meanwhile, Volkov was still at large, out on the hunt with his two sidekicks like feral creatures in the woods. Emil needed to take special care to leave as few tracks as possible as he moved among them all.

Then there were the Americans. So much hinged on what they did on Monday. Even if they complied with his wishes, would any further contact be compromised? He had already concluded one thing: The woman he had passed the note to was not the one who had called Lothar's dacha to set the time for the initial rendezvous. Their voices were too different. Was that where Lothar had gone wrong—some leak on the American side? At least he had the coming weekend to think about it, and prepare.

The other wild card was Andreas Plotz. Emil had hoped to never have to contact that difficult man ever again, directly or indirectly. But now he had promised both Dorn and Krauss that he would give it a try. Just as well, he supposed, because he had his own reasons for doing so, even though any attempt was likely to be risky.

It was too much, all of it—too much for one man to take upon his shoulders. But there was no one he could possibly recruit to assist him.

Those were his troubled thoughts as he turned the Wartburg onto the dirt lane toward the Bauersee, its headlight beams tunneling through the darkness.

Emil craved a steaming mug of coffee, a comfy seat next to Karola on a warm couch, a quiet chat about anything other than these concerns. But by the time he rolled up to the dacha, all the windows were dark.

He stepped out into the cold, alone with his burdens.

24

Bill Gentry placed a hand on Claire's elbow and steered her toward a quiet table in a corner of the hotel bar.

Freed from the decorum of the workplace on a Friday night, his movements were more aggressive. He had practically pounced on Claire the moment she stepped off the elevator from upstairs—a hug of greeting, a squeeze of her shoulder, a hand to the small of her back as they crossed the lobby. He nudged her toward a chair, and then slid his own chair closer.

"Lindsey is quite impressed with how you're handling this, the way you were able to salvage a contact." He leaned across the small table until their foreheads were practically touching. Claire fought off an impulse to back away. She glanced down at the table to avoid his gaze.

"Not much to be impressed with, really. He made the approach."

"Yes, but you kept your cool, didn't spook him, phoned it in right away. And I could tell she liked your ideas for follow-up."

"I thought she seemed a little wary."

"Well, maybe this morning. Maybe initially. But I can tell you first-hand that by this afternoon she had warmed to the whole idea. She's bringing in some help over the weekend, just in time for your contact on Monday. Not that you heard that from me."

"What kind of help?"

"That will have to come from her. I think she's eager to person-ally make the introduction. Probably tomorrow, so hang loose. He's another outsider, due in at Tegel overnight." Gentry checked his watch. "In about two hours, in fact."

"Good to know. Thank you."

Bad news for Baucom, she supposed, although their partnership would remain in play at least long enough for the trip to see Markus Wolf. Baucom had phoned her only an hour ago with further details of those arrangements. A second fax from the cutout "Roman" had curled onto his floor that afternoon, leading to a phone call that had revealed at least part of Wolf's reasons for seeking a meeting: Someone from Langley had reached out to him, also through a back-channel connection, and was seeking a personal audience.

Claire had asked Baucom if that someone might be Lindsey Ward.

"Doubtful," Baucom had answered. "This person is even higher up, or that was Wolf's impression, anyway. Whoever it was made it a point to say they'd been 'sent by Webster.'"

As in CIA director William Webster.

And now Wolf was hoping Baucom could give him a better idea in advance of what this high-ranking visitor would want from him, apart from the obvious items that Wolf had already made clear he wouldn't be offering.

"But I have no idea what they want, of course," Baucom had told her. "So if you pick up anything around the salt mine . . ."

"Sure. As long as you're still taking me with you."

"I tendered that request via Roman. Told him you were an academic researcher, working on your thesis."

"Is that supposed to impress him?"

"Don't knock it. The East Germans have always had an affinity for our academics. They can't believe we actually give eggheads so much access, so they're convinced they sometimes know as much as the spies do."

Wolf wanted to meet as soon as Sunday, which would certainly make it easier for Claire. She could tell Gentry and Ward she'd gone off for an afternoon in the country, to clear her head before the important Monday meetup.

Her briefing that morning with Ward—the one Gentry had just characterized as an unqualified triumph—had felt precarious at times, but Claire had at least learned a few things. Ward had confirmed that there was indeed a direct competitor—the aforementioned "Leonid"—who was offering a product comparable to whatever Lothar Fischer had proffered.

To Claire, that made Leonid a likely suspect in Lothar Fischer's death, and she had said so. Ward, somewhat defensively, had voiced skepticism, and she had not volunteered any further information on Leonid. That was another reason Claire had agreed to meet Gentry this evening, in spite of his obvious ulterior motives. Ply him with drink, flatter when necessary, then sit back and listen. It was shocking how often that still worked, even among professionals.

The waitress approached to take their order.

"Two whiskies, neat," Gentry said. He got out a credit card, but Claire gently nudged it aside.

"I'm the one on a per diem, so how 'bout if I run the tab?"

"Oh. Sure."

He sounded disappointed to have lost control of that aspect of the evening, although he did seem pleased by her touch. When the waitress returned with the drinks, Claire smiled, tapped her glass to his, and nudged the conversation in what she hoped would be a more productive direction.

"Must be exciting to be fielding so many high-grade offers for quality information. A real feather in your cap if we pull it off."

"But there's always the danger of bad-faith dealers. The old postwar days of the Berlin 'paper mills' come to mind. Con artists who would type up whatever they thought we wanted to see, as long as we were offering a few cartons of cigarettes in return."

"Except this time we know the records are actually there for the taking. The ones that haven't already been tossed out the window, anyway."

"Or shredded. Or carted off to Moscow. But, yes."

"It doesn't take a genius to see that at least one bidder must have KGB connections, given those skeevy men in leather I ran into. Plus the name, Leonid."

He nodded but said nothing. Claire saw that his glass was empty and signaled for a refill. The color was up in his cheeks, and he had loosened his tie.

"Who's Leonid's contact on our side?"

"Oh, I'm not privy to that. Lindsey has personally taken charge of that side of the action. The initial approach was in Warsaw. Went straight to our embassy."

"A cold caller?"

"Or his cutout. Dropped a sample over the transom, with the understanding that any further transactions would be conducted here."

"I suppose by now we must at least have his true identity, right?"

"I'm not at liberty to say."

"Of course. I'm probably overestimating our ability to connect the few dots Lindsey Ward has chosen to draw for us."

"Oh, I've managed to coax more than a few *dots* out of her." He laughed smugly.

"I should have guessed you'd be on top of that."

"Not that I can brief you fully, of course."

"Understood. At my level I'd be satisfied with just a dot or two."

He smiled and seemed on the verge of saying more. Instead he picked up his drink for another sip, as if to keep his mouth too busy to misbehave. Claire didn't give up.

"I guess it's obvious he must be based at Karlshorst, not Warsaw."

"What makes you say that?"

"Well, you're an ex–field man, Bill. Isn't that how you'd play it if you had some dangerous information to peddle? Make first contact in someone else's backyard, a place you'd be less likely to be seen by your own people. But for any further business you'd want to be working on your own turf, because that's where all your help is. Your muscle, like those lovelies in black leather."

"Not a bad assumption." He seemed mildly disconcerted that she'd connected those particular dots. "But that's all I should say for now on that front."

"Of course."

Someone from Karlshorst, then, and probably from the higher ranks of operatives and supervisors. That would only narrow it down to a few dozen people, and she wasn't familiar with the personnel there, but it was a start.

Gentry again leaned forward, back on the prowl. This time he took her hand before she could pull it out of reach.

"So, then. Now that it's the weekend and we can let our hair down a bit, I was pleased to hear you say the other day that you weren't currently involved with anyone."

"Not in Berlin, anyway. I believe that's how I put it."

"Nor in Paris, according to Marston."

Marston was her station chief. Gentry had obviously scouted her out in advance of her summons to Berlin—not just for operational fitness, but for her potential as a personal conquest in his new life as a bachelor.

"Which only goes to show that Marston knows less about me than he thinks."

"Oh?"

She nodded.

"I'm sorry to hear that. Still, you strike me as the type willing to play by different rules when you're off your home ground."

"Do I, now?" She smiled, not yet ready to crush his feeble hopes. Or not until she'd had a chance to ask about Markus Wolf. "Well, at the very least I'd say this calls for another drink."

"Right, ho."

He said it with a jolly British accent and signaled to the waitress. Claire tried not to feel too queasy about Gentry's smile as it widened into a leer. Maybe if she got him telling old war stories he'd stray from the main objective.

"Here's a question I have for all of you more experienced Berlin hands. Did you often run into your competition in places like this?"

"Not the known ones. But you always had to be careful. And still do, where the Russians are concerned. Look at this place tonight, for example. Dead as can be. I suppose our waitress or bartender might potentially be on the payroll at Karlshorst, but she's keeping her distance except when we call for her."

"How about the East Germans?"

"Oh, their people were everywhere, and they were always listening."

"Was that mostly Wolf's doing? The fellow we couldn't manage to get a picture of for so long?"

"Markus Wolf, yes, the Man Without a Face. Finally retired a few years back, thank God."

"Have we ruled him out as a possible co-conspirator of Lothar Fischer's?"

"Oh, absolutely. Ideologically he's as pure as the driven snow. He'd never give us anything that would reveal the identities of his own people. But, well . . ."

"What?"

His smile was now more conspiratorial than salacious.

"Apparently the thinking on Wolf is that he might be more useful with regard to what he knows about our mutual friends in Moscow. Especially if they refuse to lift a finger to protect him or his people from prosecution. And that squares with recent events."

"Like what?"

"Some strange doings at Harnack House."

Harnack House was a stately old building in the U.S. Army compound in Dahlem, only a few blocks from the CIA base. It was home to the local Officers' Club, with a restaurant, a few bars, and limited lodging for privileged guests. Lindsey Ward was currently staying there.

Gentry lowered his voice, his eyes alive with the excitement of privileged information.

"Lindsey got bumped out of her suite yesterday."

"They gave her a whole suite?"

"The Brigadier's Suite, yeah. But she's been relocated to another floor. To make room for someone higher up the ladder."

"How much higher?"

"Top floor, or that's what Lindsey heard. Some recent heavyweight of counterintelligence, dispatched by the director himself. Due any day now."

"And you think this is about Wolf?"

"Who else would rate that kind of visitor?"

There was a sudden burst of noise from the entrance. Five men in suits—all of them late twenties, all speaking English in British accents—traipsed loudly toward the bar and took seats at a nearby table. When the waitress approached, they ordered pints in this land where beer was measured by the liter. So much for any further privacy, and it was just as well. Claire had gotten all the information she was likely to receive.

Gentry gave her hand a squeeze and said, "You know, we could always retreat to a more secure location. Does your room have a minibar?"

She smiled and pulled her hand free.

"It does. But Jacques is supposed to be calling in about half an hour."

"Jacques?"

"A friend. In Paris."

"Ah, of course. That damn Marston. No wonder he can't land a posting as important as Berlin. No aspersion on your own capabilities, of course."

"Of course."

She caught the eye of the waitress and mouthed a request for the check.

"Thank you for a lovely evening, Bill. It's been nice to unwind. Looking forward to meeting the new arrival tomorrow."

"Yeah, sure. And, well, if you happen to change your mind later about the need to unwind further . . ."

She smiled again but said nothing. The waitress handed her the check. Claire signed it and rose from the table.

They said goodbye a few moments later in the lobby, where she preempted another hug by holding out her hand for a farewell shake. Gentry offered a halfhearted squeeze along with a wan smile, then departed into the revolving door. Claire watched it eject him onto the street before turning toward the elevators.

She checked her watch.

There was no actual Jacques currently in her life, although there was an Henri. But the man next on her call list was Clark Baucom, because there was still work to be done.

25

Grimm knew firsthand that Andreas Plotz was an incurable night owl and a late riser, so he rose at dawn on Saturday to drive to Plotz's apartment in Marzahn. Catching the man asleep might be the only way to jolt some honest answers out of him.

Emil knew this because long ago he had trained Plotz in the arts of deception, and by now the fellow had lived so many lives under so many identities that lying came to him as easily as breathing.

He had first known Plotz by the name his parents gave him, Thomas Eberhardt. Emil had spent six months preparing Eberhardt for his first mission before sending him to Brussels, where under a new name he quickly landed a job as an office clerk at NATO headquarters. Thus was Agent "Schumacher" born, and under that identity Plotz steadily climbed the ranks of the NATO office pool until he was promoted to archivist, giving him access to some of the organization's most sensitive documents.

Two years later, after a wildly productive span in which he had given the HVA a stunning array of secret NATO reports, maps, and orders of battle, Schumacher began growing a bit too enamored of his increasingly louche Western lifestyle. He stayed out late, drank too much, broke too many hearts, and talked freely to too many people he barely knew.

Recognizing the warning signs from previous failures, Emil began planning for the worst. By doing so was he able to engineer an extraction operation on only two hours' notice after learning that Schumacher's cover had been blown. The operation smuggled him safely across the border just as authorities in Brussels were breaking down the door of his apartment.

Emil then did what he always did with his damaged goods. He bestowed on him yet another new name, moved him to Berlin, bought him a car, and inserted him into a dull but steady job within the East German bureaucracy—in this case, a low-level slot in the HVA's Department Twelve, official records, where Eberhardt/Schumacher was reborn as Andreas Plotz, file clerk.

Again he rose quickly through the ranks, although Emil hadn't realized quite how high until a few months earlier, when he had learned that Plotz was running the emergency Task Force 7, created to secure and dispose of the HVA's most sensitive records.

Emil heard this news from none other than Lothar Fischer, who told him over a few beers on a sunny Saturday in early December, just after they'd chopped some firewood for Lothar's dacha. Due to their usual "need to know" strictures, Lothar wasn't aware until then that Plotz had once been one of Emil's agents. Emil later wondered why he had decided to tell Lothar even then. Was it an indiscreet outburst of professional pride? A feeling of futility about his future? Maybe both. Or perhaps it was a simple case of opportunism, because after a few more beers he and Lothar had concluded that Plotz's access and skills made him a uniquely valuable asset with regard to their hopes for a more secure future. Especially since, as they both knew, the last thing Plotz needed now was for any authorities in a reunified Germany to find out he'd once been a Stasi spy.

Lothar's willingness to proceed with their scheme had taken Emil by surprise. Lothar had always been far more vocal than Emil about his loyalty, not only to the HVA but also to the party, the nation, the cause. It had made him prone to windy, tiresome lectures whenever their colleagues gathered socially.

But his personal downfall had apparently changed all that, and on that chilly Saturday at his dacha, it had taken only one more beer for Emil to tap into Lothar's deep-seated resentment.

"That bastard Mielke cast me aside like one of these empties," he'd said, gesturing toward the spent bottles of Berliner Pilsner. "And for what? A goddamn woman? A tart who I never said a word to about anything we did? And by doing that, of course, the asshole gave license to Käthe to throw me over as well. Thirty-six years of marriage and she walks out over a single mistake. I worked hard to keep their secrets, and I did it better than anyone else, even that preening peacock, Wolf. But none of it meant a damn thing to them once I unzipped my pants without their permission. So fuck them."

Three days later, Lothar had set their plans in motion by paying a visit to Plotz—at his home, not his office. Now Emil was following the same route to Plotz's door as he turned the Wartburg onto the Autobahn, heading due south past the exit for Bernau.

Half an hour later he was steering through light traffic on Blumbergerdamm. Pale sunlight seeped into the dimness of the gray horizon to his left.

The Berlin district of Marzahn was one of the dreary "new towns" of the 1970s, born of East Germany's desperate need for housing, a creation of central planning. State engineers and architects began mass-producing high-rise *Plattenbau* apartment towers, one after the other, out of prefab concrete slabs. Minimal design variations allowed for rapid construction, and the dominant prototype was the eleven-story *Wohnungsbauserie 70*, or WBS 70, replicants of which now lined Marzahn's newer street grids like giant tombstones, with tram cars scurrying between them like mice in a maze.

The first tenants had been eager to move in, grateful for reliable heating, running water, modern kitchens, and the reasonable rent, but it didn't take long for breakdowns to begin. Then boredom set in, especially during the long Berlin winters, when bare trees and wet roadways only added to the gloom of the imposing gray monoliths.

Plotz lived on the tenth floor of a WBS 70. Emil parked a few blocks away, sighing with resignation as a light snow began to fall. His right knee was stiff from the drive, and his Pistol-M again banged against his thigh as he walked.

Not having seen Plotz in several years, he hadn't yet worked out exactly how to approach this meeting. Plotz was the sort of fellow for whom the adjective "rakish" had been invented. He was jauntily charming, handsome in the manner of a gigolo. When he set his mind to a task, his work was polished and competent. Punctual on weekdays, and a ne'er-do-well in his spare time, Plotz could juggle half a dozen lies without dropping one, which made him both valuable and worrisome as a co-conspirator. That's why Emil had insisted that Lothar tell Plotz as little as possible about their plan.

Presumably, Plotz did not yet know of Emil's involvement, which left Emil wondering how to ask questions in a way that still wouldn't reveal it. Maybe he could convince Plotz he was looking into these matters on behalf of the ministry. Emil had plausible cover for that option, since both Krauss and Dorn had given him their blessing to seek the man out. Still, this would be tricky, because no one sniffed out deception better than a deceiver. Emil was still puzzling out these problems as he rode the clanking elevator to the tenth floor.

It was quiet on the landing, a sleepy Saturday morning with no one yet stirring. Emil took a deep breath and pressed the button at Plotz's door. He heard the buzzer go off inside, but otherwise the place was silent. No TV or radio, no footsteps, no groan of misery from someone climbing out of bed. He pressed again, and this time held it for several seconds.

Still nothing.

Emil was prepared to pick the lock. If Plotz had heard what happened to Lothar, maybe he was no longer answering the door. He might even have gone into hiding.

He tried a third time. A baby cried out from a neighboring apartment, followed by a thudding of footsteps as someone went to comfort it. Emil turned the handle, and to his surprise the door was unlocked. Before entering he stooped for a closer look at the keyhole and saw signs of tampering.

Not encouraging, not at all. Emil took out a handkerchief and wiped down the handle. Then he used it to slowly push the door open. He stepped into the narrow central hallway.

It was the one-bedroom floor plan, with little more than four hundred square feet of space. Emil had been in so many of these apartments that he could have navigated the layout with his eyes closed. The bathroom was on his immediate right, with the door shut. At the far end of the hall, on the right, was the door to the bedroom. On the left side were the entrances to the kitchen and, farther along, the living room.

The place was frigid. It smelled like the great outdoors, with a stale underlay of cigarettes and cooking grease. A refrigerator rattled to life down the hall in the kitchen and began to hum, which put him on edge. He used the handkerchief to press the door shut behind him and paused to collect himself. He reached into the pocket of his overcoat to grip the stock of the Pistol-M. Then he called out loudly.

"Andreas! Are you here?"

No answer. The baby next door had stopped crying.

He let go of the gun. Then he slipped off his shoes, as any courteous visitor would do, and placed them by the door. His feet were already cold from his walk to the building, but now the chill spread up his legs to the pit of his stomach.

Emil headed for the bedroom doorway in his stockinged feet. He reached the opening with a sense of dread, but stepped into a neatly arranged room. No one was there. The bed was made, but there were signs of recent occupation.

A suitcase was splayed open on top of the bedspread. It was only half-filled, with a few shirts neatly stacked by some folded trousers. He rounded the foot of the bed and spotted the first sign of disorder on the rug by the dresser—an open shaving kit that had been knocked to the floor, its contents scattered. Toothbrush, a tube of toothpaste, a razor, a bar of soap. Everything was suggestive of someone interrupted in the midst of a quick but orderly departure.

It was even colder in here, and now Emil saw why. The window was wide open. He approached for a look, half expecting to see the body of Andreas Plotz ten stories below, sprawled and broken on the pavement. But the courtyard was empty.

A need for fresh air, even in winter, was not unusual among Germans, as Emil knew firsthand, but this was extreme. He again took out his handkerchief and gripped the sill to pull the window shut. Still using the handkerchief, he opened the drawer of the bedside table to check for further evidence of imminent travel. There were no rail or air tickets, no paperwork of any kind. Emil left the bedroom and crossed into the living room.

There, too, the window was fully open, but the furniture was neatly arranged, and the room was clean. A few newspapers and magazines were neatly stacked on a coffee table. The focal point was the usual wood-grain entertainment console, where a bulky Chromat television filled the biggest opening. On the shelf next to it was a Grundig amp-turntable combo that Plotz must have bought in West Germany. His return to East Germany had presumably prevented him from upgrading to a CD player.

Emil checked to see what was on the turntable. Guns N' Roses, their latest album.

Over by the door into the kitchen was a round dining room table, with three metal slatted folding chairs like the ones in parks and beer gardens. There was a gap where a fourth chair should've been, which troubled Emil for some reason he couldn't yet pinpoint. The radiator was on full blast, so Emil also shut this window, again using his handkerchief. He headed for the kitchen.

There, too, the window was open, and by now Emil was deeply worried by the implications. He shut this one as well and made a quick inspection. A bag of oranges from Spain was on the counter. The milk in the fridge was still fresh, and the place seemed reasonably well stocked. Pots were hung on hooks—two skillets and two saucepans. Next to the stove was one of those angled wooden blocks for holding knives, which were also from West Germany, a pricey set with white handles made by Wüsthof.

The biggest slot was empty.

When he stepped back into the hall he was enveloped by an odor that must have been masked earlier by all the outdoor air. It was coppery and sharp, a rawness verging on rancid, and it was coming from the only remaining room, the bathroom, where the door was shut.

Emil crossed the hallway and took a deep breath. He again took out his handkerchief and turned the handle. Overcome by a sense that he needed to get this over with as quickly as possible, he shoved open the door.

The stench inside was overpowering, but the sight was ghastlier—the naked body of Andreas Plotz, staring back at him from a sitting position in the bathtub, where he had been tied with butcher string to the folding chair from the dining room. He had been slashed and cut multiple times. Gallons of blood had spilled beneath him in the tub, a fetid, darkened pool that had clotted the drain.

Plotz's skin was polar white. His mouth was gagged, covered by a rag knotted tightly in the back, presumably to muffle any screams so the neighbors wouldn't hear. Cuts were on his chest, arms and genitals, although the deepest one was across the throat, a gaping wound that left his head tilting back against the white tiled wall. The arteries, muscle, and nerves of his neck were exposed like the dangling hoses of an engine that had been ripped from a car. Plotz's eyes gaped skyward, showing mostly their whites. Balanced on the rim of the tub was a bloody chef's knife. Its white handle had been wiped clean.

He now realized why the sight of the missing chair had disturbed him—because it had reminded him of the police photo from Leipzig, the one of Boyan Barkov, tied to a chair and slashed.

This scene, like that one, was the handiwork of Yuri Volkov.

26

Emil sat in the silence of his car for several minutes without turning the key. The horrible smell clung to his clothes. He should call someone. The police, maybe. Then he envisioned the hours of waiting, and all the questions, the red tape, the aggravation, the suspicion, with far too many people now tying his name to that of Andreas Plotz, a connection that would draw unwanted attention from far too many people, Yuri Volkov among them.

Dieter Krauss would probably be the person best equipped to keep this under wraps, but for all the wrong reasons. Anything he told Krauss would likely go straight to Volkov.

The sight and smell of Plotz's body had made Grimm gag. He had only narrowly kept himself from vomiting onto the bathroom floor. Then, as if in penance, he had forced himself to take a final, longer look at Andreas Plotz, even though he had known the image would trouble his sleep. Because of the horror, yes, but also due to his complicity. Perhaps Plotz had helped bring this on himself by angling for a better deal elsewhere, maybe even in a way that had exposed and endangered Lothar. But Emil had put both men in harm's way, by suggesting that Lothar contact Plotz. He had set these events in motion.

Before leaving the apartment, he had checked the bottom of his stockinged feet as he slipped back into his untied shoes. They had flopped loosely as he stepped aboard the elevator. He had wiped down the button for the tenth floor that he had pushed on his way up, and then he'd pressed the handkerchief to the button for the ground floor.

Exiting downstairs, he had shuffled along like an old man in a bathrobe and slippers, the loose shoes flopping all the way back to the Wartburg.

Now, still taking deep breaths, he scanned the street and sidewalks. As far as he knew, no one had seen him enter or leave the apartment. Hardly anyone was out at this early hour of a wintry Saturday morning.

Then he contemplated the sight of all those windows in all those apartment buildings, staring down from so many angles. He was one of only a few people down here who had parked his car and then walked around. There were too many eyes up there, all of them belonging to people thoroughly conditioned to tell what they had witnessed whenever someone from the state knocked on their doors. Yes, the state was now dead, but the Volkspolizei were not. Plus, he had seen that dangerous gleam in Dorn's eye, that of a man out for the big score. Emil had used that zeal to his advantage, but it could just as easily work against him if he got caught trying to cover up this visit.

So he decided to call it in, but not from a nearby phone. He would drive to West Berlin and use a yellow Telekom phone booth. The drive would give him a chance to calm down and figure out exactly what to say.

He started the Wartburg and pulled away.

. . .

Half an hour later Emil pulled to the curb of a busy street in Schöneberg. He still felt shaky, and his toes were still numb with cold. He had taken several detours along the way, to make sure he wasn't followed. But he hadn't yet decided exactly how much to tell Dorn. Play it by ear, he supposed.

He stepped into a yellow booth and punched in the number for the duty officer at the Bernau police station. A gruff voice answered.

"Patch me through to Lieutenant Dorn's home, please."

"No need. He's up in his office."

It wasn't yet nine o'clock on a Saturday morning. Emil sighed and waited for the detective to answer.

"Dorn here."

"It's Grimm. I've been to see Andreas Plotz this morning. The news isn't good."

"No luck on ID'ing the film?"

"He's dead. Trussed up and carved to a bloody mess in his bathroom. Someone had tied him to a chair."

There was a sharp intake of breath, followed by a pause filled with the crackling that still haunted all East-West phone connections.

"That's remarkable."

"*Remarkable?*"

"I was just looking through the Boyan Barkov police file, the one from Leipzig. They faxed it overnight and, well, your description . . ."

Emil nearly tripped himself up by saying something that would've showed he knew all about the similarity of the two murders. Instead he said, "Yes?"

"It sounds exactly the same. Horrible, but the same."

"So then it's the same person?"

"It certainly sounds that way. The killer in Leipzig was Yuri Volkov, a bit of muscle the Russians had hired. But the fellow who cleaned it all up in cooperation with Dieter Krauss had a few stripes on his collar. A KGB colonel."

"Name?"

"I was just reaching that part. His signature is all over the forms. Here we go . . . Gregor Kolkachev."

Emil knew the name, and even remembered the face. A tough KGB insider, midforties by now, a big man who had managed to survive the shakeups and purges that had seemed to emanate every few years from Moscow. He was the district chief for counterintelligence, which meant he'd have a keen interest in either saving or destroying the HVA's agent files and other sensitive documents.

"Kolkachev. I see."

"Do you know him?"

"The name is vaguely familiar, but I can check with people who'd know, if you'd like."

"Yes, that would be helpful."

"And of course now I'll need to find someone other than Plotz to tell me more about these strips of microfilm."

"Maybe it would be better if you just returned them to me."

"No, no. I have a few solid leads I'm already pursuing."

"But, Grimm, I cannot possibly—"

"I've already set the wheels in motion, Lieutenant. Too many people are now aware of a police interest in this matter for me to not show them anything. Oh, and for obvious reasons it will be better for both of us if you're the one who reports this Plotz killing. It's in a *Plattenbau* in Marzahn. I'll give you the address. I touched nothing."

"*Me*? But you're there! I don't even know the supervisor for that district. And—"

"I'm in Schöneberg now. I was too shaken up, so I had to go for a drive."

"Then you make the call! I'll get you the number."

"Do you really want to have to explain why you authorized me to go down there on your behalf?"

"*My* behalf? But you were the one who made the offer. Shit!"

"Just say you received a tip from a source about a witness of interest in your murder inquiry. If my name eventually comes up, then I'll be happy to back up your story."

"*My* story? You're being impossible, Grimm!"

"It's the only way I can remain free to help you. No other ministry source is going to do that, not under current conditions."

There was an uncomfortable pause. He could hear Dorn breathing as he made his calculations.

"I'll have to think about this. In fact, I need to reconsider our entire arrangement."

"Fine, but I don't think you'll want to explain how you let a Stasi colonel take possession of a key piece of evidence, and without even signing for it. In the meantime, you'd better report this killing before the body gets any colder."

"Goddamn you, Grimm! This is asking too much. This is—"

"What will it be, Lieutenant Dorn? Do you want me to keep working in the background to help you break this case, with all credit of course going to you? Or would you rather drag me out into the light, and have to explain why you've been making improper allowances for someone so high up in the old regime?"

Before Dorn could answer, Emil gave him the address for Plotz's apartment. He heard the scratching of a pen on paper.

"Look, Grimm, I am willing to continue awhile longer with this arrangement, but only if—"

Emil gently hung up the phone. He had no idea how much longer Dorn must have gone on, but he could easily guess the tone and character of his language.

On the drive back to Prenden, the passing sights barely registered. Thanks to Dorn, he now had a key name in his possession—Gregor Kolkachev. But every time he tried to focus on that, what he kept seeing instead was Andreas Plotz's body—the white, clammy skin, the gaping raw neck. He turned the Wartburg's heater to its highest setting, but was still rigid with cold by the time he reached the dacha.

He now had plenty of ideas, but little hope that he'd have the means or ingenuity to put them to use, unless something soon changed. He would also have to deal further with Dorn's anger, probably sooner rather than later—unless, of course, Dorn decided that he was simply too hazardous and unpredictable to associate himself with any further, and came clean with his supervisors.

As he turned up the gravel lane toward his dacha, he decided he needed a walk in the woods to clear his head, calm his nerves, plan his next actions. He was certainly not yet prepared to face Bettina and Karola. After pulling into the driveway he hopped out and headed straight for the nearest trail, where he disappeared into the trees.

He breathed deeply of the fresh air, and by the time he was nearing the top of the hill his rattled nerves finally began to settle.

But what Emil didn't yet know was that someone was tracking his progress, someone who knew these trails as well as him. So, breathing heavily, he plodded onward and upward, oblivious to the presence in his wake.

27

Claire's "help" was going to be a thorn in her side. That was her initial assessment of Ron Kent, the new arrival from points unknown. She met him late Saturday morning in the conference room, a space that Lindsey Ward had now fully colonized with file boxes, a fax machine, and an encrypted phone line that a technician had wired up for her the day before. Plus a small refrigerator with a carton of milk for her coffee. It had the look of a personal command center, and Ward kept the door locked to everyone except those she summoned.

Gentry and Kent were already there when Claire arrived. The remains of a breakfast for three were at the far end of the conference table, which told her Kent had a head start on her in the morning's proceedings, probably by design.

Baucom had warned her that Ward was likely to bring in one of her own once things began moving forward, or if they became more complicated. Baucom had called an Agency pal who he said had tracked Ward's career ascent "the way a baseball scout follows a talented young center fielder's rise to stardom," and on her way up the ladder she had cultivated valuable allies at every step, both in the field and in the corridors of power. Kent was apparently one of the chosen. So naturally he had gotten a fuller briefing.

Far more dismaying to Claire was Ward's choice of words in introducing them to each other.

"Claire, this is Ron Kent. From here onward you'll be working this op as coequals. He'll share fully in all decision making, and in case of any disagreement he'll make the call."

A demotion, then. Not unexpected, but still jarring.

Her second assessment, based more on Kent himself as the morning unfolded, was that he at least was intelligent, was not without charm, and might even be pleasant company if they ended up spending much time together.

Kent was fit and trim, late thirties, with an unadorned and somewhat preppy handsomeness that made her wonder if he hadn't come to his career via one of the old Ivy League pipelines that had supplied the Agency with far too much of its personnel in the '40s and '50s. His close-cropped haircut wasn't in style, nor was his plain wardrobe of uncreased khakis, white oxford shirt, and rumpled blue blazer. His manner was a finely balanced combination of relaxed and watchful, and he didn't seem to care if you disapproved of him or not, an attitude that lent him an air of competence, or at least confidence. She supposed she could have done worse.

"Pleasure to meet you," Kent said. "And, coequals or not, since you've already been on the ground a few days, and have actually met the contact, I'll be deferring to your judgment in our initial approach."

Claire was impressed he was willing to say that in front of Ward, although he'd certainly left himself an opening to call the shots once he got his bearings. They took seats around the table, Ward and Gentry on one side, her and Kent on the other.

"We've briefed Ron on the basics," Ward said, "and also on your progress to date. Or lack of it."

Kent had the grace to lower his head in response to that open rebuke. Gentry offered a nervous laugh but said nothing in Claire's defense.

"I've also explained to him some of the dynamics with regard to your new contact's competitor."

"Great. Maybe you should bring me up to speed on that as well."

Kent again lowered his head, although this time Claire could have sworn it was to hide a smile from Ward, who was not amused.

"Since you've chosen to press that point, I'll observe that Ron's security clearance on these matters is higher than yours. And that's a decision that came straight from Langley."

Or straight from Ward, as Claire suspected. Ward stood.

"I'm guessing the two of you will want to get better acquainted, and begin preparing for the next steps. Any further questions before you set off?"

Claire had several, but wasn't in the mood to endure further humiliations.

Gentry stayed behind as Claire and Kent left together. The moment the door shut behind them, Kent turned to her and nodded toward the exit. He waited until they had left the building and passed through the security gate onto Saargemünder Strasse before speaking again.

"I've got a car around the corner if you want to start giving me the lay of the land."

"Sure."

There was a pregnant pause. He shifted his posture from one foot to the other and then looked off to the side, as if searching for the right words.

"Lindsey's blunt like that sometimes, probably to a fault, but she knows what she's doing, and, well, the stakes of this may be even higher than you think."

"I'll take that as an assessment of whatever the Russian, Leonid, must be offering."

"Good. And for now I'll leave it at that. Look, to clear the air a little, I know Lindsey wants me breathing down your neck with every move you make, but that's never been my style. So don't hesitate to tell me to back off whenever you need some space."

She was already irritated by his familiar use of the name "Lindsey," but at least he'd made a peace offering of sorts, so she reciprocated.

"I'm all for hearing your ideas as we move along. Especially since, so far on this op, everyone seems to be making it up as we go along. Ward and Gentry included."

"Got it."

She watched Kent closely. His answer was notably noncommittal with regard to her critique of management, but she supposed that wasn't surprising. She also observed that it was impossible to look him in the eye for very long without your attention snagging on the arresting blue of his irises. They invited trust even as they fended off deeper inquiry—an observation that was probably behind her next remark.

"Maybe I'd feel even better about this arrangement if you at least told me the kind of work you normally do. All I know is that you're not based here or in Paris, and I'm guessing you've been fully briefed about my particulars."

"I'm based in Langley, but I work abroad on demand. Beyond that I'm not even authorized to tell Gentry, so don't feel slighted."

"All right. I won't." Even though she did.

"Look, we're on the same side in this, and Lindsey wants us to succeed. I hope you're not one of those Agency women who can't stand to let another female outdo her."

Whatever ground he'd gained began to crumble.

"I'm not. And I might be more open to that question if I thought you'd ever posed it to Ward. Or, excuse me, Lindsey, as you always call her." He looked down for a second, but didn't blush. Nor did he smile, thank God. "Also, I wasn't aware this was a competition, at least not on our side. If it is, maybe you could tell me what Ward has ever done operationally to give herself a leg up."

"Fair point. She's a desk jockey, always has been. But her operational instincts are solid. I've seen that firsthand, and if she believes there's something more to be had from one source than another—or, more to the point, more of a future in that relationship—then I'm inclined to trust her."

"At any cost?"

"That's her call, not ours."

"Theoretically. But you know how it works. At some point, out in the wild, we may have to make that call on our own."

"And if we do, your opinion will count as much as mine."

The words were reassuring, but his eyes were still refusing full admission. She nodded, and they headed for his car.

Despite the trickiness of this new relationship, Claire was relieved to have an official partner. She hadn't liked the look of those three Russians, and Lothar Fischer's death had raised the threat level for everyone. As steadying as Baucom's experience was, it was more practical to be paired with someone younger and fitter, not to mention fully authorized.

They decided to make a reconnaissance of the location of Monday's rendezvous. Claire provided directions from a map, although he seemed to know his way once she gave him the address. His rental was a black Opel Vectra. It would be an obvious interloper among all the Trabis and Wartburgs, so they decided to park several blocks away and walk from there. All the better to let them assess the lay of the land at a leisurely pace, and from a pedestrian's point of view.

"I'm still amazed you can just do this with a wave and a nod," Kent said, as they rolled into East Berlin across a steel girder bridge at the Bornholmer Strasse checkpoint.

"I know that the Brandenburg Gate got all the attention the night of November ninth," Claire asked, "but wasn't this where the floodgates first opened?"

"It was. This whole bridge was wall-to-wall people. You should've seen how this worked even five months ago. These old checkpoints were such quaint exercises in hypocrisy for people like us. You'd sit in your car for an hour while they pretended to check you out. We didn't let them touch or stamp our passports because we didn't officially recognize the Wall's existence, and they played along. But we played along, too, by holding up all our papers at the window for them to see as we drove by."

"And how much experience of that sort of game-playing do you have?"

He smiled.

"That's another item from the file that even Gentry can't open."

"I guess I should be reassured by that. Unless you're bluffing, of course, to make me feel better."

He smiled again, but wouldn't be baited into offering more.

"How 'bout this, then. In all your briefings this morning with Ward—the ones before I showed up—I gather you discussed this Leonid fellow at some length."

"Not at length, but his name came up. She also told me about the welcoming party of Russians you ran into the other day."

"Gentle persuasion didn't appear to be their preferred way of doing business."

"Apparently that's the new style in a certain reactionary corner of the KGB. The non-Glasnost crowd."

"She told you that?"

"She didn't need to. It's a hot topic in the high corridors of Langley."

"In your section?" A yes would have been as good as telling her he worked for the Soviet desk.

"In higher corridors generally. More implied than overt, but it's there all the same."

"How many floors do you have to climb from yours to hear this kind of chatter?"

He laughed and shook his head, which was fine. At least he took her probing in good humor. Some men would have just told her to fuck off.

"I'm not hearing it right outside my door, if that's what you're guessing. But I am invited up there from time to time. The day before I left for Berlin being the latest instance."

So at least he doled out a few rewards for persistence. Smart, because it would make them better teammates, especially if the game turned against them. As if to confirm this judgment, he then offered a roundabout confession of the gaps Ward had left in his own briefing.

"Whoever this Leonid is, he's the clear front-runner in the competition, as opposed to the shabby German who passed you that ostmark fiver the other night."

"You think she's hoping to turn him, this Russian?"

"He could certainly offer more value going forward than an unemployed Stasi man. Especially if he can deliver the same set of documents."

"He's also a higher risk, especially if he's proffering himself at the KGB's request."

"High risk-reward scenarios have always appealed to Lindsey."

"Did Ward"—Claire refused to call her Lindsey—"tell you any more about that trio of Leonid's thugs?"

"No. But I got the feeling she knows the ID of at least one of them."

"I'm not sure whether to feel good or bad about that."

"Same here."

"I'm beginning to see why you're so willing to keep humoring all my questions."

They said little more for the rest of the ride. A few minutes later he parked the Vectra on Eberswalder Strasse. Claire folded away the map, already suspecting he had never really needed it. Then Kent headed in one direction and Claire in the other, with plans to converge at the rendezvous point.

The Zum Goldbroiler restaurant was on the corner of narrow Kan-zowstrasse and busy Prenzlauer Allee, a four-lane boulevard. The Gold-broiler chain had been one of East Germany's few retail success stories. Modeled on West Germany's Wienerwald rotisserie chicken joints, its fast-food outlets had catered to budget-minded families.

This location was already looking outdated. The yellow script lettering of its neon sign popped and buzzed on the façade. The droopy lace curtains in the plate glass window were dusty and yellowed. By the time Claire arrived, Kent was seated at a corner table for two, eating a greasy drumstick and licking his fingers. Claire ordered a Club Cola, another East German brand, and sat a few tables away. Each of them took note of the layout, plus the advantages and drawbacks of every table and doorway.

He finished his chicken and she her cola. Then she followed him outside, where they spent the next hour strolling the surrounding blocks. The only nearby place of particular interest was the Zeiss Planetarium, a massive silver orb a few blocks away. Customers were lined up outside for the next showing. A busy S-Bahn station was less than a block from the restaurant, with tracks running overhead, so they familiarized themselves with its entrances and exits.

It was certainly a more effective way to prepare than how she and Baucom had done it a few nights ago, by tracing their fingers along an old map while relying on Baucom's memories, but Claire missed the old fellow and the comforts of his experience in this neck of the woods.

They agreed that Kent would arrive half an hour ahead of the scheduled time in order to set up inside the restaurant, preferably at a table by the window so he could observe the arrival of her and the German, or the German's cutout. That would also give him a heads-up in case any leather-jacketed Russians crashed the party.

"If those goons show, we abort," Claire said.

"If our contact decides to take you elsewhere, should I try to follow?"

"If we leave on foot, definitely. By car? Depends on where you park, I guess."

"Ward said she would get a Trabi for us to use, so at least we'll blend in a little better."

"Assuming a Trabi can keep up with anything besides another Trabi."

They laughed, but after what had happened at the first rendezvous

Claire was a little on edge. She wished she had gotten a better look at the German in the darkened tunnel beneath the S-Bahn, although she was pretty sure she'd recognize him.

Their last chore was to choose a fallback location where they would meet later, in case they got separated. If Claire failed to arrive there, Kent would sound the alarm to Ward.

Fifteen minutes later they crossed back into West Berlin in the Vectra. They agreed to meet again early the next morning. Sundays were always quiet in Berlin, a conducive atmosphere for reviewing plans and contingencies. Kent suggested they also go for a Sunday afternoon outing, perhaps to a *Bierstube*, or, weather permitting, a stroll in the Tiergarten—the sort of experience that someone from human resources might have annoyingly described as a "team building" exercise. But Claire already had plans for the afternoon, her off-the-books meeting with Baucom and the exalted Markus Wolf.

"Thanks, but I tend to keep to myself the evening before something like this. I may go for a drive in the country to clear my head. Maybe visit some kitschy roadside attraction to watch the locals spend their welcome money."

"Not a bad idea," Kent answered pleasantly, doing his best not to sound snubbed. "Maybe I'll do that as well. On my own, of course."

He was appealing. She liked him. It was Ward, and his willingness to unquestioningly do her bidding, that still gave her pause. They parted cordially, with a promise to reconvene at Berlin station at eight the next morning.

When Claire got back to the hotel, she took a mini-bottle of bourbon from the mini-fridge and poured it into a tumbler. She sipped and thought things over while gazing out the window toward the bustle of the Ku-Damm, a block away. Given her current available resources, there was really no reason she needed to stay so much in the dark about Ron Kent, but she didn't want to risk using the hotel phone. So she went downstairs, exited through the revolving doors, and used the nearest Telekom booth to dial Baucom's number.

"Didn't expect to hear from you today. Not getting cold feet about our trip tomorrow, I hope?"

"Wouldn't dream of missing that. But I was wondering if I could interest you in some further employment. Still unofficial, of course."

"What do you need?"

"A background check. One of ours."

Baucom's smoker's chuckle wheezed through the receiver.

"Already doubting Ward's choice for your partner?"

"Actually, I think she chose pretty well. But forewarned is forearmed."

"Name?"

"Ron Kent. Although I have a hunch it's not his real one. Probably her idea."

"Based in?"

"Langley. Don't know the desk, but he seems to be one of her regulars, just as your friend the 'baseball scout' predicted. Does covert stuff, seems to travel a fair amount with a wide portfolio, and he's no stranger to East Berlin."

"I'm on it."

"Thanks."

"See you tomorrow, then."

28

This plan of his wasn't going to work. Emil reached that conclusion quickly as he made his way deeper into the woods. Even with two of them participating it had been a long shot. He and Lothar were too old, too inexperienced in the field, and, just maybe, too overconfident. What had ever made them think they could pull it off? Hubris, probably, from more than thirty years of working high up in a ministry where even their boldest official actions had always gone unchallenged, unquestioned. Maybe they were only getting what they deserved.

And what was he even thinking with this "they" business? Lothar was dead, and Emil was alone, cast adrift in a spy's wilderness of abandonment, with no support network to exfiltrate him back to safety. He was wandering without a map, as aimless as a lost hiker in the woods, which, come to think of it, described him perfectly at that moment.

He stopped, gazed up at the treetops, and took stock of his location. Snow was no longer falling, but there was about an inch on the ground. Emil had been walking briskly for nearly half an hour, and his breathing was labored. He had set off from the Wartburg like a man possessed, forging up the nearest hillside without even stopping to let Bettina and Karola know he had returned, although surely they must have heard the car enter the driveway.

He now realized he must have taken several turns in the trail without thinking. His longest stop had occurred a few minutes earlier in a small clearing, a favorite spot of his since a few years ago, when, on a somber winter day much like this one, he had watched in astonishment as a stealthy fox caught an infant groundhog and trotted away with its bleeding trophy in its jaws. At the time he'd been exhilarated to witness this elemental display of the natural order. Now it felt like a warning, a fable to learn by, and he glanced over his shoulder, lest Yuri Volkov suddenly pounce from the underbrush. ·

Clearly their plan—*his* plan—was now as hopeless as that baby groundhog. The safest course would be to abandon tomorrow's rendezvous with the Americans, a meetup that suddenly seemed ludicrously unmanageable. With any luck the CIA still didn't know his name. Maybe by lying low from here on out he could escape this fool's errand alive.

Even then, he would still face the issue of what to do with the merchandise that he and Lothar had stashed, the prize that was supposed to have secured their future. He decided he should at least do another walk-by. Because with Lothar and Plotz now dead there was no assurance that the object in question had remained undisturbed.

First, he had to recalibrate his location. Emil took note of the moss on the trees and the position of the sun behind its veil of clouds. He oriented himself accordingly, and took the next available leftward fork. Soon he was descending to a lower plateau that looked familiar. Ten minutes later he again turned left and headed for the hunting stand.

It came into view from about fifty yards off, the boxy green hut on stilts, barely visible through the trees, its plywood roof covered by snow. Then he stopped, wavering, having spotted something that immediately made the air feel a few degrees colder.

Someone was there, dimly visible through the branches. A seated figure in a hooded hunting jacket, propped on a lower crossbeam of the stand's supporting frame. The person's head was turned away, as if he were watching something in the opposite direction. Being seated made his size hard to judge. Emil remained motionless. He still had time to double back. Even if he'd been detected, he might have enough of a lead to outrun the fellow to a neighbor's dacha, or his own.

He also had the gun. Emil reached into his pocket for the heavy lump of steel, the plastic grip. At least there weren't three goons in black leather this time, unless the other two were hiding nearby. And he had already concluded that the mystery sentinel wasn't Krauss or Dorn. Maybe it was only a weary hiker, pausing to rest.

Emil gripped the rough stock of the Pistol-M. In doing so he wondered if this had been exactly how Lothar met his end, lured to a foolish encounter by a seemingly harmless hooded figure on the trail ahead.

He drew a deep breath and set out at a slow but steady gait, but the man did not rise from his post or turn toward him. He closed to within thirty yards, and then twenty. Still the figure remained motionless, face averted. Emil's footsteps thumped against the matted leaves.

Then the man stood, stepped into the path, and turned toward Emil, face shielded by the low hood. Emil curled his forefinger onto the trigger of the Pistol-M. He stopped, waiting. The figure spoke.

"Did you think you could avoid us for the rest of the day?"

It was a woman's voice. Karola's.

Emil sagged in relief, exhaling as he released the pistol into the depths of his coat pocket. He saw now that she was wearing his hunting jacket, which she must have taken from the closet. But how had she known to come here? She must have followed him from the dacha, at least for a while, yet he had failed to detect even the slightest sign of her. Further proof that his skills were slipping, that this reckless mission was beyond his abilities.

"How did you manage to . . . ?"

"Beat you here? Without you knowing? Without you even having a clue that, for a while, someone was stalking you, especially with you being so on edge about everything?"

It was disconcerting how easily she always read his mind.

"Well, yes. To all that."

"I did it to show you that I'm qualified for what you need most right now. Help. Also to say that, whatever you and Lothar were up to, I know it has something to do with this."

She slapped a corner post of the hunting stand. The noise and vibration startled a crow perched on the roof. It cawed in annoyance and flapped away through the trees.

Emil's stomach tightened. How could she possibly have known about the hunting stand? Unless . . .

In his sudden suspicion, Emil slid his hand deeper into his pocket, yet couldn't bring himself to take hold of the gun. If Karola were to be the catalyst of his downfall, then so be it. The disappointment of her betrayal might be enough to kill him all by itself.

He then registered the pleading look of compassion on her face, the one he was already so familiar with, and he sighed at his foolishness. He withdrew his hand and set off toward her. She was not the enemy, of that he was certain. But she *was* hiding something, and possibly had been doing so for a while.

They threw their arms around each other, an embrace of relief. Then he looked into her eyes. She nodded, as if replying to his thoughts.

"Let's talk," she said.

"But not here." He nodded at the hunting stand.

"Of course."

"This way, back toward the lake."

"A walk and talk, isn't that what you'd call this? In case of microphones, or a stationary eavesdropper? Although we're definitely alone. I've checked the perimeter."

He cast her a sidelong glance, his curiosity growing. So many questions came to mind, but she spoke before he could ask any of them.

"You're going to have to tell me—tell both of us, Bettina and me—what is going on."

"That depends on how much you already know. That hunting stand, for starters. How did you know it's important?"

"Your phone conversations with Lothar. I'm a good listener, and it was pretty easy to guess that the two of you must have hidden something there."

He stopped and placed his hands on her shoulders. "See? Yet another example of how careless I've become. Which is why I've decided to cut my losses and drop all of my stupid plans. So don't worry about that hunting stand anymore, and don't worry about me."

"That's all you're going to tell me?"

"Karola, I've spent an entire career keeping my biggest secrets to myself, and for good reason. Not just for my own safety, but for the protection of those around me. This is no different."

She pulled his hands from her shoulders.

"It's *completely* different. Before you worked for the state. Now you're working for yourself and, by extension, for Bettina and me. And one thing I can see clearly, without you saying a word, is that whatever you were cooking up with Lothar—"

"I—"

"Stop! Just listen for a minute."

He nodded, a little in awe of her just then. No one at the ministry, not even Mielke in his foulest moods, had ever maneuvered him so deftly into such a tight corner.

"Whatever you two were cooking up, you need my help now that he's gone. Especially with that fellow Krauss and that detective, Dorn, both looking over your shoulder."

"Karola, you cannot possibly know how moved I am by your offer, and I say that with love, and the utmost sincerity. But, as I said, I'm backing away from this. It's not the sort of work you're equipped to handle. Me, either, apparently. Enlisting your help would only put us all in even greater danger."

"You're making a spy's biggest mistake. Making a key decision without having enough relevant intelligence."

He smiled and suppressed a laugh.

"And from what movie character did you steal that bit of espionage wisdom? Not James Bond, I hope."

"Gerhard Schulz."

"Schulz?" The name was familiar, but not from the movies. Schulz had once led the HVA's training section. He had also been a talent scout, an HVA recruiter. The implication was staggering.

"You've met Gerhard Schulz. Did he even . . . ?"

"Recruit me? Yes. When I was twenty-one. He gave a talk to one of my classes at Humboldt University. The Wall had just gone up the year before. He invited me to apply. So I did."

Emil was floored. This would have been right after he'd moved over to the HVA. For a moment, he couldn't speak. She smiled at his baffled expression and touched his arm.

"There are many things about me that you don't know, Emil, from long before you knew me. Long before I ever lived up here. Long before I was married."

"If you started in '62, then I probably saw you and your classmates passing in the halls, on your way to the cafeteria."

"Oh, you did more than that. You hopped onto a paternoster with me once. It was passing your floor and you were going downstairs for coffee. You were studying some notes and barely looked up at me."

"I must have been blind."

"No. You were happily married, that's all. You only had eyes for Bettina. She has told me about those years."

Emil realized then that his wife must have known these things about Karola for ages.

"You've told her about all of this, haven't you?"

"Of course. She was the first one to suggest I should help you."

How Bettina could have conveyed that wish in her current condition was a mystery to him, although by now he knew better than to be surprised by any sort of communication these two women still managed. It was part code, part telepathy. He knew he would never master it, and he envied them for it.

"Did you complete the training?" His tactful way of asking if the HVA had deemed her worthy of employment.

"I did. I even got to meet Wolf. He interviewed me personally. Of course now, whenever I see him or that very young wife of his, he shows no sign of recognizing me. But I suppose that's not surprising, since I never really saw him again. Not on Normanenstrasse."

"You were never activated?"

She shook her head and looked down at the ground.

"He—Schulz, I mean—was moved up from training after our class. And they made him my handler, my case officer."

"He must have chosen you personally, then."

"He did, yes."

"That's quite a feather in your cap."

"It wasn't." She looked off toward the lake. "He was . . . not a good fit for me as a boss. It was awkward. Worse than that, really."

"I see."

It was then that Emil remembered the talk around the office about Schulz—the way he often took a shine to some of his young female recruits, to the point of continuing their "training" after hours. When word of it had reached Mielke, Schulz had been transferred to field work, as a case officer, with the reasoning being that at least then his sexual targets would be a few years older, and better equipped to fend him off. But the timing of the move had been exactly wrong for Karola.

"Yes, I see." Now he was the one looking off into the trees.

"There was no escaping him. And he was a large man, and strong, so . . ."

"I'm sorry. You should have reported him."

"I did. That's why they let me go."

He thought of Mielke, supposedly the fussy schoolmarm, the moralist. But only when it came to adultery, apparently. Schulz had been a single man, so in his case Mielke had undoubtedly taken the attitude of "boys will be boys," because a few years later Schulz had been promoted.

"So you see?" she said. "It was a long time ago, but I'm trained, I'm qualified. Who knows? If I'd stuck it out, I might have ended up working for you, and now seems as good a time as any to find out how that would have gone."

Emil smiled. The offer was tempting but perilous. He'd be putting Karola in harm's way. And if she became vulnerable, then Bettina would as well. Karola again tuned in to his thoughts before he could put them into words.

"I know. I have reservations, too. But at the very least you should tell me what this is all about, so I can decide if it's worth the risk. And if this whole thing is only about money, or our financial future, then it's not worth it. West Germany will pay for her care, you know."

"I know. And it isn't about money. Maybe for Lothar it was. But for me it's more of an insurance policy, like one of those cards you draw in that capitalist board game they play in the West, the one we all used to make bootleg copies of when we were teens."

"Monopoly?"

"Yes! And if you landed on the right square, sometimes you got that card that said, 'Get out of jail free.' Remember? This is what Lothar and I were working toward, by offering something the Americans would want so badly that they would agree to protect us. From Bonn, from our old colleagues, all of that."

Karola's mouth flew open in surprise.

"The Americans? The *main enemy*? That's who you've been dealing with?"

She used the German word *Hauptgegner*, a term the HVA had translated from the Russian words *glavni protivnik*. The main enemy.

"That's a betrayal of everything you ever worked for."

"Of course it is. But we've lost that struggle. And as even Wolf would admit, the Russians have thrown us to our fate. So, yes, I'm willing to sell out to our old enemy, because now I'm working only for the three of us. If Bettina were healthy, the prospect of spending a few years in jail wouldn't be so terrible. But a few years are all she has left."

"And if you disappeared into some prison, she would stop fighting."

"I know. I am quite aware of that."

They walked another twenty yards in silence before Karola spoke again.

"Then you must do this. And I must help. But first, you have to tell us everything. Both of us."

His first instinct was to say no. In his profession, there were two reasons for withholding information from your spouse: to keep them from telling others, and to keep them from being targeted for their knowledge.

Bettina, however, could no longer tell anyone—apart from Karola, it seemed. And in her current locked-in state of mind, probably the only thing more stressful than worrying about Emil was worrying about him in a state of ignorance. An informed Karola would be better equipped than him to reassure Bettina that things were okay, even when they weren't.

So Emil agreed to her terms, and they walked back to the dacha. He made a fresh pot of coffee to warm them up while Karola brought Bettina up to date on what had just transpired in the woods. Emil joined them, cleared his throat, and settled into a bedside chair. Overhead, some small creature stirred with a skittering noise, somewhere above the ceiling. Karola frowned.

"You really should deal with those critters. I worry they're in the rafters, and it gives me the creeps every time I hear them. Bettina, too."

Bettina blinked once in affirmation.

"Soon," he said, nodding. "But as you've observed, I've been rather busy lately."

He then spent the next hour telling the women everything, from start to finish, including the gruesome discovery he had made a few hours earlier at the apartment of Andreas Plotz—minus a few graphic details, of course. And minus the names of Yuri Volkov and Gregor Kolkachev, because, even now, that was the sort of knowledge that could get you killed. He nonetheless saw the color drain from his wife's face as he described the fate of Plotz. Karola lowered her head as if in mourning.

They unanimously agreed to several immediate changes in their living arrangements. Emil would call the other caretaker, Frau Adler in Berlin, and arrange to bring her here tomorrow. That would free up time for Karola's new duties, and Frau Adler would remain on standby for any and all other times Emil might need Karola's help, as circumstances demanded. In the meantime, Karola would move in with Emil and Bettina, at least until Emil's plans were on firmer ground.

Then, as Bettina watched and listened, Emil unfolded a map of Berlin at the foot of the bed. He and Karola began making plans for Monday, and their meeting with the Americans.

29

The instructions for the secret appointment with Markus Wolf had advised them to dress for a day in the country, a bucolic escape into the Brandenburg woods, so that's what Claire did. She showed up at their departure point in jeans, a flannel shirt, a pair of running shoes, and one of those puffy down coats that made you look ready for an assault on Everest.

Baucom had stuck with his usual wardrobe: baggy wool slacks, rumpled white oxford, and a pilled wool navy overcoat, although his shoes at least had crepe soles. Claire found him seated in a booth in an otherwise empty Chinese restaurant in Ruhleben, on a tree-lined residential boulevard. His cup of coffee had already left a brown ring on a paper placemat depicting the Chinese zodiac, and he began grumbling about the day ahead the moment she arrived.

"Check out this map Roman sent me."

He slid forward a sheet of fax paper with a hand-drawn diagram of various roads and landmarks, with an X marking their rendezvous point.

"Like something for a goddamn Boy Scout treasure hunt," he said. "We park at a clearing, bushwhack our way through the forest, then meet a cutout on a log bench by a drippy fucking lake, near some cabin of his."

"A dacha, I suppose he calls it."

"Probably 'cause the roof leaks and there's no central heating."

Claire smiled and stole a sip of his coffee, which was cold and terrible, so she handed it back. They would be taking his car, a beige BMW several years past its prime. Claire had just walked a half mile from an S-Bahn station. The path had taken her by the Olympic Stadium, which made her think of Jesse Owens sprinting to victory while Hitler frowned down at him from the viewing stand. It was still as imposing as it must have looked in 1936—all those marble columns stacked with Teutonic precision in a massive stone oval.

Ruhleben was in the old British sector of occupation. Baucom chose it because they'd be less likely to encounter any Agency colleagues, although it would lengthen the drive to their destination. He checked his watch. At noon on a Sunday most Germans were either at home or at church, and traffic would be light.

"Guess we better get going. I was hoping he'd invite us to his duplex on the Spree, in the heart of the city. Supposedly the nicest digs this side of Honecker's house, with a solarium and all the best Western appliances. His retirement gift from the Stasi."

"Easier to keep us hidden out in the sticks, I guess."

"Oh, operationally it makes perfect sense, but, goddamn, wasn't this supposed to be fun?"

Claire laughed, knowing it was partly an act, because they were both excited. They were about to meet and chat with a legend of their profession—at his invitation, no less—and with the bonus of knowing he was no longer really the enemy. The afternoon loomed as an adventure, a field trip to help her relax before tomorrow's rendezvous. With any luck she might even pick up a useful item or two for the days ahead.

They piled into the BMW and Baucom pulled away from the curb. He asked how her new partner was working out, and what they'd cooked up for tomorrow. Claire, uncomfortably, found herself scrimping on details, not that it fooled him for a second.

"I get it. I'm out of the loop now, so you can't share. Still, as events move forward maybe you could toss a few scraps to the guy who saved your ass."

She smiled but made no promises.

"Why don't we talk instead about Mischa Wolf. Do we know what he's been up to since November?"

Baucom had managed to pick up a few helpful details from Roman, the go-between.

"This dacha is up near a town called Prenden. Roman's been there, and without any prompting he told me a couple other top HVA guys also have places up there, including, well, take a guess."

"Lothar Fischer?"

He nodded.

"Did Roman know Fischer was dead?"

"If he did, he wasn't saying."

"Who's the third guy?"

"Roman didn't say."

"Probably someone on that flow chart Lindsey Ward showed me. Maybe if we get a chance, we can snoop around afterward."

But to get there they'd first have to confront the Cold War version of the troll at the bridge—a highway checkpoint run by the Russians and East Germans that monitored all West Berlin vehicles crossing into East Germany. Within minutes it loomed formidably on the horizon, a massive complex of guard towers, low concrete buildings, and tollbooth-style passages that spanned the highway from shoulder to shoulder.

Five months ago they would have been delayed for hours while officials searched their car and pulled them aside for questioning. Current conditions seemed to be changing by the day. Baucom had heard that searches were no longer occurring, but Russian soldiers were still sometimes stopping cars with West German or diplomatic tags, not to harass or question them, but to sell them military watches and other memorabilia.

"Well, let's see what kind of rules they're playing by today," Baucom said, slowing down.

None at all, as it turned out. No one was even manning the booths, and they breezed through without so much as a wave.

"Anyone on our tail?" Baucom asked.

"No. And I've been watching."

"Guess we'll know for sure when we hit the exit for Bernau."

"How are you set for East German road maps, by the way?"

She reached forward to flip open the glove compartment, where she found the map right away, stacked atop the car registration papers and an owner's manual. Buried behind all that she also found something else.

"Well, now. How long has this been here?"

She pulled out a slender, long-barreled pistol that looked like a relic from a firearms museum. There was a suppressor screwed onto the end.

"What do you even call this thing, other than contraband?"

Baucom sighed.

"Shit. Forgot that was even in there. Probably should have hidden it beneath the spare."

"Or turned it in when you retired."

"Oh, the Agency lost track of that ages ago, when they gave me a Beretta, which I handed in like a good boy, all signed and proper. That's from the '60s, but they go back even further. A High Standard HD 22. I doubt it even works."

"That's some sandbagging if I ever heard it." The gun looked well oiled and maintained, although she decided out of decorum not to check if it was loaded. She slid it back under the papers and shut the compartment. "Don't worry, I never saw it. But I doubt a German cop would be as forgiving."

"I'll keep that in mind, Mom."

They reached the exit for Bernau not long afterward. By then traffic was sparse, and no one followed them off the Autobahn. They came to a junction with a two-lane road that went right toward Bernau or left into the woods. They turned left.

"Bernau," Baucom said, shaking his head with a smoky chuckle. "Now that's a story.

"Lester Diggs actually had me set up a safe house there a few years back, when he thought he was about to reel in a valuable agent, some handyman type who worked on the villas of all the muckety-mucks over in their Waldsiedlung compound in Wandlitz, a few klicks from here. I used a cutout to rent an apartment a floor above the town's only antique shop, mostly because the shopkeeper was deaf and would never hear a thing, and the store almost never had any customers. It was just inside the old medieval ramparts. We liked the building because it had those thick old walls from the 1600s, not that cheap prefab shit they were building everywhere else."

"Did it get much use?"

"That's the funny part. None at all. By the time we got it set up,

Diggs had discovered that his asset, like every other agent he ever recruited over here, was reporting back to the Stasi. But he never bothered to shut the place down. Wishful thinking, maybe, in case he ever got a clean hit. By now the place is probably an inch deep in dust."

He wheezed with low laughter.

Soon they were rolling through beech and pine forest beneath a heavy gray sky. They passed a village and a few farms, but the only sign of vibrancy was a wet field where mud-spattered boys were playing soccer, their breath huffing in tiny cloudbursts.

"Wonder how this place will look in another ten years?" Claire asked, as the car jolted through a deep pothole.

"Goddamn roads will be smoother, that's for sure. This must be Prenden."

A huddle of tan homes and outbuildings loomed up on their left. Half the houses looked like they'd been built since the war. The others might have been around since medieval times. Claire checked the hand-drawn map.

"Our turnoff is the next right."

Baucom eased onto a narrow paved road that led into the woods. They hadn't even gone a mile when it narrowed further and turned to dirt, with a bed of pine needles to soften the way.

"Another right coming up. See it? That's the road to the parking lot."

No one else was back here, either on foot or in a car. A roe deer darted through the trees to their right, and a hundred yards farther on they scattered a group of crows that were picking at the carcass of some flattened furry creature. The birds lifted briefly in a flutter of black wings, then resettled to their work with a few caws of protest.

The parking lot came into view on the left. It was a little more than a turnout carved into the trees, wide enough for maybe four vehicles. There were a few muddy tire tracks, but no other signs of any recent visitors. The moment Baucom cut the engine they were enveloped in silence.

"Cozy," Baucom said disdainfully. "One of those must be our trail."

Two paths ran into the woods. One went right, the other straight ahead. Claire checked the map.

"The one going straight, that's what we want."

"Do we look for breadcrumbs marking the way? Or has the witch already eaten them?"

"I believe birds were the culprits in that one. The witch was waiting at the end."

"Oh, right. And the big bad Markus Wolf lived happily ever after, but only because he was nice to the two little lambs from CIA."

"We never really decided on the best way to bring up Lothar Fischer, unless he does it first."

"Why don't you handle that. But make it toward the end. He'll be more forgiving of any prurient curiosity coming from a historian."

"You think he'll really believe that cover story?"

"Once we're in his house, it won't matter. At this point he must need us more than we need him, or we wouldn't have been invited."

They climbed out into the raw and bracing air. Claire was eager to get moving, but Baucom needed a few seconds to groan and stretch. They set off down the trail, with Claire leading the way.

The flurries of the day before had left a thin coating of snow. Only one other set of footprints was on the path—a man's, judging by their size—but there were plenty of animal tracks. The cloven hooves of deer, the skid marks of a hare.

"Germans and their enchanted forests," Claire said. "All this reminds me of something in a William Manchester book."

"The one about the Krupp family of arms makers?"

"Yes. He goes on and on about their love of the primeval forest. Ties it to all their worst behavior, their national legends. Then he closes with a line that still makes me laugh. Something like, 'Even today, give a German an afternoon off and he'll pack a lunch, assemble his family, and vanish into the trees.'"

Baucom's laughter rumbled up into the drooping pines. Claire came across the prints of a larger animal and paused for a longer look.

"What do you think made these?"

Baucom stooped lower to examine it.

"Wild boar. They're all over these woods. Germans like to shoot 'em. Of course, for a while there, Germans liked to shoot pretty much anything . . . Sorry, I suppose that's uncharitable considering how *betroffen* they've become lately. But I tend to get in that mood whenever I visit the Worker's Paradise. The bastards."

"You must've had quite a few run-ins with Wolf's people."

"My agents did. Lost a lot of them over here. You know, it's funny about these German commies. For a time they were the most passionate anti-Nazis on the planet. Died for it by the thousands. Or, like Wolf's family, fled for their lives to Moscow. Then, after the smoke cleared, all it took was a few years of studying under the KGB to become as good at snooping on their own people as the Gestapo. Better, even."

They walked in silence a few seconds longer before Baucom spoke again, this time with a note of regret.

"But who are we to talk? Forty-five years ago we were happy to make nice with any Nazi who knew how to build a rocket. Now here we are again, chasing another set of ogres through the bush. I'm guessing we'll forgive any of them as long as they've got something we want."

"Wasn't Wolf an advocate for reform?"

"Supposedly. But he knew when to avert his eyes. All his people did, or they wouldn't have kept their jobs. And the system treated them well. Bigger apartments, foreign travel, all those special stores. Hard to feel too sorry for the bastards, even the smart ones who played the game better than we did."

"Maybe he's still playing the game."

"That's what we're here to find out. Provided I survive this goddamn death march."

Baucom paused, wheezing. He took out a handkerchief to blow his nose, then nodded toward a shimmer of reflected light downhill through the trees. "Is that the lake we're looking for? What's it called again?"

"The Bauersee. When we reach it, we turn left, then follow the trail a hundred yards to a log bench by the water."

As they set off down the hill, she noticed a second set of footprints that had joined the man's on the path, side by side. Small enough to belong to a child or a woman. A hiking companion, perhaps.

Baucom nearly slipped on the mud as they reached the bottom of the hill. His crepe-soled shoes weren't much good on this terrain, but the bench soon came into view. It was little more than a stout log that had been bolted to the ground, with a flat surface cut into the top for seating.

"Well that's a lovely sight," he said. "Looks wet and cold."

"The directions say to sit and wait. In a few minutes someone's supposed to come down the hill from up that way and ask if we're Stefan and Hilda."

"I look about as much like a Stefan as you look like a Hilda. But thanks for the reminder."

Baucom used his handkerchief to dry off a spot for them, and they sat side by side, admiring the view. Across the water and to the right was a marshy shoreline where an incoming stream fed the upper end of the lake. The shoreline directly opposite was nothing but trees until you got farther to the left, where the rooftops of a few rustic houses were visible through the branches. Claire smelled woodsmoke, a cozy scent on such a clammy day.

With the appointment now imminent, they lapsed into an expectant silence. A few minutes later they heard the crackling of twigs and the sound of approaching footsteps. Claire turned to see a small, attractive woman, late forties, with blonde bushy hair, shoulder length. The woman offered a tentative smile and then, exhibiting some caution, stopped about twenty yards away. She greeted them in German.

"Stefan und Hilda?"

"Ja," Baucom grumbled. He lumbered to his feet like a gentle beast of the forest. Papa Bear, addressing an aging Goldilocks. "And you are?"

"Andrea Wolf. My husband is waiting. Follow me, please."

She turned and headed uphill, and they set out in her wake. Claire glanced quickly to either side. She could have sworn she had spotted movement off to the right, uphill and through the trees, near a big beech with smooth pale bark. Otherwise, this patch of woods seemed empty apart from them. She kept glancing in that direction as they ascended, but nothing seemed out of the ordinary. Probably just a squirrel or a bird.

At the top of the hill they came into view of a fairly large A-frame house next to a garage and a few outbuildings, a compound surrounded by a tall wooden fence with barbed wire along the top. Andrea led them around the left of the fence until they reached a locked gate on the far side. The lens of a security camera gazed out from a birdhouse mounted on a nearby tree. Claire had little doubt that Wolf was now watching their approach on a screen inside his house.

As if to affirm this, a buzzer sounded as Andrea gave a wave. She pushed open the gate and motioned Claire and Baucom down a walkway. The dacha looked like a Tyrolean hunting lodge, and an impressive set of stag antlers was mounted high above the front door. Baucom sidled up to Claire, whispering in English as they followed Andrea.

"I feel like Siegfried, summoned to Valhalla."

"As long as I don't have to be Brünnhilde."

He smiled crookedly but said no more, now that it was time to be on their best behavior. But she, too, felt the unreality of the moment. It wasn't every day you were invited to huddle beneath the trees with spydom's most storied practitioner. Wolf's legend had been romanticized almost to the point of superhuman, so she was fully expecting a letdown upon meeting the genuine article.

The door opened, and there he was, tall and handsome, with healthy coloring and probing eyes. In spite of all the buildup, she was impressed. Yet she also detected a hint of uncertainty in his eyes. Like them, he was a little on edge.

"Welcome, and please come in."

He stepped aside to let them enter.

Shoes were lined up neatly in a row just inside the door, and Andrea had already removed hers in favor of a pair of house slippers. Claire reached uncertainly for her sneakers, but Wolf waved off the gesture and motioned her forward.

"Please. It's a dacha, not a palace."

Claire crossed the threshold, and entered the woodland lair of Markus Wolf.

30

Emil waited until they had moved out of sight and out of earshot as he tried to make sense of what he had just seen through the trees. It was the CIA woman, the one he had passed the note to, the one he was supposed to be meeting tomorrow in Berlin. The older man with her was the fellow who had hailed the taxi for her narrow escape on Frankfurter Allee. And now they were together again and practically in his back garden, while being led through the trees by none other than Andrea Wolf, presumably as prelude to a secret meeting with Mischa himself. Wolf's personal guests, invited to his dacha.

What the hell could it mean, and how did it affect his plans for tomorrow?

All Emil knew for sure was that bringing Karola into his confidence was already paying dividends, because otherwise he never would have been snooping around out here this afternoon to find out what Mischa was up to.

Karola had aroused his curiosity after returning from a Saturday trip to the market in Bernau. She had brought back a canvas sack of groceries and a breathless bit of gossip.

"The Wolfs are expecting company."

She had announced this even before setting down the bag.

"Company? Did you talk to them? Were they passing on the lane?"

"No, no. I saw that much younger wife of his, Andrea, in town while I was shopping."

Her words amused him, because Bettina had also habitually referred to Wolf's second wife, Christa, the same way. *That much younger wife of his*, and always with a note of scorn. Granted, Bettina was four years younger than him, and Karola seven. But the difference between Wolf and Christa had been at least twenty years, and Andrea was younger still. It was as if, four years ago, Wolf had traded in Christa for an updated and slightly more compact model, after an affair that had begun right here on the Bauersee, during a weekend visit by Andrea and her previous husband. The delicious little summer scandal had rippled across the lake like a thunderstorm, with repercussions reaching all the way to Normanenstrasse.

Wolf had to weather a scolding from Mielke, who, in a moment of rank hypocrisy, suggested that the ministry would be better off if Wolf remained married to Christa, who was also a Stasi employee, and simply set up Andrea as a kept woman in a Berlin love nest. Wolf refused, and once the divorce became final, Mielke put Christa under surveillance out of fear that she might defect and tell all.

"Andrea told you they were having visitors?" Emil asked.

"Oh, no. She'd never talk to me. I doubt she even knows my name, although she knows I'm someone who takes care of Bettina. She didn't have to tell me, because she was ordering around the poor grocer's boy like she was royalty, like she had just stepped into the kitchen at Charlottenburg Palace to boss the cooks. 'We must have this, we must have that.' Olives and crackers and cheese, slices of their best cured ham. Items they've only had in stock for a few weeks now, and she was practically cornering the market on them."

"Interesting."

"Yes, I thought you'd think so."

"Are these visitors expected this evening?"

"I doubt it, because she was asking how well everything would keep overnight, the best way to wrap it in her fridge, that sort of thing. I guess with everything closed on Sundays she had no choice."

So these visitors were coming Sunday, then. And with Wolf only just returned from Russia and supposedly lying low. Yes, this could be something—or someone—important.

"Very good, Karola. Nice work."

Emil had then gone for a walk to consider the implications of this intelligence, and how he could best put it to use.

Who could it be? Emil quickly ruled out Dorn and Krauss. Wolf would never put on such a spread of hospitality for a mere policeman, and certainly not for a representative of the despised Spezialkommission.

One thing Emil knew for sure from years of working for the man was that, for Wolf, every professional relationship at some point became a courtship for one side or the other, a moment at which special care and handling were needed to keep everything in balance. Sometimes Wolf had to be wooed—by Emil, by others who worked for him, or even by Mielke. At other times he was the suitor, and he had tended to reserve his most aggressive tactics for weary or dispirited agents, to keep them productive and loyal.

He would treat them to meetings in exotic and sunny locales. Those he especially valued might even be invited to his apartment in Berlin, where he would turn on the charm and personally prepare for them his favorite traditional Russian dish, *pelmeni* dumplings stuffed with sausage.

Emil decided that if Wolf had visitors on a Sunday, they almost certainly wouldn't be arriving until after noon. Germans simply didn't have guests on Sunday mornings, and Wolf liked to sleep in on weekends. Early afternoon was certainly possible, given the items his wife had bought. In fact, that was a more probable time than the dinner hour, or else she would have bought a roast, or even the makings of *pelmeni* for him to prepare. The array of foods made him believe these were guests that he wished to make welcome, but not necessarily impress. Maybe, in Wolf's eyes, they needed to make a better showing than he did.

In any event, Emil had decided to do some raking and clearing of brush on a portion of his lot with a vantage point of the approach to Wolf's dacha, and with his trusty viewing scope in his pocket. And that was how he had first heard the door shut at Wolf's house, and then saw Andrea moving into the front lane and around the far side of the lot, toward a trail that led downhill to the lake.

Emil had dropped his rake and stealthily gone out his back gate, heading through the trees until he spotted Andrea as she descended. He then hid behind a large beech, his nose running from the cold. A few minutes later he had watched through the scope as the American man and woman followed Andrea back up the hill. The woman had glanced in his direction, forcing him back into cover, but he was fairly certain the other two hadn't seen him. He waited for them to disappear around the far side of Wolf's dacha before heading back home. By then his feet were wet and numb from the last of the snow, but his mind was active, fully engaged in speculation on what his old boss could be seeking from the two Americans, or they from him.

Had the woman, possibly, told Wolf what he and Lothar had been up to? Or, alternately, had she offered enough hints for Wolf to figure it out on his own? Or maybe Wolf had invited his visitors for some other reason, completely unrelated to him or to Lothar. CIA people were now scurrying all over the Berlin area, seeking to make friends of their old enemies in hopes of prying loose their secrets.

But if that's what this visit was about, why was Wolf laying on the charm and hospitality? Shouldn't the Americans be the ones bearing gifts, the better to woo him?

Emil would never reach any conclusions by lingering out in the cold. And he was certainly not willing to hop the fence of Wolf's compound to snoop around further, so he went back indoors, where Karola greeted him with a steaming mug of herbal tea and a burst of questions.

"Did you see them? Who was it? Did you recognize anyone?"

"One at a time, please."

He took a swallow and felt the warmth reach his stomach, but not his toes. Then he led Karola back into Bettina's bedroom, and briefed them on what he had just observed.

It was remarkable to him the change that had come over his wife since he had admitted her and Karola into his inner circle of secrecy only a day earlier. Her eyes sparkled with energy. Her skin had taken on some of its former glow. Obviously, she was thinking deeply about all of this. He saw that clearly, without having to rely on Karola to interpret it for him. In some elemental way, they were closer again. He took her hand and squeezed it, and she blinked up at him. Maybe he should have done this sooner.

"Well, what do you think, then?" Karola said. "Should we still go through with this?"

"We will keep the appointment. But we will change our plans. Or our plans for your role, anyway."

She frowned. Bettina narrowed her eyes.

"Surely you need a lookout and backup more than ever now. I refuse to let you do this alone."

Bettina blinked rapidly in emphatic agreement.

"I'm not canceling your role, Karola. I'm expanding it."

Karola glanced at Bettina, who seemed to approve.

"All right, then. So tell us."

Emil again got out his map of Berlin, and again spread it across the foot of the bed. Then, pointing as he progressed, he explained to them how everything was going to work.

31

From the moment they entered Wolf's dacha, the encounter felt a bit surreal, and not just because of who they were there to see.

For starters there was the furniture. Not the rustic items Claire had expected in a country home, but a stylishly comfortable look, in a dated, mid-'60s sort of way, with couches and chairs that had obviously been imported. Large windows were built into the steeply slanted ceilings, giving the great room a light and open feel, even beneath a leaden sky. Covering one wall were abstract etchings and oils, which hung alongside the de rigueur photos of Wolf with celebrity leaders of the communist world. Brezhnev, Castro, Honecker. The other wall was filled with bookcases. At a glance Claire saw several titles that had almost certainly been banned in East Germany. Wedged between the spines were components of a state-of-the-art stereo system, which, it occurred to her, probably concealed a taping system that Wolf had switched on the moment she and Baucom stepped through the door.

Then there was his wife, Andrea. Claire had expected her to discreetly retire to a bedroom to let the spies go about their business. Instead she curled up on the couch next to Wolf, practically purring as she smiled at their apparent surprise. Not that Andrea had neglected her duties as a hostess. Laid out on a glass-top Noguchi coffee table was a tray with cups, saucers, and a thermal carafe of coffee.

"There is also herbal tea, if you prefer," Andrea said.

Well, of course there was. And it was then that Claire realized what was causing her momentary buzz of cognitive dissonance. The whole setup felt more like the country getaway of a dissident playwright than of a spymaster for one of the world's most oppressive regimes. If Wolf had a weakness, it was probably his desire to be seen as more enlightened than the people he had once worked for. Maybe they could use that.

"Coffee for me," Claire said. "Black."

"Same," Baucom said, and with a glance Claire realized he was having a similar reaction. His observant eyes scanned the room in apparent wonder.

They made small talk for a minute or two, discussing the local scenery, the snow, and the recent avalanche of change that had overwhelmed their lives, his country.

Andrea leaned across the table and whispered to Claire.

"There are a few more items to bring out. Would you mind helping me?"

Ah, yes. The inevitable relegation to domestic servant. But to refuse would risk upsetting the social balance. Besides, Claire had already seen that, so far, Wolf only had eyes for Baucom. Perhaps he had bought into her cover as an academic researcher, who had come along only to listen and observe.

The adjoining kitchen had a wide opening that at least allowed her to keep an eye on the two men. Andrea had prepared another tray with pastries, crackers, bread, jam, cheeses, olives, and sliced ham. There was also a stack of small plates with cutlery and linen napkins.

The two men were leaning closer now, and they had both lit cigarettes. Claire couldn't make out the words, but from their animated movements she guessed they were swapping old war stories, perhaps even the one of their initial meeting, when they had both fooled the pompous Russian general. They held crystal tumblers with some amber liquid that Wolf must have poured from his private supply. A dusty bottle sat on a side table, and a cloud of pale blue smoke was already forming above them.

She couldn't help but smile, even as they excluded her. Claire had spent much of her early career battling this old boy mentality, fending off their affronts and their advances even as they had fended off her curiosity, keeping to themselves when it mattered most.

But apart from this reunion with Baucom, her only recent contact with the species had been her attendance at their boozy retirement send-offs, where she listened to their farewell speeches. Each one that fell by the wayside took a little knowledge with him, much of it invaluable. She couldn't say she venerated what they'd accomplished—at best, a stalemate in which they'd never flinched from sacrificing any poor sap caught in the middle—but there were lessons to be learned from their successes, as well as their failures.

"Look at them," she said to Andrea. "It's like walking through your woods and coming across an endangered animal."

"Or a wounded animal, maybe, in Mischa's case. You're not really an academic, are you?"

Claire could have easily parried the remark, maybe convincingly so. But having reached the epilogue of this competition, what would be the point?

"No. I'm not."

"I told Mischa this, but he laughed me off. He said the Americans would never send a woman on such an important assignment. Maybe he was only projecting his own feelings."

And his own vanity, she thought. But what she said was, "Shall we rejoin them?"

Andrea carried in the tray. Claire took the plates and cutlery. They reached the coffee table just as Wolf reared back with a roar of hearty laughter. Baucom joined in at an octave lower. They were a duo in concert, perfectly attuned. Wolf refilled Baucom's glass with the bottle from the side table. He did not ask Claire or Andrea if they wanted any. Wolf then capped the moment by using the familiar *du* pronoun as he addressed Baucom, instead of the more formal *Sie* he had used earlier.

"It is too true, what you're saying, my American friend. All of us shall be obsolete quite soon. And it's not just the space satellites with their wondrous cameras. Not long ago I was talking to a colleague from our Technical Operations Sector."

"The bunch that came up with all those great gadgets your people always had?"

"Yes! Cameras and microphones that would fit inside a fountain pen, or hide behind your necktie. And that spy dust, for tracking everyone who touched the doorknobs of your safe houses. But this fellow told me your people are developing unmanned aircraft that can be piloted from thousands of miles away, and will be able to transmit live images of all their surveillances."

"Incredible."

"And that's nothing compared to the flood of information that's coming. This World Wide Web, as he called it. Before long an office clerk in Shanghai will have more power to pry into your personal affairs than our ministry does today. Once that comes to pass, why even bother with a million informants?"

"Did you say a million?" Claire asked. "In your own country?"

Wolf seemed taken aback by the question, as if he had just become aware of Claire and Andrea's return. But the number, if true, was shocking. East Germany's population was sixteen million. Had one in every sixteen of them really reported to the Stasi?

"Well, not *quite* a million, but it was close, there at the end. Of course, that was the doing of the other side of the ministry, not ours. I remember a year or so before I quit, Comrade Mielke told a group of us with great pride that we had just surpassed 750,000 informants. I was there with three of my colleagues from the HVA. We were dumbfounded, even ashamed."

There it was again, Wolf setting himself apart from the excesses of the people who had paid his salary. He then pivoted to the subject that he had supposedly summoned them here to discuss.

"But I doubt this is the sort of information your Director Webster is seeking from me, assuming I consent to meet his representative. Would you agree, Herr Baucom?"

"I would. Prost!"

They tapped glasses for another swallow.

"Any idea of what he wants? Because if his interest is the identities of our agents—*my* agents—he will be wasting his time. Those people entrusted their lives to me, and I won't betray them. Not at any price, even that of my freedom."

The words sounded rehearsed. Someday, Claire supposed, they would turn up in a Wolf memoir, for which he would almost certainly be richly rewarded by a Western publishing house.

"I'm told it's a bit more complicated," Baucom said. "It has more to do with your knowledge of your sister agency in Moscow."

Baucom had worded the remark perfectly, Claire thought. By referring to the KGB as a "sister agency," he had placed the Stasi on an equal footing, an appeal to Wolf's ego, even though Moscow had never felt that way.

"All I know for sure on that score," Wolf replied, "is that your own people have had a rather rough time in Moscow in recent years."

It was an understatement. Claire, like most field operatives, had been vaguely aware of the scope of the calamity, but Baucom had filled her in on more of the details. In the past four years, CIA's Moscow station had endured one blown agent after another, each of them brutally rounded up by the KGB—a level of betrayal that could only be explained by the presence of a mole.

"Yes, rather rough. And the high muckety-mucks have concluded that, in all likelihood, the problem lies very close to home."

"I see. A mole within your headquarters. Well, what I would tell Mr. Webster is that, sister agency or not, that's the sort of deeper secret the KGB would never share with anyone on Normanenstrasse. Not even Comrade Mielke."

"Understood. But as you know, there are always other considerations. Shared intelligence which could have only come from a limited number of sources. Favors they might have asked in servicing or even vetting this person. Surely you must have seen items and requests that made you wonder. I doubt they'd ever expect you to give them a name, even if you knew it."

"And I don't."

"Let's assume that's true. It's those other items they're after. Any hint or anomaly to help them narrow their search."

Wolf nodded. A few seconds of silence followed. Baucom sipped again from his tumbler, but Wolf only stared at his, as if seeking counsel from a crystal ball.

"I'll think about it. I suppose agreeing to meet won't do any harm, provided the arrangements are circumspect. But I doubt I can help them."

"Unable or unwilling?"

Wolf smiled.

"That's a matter for further thought, too, even though our Russian friends have been, well . . . less than helpful in our hour of need."

"They won't intervene in Bonn on your behalf?"

"No. Although you didn't hear that from me."

"Of course."

It was a juicy item of intelligence. Wolf's little gift to Baucom, Claire supposed. The trick would be figuring out how to pass it along without admitting they'd participated in an unauthorized meeting. She certainly couldn't be the conduit.

Wolf nodded at Andrea, who picked up the coffee tray and headed for the kitchen, an action that Claire read as a motion for adjournment. She looked at Baucom, who responded with a slight nod. Time to ask her question.

"Going back to that meeting you just mentioned, the one with Comrade Mielke."

"Yes?"

"You said three of your colleagues were with you. Was one of them Lothar Fischer?"

The light went out in his eyes. Andrea went still in the kitchen, the clatter of dishes halting as if someone had flipped a switch.

"So. This terrible news has traveled quickly, I see."

"Although we don't yet know as much as we'd like to about how his death occurred."

Wolf shifted uneasily on the couch, so Claire upped the ante.

"His murder, I mean."

He sighed, as if to concede the point. Then he glanced toward Andrea, who stared back from the kitchen with a knowing look that said, *See? I told you she was trouble.*

"We don't know as much as we'd like to, either. Or *I* don't. The ministry is no longer functioning, not really. At first it looked like a suicide, but yesterday I learned that has been ruled out. Is this what you're hearing as well?"

"We're wondering if the Russians were involved."

His eyes widened. It was clear that her remark had surprised him.

"I have no answer to that. Or none that I would be comfortable with. It occurred here, you know, not so far from that bench where Andrea came to fetch you."

Claire tried to hide her surprise as Wolf kept talking.

"It's the one reason I hesitated to invite you to the dacha, even though our home in Berlin would have been out of the question. Too many eyes and ears along the Spree. But I concluded that whoever came for poor Lothar must have completed their business and moved on. All the same, take care in your movements as you depart. If you were thinking of, well, exploring further in this neighborhood—because, believe me, I know all of the reasons you might want to—perhaps you should reconsider."

"Thanks for the advice."

"I think all of us are tempted now to lower our guard, especially with so many checkpoints and barriers coming down. But perhaps the time is not yet right for that. We shall see."

An awkward silence followed. Claire couldn't help but recall the earlier moment outdoors, when she thought she had noticed something—or someone—moving through the trees as they'd climbed the hill from the lake.

The mood now was somber, but Wolf wasn't finished.

"In a way I suppose it is a good thing that you brought up this sad subject of Lothar Fischer. Of all the people who I thought might betray our secrets to, well, people like you, he was high on the list. Or so I've been led to believe, by people who should know."

"Based on what?" Baucom asked.

"His recent movements and activities. These are not things I know firsthand, so perhaps they are not completely reliable. But one thing I can tell you with certainty is this: Anyone promising to sell you a file containing the identities of our agents is offering you something they cannot actually deliver. Because such a file does not exist."

His smile returned, this time with a hint of smugness.

"Surely you and your people didn't keep all of that information in your heads?" Baucom said.

"Of course not. Let's just say that the system I set up for these things, years ago, was far more complicated than that."

Baucom seemed momentarily befuddled, but Claire knew what he was talking about because of what Lindsey Ward had told her, and she decided to let Baucom in on the secret.

"Because you set it up like pieces of a puzzle," she said, "and you need every piece of it before you can actually identify the agents."

Wolf seemed impressed, and a little of the smugness drained from his expression.

"Perhaps. And maybe some of the pieces of this puzzle have already been taken away or destroyed. So if anyone makes an offer to you, well, caveat emptor, as your consumer specialists like to say. Let the buyer beware."

"We'll certainly keep that in mind."

Wolf then slapped his hands on his knees, his upbeat mood restored.

"Please. Before you go you must help us finish some of these wonderful foods Andrea prepared for us, so that at least you will leave with a full stomach."

"Fattening us up for the kill, Mischa?"

Baucom said it with a jolly enough tone, but the ensuing laughter was forced. For decades they had been mortal enemies. Maybe in some ways they still were.

Wolf reached for a piece of bread and a slice of ham. He forked a slice of cheese on top, his appetite seemingly undiminished. Then again, he wasn't the one facing a mile-long walk back to his car through what suddenly felt like hostile territory. Yes, Claire thought again, the Germans and their enchanted forests, populated by so many ghostly horrors.

She watched Wolf closely. He was four years into retirement, with only months remaining in the life of his country. Yet she supposed he might still be playing the oldest of games, unable to quit.

She pushed away her plate, her appetite gone.

32

Claire was reassured by the absence of any additional footprints as they hiked back through the trees to the car, although by then the sun was out and had melted most of the snow, so she couldn't be sure.

Neither she nor Baucom said much until they climbed into the BMW. He collapsed into the driver's seat with a wheeze and immediately fired up a cigarette.

"Well, that's something to tell your grandchildren about. Not that I'm advising you to marry and have children, so don't blow the whistle on me to HR."

"Only if you don't object to poking around the neighborhood a little more, now that we're back in the safety of your chariot."

Baucom snorted a laugh that sent smoke out his nostrils.

"You know, I guessed you were going to suggest that the moment Herr Wolf advised us not to linger."

"He did seem a little too eager about that, didn't he? Doesn't want his Stasi neighbors knowing he's meeting with the enemy, no doubt. Same reason he had us park way over here. Which means the least we can do is meander around the lake awhile longer. See what there is to see before heading back."

"I was kind of hoping to stop off at the Waldsiedlung compound on the way home, the gated community for the party elite—Honecker, Mielke, more than twenty of them."

"That would be fun, too."

"Except Roman told me it's been sealed up tight while a bunch of corruption investigations get under way. I suppose a bribe or two might get us through the gates for a little rubbernecking, but the last thing you should probably be risking is an arrest for trespassing by the Volkspolizei."

"Lindsey Ward might frown on that. Especially if they found that gun in your glove compartment. Speaking of Roman, you said earlier he told you there were three HVA big wheels with dachas up here? Could he possibly get us the name of the third one?"

"You're thinking that might be your contact?"

"Makes sense, especially now that all these guys seem to have gone to ground."

"It does. I'll ask him."

He started the car.

"Which way, Fraulein?"

"Links, bitte. The lake is definitely in that direction. We'll look for the road that runs by all the houses. If we pass Wolf's place, we'll wave to his birdhouse camera."

Baucom gave another snort of dragon's smoke as he backed the car into the gravel lane. A few minutes later they found the road that circled the upper end of the lake, and they soon came within sight of a cluster of houses set back in the trees, Wolf's among them. Baucom slowed down and they crept by at walking speed. None of the others had any cars in the driveway until the last one, which had a mustard yellow Wartburg parked by a house that wasn't nearly as big as Wolf's. Smoke was coming from the chimney. Someone was home.

"Think that's our third guy?" Claire asked.

"A Stasi poobah with a fucking Wartburg?"

"I know, but check out the birdhouse."

"You're right. It's got a lens. And look, barbed wire on the fence. Good call."

"Slow down. I want the tag number on that car."

He obliged her. She committed it to memory, but did not write it down. Back here in the trees, the end of the Cold War didn't feel quite as decisive, and she didn't want to be pulled over by some cop who'd find the tag number of a ranking member of the Stasi among her belongings. They had already tossed the faxed directions to the rendezvous into the trash at Wolf's dacha.

As if to confirm the need for caution, a hundred yards later they passed a turnout where a dark Citroën with smoked windows was parked. As soon as they passed, its engine cranked to life. It wheeled around on the gravel and smoothly closed the gap behind them.

"Well, that's a surprise I wasn't hoping for," Baucom said, frowning into the rearview mirror.

"Friend of Wolf's, you think?"

"That would certainly be preferable to an enemy of Lothar Fischer's."

"Unless those are one and the same."

Baucom held his speed, not wanting to look panicky, but they were both aware of how much their West Berlin tags must stand out in this remote spot.

The Citroën inched closer, following about ten feet off their bumper. The only sound was the pop of gravel in the wheel wells. Claire checked the side mirror, not wanting to give their pursuers the pleasure of seeing her look over her shoulder. She committed its tag number to memory along with the one for the Wartburg.

Not long afterward they reached the paved road to Prenden. Baucom turned. The Citroën did not follow. Half an hour later they were back in West Berlin.

33

It was finally Monday, with zero hour approaching. Emil had never before been this nervous about an op. Then again, he had never played such a leading role, and Karola's participation raised the stakes even higher.

They were in the Wartburg, a few miles from the target destination. Already there had been a complication—the dark Citroën had returned, and had tailed them out of Prenden. Emil, never an expert at crafty driving, had relied on Karola to direct him, and they had finally lost their pursuer in the streets of Pankow.

The need for evasive action had put them a few minutes behind, and Emil, a man of promptness who took comfort from sticking tightly to a schedule, had become uncharacteristically flustered, which led him to go over their plan for the third time since they'd left Prenden.

"Remember. If they insist on their own vehicle, refuse. It's ours or nobody's. We set the rules, and—"

"And we control the access. You don't have to tell me again, Emil. You need to calm down. I'm ready. I'm up to the job."

"But if—"

"We've covered all of the buts and contingencies. In fact, we've covered everything except what to do in case of a hailstorm, or the Second Coming, and if one of those happens, I'll improvise."

He went quiet for a second, then swerved to avoid a Trabi as it cut into his lane from the right. Emil shook his head and settled deeper into his seat, trying to calm himself.

"Sorry. I'm not usually such a micromanager. Or haven't been till now."

"I *have* been wondering how your agents must have put up with you."

"Oh, I'd be a little on edge whenever a big moment was coming up, of course. I'd jump whenever the phone rang. But it was nothing like this." A brief pause, then, "Of course, I was never so close personally with any of them, so . . ."

She gave his thigh a gentle squeeze.

"We'll be all right. It's a good plan, that's what matters. And look out for that damn tram car."

The tram driver rang his bell as he swerved the lumbering trolley in front of Emil. The Wartburg bumped and rattled across the rails in the pavement and tucked in behind.

"We're back on schedule, or close enough. I'll circle the block and let you out on Prenzlauer Allee. Then you'll need to—"

"I know. I'll need to pace myself so that I don't arrive too soon."

"Yes. Correct. I'll watch from two blocks away to see who else they might have in the area, then I'll get into position. I'll be where I'm supposed to be by the time you've done what you need to do."

"And you have the package?"

Emil patted the breast pocket of his jacket for at least the fourteenth time that morning.

"Yes. I have the package."

"We're good to go, then. You've done all you can do. And I know you hate to hear this, but the rest will depend on them."

"I know. I know that."

And, as he also knew, it would depend as well on whether any uninvited guests showed up—his greatest fear, and the item he had the least control over. As if reading his thoughts, Karola addressed the subject that neither of them had yet wanted to discuss.

"Those other people. If they come, they should at least be easy to spot, yes?"

His stomach went cold. He swallowed with difficulty.

"Yes."

"Black leather jackets? Dressed like thugs, probably three of them?"

"Yes."

"I'll keep an eye out."

"And abort if necessary."

"But only if necessary."

And that's what worried him most, the idea that Karola would have a more daring idea of necessity than he would. She had only heard secondhand what Kolkachev, Volkov, and their people were capable of. Emil had seen it up close. He had touched it and smelled it. He had retched in its presence.

His foot tapped the brakes. One mile to go.

It was then Karola's turn for doubts. Her hands were in her lap, and from a sidelong glance Emil saw that she was picking at her nails.

"It's only a meeting, Karola, and it will be quick. I'll give her the item and be gone."

"It's not that. It's Bettina. We're leaving her so much now in the care of Frau Adler."

"Frau Adler is qualified."

"But to her it's only a job, and Bettina knows that. And if something should happen to both of us . . ."

"This was your choice, to help me."

"I know, and it's necessary. Still . . ."

He took his hand off the shifter and patted her thigh. She placed her hand over his and held it in place, a comfort to them both until he approached a stoplight.

"Karola, I have to downshift."

"Yes, of course."

She smiled nervously and removed her hand.

They were almost there.

34

Baucom wasn't supposed to be there. Maybe that's why he was enjoying himself so much, seated with a thermos of coffee in his chilly BMW, three blocks from Zum Goldbroiler, watchful and alert at the north end of what he once would have called the operational perimeter.

In the prime of his career a mere surveillance chore like this would've bored him to tears, and he might have laced his coffee with whisky to make things bearable. But this morning at thirty minutes before zero hour he was feeling alive and useful in a way that he hadn't in months.

He had come here partly out of worry on Claire's behalf. Not because she wasn't up to the job, but because, well, it was clear from what he'd already heard and witnessed that Russians were involved.

Baucom had made one last contact with Claire, right around dawn, after his pal Roman had faxed him overnight a single name, that of the third Stasi officer who kept a dacha in the woods near Prenden. He phoned her room, told her the name, and wished her well. Moments after he hung up, he lit the day's first cigarette while still in his PJs. That's when he decided, what the hell, he would drive on over and serve as an extra set of eyes whether Claire wanted his help or not.

The visit to Markus Wolf's dacha was also to blame. Meeting his old foe had made him realize that while East Germany was dead, the struggle wasn't, not really, because in between their laughs and war stories both men had been probing for weaknesses, like old generals inspecting a battlefront. Baucom thought about it all through the evening and on into his dreams, and by sunrise he'd concluded that these were people who could never be trusted as long as they maintained their ties to Moscow.

Here he was, then, uninvited and probably unneeded, and already he had spotted something interesting. Only ten minutes earlier the mustard yellow Wartburg had crossed the intersection just to the south. Baucom, too, had memorized its tag numbers the day before, and these were a match.

He caught a glance of the driver as the car braked for a stoplight—no smoked glass in these cheap old Wartburgs, thank goodness—and from the shoulders up the fellow had matched Claire's description of the fellow who'd handed her the note. A man in his late fifties with unruly gray hair poking out from beneath a wool flat cap.

Normally Baucom would have worried about being spotted, but the fellow was talking to someone, and when the car rolled forward through the intersection he had been surprised to see a passenger— a woman, no less. He debated for a moment whether to try to follow, then decided to sit tight. Five minutes later he saw the car again, turning back onto Prenzlauer Allee a little to the south. It rolled past the Zum Goldbroiler and pulled to the curb a few blocks later.

The passenger door opened and the woman got out, but she walked away from the restaurant. The car pulled off and took the next right, and he had not seen it or the woman since.

Baucom poured more coffee and checked his watch. It was ten minutes before noon.

A little earlier he had gotten his first look at Claire's new operational partner, Ron Kent, who had arrived on foot and entered the Zum Goldbroiler at about 11:30 a.m. Baucom still had no further word from his source on Kent's reputation, or why Lindsey Ward would have selected him for this role.

But it wasn't all that hard to see how Ward must view this op—not as an entity unto itself, but as part of a tandem with the competing offer, which supposedly involved a Russian. He knew from experience the temptations involved once a supervisor got the idea they might be able to reel in someone from the KGB. Even with the Cold War on the wane, that would still have plenty of allure, a temptation great enough to make any manager get a little fast and loose operationally. And the Russians, for their part, had always been masterful at exploiting these kinds of hopes and ambitions.

A couple of hours ago Baucom had again phoned his old colleague—the baseball scout, as Claire had called him—to chat further about Ward. His friend had described her as the single most competent boss he'd ever worked for. Once she settled on a goal, she became utterly focused, perhaps to the point of ruthlessness. And unlike many males with those traits, she was quite deft at attuning her own wants and desires with those of the Agency, so that her own successes made those above her look good as well. While that was great for advancement, it could be dangerous for anyone ranked beneath her, since they were more subject to risk.

As someone who had run a few agents of his own on the other side of the Iron Curtain, Baucom couldn't help but sympathize with Ward's dilemma. Yes, the CIA had been duped before by fellows like Leonid—tasty offers that had turned into poisoned apples. But the Agency also had a history of turning away—or even jailing—KGB defectors who had turned out to be the genuine article. And at this early point who was to say whether Leonid was the former or the latter? Ward would be remiss if she didn't at least try to find out, and she could only do that by playing his game awhile longer.

Would she consider an obsolete old East German to be expendable in order to do that? Absolutely. Two Germans, even? Probably. Would this cavalier attitude also apply to her own people? No, because that could ruin her career. But in her zeal to land the big prize, or at least to thoroughly vet its potential, she might lose focus on their safety long enough for terrible accidents to happen. And that, too, was why Baucom was here, as a self-appointed safety valve for his friend and colleague.

The good news was that, so far, he'd seen no sign of any Russians. Whoever had leaked the news of the first rendezvous had either been silenced or shut out of the loop for this one.

And now, a few minutes before the appointed hour, there was Claire, approaching the destination on foot from the south. In through the door she went, the trigger event that would set others in motion.

Baucom kept watching, as alert as he had been in ages.

35

Claire spotted Ron Kent at a table by the window the moment she walked into the Zum Goldbroiler, exactly at noon. He opened a newspaper, the signal that he had not yet seen any sign of their contact. The place wasn't even half full, so she sat at a corner table and opened a menu.

The place smelled a little bit like her mom's kitchen on Thanksgiving morning—the aroma of a roasting bird with its juices smoldering in the pan. In glass cases behind the counter, plump browned chickens were lined up on rotating rods, turning slowly as they dripped and glistened.

The employees looked listless, as if sensing their days might be numbered. A lot of places on this side of the Wall had that feel now. As the euphoria from November 9 wore off, people had begun to worry about what would become of their apartments, their jobs, their neighborhoods. The only people who still seemed excited were the squatters, pouring in now not only from West Berlin but from the bohemian pockets of Western Europe and beyond.

The door squealed open. A woman, late forties, maybe older, walked in and eyed the counter, then scanned the room as if looking for someone she had come there to meet. Her eyes settled on Claire. She approached the table, leaned closer, and in a lowered tone said, "That grandchild of mine you wanted to see is waiting. Shall we go?"

It was an unexpected turn, but not all that surprising. Their contact was bound to be taking extra precautions after Lothar Fischer's death.

"Certainly."

"And your handsome friend by the window needn't come with us. My grandchild is still a little frightened by too many visitors at once. Unless of course you'd like to postpone to another day?"

The woman smiled, quite relaxed. If anything she seemed to be enjoying herself, and she had certainly spotted Ron Kent right away.

"No. I'm fine with today. Let's go."

Claire glanced at Kent and gave a slight shake of her head, and when she rose to leave, he remained in his seat, although she knew that after a decent interval he would still try to follow.

They headed out the door and turned right, south on Prenzlauer Allee, which took them beneath the overhead S-Bahn tracks. The walk gave Claire time to take the measure of this attractive older woman who was leading the way.

She realized that, up to then, her idea of East German womanhood had been unduly shaped by the country's Olympic swimmers, fearsome specimens with massive shoulders and bulging eyes. This woman certainly had an air of capability, but her grooming, her plain but neat clothing, and the laugh lines around her eyes suggested more brains than brawn.

They continued for two more blocks and turned right onto Stargarder Strasse. Claire glanced behind her as they turned, but saw no sign of Kent, although he was probably back there somewhere. Her escort looked that way, too, so it was just as well that he was out of sight.

They picked up the pace and turned right on a side street among battered, drab apartment buildings. The woman pulled a set of car keys from her coat pocket, and half a block later they stopped by a mustard yellow Wartburg. Claire checked the tag. It was the car that had been parked at the dacha, Wolf's neighbor. She felt like she had just gained a small advantage.

"Sit up front, where I can keep an eye on you."

The passenger door was unlocked. Claire angled a backward glance as she climbed in, and her escort noticed.

"Oh, he's back there, but he won't be able to keep up with us now." She started the car.

The car rumbled like the banged-up old Chevelle Claire's younger brother had driven as a teen in north Georgia. Out the back window she saw blue smoke drifting into the breeze.

"See that ticket on the dashboard in front of you?"

"Yes."

"Take it. You'll need it soon."

The ticket was for a show at the Zeiss-Grossplanetarium, the big globe-shaped building only a few blocks away. So at least they wouldn't be going far. Why the car, then?

She got her answer soon enough. The woman headed directly south, accelerating quickly away from the restaurant and the planetarium. Kent had parked in the opposite direction. There was no way he'd be able to keep up. The Wartburg traveled about a quarter mile before turning east on Danziger Strasse. They then made a wide circuit around Ernst-Thälman Park, heading north and then west as they doubled back toward the grounds of the planetarium, on the opposite side of where Ron Kent was probably still looking for Claire.

The Wartburg pulled to the curb.

"Your ticket is for the 12:30 show. They've already opened the doors, so you'll be able to go straight in. Don't linger outside, or the meeting is off. When you enter, take the left aisle and look toward the section to your right. Third row from the back, two seats in. There will be a gray wool coat holding the seat for you."

Claire climbed out. The door slammed behind her, and the car rattled away in another burst of smoke. The planetarium loomed like a gigantic silver ball a few hundred yards across a grassy expanse of parkland. She did as she was told and made a beeline for the entrance, where patrons were lined up for tickets and filing in for the show.

Inside, the place was already about half full. Eight rows of seating curved in both directions, forming almost a full circle around the star projector, a buglike contraption mounted in the middle. Claire headed left. She took the first aisle, sloping downhill, and spotted a gray wool coat draped on the second seat of the third row down.

She wasn't sure what to do with the coat, so she set it onto the aisle seat and eased into place. Most everyone else was staring up at the domed ceiling, lit to resemble twilight, so she did the same. Only seconds later, the old fellow from the previous Thursday evening grabbed up the coat and settled into the aisle seat. He was wearing the same wool hat, and smelled like the outdoors, an essence of loam and wet leaves. Claire flashed to her memory of the darting, watchful presence among the beeches and pines as she and Baucom had climbed the hill to Wolf's dacha.

She did not turn to acknowledge his presence, and he, too, looked up at the man-made sky. The lights dimmed further, and a hush fell over the room. He leaned closer and whispered, his earthy scent even stronger.

"It occurs to me that I have seen this particular show, so why don't we take a walk."

"After you."

She expected him to head back up the aisle. Instead he went farther downhill and cut left toward the red-lighted "Ausfahrt" sign above an emergency exit, which led into a concrete stairwell with a fire door on the opposite side. He pushed through it, back into the outdoors, and she followed.

He turned and watched her as he put on his overcoat. The same fellow for sure, but daylight offered a clearer look. He was about six feet tall, thin and in decent shape. Mid- to late fifties, which meant he would have come of age in a time of postwar deprivation, in rubble and ruin, and probably in the Soviet sector of occupation. His mother and any sisters would have been targets for rape. Odds were that his father had been a combat casualty, either physically or emotionally.

But unlike many East Berliners, who seemed overly pale or, if more privileged, flabby from the perks of their party status, his skin was ruddy, his features toned.

"Let's walk," he said, pointing across the grounds in the direction Claire had come from.

They fell into step, side by side. At first he seemed to have a slight limp, but his stride quickly loosened. He then surprised her by gripping her arm with what felt like a little too much force, maybe even a touch of anger. His next words were insistent and carried some heat.

"I have a sample I'd like to give you, to convince your people of the authenticity of what I'm offering, but I will do so only if you fully and honestly answer one question."

"Maybe you could start by letting go of my arm."

"That, too, will depend on your answer."

"Ask me, then."

"Why were you and your friend meeting yesterday with Markus Wolf?"

It threw her, but only for a second.

"So that was *you*, then, watching us from up there in the trees."

His grip loosened, as if she had knocked him off balance. She spoke again while she still held the advantage.

"Which means you must be Emil Grimm."

He released her arm, and she dared a sidelong glance. He wore a worried frown, and his breathing was uneven.

"Let's find somewhere to sit. This is going to be more complicated than I thought."

"I quite agree."

He glanced back at her, then quickened his pace toward a bench fifty feet farther along. He sagged onto it with a sigh, and Claire sat to his right. She surveyed the landscape. Ron Kent was nowhere to be seen. The Wartburg that had dropped her off was also gone. The only other people in the park were mothers and children, a few shoppers strolling home with their bags. The sun poked through the clouds, casting long shadows even at this hour, although she was grateful for the extra warmth.

She turned to see Grimm staring at her. Then he broke into a rueful smile and shook his head.

"We appear to have arrived at the unlikely destination where both of us know too much about each other—or more than either of us is probably comfortable with."

She couldn't help but smile back. This was indeed one of the oddest operational moments of her career. Encounters like this were usually brisk and businesslike, with few words spoken before both parties exchanged whatever needed to be exchanged and melted back into their surroundings. This time it already felt like they were trying to reach an accommodation beyond the usual rules; perhaps also beyond the usual supervision. The latter aspect would be easier for him to manage since, presumably, he was no longer reporting to anyone. As for Claire, well, she had been straying from her tether from day one of this op, first by bringing Baucom into the mix, and then by visiting Wolf. And now it was clear that this fellow, Grimm, her presumptive adversary, already knew more about both of those moves than either Lindsey Ward or Bill Gentry. While Claire, in turn, knew Emil Grimm's name and where he lived, and she had spent part of the previous day with his longtime boss.

"You're right. We're both at a disadvantage."

"And you still haven't answered my question."

"We went at Wolf's invitation. It was unofficial. Apparently, someone higher up in my chain of command is seeking a formal meeting with him, and he wanted to know why."

"And?"

"The reason isn't relevant to you."

"Did Wolf give you my name?"

"No. He didn't mention you, not even in passing."

He paused to digest this and gave her a long look, as if to assess her honesty. Claire looked right back. It was another unlikely moment—two people trained to mistrust, searching for any sign that it might be safe to do otherwise. She spoke again.

"Maybe if you came here to give me something, you should just do it."

"Even though someone else is offering your people the same goods?"

"That's not for me to say or to judge."

"I am pretty sure his name is Gregor Kolkachev, in case your superiors don't know, or haven't told you. And the name of his chief thug, the one who came after you on Frankfurter Allee, is Yuri Volkov. Kolkachev is in charge of KGB counterintelligence for this district, based in Karlshorst. I suspect he is playing your people, because that has always been a part of his job description. Tell them that."

"I will. But of course you'd say that, wouldn't you, because otherwise it's pretty clear how he'd be able to make his offer more attractive than yours."

"Yes. Attractive enough for them to look the other way while he arranges for all his competitors to be killed."

"Risk isn't something I can manage for you. Except when you're with me."

He glanced around, as if risk was suddenly his top concern. Claire did the same. The mix of people in the park hadn't changed. No one seemed to be paying them undue attention, although there was also no sign of his backup, or of hers.

"Considering your evident lack of resources in these encounters, I'm not so sure you can manage it even when we're together. And if I am in danger, then so are you. Although I suspect you're already aware of that, after your near miss."

So he must have watched the whole thing, yet had lived to tell her about it.

"I'm impressed. And I'm guessing that Kolkachev—if he's indeed your competitor—doesn't yet know your name."

"I doubt I would be alive if he did, and I'd like to keep it that way. Does everyone on your side know my name now?"

She debated whether to level with him, then decided to do so.

"No. Just me."

He sighed, seemingly in relief.

"Then perhaps you could wait awhile longer before telling them, because, well . . ."

"You think we have a leak?"

"Oh, you have always had leaks. Wolf would have happily told you that, if he had been in the mood to boast."

With each such prod and response they moved deeper into the underbrush. Claire suspected they would soon reach a point from which neither of them would be able to return without being compromised or badly hurt.

"I'll do what I can, but I can't offer any guarantees."

He nodded, reached into his coat pocket, and withdrew a sealed envelope. He started to hand it over, then hesitated.

"I'm offering you this. Your people will know what it means, based on information contained in previous communications."

"From Lothar Fischer?"

He sagged a bit at the mention of the name. His eyes looked weary, a little sad. "Yes. I will proceed based on how they respond. Unless, of course, you believe my case is so hopeless that I should bow out while I still can. If so, tell me now."

Claire wasn't sure how to answer. At the very least, she supposed Ward would want to keep Grimm on the line if only as leverage for dealing with Kolkachev. Not that he would want to hear that. She had come here to retrieve what he was offering, but she didn't want to get the man killed.

"My advice, since you asked, is that you find some way to add value to your offer."

"I see."

He nodded and thought it over as he continued to hold the envelope between them.

"And if I manage to do that, what will be the added value of my compensation?"

"Impossible for me to say, even if I knew what was already on the table. Which I don't."

"Tell them this, then. In addition to what I've already requested, any 'added value' will require similar considerations for two additional people. And since my original partner is now . . . gone, we're really only talking about compensation for one additional person. Three of us, instead of two."

Upping his price, then. Maybe, after all, he was just another grifter in the game of betrayal, cashing in while the market was hot.

"Why not just make it easy for both of us and give me a number."

"A number?" He looked puzzled. Then her meaning seemed to dawn on him. "Ah, an *amount*, you mean, of money. No, that's not what I'm seeking. Your people initially mentioned a figure, but that's secondary to me. That was Lothar Fischer's request, not mine. My primary interest is safe harbor, and now I want it for three people instead of two. Including one with, well, a medical condition. Someone who may need special assistance in . . . in going free."

Her opinion shifted again. He came across now as more desperate than opportunistic. More of a refugee than a spy, although Claire knew that was likely naïve, given his longtime employer and his high rank. She wondered if the woman who had driven the Wartburg was one of the two additional people, and if so, who the third one could be.

"I'll tell them. I know they'll be surprised by one thing. Your use of a woman. Someone who supposedly knows the way your side does things had assured me that almost never happened."

He shifted on the bench and withdrew the envelope, clearly troubled by what she'd said. The disadvantages for each of them had now accumulated to the point where neither could afford to violate the trust of the other. Maybe the deal was off.

"Are you ever going to give me that envelope, or have you changed your mind?"

He looked her in the eye. She stared back. He again held forward the envelope. "Here. But do not take it unless you are willing to meet me again, sooner rather than later, and no matter what your superiors say."

Committing to that would be a leap beyond Ward's supervision, but after what Claire had already done during the past few days it didn't feel like much of one.

"I'm guessing you already have a time and place in mind."

"Noon tomorrow. In Mitte, my side of the Wall. There's a big vacant building on Oranienburger Strasse, a leftover ruin from the war that artists have begun moving into. They're calling it Tacheles."

"Tacheles?"

"I'm told it is a Yiddish word, meaning 'straight talk.'"

"Perfect for us, then."

She took the envelope and put it in her bag without averting her gaze.

"It's a five-story building. There's an arched passage that cuts through from the street to an empty lot. Look for me there, waiting in the passage. Squatters have been swarming to the place like termites to a rotting log, and a lot of them are foreigners, so nearly everyone there speaks English. We'll do the same. If you want to fit in, don't comb your hair, and dress to look careless and bohemian."

"Meaning you'll come as you are?"

He surprised her by breaking into a laugh, and this time his smile was mirthful. Then he stood. Claire did the same. She again noticed that he seemed to favor his right leg. He flexed the knee while checking in both directions, and turned to face her for a final word.

"I am probably a fool to do this, but I have decided to trust you. Three lives are now in your hands."

A sober and even noble response seemed to be in order, but words failed her. Here was an adversary whom she now felt duty bound to protect, an unfamiliar position. Then again, she had never before dealt with an adversary whose side had already been defeated. Their employers were supposedly at peace, dickering only over the terms of surrender. It was his longtime ally, the KGB, that was still a threat to them both.

"I'll keep your name to myself as long as I can. If this offering of yours passes inspection, you'll be helping us both if you can come up with something more. The sooner, the better."

He nodded.

"I'll work on it."

He turned and strolled away, limping then not limping. Claire saw that the yellow Wartburg was now waiting for him on the far side of the park, engine running. She headed in the opposite direction, already wondering how much she could or should reveal to Ron Kent. The concepts of duty and loyalty had never before felt so complicated.

36

Emil climbed into the Wartburg with a sinking feeling, knowing that now he'd have to look Karola in the eye.

She was bright-eyed, excited, pleased to have done her job well. He was heartsick that he had made her a part of this. He had put her in the line of fire, inexcusable, especially now when it seemed clear that his offer was going to fall short. Added value? What did that even mean when your competitor was a KGB man with access to all sorts of secrets beyond Emil's reach? Anything that Emil could offer had an expiration date, and from this point onward its value would only begin to decline.

And while the American woman seemed to mean well, he doubted she could keep his identity secret forever. Inevitably, perhaps soon, he would become vulnerable.

"How did it go?"

Fortunately, Karola was checking the mirrors, alert to traffic and possible pursuers, which bought him time to muster a smile and inject a note of hope into his voice.

"As well as you could expect, I suppose."

He didn't have the heart to tell her that the American had known his name.

"What did she say about Wolf?"

"That he had invited them, but that they didn't talk about me. Wolf did mention Lothar, but she didn't get the idea he knew for sure what Lothar had been up to."

"Do you trust her?" Then, as if realizing that wasn't ever really a question you could answer with much accuracy in this profession, "I guess what I really mean is, do you think she's reliable?"

"As far as it goes. I do believe she wants this to work out safely for all parties, and she seems fully aware of the risks. So that's a start."

"And?"

Karola was watching him, so he turned toward her. He could only manage a shrug.

"She thinks our competition may outbid us. I'm inclined to agree."

Karola was silent for a moment. When she next spoke she sounded more subdued. "A competitor." She went silent for a moment. "The one who killed Lothar, then. And Plotz."

"Probably a safe assumption."

"Did she have a name for this competitor?"

"She did not, nor would I expect her to." He was relieved he didn't have to lie about that part, or even the next. "But I think we can safely assume it's someone with the KGB."

"Yes. Of course."

There was still no way he was going to reveal Kolkachev's and Volkov's names to Karola.

"Is there anything we can do to improve our offer?"

He noted her use of "we" and "our." He would never be able to convince her to withdraw from this, even though that was now his inclination. She'd be insulted if he even tried.

"I'm open to any and all suggestions."

The answering silence was oppressive. Emil then decided that after tomorrow's meetup at Tacheles he would limit Karola's participation as much as possible. Now that the Americans had his sample, the odds would only increase that his name would leak to Kolkachev. The less exposure for her, the better. He still didn't know what purpose the meeting would serve, except as a delaying action. But if he had nothing new to offer by then, well . . .

"What's wrong. Emil?"

"Nothing."

"You look like you think it's hopeless."

"No. I'm just thinking. We're not out of the game yet."

"Will you be meeting them again?"

"Yes. You'll only need to drive me. We'll discuss the arrangements later."

She again looked over. Emil avoided her stare for as long as he could, and then managed a weak smile.

Karola shook her head, unconvinced.

They drove on in silence.

37

Baucom hung back in his old BMW as far as he could without losing contact with the Wartburg. He tracked its progress by the blue smoke from the tailpipe, although that advantage soon vanished in plumes of competing smoke from two intervening Trabants, so he accelerated to close the gap, weaving past a tram before settling in a block behind.

Fortunately his goal in this pursuit was limited. He only wanted to find out the old fellow's preferred route to and from Prenden, in order to choose the best possible chokepoint for a future surveillance.

He doubted Claire would let him know if they planned to meet again, and she certainly wouldn't tell him the time or place. But Baucom was betting that an old hand like Emil Grimm would plan his assignations with a certain regularity, and based on today midday seemed to be his preferred time.

Grimm would almost certainly change the location, and Baucom figured he could work around that gap by setting up shop at a traffic surveillance point at around 11 a.m., or maybe a little earlier—some spot where he'd be likely to see the Wartburg pass by on its way back into the city. He would do that every day for at least a week until he got a hit. But first he needed to determine the route and pick a vantage point.

Fortunately, Baucom had spotted Grimm on foot shortly after noon, not long after he had lost sight of the Wartburg. By moving his car down the block he had seen Grimm just as he'd entered the grounds of the Zeiss Planetarium. Baucom had decided to take up an observation post on the far side of Ernst-Thalmann Park, which proved fortuitous when, a few minutes later, the Wartburg rolled into view and dropped off Claire. It then returned to pick up Grimm, and Baucom had set off after them.

Now the Wartburg was heading out of the city on Greifswalder Strasse, which was part of northbound Highway 2. Baucom knew it went straight to the entrance of the Autobahn that led to Bernau and Prenden, so he began dropping back to let the Wartburg move out of range.

His BMW, even in its dilapidated state, stood out a bit among the East German cars, so Baucom decided that tomorrow he would borrow a friend's car—a particular Opel compact came to mind—to blend in better.

He spotted the ideal vantage point a few minutes later, just past the tram stop for the bathing beach at the Weissensee, another of Berlin's many small lakes. There was a gas station a couple of blocks farther along where he would have a full view of incoming traffic, with easy access to the road. He could give himself an excuse to linger by popping open the hood, like a motorist checking the engine. Doing that several days in a row would be suspicious, so he would employ other tactics as the days progressed, whether Claire wanted him to or not. Because if his many years of Berlin experience had taught him anything, it was that you could never have too many eyes and ears on your side.

In the meantime, he would keep digging with his old source for any further insights into the character of Lindsey Ward and her chosen operative, Ron Kent. Because the more information he could get for Claire, the better. And also because, well, Baucom was enjoying himself too much to quit.

His work done for the day, Baucom took the next left turn and headed for home.

38

By the time they reached the dirt road along the Bauersee, Emil was exhausted from trying to maintain an upbeat demeanor, and by his awareness that Karola wasn't buying it. This made it all the more dispiriting when they rounded the final curve through the trees and saw a green-and-white *Polizei* car parked in the driveway behind Frau Adler's brown Škoda. Although at least the Citroën was gone. He wondered if the two events were related.

"Is it that lieutenant again?" Karola asked.

"Yes. Dorn. He's waiting by the door."

"He doesn't look pleased."

"He almost never does. Here." He pulled the Wartburg onto the shoulder and got out his wallet. "Go inside and pay Frau Adler. I'll deal with him out here."

She eyed him suspiciously, but he had to keep her from hearing the conversation, especially if Dorn started throwing around names of Russians.

Dorn nodded curtly as they approached the door.

"Frau Weber. Herr Grimm."

He at least had the sense to wait until Karola was inside to get to the point of his visit.

"The evidence, Herr Grimm. Those strips of microfilm. You must return it to me this instant." He held out his hand in an impatient manner.

"I have good news on that front, Lieutenant. Only this morning I was able to put it into the hands of archival experts who will be able to determine its provenance, and probably also its importance."

Dorn sighed and dropped his hand.

"I was afraid you would say something like that."

"Soon, Lieutenant, soon. And since there is no paperwork to link its disappearance to either you or me, we are both quite secure on that matter as long as no one begins asking about it. And, of course, as long as you don't make an issue of it with your superiors."

Dorn pressed his lips together in a seam of repressed anger, but did not answer. Emil changed the subject.

"Krauss's people have been sniffing around here again, I'll have you know. Posting a car, following me. Have you managed to have a word with him yet?"

Dorn beamed and rose up on his toes for a second. Obviously, Emil had chosen the right diversion.

"Krauss and his goons have been placed on notice, Grimm. I have seen to that."

"So he talked?"

"No. I went to his new place of work, the address you gave me. Four of us, like you suggested, just this afternoon. When he came out for lunch, we pounced."

"And?"

"He refused to be questioned, but he listened. Oh yes, he listened, and he was not at all pleased by what he heard."

Emil wasn't sure he was going to be pleased, either, especially since it had been his doing to send Dorn after Krauss. Maybe riling the man up wasn't such a good idea, especially now that his own work had reached such a delicate moment.

"What did you say to him?"

"I flushed him from cover, him and his Russian friends, like a brace of partridges. I considered taking matters to their embassy, of course, but for that I would have had to ask my chief inspector, Bilke, and he would have then gone to the new interior minister, Diestel, and, well . . ."

"Yes, far too many ripples in the pond. Good decision. But what did you say to Krauss?"

"I told him that Lothar Fischer's death was a murder, and that he was officially a suspect in either the commission or the cover-up of this crime. Further, I told him to inform Herr Volkov and Herr Kolkachev that these acts were committed on the soil of a sovereign nation, and that while actions like this might once have been overlooked or even tolerated before, under the old regime, they will not be tolerated now. So, even though I may not be able to arrest them directly due to diplomatic considerations, well, they have at least been put on notice."

Yes, Emil thought, meaning now they would move deeper underground, and become stealthier and more careful in their actions. No more blunt force killings, perhaps, but they were certainly capable of more diabolical methods. But to lecture Dorn on this point would only reveal his own knowledge of the darker arts of his profession, the black bag capabilities that all of them—German, Russian, American—had sometimes employed during the Cold War. He sighed wearily.

"I see. You didn't mention my name at any point, I hope."

"Of course not. Not that you've done anything lately to earn such loyalty. Are you certain you'll be able to return that evidence in a timely manner?"

"As I said, it is being examined by experts. They hope to return it to me in the next few days, but certainly no longer than a week."

"A *week*? This isn't permissible! That is far longer than what we agreed to."

"Their work must be done properly, Lieutenant. And when you do get it back, you'll have the satisfaction of knowing its true nature and genuine provenance. It will be even more valuable as an evidentiary tool."

"Evidentiary tool! Listen to your bullshit." He sighed loudly. His hands were tied, and he knew it. "You are to inform me the moment it is back in your possession."

"Of course."

"And you might at least thank me for getting Krauss off your back. One of his men was parked here in the lane when I arrived. I gave them a long look, and they took off."

"Very good. Thank you indeed, Lieutenant."

Dorn nodded, but still looked upset about the microfilm. Then, without a further word, he pivoted on his heel and headed for his car.

He left literally in a cloud of dust, with a sudden acceleration that sprayed gravel onto the parked Wartburg.

Emil watched until the police car was out of sight. He half expected to see a Citroën come creeping down the lane to replace it, but all was quiet. A few crows circled overhead, never a good omen, but he was relieved to finally have a moment of peace.

He reached into his coat pocket. The old pack of Juwel cigarettes was still there. Emil shook one out, fumbled for his lighter, then lit it. It went out almost as soon as he began to inhale. He tried once more, failed, then angrily tossed the cigarette onto the lane.

Frau Adler left shortly afterward. The mood in the dacha was subdued. Karola brought Bettina up to date, painting the rosiest possible picture, but he was certain that his wife saw through their optimistic words, if only by reading their faces.

He bathed her, fed her, and then read her another Stefan Heym short story while Karola cooked a rustic dinner for two of *Spaetzle*, pork, mushrooms and cream, which they washed down by splitting a liter of Pils.

Emil had little appetite, and his plate was still half-full when he pushed it away. Karola barely noticed, lost in her own thoughts.

It was all catching up to him, he supposed, all of his lies and misleading behavior with Dorn, Krauss, Wolf, and even the Americans—a tottering structure of deceptions that might collapse upon all of them at any moment. The path forward seemed narrower than at any other time in his life.

It brought home to him how his agents must have felt as they had lived their double lives on his orders, out there in the West for years. Such a strain to keep all of your fictions alive and in proper order.

Yet he felt a certain giddiness as well. Earlier with Dorn, for instance, he had mildly enjoyed yanking the man further along while still keeping him partly in the dark. So there was pleasure in this spying life, too. And now, at least, instead of having to be a good employer who kept other people's secrets, he was working instead for his own Nation of Three. In retrospect, perhaps it was the only worthy cause he had ever served.

"I thought you were hungry?"

Karola was frowning at his plate.

"I thought so, too, but . . ."

"Yes. I know."

She began clearing away the dishes. Emil stood to help. When he was halfway to the sink, someone began banging on the front door, loud and insistent—five knocks, then silence. Instantly alert, Emil switched off the kitchen light and looked out the window, but the porch was in darkness. The Wartburg was the only car he could see.

"Who is it?" Karola whispered. "How many?"

"I can't tell."

The banging began again. Five more rapid, heavy knocks.

"Go into Bettina's room and lock the door," he whispered. "Stay as quiet as you can!"

Emil looked for his coat, spotted it draped across the back of the couch, then hastily reached inside for the Pistol-M. He walked as quietly as he could to the door, but whoever was on the other side must have heard him approaching.

"Grimm, open up!"

A deep baritone. Not Dorn, and not Krauss. Was there an accent? He didn't think so, but in his frazzled state of mind he couldn't be sure. He took a deep breath, eased the gun behind his back, and used his left hand to turn the handle of the door.

39

Lindsey Ward paced like a caged panther, claws bared, irritable and impatient with what she was hearing from Claire about the meeting with the East German. She stopped, leveled her gaze, and pressed her question yet again.

"So he still hasn't given us a name, not even a fake one?"

Claire, feeling like a slab of raw meat hanging just beyond the panther's reach, held her ground and answered.

"He hasn't."

Technically, it was true. Emil Grimm *hadn't* offered a name, even if Claire had figured it out for herself. But that was an item of intelligence she hadn't revealed even to Ron Kent—it was the first thing he'd wanted to know as well, when they'd met at the fallback location—so she certainly wasn't going to tell Ward, not with Kent sitting right beside her.

"And he didn't offer any indication of what this upgrade to his offer was likely to involve?"

"None."

"Well, then we certainly can't yet assume it's of any real value. And we definitely can't yet extend our offer to cover two extra people."

"Only one extra, actually, now that Lothar Fischer is off the board. That was his argument anyway."

"Are you his contact or his advocate?"

"I'm a conduit, passing along what he said."

True as well, although Claire couldn't help but marvel at how protective she felt of the fellow. Someone in his position had undoubtedly authorized plenty of actions she would have considered abhorrent. The Stasi itself was abhorrent. Why, then, did she indeed feel more like his advocate than his adversary?

Her run-in with Grimm's competitors—those tattooed thugs in black leather—was part of it. The KGB wasn't a former enemy, they were the current one. Sacrificing anyone to that crowd seemed unforgivable.

Maybe she'd also been impressed by his apparent lack of greed, or the vibe of his chosen accomplice, the competent and calm woman at the wheel of that pathetic car. Claire was brokering a deal with the underdogs in this arrangement, there was no doubt of that. But it was also possible she was being played for a fool, especially if some fellow from the KGB, no matter how ruthless, or motivated by greed, was additionally offering genuine inside intelligence that, in the long term, would be far more valuable than what Grimm could give them.

Ward opened her mouth to speak again, so Claire preempted her. "Have our technical people said anything yet about his submission, the microfilm?"

"They say full verification will take at least a day, but their initial reaction was positive. They think it's almost certainly a genuine piece of the puzzle we're after, and in all probability a reliable indicator that he has every piece that we want."

"Then why is his identity so important?"

Ward's voice rose in volume, and she again bared her claws.

"We're in a fast-moving marketplace for information, in case you haven't noticed. The more of it we can acquire, the more leverage we'll have with other possible contributors."

"So you want his name as a bargaining chip for . . ." Claire paused, but only for a second. The name "Kolkachev" was on the tip of her tongue because she knew it would be an effective goad. But it would also be further evidence to Ward that she was withholding intelligence, and maybe also that she'd been venturing out on her own. So instead she concluded her question with the code name "Leonid."

"Only because Leonid is offering the same product, plus future access to more and better information than what this old hack from the Stasi is offering. It's a pragmatic calculation, and it's a sound one. And, as I said, we certainly can't offer any further assurances to your contact unless and until he can show tangible proof he can give us something better."

Claire nodded and sighed. Ward's point was valid. They were not in the business of choosing between personalities, or motives. It was all about information, intelligence. She felt some of the heat going out of her argument on Grimm's behalf, and her next words emerged in a tone of resignation.

"I think he probably expects that kind of an answer for now. I got the impression he was mostly hoping to keep the channels of communication open."

"So you think he might be blowing smoke about upgrading his offer?"

"I'll have a better idea after I meet him tomorrow at Tacheles."

"Then maybe *you're* the one who's buying time."

"Are you saying I shouldn't meet him?"

"I'm saying it sounds like you've gone soft on him."

Ward could be right. Hell, she *was* right. And Grimm might be playing her with his poor little underdog pose. Maybe he was already back in his dacha, laughing with his lady friend about how easily they'd just handled the naïve American.

As if sensing her doubt, Ward reached into a folder for a sheet of paper, which she handed to Claire.

"Here. Take a fresh look at this."

It was the flow chart of HVA leadership that Ward had showed her the week before, except Lothar Fischer's name had been crossed out in red ink, and each of the other names had been supplemented with further information about their operational duties.

Claire wondered who had provided the additional intelligence. Kolkachev? Someone in the Stasi? One of the other names on the chart, even? She supposed that even Markus Wolf could have supplied it, but only if someone at the Agency other than her and Baucom had been in touch with him during the past few days.

Claire made a show of carefully reading every thumbnail description. Emil Grimm's name was right there at number six on the chart. He had run their ops at NATO. God knows how many of their vital military secrets he had uncovered. That alone was grounds to mistrust him, she supposed.

"Anything new in there that makes one of those names a better match for your contact?"

"Sorry. No."

Ward narrowed her eyes, and they engaged for a moment in a ridiculous staredown. Ron Kent, who'd remained silent throughout, lowered his head and crossed his arms, as if not wanting to attract any crossfire. Ward gave him a sidelong glance and frowned, as if in disapproval of his show of neutrality.

He then spoke up.

"For all this talk of added value, these agent records by themselves would be a major acquisition. We'd know the identity of every East German asset who ever worked in West Germany, at NATO, and even in the United States. With hundreds, maybe even thousands of names, a lot of them still out there, still unknown. That's huge. That's as big as anything we've ever landed."

"Are you saying I've lost sight of that?" Ward said.

Kent seemed taken aback.

"Not in the least."

"Good. Because I haven't. Yes, it's vital material, all of it. But if we can get the same from Kolkachev, plus more, then we do that. Especially if the bonus information is about an adversary that's still active and fully functional. Don't lose sight of that."

"I haven't."

"Good. See that you don't. Both of you."

Claire said nothing, content to let the tension between Kent and Ward take center stage for a moment.

Ward walked around to the other side of the table, where she opened another folder, glanced at some pages, and then, without looking up, said pointedly, "And how are things working out between you and Ron, Claire?"

"I suspect he has already given you a pretty good idea of that."

"Yes, he has."

So there was that issue out in the open. Kent again had his head down, although his ears were red, which Claire decided was a point in his favor.

"Well, if you're going to go through with this meetup tomorrow, then the two of you had better start planning logistics."

"Agreed. Absolutely."

"This time don't be such a pushover. Press him on every point, and make sure Ron is close at hand."

Claire stood. Kent did the same. Ward wasn't finished.

"Ron, I'd like you to stay behind for a minute or two. Some of your paperwork from Langley needs attending to."

Another show of force, to put Claire on notice that Kent was still Ward's preferred option, even though he didn't seem pleased by the move.

"I'll leave you two to your paperwork, then."

And with that, Claire departed. The last sound she heard as she shut the door behind her was Ron Kent, clearing his throat.

40

When the door opened, Emil saw that it was Markus Wolf out there in the night. He felt like a fool for having panicked. He slid the gun out of sight on a table by the entrance and made way for his old boss to enter.

"Come in, Mischa. Sorry to make you wait."

Wolf stepped gingerly across the threshold. He surveyed the room carefully, as if perplexed by all the darkness.

"I hope I didn't wake you."

"No, no. I'd just finished a late dinner." The remark only seemed to perplex him more. Emil switched on a light and mustered a thin smile. "Can I get you a drink?"

"Actually, I was hoping to lure you out for a drink."

"Oh, yes? At your dacha?"

"At a bar near here. A little place on the road into Bernau. But if you need to stay here with Bettina . . ."

"No. I have help." He was reluctant to mention Karola's name, worried he might shake loose Wolf's memory of her brief period of employment with the HVA. "I just need to tell them I'm heading out, then I'll join you."

"I'll wait for you in the lane."

"Certainly."

Wolf took a final look around and went outside.

Emil's heart was beating at twice its normal rate. He put the gun back into his coat pocket, then thought better of it and took it to his bedroom, where he opened the top dresser drawer and slid the pistol beneath his socks. Stepping through the shared bathroom, he saw Karola at Bettina's bedside. Both women were wide-eyed and silent in the dark.

"I heard," Karola whispered, saving him an explanation. "So, then. I suppose that now the Wolf *is* at the door."

He smiled weakly, wishing he could respond with a laugh.

"I need to calm down, or he'll wonder what's up. He always notices these things."

"Do you think he wants to talk about Lothar, or, well, *any* of this?"

"I don't know. But he must not want even Andrea to hear us, or we'd be going to his place. And from all I've heard he shares everything with her."

"So it seems."

She said it archly, Karola again expressing her disapproval of Wolf's third wife. Their little lakeside community could be as gossipy as a rural village.

Wolf's Volvo was parked down the lane instead of in the driveway, which explained why Emil hadn't seen it earlier. Wolf had once had a driver to take him everywhere he needed to go. That perk had disappeared along with the Wall. Emil wondered who the chauffeur was working for now. Maybe he, too, was out of a job.

"Where's this place you're taking me?"

"Sort of a roadhouse tavern. I used to go there from time to time whenever I wanted to meet someone up this way and not be noticed. It's almost never crowded, so any outsider stands out, and they're usually playing music loud enough to talk without being overheard. Kitschy Bavarian schlock from the jukebox, but still. The liquor selection's terrible, so I hope you're in the mood for a beer."

They arrived a few minutes later, and Wolf's description was right on the mark. The lighting was dim, and the only other customer was an older fellow slumped over a whisky at the far end of the bar. Wolf led them to a table—one of only five—at the opposite end. The concrete floor was damp and littered with peanut shells. The walls were decorated with Dynamo Dresden football posters. Here, at least, Erich Honecker's framed photo still had a place of honor, although it had been knocked askew.

Tonight a television up behind the bar was playing instead of the jukebox. It was showing an episode of *Unser Sandmännchen*, the nightly children's bedtime tale starring a stop-action puppet with twinkly eyes, the face of a cherub, an elfin cap, and a pointy white beard. He was one of East Germany's sweeter creations, with a calming theme song sung by a children's choir and accompanied by a flute. Bettina had always gone quiet whenever Sandmann appeared on their screen, probably because he made her think of the child they never had.

The bartender, a big fellow with rolled-up sleeves, tattooed forearms, and a silver buzz cut, nodded familiarly to Wolf and brought over a pair of foaming glasses of Berliner Pils. He waved away Wolf's ostmarks and retreated without a word. When he got back to the bar he reached up and switched the channel. The blare of a car chase across Turkey replaced Sandmann's flute music. Wake up, boys and girls.

"He knows you," Emil said.

"Rudi, you mean. Yes. I used to do business here from time to time. I once brought Gaby Gast. She loved the place."

Gast was one of Wolf's few female agents, and probably the most famous. She had infiltrated not only the West German government, but its spy agency, the BND.

"One of your favorites, wasn't she?"

Wolf waggled his hand.

"Productive, but difficult. That tended to be the case with the women. Too much special care and handling."

Yes, Emil thought, especially when you let their training officer prey on them like lambs in a meadow, and then fired any lamb who asked for help. He swallowed some beer to wash away that thought.

"Rudi's a good man, but he's in a bad place now. He's worried he'll lose the bar once the West begins selling state assets. So I put in a word for him, for whatever that's worth anymore. Less than he thinks, probably."

"But an effective way to continue buying his silence."

"Please, Emil. His *discretion*. A more refined word."

Wolf, who hadn't yet touched his beer, then leaned forward and lowered his voice, as if to signal they had reached the main business of the evening.

"Our little visit the other night really got me thinking, Emil."

"At Lothar's dacha, you mean?"

"Yes. It stirred up all sorts of old memories, quite unbidden, and there was one in particular I wanted to ask you about."

Wolf had always gotten straight to the point, but even for him this was quite direct, which put Emil on his guard.

"It's about a matter you handled, if I'm remembering correctly, during that brief period when we were grooming you for the USA posting."

"Things were pretty slow at that time on the American front, I seem to recall."

"Well, of course. That's why I wanted to send you over there, to stir things up. Maybe that's why this case stood out to me, even though, on the face of it, it was the smallest of matters. A favor for our friends."

"Favor?"

"Of a logistical nature. For our comrades in arms."

The KGB, he meant. The reference stirred something vague at the corner of Emil's memory, although any task they would have carried out for the Russians in the United States would have been of the most menial sort. Besides, all of Emil's recollections from his brief stint on the America desk were still clouded by the event that had knocked him back into his old job—Bettina's diagnosis of ALS.

"I like to think I have pretty good recall for operational detail, but this matter isn't coming to mind."

"Not at all surprising. In fact, I think it may have initially been handled by the weekend duty officer—the logistics of it, anyway. But there was a bit of housekeeping in the aftermath, something to do with the file, and I believe that fell into your lap. The only reason any of this came to mind is that Mielke took a personal interest."

Ah, yes. Now Emil remembered. The episode in question had occurred the very weekend that he and Bettina had learned the test results from the doctor, so by Monday morning he had been somewhat distracted when Mielke's personal assistant had come to his desk for the thin file—so distracted, in fact, that Emil had brusquely sent the fellow away and told him to return with written authorization. Probably the only reason he remembered any of this was that later that day an irritated Mielke himself had come for the file. Visits like that stuck with you, even when you were going through a personal ordeal.

"Of course. I do remember. Mielke was angry with me because I'd blown off his assistant. So he actually rode the paternoster down to see me. Wasn't this about some mailbox we cleared for them?"

"A dead drop, yes. Exactly. I knew it would come to you. The Russians were shorthanded that weekend, for whatever reason, and they had an urgent need to clear a dead drop for one of their agents. They never said why the agent couldn't take care of it himself—or I suppose it could have been a she—but we were happy to do it, of course."

"The location was in some park, wasn't it?"

"Correct again. On the outskirts of Washington. Under a pedestrian bridge in a park area, along a road called Little Falls Parkway."

"That's a lot of detail. Sounds like you've been doing more than just reminiscing."

Wolf shrugged.

"I remember that we handled it promptly and smoothly. An easy matter. But I was wondering if you remembered what our old boss, Mielke, said he was going to do with that file? Because, well, I'll confess, his action of personally taking charge of things made me believe that maybe this was a bigger item than we had thought. Or connected to something bigger, anyway."

"Yes, that's possible."

"Did Mielke say he was handing the materials over to them?"

"To the KGB?"

"Yes."

Emil thought about it for a minute.

"I don't think so. I don't recall him saying he was going to give it to anyone."

"Then why didn't he just let your people file it as a matter of course, along with our other materials in the American section?"

A good question. Emil took a long swig of beer and thought it over. He also thought a little about Markus Wolf, and his sudden interest in this "bit of housekeeping," as he had just described it. And with his memory astir, Emil now had a hazy sense that something other than the location of the dead drop had ended up in the file. Something quite valuable, perhaps, even if he couldn't recall exactly what. Besides, at the moment he was more interested in figuring out what Wolf was really up to.

Emil knew plenty about the man and his motivations, but the two most salient details with regard to Wolf's current state of mind seemed to be that, one, he was deeply disappointed with how he had recently been treated by the Russians, and, two, he had begun meeting secretly with his old foes, the Americans.

In that context, Wolf's reason for wanting to know more about an item like this seemed all too obvious—as a means of either prodding his old friends to treat him better, or of spurning them by helping the Americans. Since neither option would involve betraying his own agents, Wolf would feel perfectly justified in taking either course of action.

But the KGB had never responded well to being leveraged in that way. They almost certainly wouldn't like it in this case, even if the instigator was their homegrown German, the former wunderkind Mischa Wolf. While Emil doubted they would go so far as to squash him like a bug on their windshield, he doubted seriously they would respond in the way Wolf wanted, by applying pressure on his behalf with the West Germans.

That left the other option.

Giving the Americans the possible key to a potentially important Russian asset working in the Washington area, well, that could be valuable indeed, especially if it helped Wolf earn a new, clean-washed future somewhere in the West, free from prosecution and economic worries.

But why give it to Wolf, when Emil needed it more?

"Well?"

"I'm sorry, Mischa. I'm drawing a blank. It was a difficult time for me, as you remember, and . . ."

"Yes, yes. Of course. But did Mielke at least say whether he planned on keeping the file? Did he offer any possible hint of its destination?"

"As I said, it's a blank, almost everything from that period. But maybe if you knew some of the possible destinations, it might jog my memory."

Wolf waved away the suggestion and finally drank some beer, but only a single swallow. He was here to retrieve information, not dispense it. A one-way street, which had always been his preference. Emil was reminded of one of the reasons why Wolf's reputation had sometimes bred resentment among his colleagues. He was a hoarder, stingy with the good stuff, and stingier still with any credit due for the HVA's operational successes.

But this time Wolf was at a disadvantage. Obviously, he badly wanted this item. So, maybe, just this once, he would have to give some to get some. Or that was Emil's thinking as he polished off the last of his beer.

Rudi the bartender looked over. Wolf shook his head. No second round, then. Emil supposed it was now or never, but there was no way he was giving up anything further unless he got something first.

Wolf took another sip of beer, then leaned across the table, coming even closer than before. There was an intense look in his eye, and his voice emerged in a whisper.

"Did Mielke perhaps happen to say anything to you then about the Bülowplatz materials?"

"Bülowplatz materials?"

"Yes. They were a personal holding of his. He kept them in a safe. In his villa."

"At Waldsiedlung?"

"Of course."

"No. He made no mention of Bülowplatz. In fact . . ." Emil let his voice trail off. He gazed toward the bar, as if lost in thought.

"Now I remember!"

"Wunderbar!"

"He said he was sending the file to be shredded, that very afternoon. In fact, he said he was going to deliver the file himself, and then personally witness its destruction. As a favor to our comrades in Moscow, he said."

"You're certain of this?"

"Quite certain. Thank you, Mischa. I never would have recalled it without your help. But, yes, that's what he did. So if the idea of that file still floating around somewhere unsecured has been keeping you awake at night, well, rest easy. It was taken care of."

"Yes." Wolf smiled weakly. "We should all be thankful for that."

Wolf slumped back into his seat, his eyes no longer alive with hope. Then he checked his watch. His beer glass was still nearly full, but he was ready to leave.

So was Emil, because he now had the means to possible salvation, even though it was quite a long shot, and would certainly involve difficult and even dangerous actions. He at last knew what his big boss Erich Mielke had been talking about all those years ago when he had angrily come straight to Emil's desk to demand the file. And he knew because now he remembered their conversation perfectly.

"Of course, sir," Emil had said, already reaching into a drawer to retrieve the file in question. "For transport to our comrades, sir, or for destruction?"

"No, no. Neither of those."

Mielke had then grinned like a mischievous boy keeping a secret from the teacher. "This is a Bülowplatz matter, Grimm."

"Bülowplatz, sir?"

"Yes. And that's all you will ever need to know about it."

So Emil, with no idea at the time of what that meant, had handed him the file, and Mielke had carried it away. And now, thanks to Wolf, Emil knew that this possible key to the identity of a KGB asset, operating somewhere near the heart of the U.S. government, could be found locked in a safe inside Mielke's empty villa in the piney woods of Waldsiedlung.

That was less than ten miles from where he and Wolf now sat. The question, then, was how to acquire it, safely, and without being caught.

A tough question, indeed. But Emil was already working on an answer.

41

Tacheles was a revelation, a glimpse forward at the freewheeling East Berlin that might yet rise from the crumbling gray ruins of the old one. Claire saw right away why Emil Grimm had chosen it as their meeting site. Already it had become a squatter's paradise, and most of the new inhabitants were artists from across Germany and Western Europe. Looking for suspicious characters? Take your pick. Everyone here seemed worthy of curiosity, and, as Grimm had foretold, almost all of them were speaking English. Claire and Grimm wouldn't merit a second look.

The massive five-story building seemed on the verge of collapse. Long ago it had been a department store, a vibrant center of commerce in the city's Jewish quarter. Then the Nazis had taken away the Jews, and bombs and artillery shells had blown apart the store. In the forty-five ensuing years the East German government had done virtually nothing to restore either, although a grandly domed synagogue just down the block had been rebuilt and was looking almost as good as new.

At Tacheles, on the other hand, much of the rear wall was still missing. The rooms along the back were open-air chambers gaping onto a vast dirt lot. Claire easily spotted Grimm, who stood in the open archway of the passage connecting Oranienburger Strasse to the dirt lot out back, where artists had already piled up plenty of items for their own use—scrap metal, junked cars, planks of wood.

Ron Kent was there, too, posted off to the side of the lot as he kept a watchful eye on her and everyone else.

Claire lingered in the empty lot, deciding to let Grimm come to her. He was bareheaded today, his graying hair looking more unruly than ever in the light breeze. She listened as a couple of nearby artists argued about which of them was going to take up residence in one of the open-air rooms looming above.

Grimm sauntered up to them, as if preparing to add his own opinion, then, pretending to notice Claire for the first time, he arched his eyebrows and walked over.

"I see your new boy over there, eyeing me from across the way. Didn't expect to see the older one again, though. He looked a little tired. But I'm guessing he's been around the block a few more times than even me."

Baucom was here? It was news to Claire, but she tried not to show her surprise. How had he even found out about this meeting?

"Should we go upstairs to one of those, well . . ."

"Studios, I believe they're calling them. Or ateliers, if you're inclined to be snooty. Complete with running water, straight from the sky. That's a joke I heard one of them telling. No, we'll be fine right out here. The authorities, such as they are anymore, are scared to death of these people, mostly because they have no idea what to make of them."

The two arguing artists had apparently settled their dispute. Now a taller man named Martin was berating a grizzled young fellow with a beard over his treatment of a nearby woman with an orange buzz cut and torn purple tights. The woman, named Griselde, didn't seem the least bit perturbed by either man, perhaps because she was smoking a hand-rolled joint as big as a cigar.

Claire was still a little off balance from learning that Baucom was on the premises, although she supposed he would at least be serving as an extra lookout for any interlopers in black leather. To her dismay, Grimm wasn't carrying any sort of bag or parcel. Maybe he had only come to beg for more time.

"I was hoping you'd brought something new for me. Because I have to warn you, my superiors are short on patience. They've decided it's a buyer's market, so if you're going to give them an upgrade it had better be soon. Preferably now."

"Oh, I have an upgrade, all right. But first I have a question about your meeting the other day with Wolf. Did he promise you something as well, perhaps? Or at least the possibility of something? Particularly with regard to a Russian asset who might yet be operating on American soil?"

It was an impressive question, freighted with all sorts of interesting possibilities.

"No. He didn't. But . . ."

"What?"

Should she tell him? Probably not. *Certainly* not. But she did, if only because she disliked and feared his Russian competitors as much as he seemed to.

"The whole reason Wolf wanted to meet us, or so he said, was that he'd gotten a back-channel invitation for a visit from someone quite high in the Agency, maybe even director level, and he was hoping we could tell him what they wanted from him."

"Could you? Did you?"

"Only in the most general sense."

"And?"

"Understand, I'm only telling you this because it follows so naturally from your question. But apparently they want to ask him if he knows of any Russian assets—one in particular—working within our organization."

"A mole, then. Inside the CIA, possibly at headquarters."

"Yes."

"Then what I have for you may be valuable indeed. Especially if, as I suspect, our mutual friend Kolkachev is merely offering something false, intended to lead you astray."

"Because he works in counterintelligence, you mean."

"Precisely. It's his nature to misdirect the opposition. And if he can make a small fortune while doing so, and also while giving you our agent files as his sole authentic offering, all the better for him and for the KGB."

"Unless, of course, he's the real deal, a possible defector in place. In which case, you'll need to up the ante. So what's your contribution?"

"The location of a dead drop near Washington, and a file about a small operation to service it that our people carried out several years ago. They cleared the box when our Russian friends were unable to do so, presumably due to some sort of crisis. All of which leads me to believe that it is, or was, a favored communications point for this asset."

"Interesting. But that would only be valuable if the asset is still using it."

"My thoughts as well. Then I recalled this morning that in carrying out this task our people on the ground also took the liberty of making a copy of the items they collected at the dead drop. Not because our comrades asked us to, but because that is what spies do. Only a few documents were involved, and while I don't recall their substance, I do remember they came with the usual trappings of office correspondence, including a circulation list of names. One document only had four names, total. Those copies also went into the file. So if you're looking to narrow the field of suspects, well . . ."

"Added value indeed."

"Pleased to know you agree."

"Then let's have it."

"Gladly. As soon as I have obtained it, with your help."

"There's always a catch."

"Only a small one. Although it will involve night work."

"Which night are we speaking of?"

"This one. Very late. But if you agree to this, I can put the item in your hands before the sun rises, at a safe location where you can help me exit safely and securely."

"That's more than a small favor."

"Perhaps. But I'll be doing the hard part." He glanced back to where Ron Kent was now drifting along, some thirty yards in their wake. "All you'll have to do is wait in the woods for an hour or so while I retrieve the item. You can even stay in your car, if you like, although don't bring that silly Trabi, which fools no one. The place I've marked will provide ample cover even for a Mercedes."

"So you brought me a map?"

"And instructions."

He pulled a folded sheet of paper from his pocket and casually handed it to her. She immediately put it in her purse as they continued to stroll the grounds. They were approaching a sandy area where two bearded young men in jeans and wool sweaters were working with shovels to bury an old Trabant at a forty-five-degree angle. Claire was guessing they'd end up calling it an art installation.

"Will your lady friend be helping?"

"Don't ask about her."

His reply was curt, a little chilly. Her hunch had been correct, then. The connection was both personal and professional.

"I'll have to ask permission, of course. From my superiors."

"When you do, also mention that I don't expect you to arrive empty-handed."

"Money?"

"Not important, or not yet. I know there was a price mentioned earlier, but the greater urgency is for two passports. West German."

"Only two?"

"I have my own set of documents available for this sort of thing, and they are still current. What's important is that you bring me two West German passports using these photos, names, and dates."

He handed her another folded paper, which also went straight into her purse.

"I will also expect your Agency's assistance in putting these passports to use, and in providing us with accommodations during our transition to another life."

"And you want these passports tonight? That's asking a lot."

"It is, but I know from experience that your people are capable of it, just as ours were. With the proper sense of urgency, almost anything is possible in our business. I suggest that you be in place by four in the morning. That gives you plenty of time to get this done."

"You'll get no argument from me."

"So it's your superiors that are the problem? The ones who have fallen in love with Kolkachev?"

"Yes, but maybe this will turn their heads. Maybe I'll also pass along your observation about how much he would enjoy stringing us along. Come what may, I expect you'll be seeing me, late tonight."

"Do not arrive empty-handed."

"I don't intend to."

"That isn't exactly a promise."

"I'm aware of that."

Then, as if to at least acknowledge her honesty, he tilted his head and gestured with his hand as if tipping a cap, before turning to walk away, off toward the archway where she had first seen him. Thirty yards to her right, Claire now saw Ron Kent standing behind the buried car, pretending to admire it even as he watched Grimm intently, as if memorizing every feature.

42

Once Baucom determined that the area was free of any dangerous interlopers, he eased into his chosen hiding place and waited for the main characters to assemble on the stage. Following Emil Grimm to the scene had been a snap once he spotted the incoming Wartburg, again driven by the woman, although he was pretty sure Grimm had spotted him once they were on foot. No matter, he supposed. It hadn't seemed to have scared the fellow away.

Already he had enjoyed a chuckle or two about this strange and wondrous place called Tacheles. Indeed, the whole neighborhood had been a pleasant surprise. It was being colonized by young people of all ilks, chatty and on the make. Just across the street, an opportunistic tavernkeeper had taken possession of a vacant fruit and vegetable market, with its old name still displayed on the faded sign, *Obst und Gemüse*. Spartan furnishings but plenty of customers, and not one of them looked over thirty. The atmosphere reminded him fondly of a trip to Greenwich Village in the late '50s, when he was in his twenties and the Beatniks ruled the streets, enlivening every block with their music, their lingo, their quirky little bars and coffeehouses. This had a similar vibe, full of promise and pretension. Maybe the Germans would finally get it right. God knows they were long overdue.

He climbed the crumbling stairway toward a higher vantage point. A waif of a girl on her way downstairs, not even twenty, eyed him curiously as he approached. And why not, because he was the oddball here. His overcoat and gray flannel trousers marked him as a stuffy leftover of the establishment, whether East or West. Although his French cigarettes fit right in, so he offered one in passing.

"Danke," she said, then quickly added, "Thank you."

He grunted in reply, climbed two floors, and stepped out onto a ragged precipice of dusty concrete, into a room that had probably been exposed to the elements since some horrible night of bombing in 1945.

Scanning the grounds, he quickly spotted Claire, already in conversation with Grimm. No goons in sight, but Ron Kent was almost directly below, lagging back to observe. Only a few hours ago Baucom had again heard from his old colleague, the baseball scout, who'd offered a full report on Kent. The results were reassuring. Claire had a competent partner, high marks across the board. Perhaps, then, it was time for Baucom to let go. Maybe he was only still in it for the fun, the cheap thrill of lurking on the fringes of something secretive, and possibly quite important.

Then he contemplated the ease with which a trio of KGB thugs, mobbed up or not, could bring trouble and mayhem to a placid field of play like this one, and decided he'd stick with it for another day or two. Then he'd quit the game for good. Scout's honor.

He smiled, lit another cigarette, and eased back into the shadows.

43

Claire did the driving on the way back. The mood in their borrowed Trabant was upbeat. She and Ron Kent had agreed that this was a potentially exciting breakthrough, not just for them but for the Agency. Better still, to Claire's mind, Ron seemed fully on board with the need to sell Lindsey Ward on the idea of following Emil Grimm's instructions for a wee-hours rendezvous on hostile ground. Because without his endorsement, Claire doubted Ward would ever go along with it.

But she was not naïve enough to believe he had shifted his loyalty. It still annoyed her that he continued to refer to Ward as "Lindsey," like they were old buddies. He'd also been taking notes after they got back into the car, and the few words she'd seen were descriptive terms that applied to Grimm. Even if she continued to hoard the German's identity, Kent's work might yet unveil it.

He was a little too silent for comfort as they headed back to Berlin base.

"What's wrong, Ron? You seem preoccupied."

"Oh. Well." He hesitated. "Tell me, did you, or maybe even Lindsey, arrange for any, well, extra help back there?"

Had he, too, seen Baucom? Would he even have known who Baucom was? If so, was she now in trouble? At least this time, she didn't have to lie about it.

"Absolutely not. And I doubt Ward would have done it without telling you. Why?"

He shook his head.

"Just a feeling. Probably nothing."

"Grimm definitely saw you, if that's what you mean."

"No. Someone who looked American. A man."

Claire suppressed a smile. Naughty Baucom. She almost wished that she *had* asked him to keep working on her behalf. The idea of Ron and her waiting for hours in the woods of East Germany for a delivery that might never happen was a little daunting.

She suspected that Grimm and his driver, the woman, were also on their own. Why else would he need their help tonight? The man was shorthanded. They were, too. The Russian had more resources, and perhaps a genuinely better offer. Why, then, did it still feel imperative that she and her contact win? She had personalized the fight, which could be dangerous in itself.

Kent was now looking at the two passport-sized photos Grimm had given her. One of them was of the woman who had driven the Wartburg, so obviously there was a personal connection. The second photo was also of a woman. Their last names—obvious fakes—were different.

"Too bad he didn't include one of himself," Kent said.

"You think Ward has someone who could identify him from a photo?"

Kent shrugged. She suspected he knew more than he was willing to say. He again lapsed into silence. Maybe he, too, was worried about tonight.

"What do you think of these instructions?" she asked. "This map he drew for us?"

"Risky. A little slapdash. I get the idea he's smart, but that he's always been a desk man. And now he's having to do everything himself and plan it on the fly."

"Yeah. Same here."

She was about to add that his title and previous duties certainly supported that assessment, but that would show she knew his name. She hoped she wasn't letting the German play her. Or not inadvisedly so. But, more so, she hoped that he and the two women would at least manage to survive this affair, and she wasn't at all sure she could help him with that. Officially, it wasn't even her role to try. Unofficially? She would do her best, even if his offer fell short.

To her right, Kent was again scribbling notes, this time with the pages angled so that she couldn't see them.

44

Emil hiked slowly through the woods. Soon he would commence his long night of darkness and confinement—ten hours without light, fresh air, or freedom of movement—so he wasn't in a hurry to get under way. He was also worried about what the morning would bring. Capture and arrest? A violent and agonizing end, like the ones that had befallen Lothar Fischer and Andreas Plotz?

But what was the alternative? Wait for Volkov to come for him? Or, even if that threat passed, the federal prosecutors from Bonn? He trudged onward.

Emil had set his plan in motion the night before, on the way home from the bar, when he had asked Wolf to drop him off shortly after the Volvo turned onto the dirt lane by the Bauersee.

"Let me out here, if you don't mind."

"Here? It's at least another four hundred meters to your dacha."

"I need the exercise after all that beer, or I'll never sleep properly."

Wolf sighed and braked the car.

"Very well. Age does it to all of us, I suppose."

Emil climbed out and waved farewell. Wolf eyed him curiously before shutting the door, as if certain that there had to be more to this than a need for exercise.

"Goodbye, then, Emil."

The words had a ring of finality. Or maybe Emil only felt that way because he knew what he was about to do next.

"Goodbye, Mischa."

As soon as Wolf's taillights winked out of sight, he turned in the opposite direction. Fifteen minutes later he reached Prenden, where he took the spare key from beneath a flowerpot and let himself into Karola's empty house. He made his way carefully to the kitchen without turning on a single light, located the telephone, and felt his way around the rotary dial until his forefinger reached the right slots. Karola would not begrudge him this clandestine use of her house, but she certainly would object to his reason for doing so. Emil was here because he needed to make a call that would not be overheard by either of the two women in his life. The hiss and click of the turning dial were the only sounds in the house until someone picked up at the other end.

"Hallo?"

"Moritz? Grimm here. Hope I'm not disturbing you."

"No, no. My wife is out with her sewing circle, which means what they're really doing is drinking a lot of wine. So I'm having a rare night of controlling the television. Let me turn it down."

Emil heard the blare of a car chase. It was a scene from the same cheesy movie that had been playing in the bar.

"There. What can I do for you, Emil?"

"A big favor, actually, so it's probably good your wife isn't there to listen."

"I see." A long pause. "Well, if it weren't for you . . ."

Emil had known that would be his reaction, because Moritz Waldman was that kind of fellow, one who never forgot a favor—or, in this case, a break that had gone his way after Emil had helped him. Long ago he had been the handyman at Emil's apartment building on Frankfurter Allee. For any kind of problem—plumbing, wiring, heating, television repair, even carpet cleaning and upholstery—Moritz solved it, quickly and competently. So when Emil heard that the powers-that-be at Waldsiedlung, the party elite's wooded refuge north of the city, were looking for just such a person, he had recommended Moritz without reservation, even though it was a loss for him and his neighbors. Moritz got a hefty raise and all sorts of new privileges, and Emil got a reliable source for the doings at the compound. In the waning years of the regime, Emil had begun to feel like that was almost as important as having a good source at NATO. Had that been prescience? No, more like disillusionment, he supposed.

"You can still say no if you like, Moritz, I hope you know that."

Emil said it because he knew it would only add to Moritz's sense of obligation.

"I understand, Emil. That's one reason I always liked working for you. Maybe you should just tell me what you need."

So Emil did.

Moritz asked a few questions and concluded that his role wasn't all that difficult, mostly because Emil would be taking the bigger risks, and by that time Moritz would be safely in his bed. He agreed to do it.

Now, twenty hours later, Emil was on his way to the parking turnout a mile from his dacha, heading down the trail at dusk after having sent Karola to the market. When she returned, she wouldn't know where he had gone.

He also hadn't told Bettina about his plans or his destination. He had kissed her and said, "I am leaving the house for a while. I will be gone for most of the night, maybe all of it. I haven't told Karola about this either, because matters have progressed to the point where it has become too risky to involve her further. She'll be back from the market in half an hour. I am not taking the car, so if anyone comes later to watch the house, they will believe I am here, which will be safer for you. All right?"

Bettina blinked once, but her eyes widened in alarm. He took her hand.

"I will return by morning. Even though I just mentioned risk, nothing that I will be doing tonight is inherently dangerous. Nor will I be crossing paths with any of the Russians. I am confident things will go well."

He kissed her again, then exited through his own room, where he took his coat from the hook and the Pistol-M from the sock drawer before leaving the house. He was relieved to see that there was still no Citroën parked along the lane. Maybe Dorn's lecture to Krauss, no matter how ill-advised, had helped.

Now Emil was approaching the place where Moritz was supposed to be waiting. His biggest worry was that Moritz wouldn't show. That would be the end of things, he supposed. And the Americans would never forgive him, because they'd wait for him until dawn, and go home empty-handed.

Then his heart lifted, because up through the pines he saw the blue-and-white panels of Moritz's repair van parked at the turnout, and then Moritz himself, smoking as he stood beneath the trees.

The van was a Barkas B 1000, of course, because that was pretty much the only van an East German could get. It was an unfortunate choice for Emil, all the same, because the Stasi had used a modified Barkas as a collection vehicle to round up troublesome citizens for interrogation, detention, or worse—something he would prefer to forget.

"Moritz. Right on time as always. Thank you for doing this."

Moritz shrugged and tossed aside his cigarette. Emil climbed in. He felt a little awkward because the man hadn't yet spoken. They looked at each other as Moritz slid the key into the ignition.

"I assure you, Moritz, that after tonight I will never again mention this episode. To you or to anyone."

"I know, boss. You're a man of your word, so I'm not worried. Really. And I didn't tell my wife, of course."

"Good man."

"Like I said on the phone, the whole place has pretty much emptied out, what with all the bad press it's been getting, and, well, all the rest."

"Yes. All the rest."

The bad press was a reference to newspaper stories that began appearing only a few weeks after the Wall came down, breathless exposés about the untold luxuries of the hideaway homes of Waldsiedlung, with their sleek bathroom fixtures, modernized kitchens, priceless art plundered from national museums, and—gasp!—cable television hookups with access to all channels from the West.

Emil found it a bit laughable. Waldsiedlung had twenty-three houses in all, and nearly all of them looked the same—plain, two-story stucco homes on half-acre lots, lined up neatly on three wooded lanes. But even that could seem quite regal, he supposed, if you and your neighbors were crammed into bleak apartments that were too cold in the winter and too hot in the summer, and you had to wait years just to buy a crappy Trabant.

There were also plenty of perks—a health spa with tennis courts and a swimming pool, a private restaurant, a shooting range, a movie theater, a hotel for honored guests, and barracks for all of the maids, cooks, and servants, although Moritz had kept his old apartment in

Pankow. Surrounding the ample acreage was an inner fence that kept out even the residents of the barracks. On a wider perimeter there was an outer wall topped with barbed wire, set well off into the trees.

Emil had been there for a few party cookouts, official gatherings where you were supposed to relax, even though the laughter was always an octave higher than normal. He always woke up the next morning with a headache, and not from a hangover. But to his mind, the most distasteful aspect of the place was its origins. Party officials had built it in 1953, well before the Wall went up, after riots by dissatisfied work-ers that year in Berlin had convinced them of the need for their own Winter Palace in the woods, a refuge where they'd be able to ride out any future insurrection. A lot of good that had done them.

"Anyone still living there?" Emil asked. "I know Mielke is in jail, and Honecker is holed up in some vicarage in Bernau. But what about the party chiefs, the heads of the ministries, the leaders of the Politburo?"

"All gone except for one or two, and even they're under house arrest, so I hardly ever see anyone unless they call me to make a repair. You should be fine. Almost all of the guards are gone now that there's no one left to protect. The security people still have me checking on everything, of course. They don't want any frozen pipes ruining the houses, or leaky roofs or any of that. There's been talk about turning the place into a recovery campus for the disabled."

"Well, I hope you'll still have a job, at least."

Moritz shrugged, his future as uncertain as everyone else's.

"I tell you one thing that's a shame."

"Yes?"

"All of that choice wine and liquor that's impounded in those houses. So if you're going to take something out of there tonight, get some for me."

Moritz laughed uneasily, as if only now he was realizing that he might be abetting an act of grand larceny against the state.

"I'm not doing this for personal enrichment, Moritz. I can assure you of that. But that does remind me, did you bring the tools I needed?"

"They're in the back, under the tarp. There's also an extension cord. I didn't have the right blade, so I bought one and installed it. Twenty West German marks."

"I'll reimburse you for it, of course."

"You wouldn't happen to have it on you now, would you?"

The message was clear: Pay now, in case you're caught. Emil got out his wallet and handed over twenty D-marks, some of the last of his welcome money.

"Have you decided how you'll explain leaving behind the van?"

"Relax, Emil. These people trust me. They also know this Barkas is a piece of shit that is always breaking down from one thing or another, and they know I don't even have a spare. It will all seem perfectly normal. I'll leave it parked exactly where you asked, and I'll walk to the guardhouse, where I'll use the phone to call my wife for a ride."

"Yes. That's good. And now I'll forget you ever told me that."

Moritz sighed and shook his head. For a fraught moment he seemed ready to stop the van. He looked straight ahead as they drove onward another mile or so, hands clamped tightly to the wheel. Then his hands relaxed, and he turned to Emil again.

"It's not much further to the guardhouse. Maybe you'd better get ready."

Emil nodded and clambered into the back, where the tarp was already spread on the cold metal floor next to a massive toolbox and a pile of clamps, a stepladder, and other items. When Emil threw back the tarp, he saw the circular saw that he had asked Moritz to bring, and its shiny new blade. He lay down as the van bumped through a pothole, his hips already uncomfortable against the hardness of the floor.

"Thank you again, Moritz."

"Please. The less said, the better."

Emil lay down and threw the tarp across his body. It was dark and musty underneath, smelling of paint and machine oil.

A few minutes later they came to a stop. He heard Moritz rolling down his window, and, even beneath the tarp, felt the coolness of the outside air as it spilled into the van. Emil briefly heard a radio playing American music as someone opened and shut the door of the guardhouse. There were footsteps across gravel, followed by the loud voice of a sentry, raspy and collegial.

"Back for more punishment, comrade?"

"Checking the plumbing at some of the houses down at the far end." Emil heard a shuffle of papers, as if Moritz was consulting a job order. "Nörden's house, then Naumann's, then Mielke's."

"I'll get you the keys."

There was a pause as the sentry went back into the guardhouse, then a jangling noise as he returned and handed Moritz the sets of keys for each of the three houses.

"Bring me back a bottle of schnapps, if you think of it. I think Naumann has a particularly nice brand."

The two men laughed. Emil heard the squeal and creak of heavy metal joints as the iron security gate rolled open.

Moritz shut his window, they eased forward, and, after a couple of twists and turns that took only a few minutes, the van stopped and the engine shut off. Moritz climbed out and slammed the door behind him without uttering a word. Not long afterward, Emil heard the hiss of air being released from the right rear tire. That side of the van sagged beneath him.

Then, silence. It was already dark beneath the tarp, but in another hour or so it would be dark outside. He had set the alarm on his cheap watch for 3 a.m., so he rolled onto his back and tried to relax. Nearly ten more hours.

Emil began feeling a little sorry for himself, until it hit him that this was Bettina's life, each and every day, and with every waking moment. Only in her dreams, or when they bathed her, or wheeled her outdoors for a walk, or perhaps also when he read to her, did she ever escape this sense of confinement. It was like living in a room-sized tomb, with your body for a coffin.

The best escape from these thoughts would be to sleep. But it was cold, the floor was hard, and his bones were already aching. Emil vowed that after tonight, he would read more to Bettina. He would take her for more walks, even though she had to be strapped into the chair, which looked horrible, and the paths were bumpy. She would shiver in the winter cold, but now he realized that for her even that level of discomfort was at least a respite from this sort of existence. So, yes, after tonight he would do more. Provided, of course, that there *was* an after.

Emil had brought a water bottle, but he decided not to drink any, not yet, because then he'd need to pee. He went still and shut his eyes, but it was hours before he was able to sleep.

45

Shortly after sunset, at a little before 6 p.m., Claire sat on the end of the bed in her hotel room, watching an American movie dubbed into German while she waited impatiently for Ron Kent, who was in turn awaiting delivery at Berlin base of the two West German passports requested by Emil Grimm.

She was eager to get under way, figuring that the later they crossed over, the more likely they were to attract unwanted attention, especially if the Russians were still keeping an eye on some of the old checkpoints, as Ward seemed to believe.

There was a small overnight bag at her feet. Their plan was to check in to an inn near Bernau that they had already identified as a safe spot for a brief wait, partly because it had a rear exit onto an alley. They would park in an underground garage several blocks away, eat dinner at a nearby restaurant, return to their room, and then wait until a few hours after midnight, when they would slink quietly out the back and walk to the garage before driving off into the night, via back roads, to the dirt lane in the woods where Grimm had said they should wait for him. The only irritating wrinkle in their plans was that Kent would maintain control over the passports. He alone would decide if Grimm's contribution merited payment. That had been the decree from Ward, who obviously felt Claire had gone soft on the old East German. She was right, but it rankled all the same.

The phone rang.

"Miss Walker?" It was the name she was registered under, complete with her own set of false documents and a credit card on which she was running her tab for both the room and the downstairs bar.

"Yes?"

"Someone has left a note for you at the front desk. Shall I have someone bring it up?"

"I'll get it myself. Be right down."

"Thank you."

She switched off the TV. Should she take her bag? No, because this wasn't the drill they'd agreed upon. Kent was due to arrive at any moment, but he was supposed to announce himself to the front desk as a personal visitor, Mr. Andrews. The desk would then summon her downstairs. Had he changed their plans on the fly?

Moments later she approached the front desk.

"I'm Miss Walker. You called about a note?"

The desk clerk was a German woman in her early thirties, crisp and businesslike in her movements, with a ready smile for the clientele. She turned and took an envelope from a slot with Claire's room number.

"Here you are. An older man dropped it off just a moment ago."

Grimm, perhaps? Was he canceling on them?

"Thank you."

She took the envelope, impatiently rode the elevator back upstairs, and, in an excess of caution, took it into the bathroom to open it. Enclosed was a page of blank stationery, nearly filled with handwritten English, cursive. There was no signature, but she knew right away it had come from Baucom.

Her first thought was that he was becoming entirely too intrusive. First, he'd shown up uninvited at Tacheles, and now this, when he might easily have crossed paths with Ron Kent, raising all sorts of unwanted questions.

As she carefully read the message, her assessment shifted. Useful information, she supposed, and reassuring.

It was a summary of Ron Kent's career. Top of his class at the Farm, high marks across the board ever since. Ward's protégé for sure, but not what you'd call a yes-man. She liked him, too. Under other circumstances they might even have become friends. She realized that now as she was reading.

Fifteen minutes later the phone rang again.

"Miss Walker? Sorry to disturb you again, but there's a visitor here. A Mr. Andrews?"

"Tell him I'll be right down."

She picked up her overnight bag, shut off the light, and headed for the elevators.

It was time to cross over. A night on hostile ground loomed, with an appointment in the forest set for around 4 a.m. She hoped Emil Grimm wouldn't keep them waiting.

46

Maybe the Barkas van was to blame. Not the discomfort of its cold, hard floor as much as its track record as a Stasi vehicle of doom. Emil's nerves also played a role, no doubt, especially in the absolute darkness of the haunted location, tucked among the homes and trees that had once sheltered the overlords of this fallen kingdom.

Whatever the dark alchemy of that tormented night, at some point Emil slipped into a dream that may have been no dream at all, a recapitulation of his most shameful moment as a servant of the state. He watched it play out in that half-conscious state between wakefulness and sleep. Later he couldn't have said for sure whether his eyes were open or closed, only that everything was as vivid as the day it had happened, five years earlier.

The whole episode had begun with a chance encounter in the corridors of Normanenstrasse, when a colleague from internal security, Klug, had stepped off the paternoster and drawn him aside. The subject was Emil's neighbor, Frau Holbein, mother of two, the same woman whom Emil had recently taken pains to avoid when he had sneaked back into his old apartment on Frankfurter Allee.

On the day Klug accosted him, Emil and Bettina were happy and healthy, facing a cloudless horizon. Professionally, Emil's star was on the rise.

"Magda Holbein, you mean? She's not in trouble, I hope?"

"No, no. It's what she's been saying lately. About your wife."

"Bettina?"

"Yes. Nothing terrible really, but—"

"Wait a minute. Saying to whom?"

"Her, well . . ."

"Her reporting officer?"

Klug nodded.

"I see. So Magda's an informant."

"A careful citizen, yes, doing her duty. But perhaps a little overzealous, so I thought you should know. Supposedly she's in some social club with your wife?"

"Yes, in our building. They play cards, swap stories. The women bring their children, and that's one reason Bettina goes. She enjoys seeing all the kids playing in the other room."

What Emil didn't add was that Magda Holbein was one of Bettina's least favorite neighbors, even though she adored the Holbein children. Bettina had told him Magda was a shameless gossip, a busybody. She would smile at you in the morning and trash you to the neighbors an hour later. So he wasn't at all surprised to learn she was an informant.

"Apparently your wife is quite outspoken at these gatherings. Or has been lately. Something about criticizing the State Planning Commission for not building enough bakeries, which then led to a joke about our party's general secretary."

"Honecker?"

Klug looked around nervously, as if worried they'd be overheard.

"Yes."

"As you said yourself, it was a joke. We've probably heard worse in our cafeteria."

"Of course, but now it's in her file. And, by implication, part of yours, so you might have a word. Maybe tell your wife to moderate her words. At least whenever she's around this neighbor of yours."

Emil had considered doing exactly that. But by the time he got home that night he couldn't bring himself to do it, or even tell her about the report, not when Bettina was so personable and well-meaning, a helpful neighbor who gave treats to everyone's children, Magda's included. And she had already made the sacrifice of cutting off all contact with members of her family in the West. No, it wasn't fair, and the more he thought about it, the angrier he got. So instead he made a few calls, and then he waited. Two days later, the phone rang on his desk.

"The Barkas arrived outside her apartment half an hour ago, sir. She was with her children at the playground. She's now on her way."

"To Hohenschönhausen?"

"Yes."

"How long before she arrives?"

"The route is twenty minutes, but they always like to drive them around a few hours while they're blindfolded and don't know where they're going."

"I see." He'd known that, but the reminder was a little jarring.

"And on arrival, of course, they'll give her a strip search and put her in a jumpsuit."

Then, as he also knew, they would put her in a cell where she would have to sit perfectly still while they watched her through a slot in the door.

"So, when should I arrive? Two hours, maybe?"

"Make it four."

Emil had blanched a bit, but didn't raise an objection.

Hohenschönhausen Prison was the Stasi's main holding area for political criminals. It was, by design, a bleak and unwelcoming place. The cells doubled as interrogation chambers. Each was equipped with a narrow bed, a sink, and a toilet, and also a desk and an office chair for an interrogator. Uncertainty was one of Hohenschönhausen's most potent tools. Few arrivals even knew why they'd been brought there, and none knew how long they'd be staying. A few hours? Weeks? A lifetime?

That was the unsettled state of mind in which Emil found Magda Holbein when he arrived shortly after nightfall, accompanied by a guard. She wore a jumpsuit of the same bright blue as the warm-ups worn by East Germany's Olympic athletes. The resemblance was so striking that Emil half expected to see "DDR" printed in white across the back.

When he stepped into her cell she had her back to him, seated before the interrogator's desk in the mandatory waiting position, stiffly upright on a backless stool, palms wedged beneath her thighs. He wondered if she had yet been permitted to use the toilet.

Because she wasn't allowed to turn around without permission, she wouldn't know the identity of a visitor unless he spoke or moved into view. Emil cleared his throat and saw her flinch. He stepped into her field of vision and addressed her in a tone of fatherly concern.

"Magda? Is that really you, my friend?"

She turned sideways as he approached, which prompted a shout from the guard.

"Face the front!"

"No, no," he told the guard. "That will not do. Leave the room while I speak to her."

The guard departed. Emil moved closer and offered her a water bottle, but she seemed reluctant to take it.

"Please. I know you must be thirsty. And sit over here, it will be much more comfortable."

He pulled the office chair from behind the desk and gestured for her to take it. She nodded, stood stiffly, gratefully sagged into it. As she unscrewed the cap on the water bottle, she lowered her head and began to sob.

"There, there, now." Emil patted her back. "This can only be the result of some terrible misunderstanding, yes?"

"I don't know," she said, gasping between sobs. "I really don't know. They came and took me in front of everyone, like an enemy of the state. My children were there! Our neighbors."

"Yes, I know. Bettina phoned me as soon as she heard. She was so upset for you. And for your children, of course. She pleaded with me to set things right. I came as soon as I could."

"But *why*? Why has this happened?"

"I am doing all I can to find out. I have made several phone calls, and I've talked to several people. And, well, I am still not sure if I can make heads or tails of it. But . . ." He let the phrase hang in the air.

"What? What have I done?"

"Well, I confess I don't know the meaning of this. Perhaps you will. But as best as I've been able to determine, you must have made some sort of inflammatory charge in one of your recent reports, to your security officer."

"Inflammatory?"

"As I said, it's a puzzle to me, because I am not privy to those reports. But it was suggested that perhaps you made an insinuation against someone of prominence, someone of unshakable reputation. Because, you see, even in our zeal to serve the state, we sometimes say impolitic things that have a damaging effect. Do you understand?"

"No. Or . . . maybe. But I'm not sure."

"Because, you see, these files that we keep. These records. They mean that any remarks of yours, no matter how insignificant, can never be erased. They are forever. And while one such error in judgment on your part might be forgivable, if it were ever to occur again, well, next time I'm not sure I would be able to assist you. Do you see?"

She spoke in a very small voice.

"Yes. I see."

"But let me see what I can do on your behalf. Usually I am reluctant to interfere in affairs of the state. It is only because my wife insisted that I am here at all. Although you will of course be best advised not to mention this to her or to anyone else. *No one.* Do you understand that as well?"

"Yes."

He nodded. She finally drank some water, which dribbled onto her chin. "When will they let me leave?"

"I do not know. Maybe in a few days? A week, perhaps? It is beyond my control."

She sobbed again. More tears fell.

"I will do my best to see that it is less."

"Oh, thank you. Thank you!"

She rose to her feet, wobbled, and then her eyes rolled back in her head as she started to collapse. Emil lunged forward to catch her, and she heaved against him awkwardly, causing him to stumble backward and twist his right knee so that it buckled beneath him as they fell in a heap to the floor.

The guard, hearing Emil's cry of pain, rushed back into the cell and reflexively raised his truncheon at the sight of an apparent struggle.

"No!" Emil said, fending off the blow with his left forearm. "Damn you!"

"Sorry, sir. But I thought—"

"Yes, I know what you thought. Help me put her into this bed."

She revived a few moments later. Emil again promised to do what he could on her behalf and then left, limping all the way to his car. Two days later they released her. Magda Holbein was never again a problem for Emil or Bettina. And when he next saw her, pushing her youngest child in a stroller around the same playground where they had snatched her up, the fear still lingered in her eyes.

In gratitude for her salvation, she baked them a cake, even though sugar and flour at that time had been as rare as spun gold. Later, of course, she must have figured out the whole thing, and from then on, even as Bettina's health deteriorated, she had remained cold, distant, disapproving.

But the greater impact had been upon Emil, and not just because of the lingering pain of his wrenched knee. On the drive home that night from Hohenschönhausen, he had felt the shame of his actions on him like a coating of sweat or grime. For days the smell of the prison had clung to his skin and hair, no matter how many times he showered. It was that episode, he now realized, that had tipped the balance of his doubts, convincing him irretrievably that the state he served had become corrupted beyond salvation, and that he had become a willing party to its inevitable decline.

Had he responded by pushing quietly for change or reform? No. He had simply buried himself deeper into his work, which blessedly dealt with foreign threats and enemies. Professionally, his star had continued to rise. But he had no longer been a believer in the mission of his ministry, of the party, of the state.

That was one reason he didn't take offense now when his old neighbors, or people like Dorn, no longer treated him with any special respect or regard. Was it irritating, humbling? Of course. But he supposed it was also their due, and his as well.

Now Emil was back at the heart of all those forces that had once controlled this country of his, an entity that would not even live to see its fiftieth birthday. He was alone with his memories and his nightmares, neither awake nor asleep.

Or so he thought until the tinny alarm on his cheap watch sounded, awakening him to the realization that it was 3 a.m. He threw off the tarp and sat up stiffly, his right knee aching like a taunt. Outside, an owl hooted in the pines.

Emil opened the water bottle, swallowed every drop, and sat in the silence of the van, steeling himself for what needed to be done. It was time to banish these ghosts. Time to set off into the night and get what he had come for.

47

Karola, too, was having a restless night. She and Bettina were angry and upset with Emil for deserting them, and for literally leaving them in the dark with regard to his latest plans. She had no idea where he could be, and worried that when the sun rose he would still be gone. Then what would she do?

As if all that weren't troubling enough, she had experienced a worrisome encounter at the market in Bernau. She'd been pushing her cart toward the checkout when she was waylaid by Florian Pieck.

Pieck, a lumbering fellow in his late fifties, had always been a meddlesome flirt, especially in the years since her husband's death. And because he was the forest ranger and de facto game warden for the woods around Prenden, their paths sometimes crossed whenever she attended community gatherings, hiked in the forest, or went shopping.

"Karola! What a pleasure!"

He wedged his cart in front of hers like a traffic policeman preparing to issue a citation. She plastered a smile in place and began looking for an escape route.

"Florian. Yes, a pleasant surprise, but I'm afraid I'm in a bit of a hurry this afternoon."

"Ah, well. Aren't we all, now that change is coming so fast? I still haven't heard if I will be retaining my ranger post, and of course everyone's hunting status will now have to be reviewed."

"Well, best of luck to you, but if I might just ease my cart around yours?"

"Oh, certainly. Excuse me."

He cleared the way. Then his words stopped her.

"By the way, are you still working for the Grimms? I was just fielding some inquiries about Emil's hunting rights, so I thought maybe you could pass them along."

She turned back around, her smile frozen in place.

"Yes. I am. What sort of inquiries?"

"From a fellow named Krauss. Said he was a colleague of Emil's."

"Of course." The angle of her smile slipped a few degrees.

"He'd first called about Lothar Fischer, the poor bastard. I only just heard what happened to him. A suicide, this Krauss fellow said."

"Yes. So sad."

"He said he was closing out some of Lothar's affairs as a favor to the family. Apparently the poor fellow's wife had no interest." He dropped his voice and shifted to an insinuating tone. "And we all know why that would be the case."

"Of course."

"Anyway, he asked about Lothar's hunting rights, and I mentioned that he and Emil had built their own shooting stand, which I remembered because I still have their plans on file, of course. And this seemed to interest him greatly. Especially when I told him about all the innovations they'd put into their design."

"Innovations?"

"Hidden places for storage, that even the boars couldn't get to. He was quite impressed. Just as I'd been. It's really the best stand in the district."

Karola gripped the handle of her cart so tightly that her knuckles whitened.

"I see."

"And, well, he indicated he might be interested in going in as Emil's new hunting partner. Although technically, of course, anyone may use that stand as long as they register first, during the legal hunting season."

"Of course."

"But in the meantime he wanted to see if the location would be suitable to his own needs. So he's coming by early tomorrow to look at my map, and the copy of their plans. So you might mention it to Emil if you happen to see him, in case he's already lined up someone else."

"Yes. I'd be happy to."

"And, well, if you thought you might be interested in dinner sometime, then . . ."

His voice faltered, but he again edged his cart forward. Karola used hers to bang it out of her path. She pushed onward to the checkout while calling out over her shoulder, "Let me think about that, Florian. I'll get back to you."

He nodded, crestfallen.

She had rushed back to the dacha to tell Emil, only to find his note. And now he was missing in action at the worst possible time, with Krauss on his way early the next morning. Bettina had reacted with alarm to the news, and the two women had agreed on the need for preemptive action. So Karola had done the best she could under the circumstances, but now her worries were running in an endless loop of thoughts about what the morning might bring for Emil, for Krauss, for all of them.

For several hours she couldn't settle to sleep. And every time she turned in Bettina's direction, she saw that her friend's eyes were also open, shining in the dark. Eventually she heard the steady, easy breathing that told her Bettina was finally asleep. And now, quite late, Karola was at last drifting toward joining her, as her own breathing slowed and steadied.

A skittering noise from overhead nearly brought her back to the surface—the damn squirrels and chipmunks, at it again in the rafters—but she continued to drift downward. A minute or two later, a heavier thump jolted her as well. Had a limb fallen from a tree? But by that time her weariness had tugged her so deeply that it didn't matter. The varmints could wait. Sleep could not.

Karola sank into oblivion. The overhead noises, quieter now, soon subsided.

48

Emil stooped beneath the cramped ceiling of the van and reached for the heavy circular saw. He lugged it to the back, unlatched the rear door, and then hopped awkwardly to the ground. He set down the saw, his right knee burning with pain.

The cold air was a welcome jolt to his senses. It smelled like pine needles. Far off in the trees, the owl hooted again, his companion for the night. The streets were empty of cars, and all the windows of the houses were dark. Emil hoped the Americans would soon be in position, waiting for him. He thought of Bettina and Karola, and felt badly about leaving them alone and unawares. But if all went well, he'd be seeing them in a few hours.

Moritz had parked the van between the last two houses on the outermost lane of the complex. Mielke's villa sat on the far corner, the most remote location, which seemed fitting because it meant no one here had been able to walk off into the woods without him seeing them pass.

It was a boxy two-story house with cream-colored stucco walls and a red tile roof. Windows of varying sizes were arrayed across the front, which gave it an ungainly look. Emil shut the door of the van as quietly as he could. He pulled a pair of garden gloves from his back pocket, slipped them on, picked up the saw, and then set off across the lawn, where he circled around to the back of Mielke's house.

Upstairs in the back, a terrace ran from end to end, with a railed barrier. On the ground floor there was a patio next to a sunroom with floor-to-ceiling windows. At the near end, a stone stairwell led belowground to a basement entrance that wasn't visible from the street. That's where Emil headed. Just as Moritz had promised, the heavy iron door at the bottom of the steps was propped open with a wedge of wood. Emil went in, tossed the wood aside, and shut the door behind him.

It was damp and dark, and smelled of mildew. A spiderweb brushed his face. Emil pulled a pencil-thin flashlight from his front pocket, switched on the narrow beam, and began to explore.

He stood in a one-room bunker, a place where Mielke and his wife would have taken shelter from a nuclear attack if they hadn't had time to flee to the bigger and cushier group bunker near Prenden. There were two narrow fold-up beds. A toilet and sink were in the corner. Dusty shelves were stacked with boxes of medical supplies, a Grundig shortwave radio, and lots of canned food. Emil wondered if anyone had remembered to also stock a can opener. But there was no sign of any safe, or of any documents.

He opened a door to an interior stairwell and climbed to the ground floor, where he entered the kitchen. Now he would have to be more careful with the flashlight, in case anyone passed by on the street.

Up here the smell was different—a distillation of roasted meat, cigarette smoke, discarded newspapers, of lives being lived. The refrigerator hummed. A faucet dripped in a sink. It felt as if someone might round the nearest corner at any moment, perhaps old Erich himself, all five foot four inches of him, the squatty little bastard. Emil swallowed a bubble of nervous laughter. To be inside this man's house at this ungodly hour was disturbing but stimulating, the thrill of the forbidden.

He moved on into the dining room, took quick inventory of its empty chairs and table, the kitschy knickknacks of a corner cupboard, then stepped into the living room, which was furnished garishly in a French provincial style that either Erich or his wife, Gertrude, must have thought was the height of elegance, a luxury to be hidden from the prying eyes of the proletariat. No safe. No documents.

A spacious den was next, with knotty wood-paneled walls and worn but comfortable couches flanked by a pair of big recliners. There was a large television, but surprisingly the model was not even as up to date as the one Andreas Plotz had owned. Emil passed through all of these downstairs rooms in quick succession, neither expecting nor finding a safe out in the open where any guest might have seen it.

He climbed upstairs to the bedrooms, three of them, and was exploring the first and largest one when a bright light flashed across the wall through the lace curtains on the window. Emil dropped to the floor in alarm, a pain shooting through his right knee. It was the headlight beams of a security car as it turned the corner, making its rounds. Moritz had said nothing about this possibility, probably because he had never been here at this hour, but Emil should have guessed it was likely. He wondered if the car had passed by the van while he slept.

The car stopped. Emil heard the engine idling, the slam of a door. He crawled to the window and peeped over the sill. It was parked in front of Moritz's van, and someone was peering through the driver's side window with a flashlight. Then he went around to the back. Emil heard the door open and, after a few seconds more, the sound of it shutting. The fellow must have then paused to inspect the flattened tire, because he didn't reappear for a few seconds more.

When he did come back into view, he swung his flashlight beam toward the Mielkes' house. Emil ducked out of sight until he heard the thunk of a car door and the rev of the engine as it drove away. He sneaked a glance just in time to see the car turn at the end of the block, back toward the guardhouse, where no doubt it was warmer and cozier and there was plenty of coffee, and the radio was probably still playing.

Emil waited on the floor for another five minutes in case the car made another swing through the neighborhood. Then he stood and toured the rest of the bedrooms, checking all the closets and bathrooms. Still no sign of a safe, or of any boxes of documents.

He made his way down the hall to a spacious office with a large teak desk and a leather swivel chair. He checked every drawer of the desk. One was locked. He got out his compact set of tiny lock picks, the deepest item in his coat pocket, and opened the drawer within seconds. There were old letters inside. Some were in a woman's handwriting, and some were perfumed, but they weren't what he was looking for. He resisted the urge to stuff a few in his pocket for later viewing, then shut the drawer. He needed to stay focused.

The top of the desk was neat and mostly empty, with a flip calendar, a telephone, some stray pieces of mail, an outdated report from the

Ministry of Planning, and a technical manual for a Grundig shortwave radio, probably the one in the bunker.

Behind the desk was a narrow closet door. Emil opened it and flicked on his light. Shelves faced him from floor to ceiling, crammed with cardboard sleeves for reels of eight-millimeter film, with titles on the spines. On a wider shelf to the right was a Bell and Howell film projector. Rolled up and folded away to the left was a portable movie screen, standing upright.

The film titles were in alphabetical order. Most were in English. For all his love of American movies, these were ones he'd never heard of, and he quickly guessed why.

Behind the Green Door, Big Guns, Black Throat

Emil directed his beam toward the Ls.

Let Me Tell Ya 'bout Black Chicks, Let Me Tell Ya 'bout White Chicks, Lolita: Vibrator Torture, Love Hotel

So, then. The schoolmarm had amassed a private collection of porn to keep him company through Waldsiedlung's lonely winter nights. The hypocritical toad, passing judgment on others while he watched his blue movies. There was a wooden folding chair beside the desk. Had Mielke convinced Gertrude to watch with him? Or had he recruited other female companions? The writer of those scented letters, perhaps. Emil didn't care to dwell on the possibilities, so he turned off his flashlight and shut the door.

High on the nearest wall he now noticed a framed photo of a smiling Joseph Stalin. Not at all surprising. Mielke had fondly—and infamously—made a toast to the late Soviet leader back at some party function in 1970, seventeen years after Stalin's death, and well after his violent legacy had been officially disavowed by Soviet leaders.

Surrounding it were photos of Mielke with other leaders from the communist world, plus a lot of pictures featuring him with members of his favorite soccer team, Dynamo, probably his purest passion. Although even that was tainted. He had pressured referees to look favorably on his team at crucial moments, which helped explain why they won so many East German championships but always flopped in international play.

Emil returned his attention to the desk, wondering if he could have missed something. The comfy swivel chair was well worn. This was definitely the spot in the house where Mielke's presence felt strongest. The bastard had probably spent most of his waking hours here, sagging back in his chair while the reels of the projector turned, with Uncle Joe Stalin watching from over his shoulder.

He checked the space beneath the desk. No safe there, either. He ran a finger across the smooth teak desktop. No dust. Someone was keeping the office clean. Might they also have confiscated its most sensitive materials? Over to the side was an expensive fountain pen, resting upright in a customized holder, its base inscribed in Cyrillic. Probably a gift from Moscow, perhaps the KGB. The object fascinated him— black, sleek, full of potential. Mielke might have used it to authorize all sorts of orders and decrees.

Emil pulled it gently from the holder and tested it on an envelope. Black ink flowed in a fine line from the nib. Then, almost before he was aware of what he was doing, he began to write on the middle of the teak desk. The words emerged in a smooth, flowing progression of cursive letters more than an inch high: *Erich the Murderer.*

The moment he finished, Emil experienced an intense, panicky urge to smear away the words. Maybe he should fetch a wet towel from the kitchen to wipe everything clean. Then he decided he didn't care. The moment of fear passed, his breathing slowed, and he carefully set the pen back in its holder. In only a few minutes the ink would dry, and you'd need sandpaper to remove it.

He exhaled in mild satisfaction and moved into the hallway. There was one last room, down at the end on the opposite side. He opened the door to a small study, or perhaps a private reading room. There was only a single cushioned chair beside a floor lamp, with half-filled bookshelves on two of the walls. And that's when Emil saw it, the safe, a cold gray cube, perhaps eighteen inches a side, sitting atop the shelves on the opposite wall. He could reach it, barely, by stretching on his tiptoes, but in testing the safe's weight it seemed heavy, unwieldy. He didn't want the damn thing to fall on his head, so he went back to the office to retrieve the folding chair, which he climbed onto to grab the safe more firmly.

He set it on the floor, put the chair back in the office, and hefted the safe down the stairs, all the way to the basement bunker. By then he was sweaty and excited. Now the question was whether all those training films he'd watched so many times with all his young recruits were accurate, the ones where they'd shown how easy it was to break into supposedly impregnable personal safes.

Emil placed the safe on the floor and turned it on its side. He plugged in the circular saw, used his knees to hold the safe in place, and pressed the button to start the blade. A loud, shimmering, metallic noise climbed in pitch until the blade was whirling at its maximum RPM. He pushed it into the base of the safe, and the teeth began doing their work, cutting into the metal skin with surprising ease. Beneath the metal was perhaps two inches of fire insulation and a thin plastic liner. The training film had been correct. These safes were garbage.

The work wasn't easy. It required a steady hand, and the noise was deafening. If the security car were to stop here now, he'd almost certainly be discovered. He paused a few times to listen for any sign of trouble, but heard only the ringing of his ears.

It took about ten minutes to finish, as the base of the safe fell away. Emil set down the heavy saw, the room silent. He shone his flashlight into the opening. Several file folders were inside, and he pulled them out in two batches.

The thickest one was also the oldest, and it explained why Mielke referred to this private archive as the Bülowplatz materials. It was the Berlin police investigation file on the 1931 murders of police captain Paul Anlauf and officer Franz Lenck, at Bülowplatz in Berlin. Emil, who had heard tales for years about this long ago chapter in Mielke's past, only had time for a cursory glance at the contents, but quickly saw Mielke's name on several items that mentioned him as a leading suspect. Back then, Mielke had been a young communist rabble-rouser, willing to do anything—even kill—to earn his stripes. What a strange artifact to hang on to. Perhaps Mielke had thought it could be used to blackmail others, although it certainly incriminated him as well. Emil set it aside.

There were several other, thinner files. One was about Lothar's disastrous affair with the actress, another was a dossier on Wolf's second wife, Christa, who had been deemed a security risk after her divorce.

The folder Emil sought was near the bottom, and was the thinnest of them all. It was marked "KGB Dead Drop—Little Falls Parkway." Inside was a brief after-action report, signed by Emil, describing the routine details of the operation. The other eleven pages were photo-copies of the documents that had been retrieved from the dead drop—four CIA interagency memos, each with a circulation list on the first page that contained the names of everyone who had received that memo. Whoever had given these to the KGB would almost certainly be named on each of the four memos.

Yes, this was valuable information indeed. Emil shut the folder. He stood, unplugged the saw, hefted it in his right hand, and then tucked the folder beneath his arm. He crossed the room, opened the door to the outside with a groan of metal against concrete, listened for a second, and stepped back into the night.

Now he had to move quickly and quietly, and there was still a lot of ground to cover. He checked his watch. Just past 4 a.m. By now the Americans were probably growing nervous, assuming they had come at all. If they hadn't, then he would be in for an even longer night, alone in the woods.

His first stop was the van, where he put Moritz's saw back inside beneath the drop cloth, retrieved a pair of wire cutters, and then gently closed the door. If the security car came now, he'd be caught for sure. But the streets were quiet, the houses were still dark. He hoped Moritz had the good sense to get rid of the saw, or at the very least the special blade. Bits of metal from Mielke's safe were still lodged in the teeth and flecked on its sides.

Emil set off across the street and into the pines, angling on a north-west heading that would take him to the rendezvous point. He was breathing heavily, carrying the folder in his sweaty right hand. Twigs snapped beneath his feet, and his trousers snagged on briars and under-brush. He stopped to pull a compass from his pocket to make sure he was staying on course, and in only a few minutes he reached a green concrete wall, cracked and crumbling, with barbed wire along the top.

He used a divot in the concrete as a foothold to climb high enough to clip each of the four strands of rusted wire. Then he clambered across. A few sheets of paper slipped out of the folder as he landed, and he plucked them from the twigs and pine needles.

He heard the rustle of other night creatures as he moved forward, and in another few minutes he reached the outer wall, which he sur-mounted in the same way as the first. He again checked his heading on the compass and adjusted his course. By his reckoning he was now within a quarter mile of where he had instructed the Americans to wait. He thought of Karola and Bettina, worried for him, and perhaps sleepless at the dacha.

Ahead he saw the pale light of a narrow clearing where the woods ended. Beyond it was a two-lane road and more trees, where, he hoped, a car with the two Americans awaited.

He peered into the darkness as he proceeded, straining his eyes to spot a glint of metal, or the welcoming flash of headlights to direct him onward. But for the moment he saw little more than trees, a forest inhabited by predators and prey.

Breathing heavily, he trudged onward, gripping the folder tightly.

49

Put two spies in a car in the woods for a few hours on hostile ground, and secrets are bound to surface. That's certainly what happened with Claire and Ron Kent as they waited for their East German contact to emerge from the trees.

It was cold, they had finished half a thermos of coffee, and they were skittish about their vulnerable position as they waited on a dirt lane twenty yards off the paved road, sheltered beneath the pines. They had arrived early, ninety minutes ago, after slipping out the back of their inn and retrieving the car from its underground spot.

While en route they'd worried about being pulled over by the authorities, or noticed by other drivers along the way. But the roads were virtually empty. No one stopped them, and few even saw them. So here they were, staring into the gloom, hoping that at any moment the rumpled old fellow in the wool cap would appear in the clearing across the road.

They knew from their map—and, in Claire's case, from what Baucom had told her the other day about the compound at Waldsiedlung— where he was likely to be coming from, a knowledge that had raised the stakes of the rendezvous. Honecker, Mielke, and all the party heavyweights had once lived in this forest, a proximity that made their presence riskier but also heightened the potential value of any item that might soon fall into their hands.

Claire had still not uttered Emil Grimm's name to anyone. She continued to guard his identity out of fear that revealing it would put him in harm's way.

Imagine her unpleasant surprise, then, when Kent said, out of the blue, "His name's Emil Grimm, by the way, although I'm betting you already knew that. I figured I should tell you, mostly because Lindsey already knows."

"What the hell! How did—"

"I picked him out from some photos she showed me this afternoon. I got a pretty good look at him at Tacheles, so it wasn't hard."

"Photos? She never showed me any photos."

"Because she didn't have any, or not until this morning. A set of five came in on an overnight fax."

"From who? From where?"

Kent sighed. Claire could tell he didn't want to say, but now he pretty much had to.

"Someone had blacked out the time signature and most of the other print, but on the third page they missed a line down at the bottom, and it was in Cyrillic."

"The Russians, then."

"Probably Karlshorst."

"Goddamnit, Ron, couldn't you have held her off at least for another day?"

"I'd already told her I got a great look at him, and Grimm's photo was clearly a match. She would've seen right through me."

"So finesse it, then. Say it also might have been one of the others. Anything to give him another twenty-four hours. What you did was totally irresponsible."

"I disagree. Grimm knows how these things work. He'll have taken precautions. And if he knows we have his ID, it strengthens our bargaining position."

"You and Ward and your bargaining talk. It's like you're negotiating an employment contract, when the man's life is at stake. Especially with someone like Gregor Kolkachev after him, which is probably who sent the goddamn fax."

"Wait. You know *Kolkachev's* name?"

"You know how these things work."

"Touché."

"I also know his thug enforcer's name, Yuri Volkov."

"Well, that's a new one for me. Maybe even for Lindsey. You should tell her."

"The problem with her approach is that she's already picked a winner, so she only values Grimm as leverage. But what if he ends up offering something better?"

"If they both have copies of the full agent files, with every piece of that puzzle, then it's pretty easy to see why she'd think Kolkachev offers greater long-term value. He's active. So is the KGB. Grimm and the Stasi are dead and gone."

"Maybe literally in Grimm's case, if she's already turned over his name."

Kent looked off into the darkness.

"I gotta admit, if he's just stolen something from where we think he is, then that's pretty impressive. Still, it's a one-off. Kolkachev could be the gift that keeps on giving. Lindsey's only playing the odds."

Lindsey, yet again. Claire was thoroughly sick of it.

"So he has agreed to be her defector in place?"

"You didn't hear that from me."

"Then why'd you just tell me?"

"Maybe I have my doubts, too."

"Why?"

"Because they've been looking for this mole upstairs at Langley for a few years now, without really getting anywhere. I was detailed to it for a while, which is one reason she brought me over for this. But the whole search has been plagued by disinformation from the start. At least half the leads from their side seem designed to lead us astray."

"Hardly surprising. And you think Kolkachev might be offering more of the same?"

Kent sighed.

"Apparently he's making the case that our problem is a communications breach. A technology thing, not a mole."

"Communications from where? What channel?"

"That's what he's promising to lay out for us."

"Sounds like another way to keep us chasing our tail. You'd think she'd at least want to see what Grimm comes up with."

"She will, if he ever comes out of the woods."

"And survives beyond the next few hours."

"That's why we're here for him. He'll be safe with us."

"Maybe. Once the sun comes up. And you've got the passports?"

Kent nodded.

"But don't go making promises we can't keep. Even if what he's got looks great at first blush."

Claire nodded back, but it still bothered her that Kent would control that part of the transaction.

"Look!" Kent said. "Across the road!"

It was Grimm. He had crossed the clearing and had just reached the road. Kent started the engine. At the sound of it, Grimm looked up like startled prey. Then he saw them and picked up his pace. As before, Claire thought she detected a limp.

"Okay, then." Kent checked his watch. "Three hours to sunrise. Time to rock and roll."

He put the car in gear and they drove out from under the trees. Grimm waited for them on the near shoulder, holding a file folder in his right hand. He looked exhausted but elated.

Their asset was in hand.

50

Claire thumbed through the pages, awestruck, reading by the light of the glove compartment. She held in her hands what seemed to be a CIA mole's contributions to the Agency's greatest enemy. The material felt special and charmed, and she couldn't wait to get it to safer ground.

But for the moment they were driving at an illicit hour through territory that, newly freed or not, still felt like forbidden ground, so she put the documents back into their folder and slid it beneath the floormat for safer keeping.

Emil Grimm was sagged on the backseat, exhausted. There were twigs on his clothes, and his eyes were red. He had remained silent since handing her the folder, when he'd said, "Here. I've done my part, now it's your turn."

She'd given him a bottle of water, which he'd polished off with a sigh. Now, perhaps getting a second wind, he leaned forward between the two front seats and eyed the road. They had just turned onto the Autobahn toward Prenden. He smelled like the forest.

"Where did you get it, if you're willing to say? Any detail like that will certainly help with the authenticity evaluation."

"From a safe. In Erich Mielke's house."

Claire looked over at Kent, who grinned back. He gave a low whistle of admiration.

"Damn, man. And you just waltzed in there after dark?"

"I had help, but those kinds of details can wait. Did you bring the passports?"

Another exchange of glances, this one with looks of concern.

"We'll discuss that when we're on safer ground."

"Safer ground? That's not the right answer."

Claire didn't want to officiate an argument. She also believed Grimm should know as soon as possible about the heightened danger he was in, so she said, "We need to start taking greater precautions, all of us. Because I'm pretty sure that by now Kolkachev has your name."

Emil's eyes widened as he absorbed the blow.

"Because your people told him?"

"It wasn't my doing."

"But your people, all the same." He was angry, and she didn't blame him. Kent, to his credit, spoke up.

"It's my fault. They showed me a photo array. I ID'ed you from that."

"What time did this happen? How long ago?"

"Around four yesterday afternoon."

"Scheisse! That was more than twelve hours ago! He could be waiting at my goddamn house by now. We need to move. Faster!"

Kent sped up, but not enough for Grimm.

"Faster, man!"

"We can't afford to get pulled over."

"I'll deal with the Volkspolizei. Just go!"

Kent floored it. The Mercedes, true to its reputation, leaped to another stratum of speed and power. They exited the Autobahn a mile later and reached Prenden only a minute after that. Because it was a farming village, there were already lights on in some of the windows, ambering the cobbled lanes.

When they reached the right turn for the dirt lane to the Bauersee, a Citroën was emerging at high speed, fishtailing and throwing gravel as it darted onto the main road.

"Uh-oh, who've we got here," Kent said. "If they stop us, we're fucked."

But the car only seemed interested in making a getaway. The driver reacted to their sudden appearance by shutting off the headlights, which felt all wrong.

"I don't like this," Grimm moaned. "Faster!"

Every window of the dacha was dark. The only car in sight was the Wartburg, parked in the driveway. Grimm bolted from the back before they even came to a full stop. He stumbled and cried out in pain, but never stopped.

Claire followed as he threw open the door of the house and disappeared inside. But she could already see there was a problem by the haze of smoke that came boiling out the open door. No flames, only smoke. She put a hand over her mouth, lowered her head, and ran inside, already hearing Grimm's voice calling out from a bedroom on the left.

"Bettina! Karola! No!"

She coughed, gasping for air, and switched on a light. The culprit seemed to be the woodstove in the middle of the main room, so she went to shut it down, closing dampers and vents. But smoke kept leaking from it, as if something had blocked it from above, or in the flue. She heard Kent behind her now, coughing.

"I'll get that," he said. "Get Grimm out of here before he collapses!"

She ran to the bedroom door, trying to hold her breath, and saw a desperate scene unfolding. Grimm stood between an angled hospital bed and a fold-out bed, bent over, coughing. There was a sleeping woman in each bed. Grimm looked torn, distraught. He stepped to the hospital bed and stooped over the still figure beneath the sheets.

"Bettina! Bettina!" He shook her. "She can't wake up. She won't open her eyes."

Claire switched on the light. She recognized the woman in the fold-out bed as the one who had driven the Wartburg. Like the other woman, she seemed to be dead or unconscious. Neither was reacting at all to the noise and commotion. Claire stepped forward, coughing, feeling faint now, and grabbed the woman beneath her arms. Then she thought better of it and turned to Kent, who had just rushed in behind her.

"Grab that end of the cot. We'll carry her out!"

It was an awkward job, but they moved fast, heaving the cot out into the fresh, cold air just in time for both of them. They sagged to the ground, coughing.

But they could still hear Grimm calling out from inside, as if his lungs would never stop working, his voice now a croak of fury and despair.

"Bettina, Bettina! Open your eyes!"

51

The police caught up to them at the hospital in Bernau. A plainclothes-man, Lieutenant Dorn, approached Claire and Kent in the small, dreary waiting room. He addressed them in German.

"Emil tells me you two were with him when he found the bodies, yes?"

"Bodies?" Claire said. "So they're . . . ?"

"His wife is dead. The other one, the caretaker, it's too early to say. She remains unconscious."

"Yes, we were with him."

It was an awkward moment, and not only because of what they'd been doing overnight, or the contents of the folder, which was still stashed beneath the floormat of their car. Both of them knew that, operationally, they should have moved on as soon as the ambulance arrived. Instead they had driven the distraught Grimm to the hospital, and felt obligated to stay for his protection, even though neither of them was armed.

Claire had tried to talk Kent into heading back on his own with the folder before they attracted further attention, but he had refused to let her shoulder the burden alone. So there they were, two hours later, with the sun coming up and a detective asking questions. Emil was off in the hospital room where they had taken the two women. Both had been alive, barely, when they'd first arrived.

Dorn nodded at Claire's answer.

"He says you've been an immense help. He asked me to leave you alone. But, well, it appears obvious that a crime has been committed, so I must question you both."

Claire looked at Kent. He sat with his arms folded and his mouth shut.

"We've done nothing illegal," Claire said.

"No, no. At the dacha, I mean. It is clear that someone tampered with the flue of the chimney, up on the rooftop. There were sticks, twigs, a lot of debris like that. I'm guessing that whoever did it wanted to make it look like the work of birds, but . . ." His voice trailed off.

"Storks," Kent said.

"Pardon?"

"Sorry. I'm kind of into birds. Storks like to build their nests on chimneys. Maybe that's what they were trying to make it look like."

"I see. I will need your names, of course. For the report."

They again exchanged glances. Then they gave him their names.

"Show me your identification."

They handed over their passports. He gave them a long look, wrote down the numbers and other details, and handed them back, which was a pleasant surprise.

"Emil did not tell me your occupations, but I think I can probably guess it, since I know his. Perhaps you could confirm this for me."

This time Kent did the talking.

"We'll refer you to our embassy for any kind of statement on that. Besides, I think we all know who's responsible for what happened to those two women."

Dorn sighed wearily and nodded.

"Yes. I suppose we do."

Claire was a little surprised by the remark. Did Dorn really know about the Russians? She had also been taken aback by the detective's apparent familiarity with Emil Grimm—calling him by his first name, readily admitting to knowing he was a Stasi spy. Obviously the two men had a history, even if it was of a recent vintage.

Dorn spoke again, this time sounding a bit wistful.

"You know, if this were the old times . . ." He caught himself, and then laughed beneath his breath. "Listen to me—the *old times*, as if they were not a mere four months ago. But if we *were* in those times, I would already be busy filing an extra report on each of you. Then

I'd have to detain you while someone made a phone call to a special number in Berlin. It would all have been very messy. Not that it feels particularly neat even now."

Claire waited, wondering what this all meant for any action he would have to take now. She got her answer right away.

"I believe that instead I will simply describe you as a pair of American friends of his. Out of respect for that, perhaps the two of you could arrange to be gone from here by, let us say, midday?"

"Yes, I think we can accommodate that request. And thank you."

He nodded. Then he shook his head like a man clearing the cobwebs, seemingly as baffled by his own behavior as by the events of the past twenty-four hours.

"I have been telling myself for these past few weeks that this new Germany of ours will be so much more open and uncomplicated than the old one. I am beginning to think that was a mistake."

"I do have something for you," Claire said. "The tag number of that Citroën we saw."

Dorn's eyes widened.

"That would be very helpful indeed. Yes, let's have it."

She told him. He thanked her and wrote it down. Then he shut his notebook with a sigh and slumped off toward the exit.

A few moments later the doctor who had been attending to the women stepped into the lobby. Claire tried to get an update, but he waved her off. She set off down the hall to the room, but a nurse barred her from entering, so she waited until the nurse came back out the door and bustled off in the opposite direction.

She entered to find Grimm standing between the two beds. He was hunched over the one where Bettina's body lay still, her face reddened, probably from carbon monoxide poisoning. Her eyes were shut.

The other woman, who she now knew was named Karola Weber, was hooked up to a respirator, an IV, and various monitors. One of them beeped steadily.

Claire took a step forward, and Emil turned at the sound. His eyes flashed, and she was poised to apologize for her intrusion when his expression softened and he nodded as if to sanction her presence.

"I'm so sorry. We'll do what we can to help both of you. But only if you want our help."

"I'm a little surprised you stayed. Even in my sorrow I have been thinking hard about what to do next, and it may already be too late. But I know one thing clearly. This will not stand. I cannot let it. So, in an hour or so, if you're still here . . ."

"We'll stay. Yes, we'll stay."

"Stand by, then. One hour, and we'll move."

Claire nodded and turned to go. A question occurred to her as she reached the door, so she stopped to speak, only to see Grimm tugging the blanket on his wife's bed, as if poised to cover her face. Then he hesitated, dropped it, and shook his head, unable to complete this act of finality. Instead, he turned toward the other bed and gently took the hand of the sleeping woman, Karola. It was a moment too intimate to interrupt. Claire left quietly and returned to the lobby.

One hour. Then they would get moving, the two of them and this deeply wounded man. She had no idea what sort of action Grimm had in mind, but she felt the same need to marshal their anger, to fight back. Sometime before the sun set again, they needed to cross back over into the West, with both Grimm and the folder in their possession, and perhaps the rest of his items as well, wherever they might be hiding.

Provided, of course, that they were all still alive by then.

52

It was his fault, of course. Emil knew that.

Yes, the Americans had spilled the key bit of information that had made him a target. But he had been too clever by half in dropping the hints that had sent Dorn in pursuit of Kolkachev, Volkov, and Krauss, which had in turn made them more careful. So instead of just coming for Emil directly, with the blunt force of a Makarov or a butcher knife, as they no doubt would have done once they learned he was Lothar's silent partner, they had resorted to a more subtle method—a chimney blockage. And with the Wartburg parked in the driveway they must have assumed Emil was home.

It should be him lying dead in this hospital room with a blanket on his face. Instead it was Bettina, and Karola had nearly joined her.

Now he wanted only to strike back, to beat them, to bring them to heel. But how? "Winning" seemed beyond reach, only because the idea of any victory under these circumstances was so hollow as to be meaningless. The only possible remaining solace would be to secure a future for Karola. The doctor said she would recover, probably with no long-term side effects. Her vital signs were improving. Bettina's frailty had made her an easy mark, and Emil would never forgive himself for deserting her at such a vulnerable moment.

What to do next, then? Kolkachev and Krauss would no doubt learn of his survival within a few hours, probably by midday. It was just after 8 a.m.

He picked up a water glass from the bedside table and took a swallow, thinking, thinking. What would he tell Karola when she awakened? *Your best friend is dead, and I was complicit.* Then his anger rose in a wave of heat in his face, and the glass shattered in his tightening grip.

"Scheisse!"

He dropped the broken shards into a trash can, and carefully brushed fragments off his palm. Miraculously, he wasn't cut. More dumb luck in his favor, when he gladly would have redirected it toward Bettina. Had he really been standing inside Erich Mielke's darkened house only a few hours ago?

A spark of doubt ignited deep in his thoughts: What if the Americans simply drove off in their Mercedes now that they had the documents? They might decide they didn't even need the rest of what he was offering. Then the spark died. He trusted them not to do that, or they would have already left. They still wanted the rest of what he was offering, he was sure of that. And the woman, at least, seemed to be on his side.

Emil's thoughts drifted along in this haphazard manner for another few seconds until he idly looked down at Karola and, to his surprise, saw that her eyes were open.

She smiled, ever so slightly, and moved her lips as if trying to speak. Emil smiled back, wiped at a tear, and stooped low to listen. Her words emerged in a raspy whisper.

"What happened?"

"Someone blocked the chimney while you slept. Probably the Russians. We got you out just in time. You're in the hospital now, in Bernau, but the doctor says you'll be fine."

She smiled wearily. Her eyes began to close, then fluttered open even wider than before. She whispered again.

"Bettina!"

It was a cry of alarm, not a question, and Emil knew he couldn't fend her off with a lie, not with his wife lying there dead, only a few feet away. So he shook his bowed head and squeezed her hand. Then he gently wiped a tear from each of her cheeks.

She rested awhile longer. He was on the verge of leaving to fetch a cup of coffee when she reopened her eyes, fighting her way back up to the surface through the drowsiness of exhaustion and the drugs of the IV drip. He again leaned lower to listen.

"The hunting stand," she whispered. "They know. They *know*. The ranger . . ."

Her voice fell away, and her eyes shut. But as she faded from consciousness she squeezed his hand, as if to communicate her urgency.

Emil was alarmed. Much of his remaining hope depended on the items buried at the hunting stand—his hopes for vengeance, for justice, and for recruiting any sort of American help in bringing them about.

He fled from the room and sprinted down the hall toward the lobby, where he desperately hoped the Americans were still waiting.

53

Clouds rolled in as they drove back to Prenden, and it was snowing by the time they parked at the dacha. Claire and Kent waited while Emil retrieved his Pistol-M, their only weapon, and his Zeiss spotting scope. They set out into the woods, with Emil leading the way.

They climbed the hill in silence. Emil's knee ached, his nose was running, his breathing labored. He was exhausted.

"How big is the item?" Claire asked. "Would they have needed help moving it? Will we?"

"No. It's quite compact. A single pilot's flight case, containing seventy-six boxed reels of microfilm. The case is a foot and a half long, a foot high, and eight inches deep. The total weight is twenty-five pounds. Even if only one person came for it, he'd have no trouble walking it out of here."

"How did Karola know they found out?"

"I'm not sure. Something to do with the forest ranger. He keeps all the plans for the hunting stands, with all the locations. She was drifting in and out when she told me, so she didn't say a lot more."

Kent spoke up.

"Any chance she was hallucinating?"

"No. At that moment she was quite lucid. I could tell by her eyes. Although . . . I suppose there's a chance she could have dreamed it."

"Let's hope. If not, someone might even be there now, digging it up."

"Or on their way, like us."

The thought silenced them as they approached the top of the hill. A few steps later, Emil stopped abruptly and raised a hand to halt them, in the manner of a soldier leading a patrol. There was a snap of twigs, the sound of plodding footsteps coming from the brush just ahead to the right.

Emil went into a crouch. He slipped his right hand into his coat pocket to grip the stock of the gun. Claire stepped off the trail, easing behind a tree. Kent held his ground.

It was a boar, blundering across the trail just ahead. It stopped and turned to face them, snow flecking its bristling dark coat. It huffed once, jetting steam out its snout, then continued into the woods.

The three of them exhaled as one. Kent chuckled.

"Well, that's a first."

"You don't usually see them in daylight."

"Maybe something on the other side of the hill flushed him from cover."

"Maybe."

They crested the hill and angled left. The snow, heavier now, began accumulating on the trail. Claire checked behind her and saw they were leaving clear prints, which gave her an eerie sense of being a stalked animal, easily trackable prey.

It reminded Emil of the night he had buried the pilot's case. Lothar had given it to him for safekeeping, and he had waited until an evening when snow had been forecast for the following morning. The moon had still been shining when he set out, but it had been covered by clouds by the time he finished. When he awakened, hours later, snow had been blowing in a high wind, and four inches were already on the ground, covering his path and the evidence of his labors.

The day before, he and Lothar had buried a decoy pilot's case in the vegetable garden in front of Lothar's dacha. It, too, had been filled with seventy-six reels of microfilm, but the labels on the boxes were fakes, and the reels were blank.

Emil had told Lothar it was the real thing, a deception that had felt necessary at the time. His reasoning was that Lothar, being their front man, the face who handled all their dealings with Andreas Plotz and other sources, would also be the most vulnerable to revealing any hiding place. And the move had paid off, of course, on the night that

Kolkachev's thugs had come for Lothar. That's why they had dug up his vegetable garden, finding the decoy case and probably not discovering until hours later that they'd been duped.

Or had they, perhaps, checked the microfilm that very night and, finding it blank, decided to torture Lothar even more before killing him and turning his body over to Krauss for his clumsy arrangement of a suicide tableaux? It was a possibility that had haunted Emil from the moment he first saw Lothar's body, and more so after Dorn told him that Lothar's testicles had been marked with clamps.

He flexed his bad knee and moved forward.

"How much further?" Kent asked.

"It's right around this next bend." Then, a few steps farther on, "There's the stand. The green one. And it's . . . Scheisse!"

"What?"

"Look at the ground beneath it! Fuck!"

Someone had dug into the dark soil, leaving an open trench that was swallowing snowflakes as they blew into the protected space beneath the stand. Down in the hole, the lid of the secret underground compartment that he and Lothar had built was propped open, and the compartment was empty. Whoever had taken the pilot's case had been in too much of a hurry to cover up afterward. Or maybe they had left everything this way to taunt him.

The only good news, he supposed, was that the theft might buy some time for Emil to move to a safer location, if only because Kolkachev would be momentarily preoccupied with validating and securing his booty. Perhaps he'd even seek an additional buyer—the West Germans, or the Brits. Sell his own copy to the Americans, and this one to someone else. Either way, the KGB man had now cornered the market on the puzzle set of the HVA's agent files. A few thousand identities, up for grabs.

Three people had died for this secret, one of them his wife. Emil dropped to his knees and gazed up into the swirling snow. Claire laid a hand on his shoulder.

"I'm sorry, Emil. I'm so sorry."

"What do we do now?" Kent asked.

Emil stood creakily and brushed off his trousers. He blinked away the snow sticking to his eyelashes.

"We go back to the dacha. We finish airing it out, and we try to think. Unless, of course, the two of you decide that I'm no longer worth the effort."

The Americans exchanged glances, but he could not get a read on their expressions. He supposed that if he were in their position, he would have driven away without delay. Take the folder, cut their losses.

But they followed him back to the dacha, and when he opened the door they accompanied him inside.

"I could use some coffee," Claire said.

It was the sanest suggestion he'd heard all day. He experienced an overwhelming desire to lie down for a long rest. Maybe the lingering scent of smoke had something to do with it, with its suggestion of death and loss. With all the windows open, the air inside was as cold as the outdoors, even though the coils of the space heater shone a bright orange. He wanted to curl up beneath heavy blankets and drift into mindless slumber.

Claire, reading his face, tried to throw him a lifeline.

"We can still make this work for you and Karola. We owe you that much."

"Thank you." But his eyes felt hollow, his energy spent. "You know, for a while, after Lothar's death I wondered, how can this be happening to people of his rank and stature, and of mine? Have all the old rules of our game suddenly become null and void?"

"The old gentleman's agreement, you mean?"

"Yes."

Everyone in their business knew of it, even though it had never existed on paper. It applied to all the major players of the Cold War spy game, especially in a contested zone like Berlin: Don't harm our people, and we won't harm yours. As for all those other poor saps who got caught in the middle, well, heaven help them. Emil continued.

"Then I realized, Lothar didn't really count anymore. Nor did I, now that our employer had been removed from the board. We'd become like all of those unfortunate souls who used to get in the way. People like Bettina." He drifted away for a second. "I never ordered anyone's death. Still, in my way, I suppose I was as cavalier with lives as Kolkachev. I'm sure your boss is no different."

"Not in the least."

He nodded, as if to confirm his judgment upon himself.

"I should make the coffee," Claire said. "Just tell me where everything is."

"The pot's on the counter. Everything you'll need is in the drawer below it."

"Ron, you want some?"

"Absolutely. Make a full pot."

Kent stepped toward the picture window on the side of the great room, where he stared out toward the birds at the feeder. He went rigid as something caught his eye, and for a lurching moment Emil was certain that something terrible was about to befall them.

"You've got a middle spotted woodpecker out there," Kent said.

Emil smiled in relief. A bird-watcher, then. It reminded him of Kent's earlier remark about the stork's nest, which in turn made him think of the blocked chimney, which made him sad and desolate all over again.

"Yes, he's a regular visitor. There's a pair of binoculars on the table, if you're interested."

"Thank you."

Kent took him up on the offer. Emil heard the clank of the glass coffee pot, the running of the kitchen faucet, the opening and shutting of drawers. Claire came to the doorway, then paused as if taken aback by what she saw in Emil's face.

"You should lie down. But, I'm sorry, where are the coffee filters?"

"Same drawer as the coffee."

"There's a box, but it's empty."

"Oh, right. Karola must have used the last one overnight."

Overnight, he thought, while he was out at Waldsiedlung, playing burglar games while they were here alone, unprotected.

"I'll get another box."

Emil stepped wearily to the pantry closet in the great room, opening the door and reaching toward the top shelf, where a box of filters was wedged between rolls of paper towels. He was so numb to his surroundings that he might easily have missed the new item down on the floor if his feet hadn't crunched against a clod of dried mud. In fact, now that he noticed, there seemed to be dirt all over the closet floor, and as he looked down to see why, his eyes alighted on the mud-smeared pilot's case, which someone had placed on the floor.

Emil shook his head and then blinked in amazement, wondering if he was seeing things. He wasn't. It was real. He felt his strength and alertness returning as if a doctor had injected him with a drug.

But how could it have gotten there?

Karola, of course. She must have retrieved it last night on her own initiative, after learning that its whereabouts had been compromised. She doubtless would have told him this at the hospital if she'd had the energy to stay awake.

Claire, coming out of the kitchen, turned to see what he was staring at. She gasped.

"Oh my God. Is that . . . ?"

"It is."

Kent put down the binoculars and watched, speechless, as Emil unsnapped the top and opened the flap. Inside were seventy-six boxed reels of microfilm. All three files were there—every piece of the puzzle. But he was still marveling more at Karola's resourcefulness under pressure.

He drew a deep breath of the bracing air. All of them were smiling. As his brain began to function again, his first thought was of Krauss, and of Kolkachev's people, his trio of killers. If they were out there now, peering into the empty hole beneath the hunting stand, their next move would be to follow the snowy footprints that led straight to the dacha.

He turned toward the Americans.

"I don't think there's time for coffee. We need to get going as fast as we can."

54

They stayed off paved roads until they reached the Autobahn, a route that took them down a series of winding dirt lanes through the trees. Emil gave directions as he leaned forward from the back, while the Mercedes bounced through ruts and potholes. Snow continued to fall, and Emil was disconcerted to see that they were leaving an easily marked trail.

"So we're looking for a Citroën?" Kent asked.

"And possibly a Volvo. Or anything expensive and foreign. Between him and Krauss, they could have all sorts of foot soldiers."

"Maybe we should have taken your Wartburg."

Emil shook his head.

"They know it too well. And if we end up in a chase, we'll want something faster than two-stroke lawnmower speed."

"It's good you know these roads," Claire said.

"From hiking and hunting. Fire roads and ranger paths. Never thought I'd use them for this. Take this right. That will bring us out of the woods just beyond the entrance ramp."

The road emerged from the trees on the downside of the Autobahn's sloped shoulder. This stretch of the highway, never busy, was now virtually empty due to the falling snow, although the flakes weren't yet sticking to the pavement. The car banged up onto the blacktop and turned right onto the southbound lanes for Berlin. No one was following. With any luck they'd be on safe ground in twenty minutes.

A few miles later, Kent braked the car as they topped a rise. Something was blocking the roadway a half mile farther on, darkened blobs visible through the snowflakes.

"Any ideas?"

Emil got out his spotting scope and leaned between the seats, focusing as the wipers flicked back and forth.

"They've set up a roadblock. A Volvo, a Citroën, and a soldier. No, two of them, Russian uniforms. No idea how many people are in the cars. And they've seen us. Look!"

The Volvo was creeping forward. Then it accelerated, shooting toward them, heading north in the southbound lanes.

Emil watched the faces of the two Americans as Kent violently swerved the wheel into a U-turn and floored it. He wondered if the same thought was passing between all of them: Only a day earlier, this tired and beaten landscape had felt like a place free of borders, a place where you could finally breathe easy. Now it was again closed off, restricted, the oxygen limited. The status quo of four months ago was back in force, and any attempt to escape might be your last.

Kent swerved the Mercedes onto the median and crossed over to the northbound lanes.

"We have to get off this road," Emil said. "If that's Krauss, then he will have set up a roadblock in the other direction as well, probably just past where we came in."

They were now on a downslope, briefly out of sight of the Volvo.

"Take that cut into the forest, just ahead on the right. Get into the trees as fast as you can."

"He'll see our tracks."

"Maybe not, if he's going too fast. Just go."

They bounced violently down the shoulder and into the narrow opening. The black Mercedes blended well with the dark, wet trunks of the heavy pines, and they came to a stop twenty yards in, where they waited motionless as the Volvo topped the rise in a burst of roaring sound.

It flashed by them at top speed, hurtling farther down the highway. The three of them exhaled as one.

"I'll be damned," Kent said, as he accelerated forward. "Where to now?"

"Deeper into the woods. Fast. When they see we've disappeared they'll double back and find our tracks."

Emil kept thinking as they moved, reviewing the possible routes. A massive birch was just ahead on the right, a landmark that helped him recalibrate. Unbidden, he remembered that Lothar had once shot a stag near here. They had gutted and dressed it on the spot. He tried to recall the route they'd taken later in a truck to retrieve it.

"There's a turnoff coming up on the right. Take it."

The going was rougher than before, the trees bigger and denser. Emil wondered if they were still on course. After another few hundred yards he spoke again.

"See that next turnout just ahead? Pull over."

"To *stop*? Why?"

"Because I'm an old man and I have to take a piss! I also need to think for a second, to make sure we're headed in the right direction."

Kent shook his head but did as he was told. They waited in silence as Emil got out and, with his back turned to the open door, peed into the snow with a patter against the ground and a trailing of steam.

"This will look good on our report after they catch us," Kent said. "Next time he's peeing out the window."

Claire couldn't help but laugh at the absurdity of it all. She kept her voice down so Emil wouldn't hear.

"Well, he did just get us out of a pretty tight spot."

"Maybe we should take the first back road we hit and make a run for the nearest border crossing."

"If Kolkachev can round up enough soldiers to block the Autobahn, who's to say he's not watching the crossings?"

"He can't possibly cover them all."

"True. But we've got no way of knowing which ones . . . unless."

"What?"

She had just remembered something Baucom had told her on their drive back from Prenden.

"There's an old safe house we can use, in Bernau, if Emil can get us there."

"One of ours?"

"From a few years ago. Never used, apparently."

"How do you know all this shit?"

"Long story. But if we stash the car back in the underground garage, maybe we can hole up long enough to arrange for reinforcements. If worse comes to worst, we could stay the night."

Emil climbed back in as he zipped his pants.

"Sorry."

"Can you get us to Bernau without getting back on the Autobahn?"

He needed only a second or two to think it over.

"Yes. Definitely."

"Then let's go. I know a place where we can wait them out."

He raised his eyebrows, impressed.

"A friend of yours?"

"Something like that."

She saw no reason to reveal an old trade secret, even if, technically, he was no longer the enemy.

He nodded.

"Stay on this road another mile. I should have us there in ten minutes."

Kent put the car back in gear, and they drove onward, deeper into the silence of the trees.

55

At nightfall, Claire and Kent began to relax as they waited in the dusty safe house. Emil, so worn out that he had nodded off several hours earlier, was slumped sideways at the end of the couch. Claire had put a blanket on him, and she now sat across from him in an armchair, too edgy to sleep.

The safe house had been exactly where Baucom had described it, upstairs above an old antique shop. Emil had known of the shop, and had guided them there unerringly. The door was locked, but Emil had made quick work of that with a small kit of tools he'd pulled from an overcoat pocket, grinning like an old magician.

It was a one-story, one-bedroom apartment, with a separate doorway next to that of the shop, which opened onto a private stairwell. It was on a quiet cobbled lane that ran just inside the town center's medieval wall. The stone wall, about twelve feet high, added an extra layer of protection, although Claire supposed it would also shut off an avenue of escape if they needed to leave in a hurry.

Claire had peeked through the glass door of the darkened shop, but saw no signs of life. No opening hours were posted, and she wondered if it were even in business any longer. Apparently they were the only living souls in the building. The furnishings were sparse, out of date, and coated in dust. It was like hiding inside a time capsule.

Their biggest initial worry was the set of footprints they'd left on their walk from the parking garage. But the snow had long since covered that trail of breadcrumbs, and other pedestrians had subsequently trampled out tracks of their own.

Kent checked the windows every few minutes, peeping out the sides of the blinds in both directions up the cobbled lane. He then looked out a back window into an alley in the rear. All was quiet. The pilot's case and the stolen folder were in the coat closet.

"Still looks okay out there," Kent said, keeping his voice low to avoid awakening Emil. "If they'd found our trail right away, they'd be here by now. I should get out on the streets to find a phone."

"To call in the cavalry?"

"Don't you think?"

Claire nodded.

"We've got one gun between us, so, yes, the sooner the better. And of the three of us, you're the least likely to be recognized."

There was no phone in the house, of course. Acquiring one would have raised too many suspicions, and there would have been a long waiting list at the time anyway. It was clear from the setup that the apartment had mostly been intended for use as an emergency crash pad.

"Probably better if you avoid any public phone boxes."

"Agreed. I spotted a takeout joint a couple streets over on our way in."

"The Turkish place?"

"Yeah. If I order food they'll probably be happy to let me borrow their phone."

"Get me a doner kebab, then. I'm starved. With yogurt sauce, fries on the side. Better get him one, too. He needs it more than we do."

"If he'll even eat."

They both glanced at the sleeping Emil with an air of concern. Now that they were at rest, and in a place of relative safety, he would be more vulnerable to his grief. And he was exhausted from his long night at Waldsiedlung. Claire hoped Karola was recovering, but was worried she'd be upset when Emil failed to return to the hospital. That would be Emil's worry as well. The longer he remained asleep, the better.

"I'm assuming you've got Lindsey Ward's direct line?"

Kent nodded. A little sheepishly, she thought, but now she was glad for his easy access to someone who could get things moving in a hurry.

"How much should I tell her on an unsecure line, other than our location and the agreed-upon distress signal?"

"Say we have our full complement of items, then stress the urgency. The problem is that, if anyone's still listening, it's probably the Russians. Think she'll send the cavalry?"

"Of course. You really don't like her, do you?"

"It's not a matter of liking or not liking. It's trust. I worry she's more loyal to the people who are after us than the ones we're with."

He sighed.

"Yeah, I get it. Maybe this folder from Mielke will tip the scale. Problem is, I can't get into any of that on the call."

"You think she might slow play this? Even with both our asses on the line?"

"I'm betting Kolkachev has assured her he's only after one man, and that we won't be harmed."

"That's a hard promise to keep once the shooting starts. Especially with a butcher like Volkov. Make the call, then. Stress the urgency."

He checked the front window. The darkness was now complete. He frowned and angled for a better look to his left, this time pulling back the shade a little, an action he had avoided up to now.

"See anything?"

"Two guys just went into the place two doors down."

"Should we be worried?"

"No idea. Not even sure if they were guys. Could barely see 'em at this angle. I'll wait a few minutes."

Claire stood and checked out the back window. The alley was still empty. The town seemed to be quiet. Somewhere—maybe next door, maybe farther down the block—a door closed with a solid thunk. Then, silence.

The snow had stopped. The streetlamps glowed amber on the white sidewalks. Under other circumstances, it would have been beautiful. Instead, it looked like another cloak of concealment for whoever might be out there, searching for them.

They waited ten minutes. Emil groaned, slumping forward on the couch. Then he bolted upright, eyes blinking as he looked first at Kent and then at Claire, suddenly awake.

"What's happening? What time is it?"

"Almost seven. All quiet, or so we think. Ron's going out for food. Is a doner okay?"

"Nothing for me, thank you."

Claire looked at Kent, who nodded. He would get enough for all of them. With any luck, help would arrive before they'd finished eating.

"Okay, then. I'm off. Good thing you knew about this safe house, Claire. It was a godsend."

He left. Emil and Claire listened to his footsteps recede, followed by the shutting of the downstairs door. From there, the snow muffled any sound of his progress.

Claire yawned. Emil did the same. For ten, maybe fifteen minutes they waited in silence. Then an expression of alarm crossed Emil's face.

"Did I really hear him say this was a safe house?"

"I wasn't going to tell you that, but yes. Never used until now, apparently."

"When was it set up?"

"A few years ago? Why?"

"They'll know about it, or Krauss will. And if they doubled back and found our car tracks through the forest, and then traced us to Bernau, well . . ."

"How would Krauss know?"

"His work with the Spezialkommission. Counterintelligence asked them to keep track of the American safe houses on our side of the Wall. There were only a few, so it was an easy job, and he'd hardly forget this one."

"But it was never used. Maybe it stayed under the radar."

"You don't understand. We knew everything your people did over here. Everything. If you set up this as a safe house, we'd know. *He'd* know."

Buried within his urgency was a note of pride. Claire reflexively wanted to defend her own side before admitting to herself he was probably right.

"So you think he'll look here?"

"If they decide we haven't gone elsewhere, yes. Especially if they find the car."

"They'll certainly know we haven't reached Berlin base."

"Your boss communicates that closely with Kolkachev?"

"That's my take. Ron's, too."

He sighed, stood, flexed his right knee, and stepped to the front window. Like Kent, he peered out the edge in both directions without disturbing the blinds.

"Let's hope your colleague moves fast. If they saw him leave, they might decide it's the best possible time to strike . . . Scheisse!"

"You see something?"

"No. But I just remembered. Krauss actually came up with a good idea about these safe houses, and it was readily adopted. For each one, we obtained access to a nearby building and connected the properties through adjacent basements. Depending on the architecture, we built interior passages up from belowground—through air shafts, between fire walls, that kind of thing, to allow for secret entry. It was all ridiculously elaborate, like so much of what we did, but Krauss received a medal of commendation from Honecker himself. Not that we ever used a single one, as far as I know."

"Until today, anyway."

"Yes. And if they used your colleague's departure as their trigger action . . ."

"Where'd they put the entries?"

"Closets, attics, wall panels."

"We better start looking."

Emil unfolded his coat from the arm of the couch, pulled out the Pistol-M, and headed for the bedroom. Claire stepped toward the kitchen, but stopped first at the front window, and this time pulled back the blinds for a clearer look just in time to see a blurred figure in a dark tracksuit disappear into the doorway below.

"Too late!" she shouted. "Someone's on his way up!"

She looked for something she could use as a weapon, and settled on a small heavy lamp on an end table. She yanked out the plug, wrenched off the shade, and backed against the wall by the doorway while holding the lamp to one side, like a batter waiting on a fastball.

There was no sound from the stairwell, either from the shutting of the downstairs door or from approaching footsteps. She kept her eyes on the handle as several seconds passed. Emil hadn't said a word from the bedroom, which was worrisome, but she needed to stay quiet.

The handle began to turn, slowly. She tensed, tightening her grip on the lamp.

A grunting noise came from the direction of the bedroom, although it sounded as if it were coming from behind the walls. The door in front of her flew open. Claire swung the lamp as hard as she could, but the intruder fended off the blow with a deft move of his forearm that knocked the lamp to the floor. It was one of the men who had tried to trap her at the café on Frankfurter Allee, the big one, beefy and tattooed. He held a gun but kept his distance, poised to fend off any further blows.

"Where is he?" the man asked in heavily accented English. "We don't want you or your colleague, but if either of you tries to stop us, we will respond with force."

Claire said nothing. She began to back away to block his path to the bedroom, which had gone silent. She hoped Emil was still on the prowl.

"Stop now, or I will shoot you."

His tone, and what she already knew of their handiwork, convinced her to do as he asked. He pivoted and moved against her from behind with alarming suddenness, wrapping a heavy forearm around her neck and pulling her close enough to speak directly into her ear. His breath smelled of alcohol and onions.

"Just because we've been asked to keep you alive does not mean we will succeed. Nor does it mean we can't enjoy you first. All of us. Now, tell me, where is Emil Grimm?"

Before she could answer, there was the sound of a struggle from the bedroom, followed quickly by a gunshot.

56

It had occurred to Emil as he entered the narrow bedroom that he already knew how Kolkachev's people would approach an assault on this safe house. He knew because his own agents had learned the same techniques, borrowed from the same KGB doctrines, and the guiding philosophy in an action like this was simple enough: Come at your enemy from as many directions as possible simultaneously. That way, one of you will almost certainly strike at a weak spot, if only by default.

And because he also knew the likely players would be Yuri Volkov and his two minions, two approaches already seemed obvious—through the main door, and through whatever secret entry Krauss must have told them about. The third direction? His mind was still working on that, although for the moment he was preoccupied by a grunt of effort and a scraping noise coming from behind the wall of the bedroom closet.

He carefully opened the closet door just as Claire shouted from the living room that someone was headed up the stairs.

So that was one of Volkov's men accounted for, and now a second one, as two feet emerged from an opening in the side wall of the closet. Emil knew that the most effective response would be simply to shoot the man as he emerged.

His calculation changed as he heard the sound of a brief struggle from the living room, and then a man's voice speaking to Claire. He couldn't make out the words, but at least she hadn't been shot.

In the closet, the legs emerged, then the arms and torso, and finally the man's head. He was holding a gun, and as soon as he saw Emil he rolled onto his side to try and get off a shot, so Emil fired first, into his chest. The man crumpled, moaning. His gun fell to the floor, and Emil kicked it away.

Footsteps were approaching from the living room. It was at that moment that he realized where the third approach would come from, as his mind seized on a memory from an HVA training manual: the rooftop, of course. They would use a grappling hook and a stout line to rappel down to the rear window and swing through, feetfirst.

Just as this occurred to him there was a loud crash and a cascade of shattering glass to his rear, and before Emil could even turn around he was jarred off his feet by the impact of heavy boots into the small of his back. The Pistol-M went flying as he caught his fall. Someone was now on his back, grabbing the neck of his shirt, the belt of his trousers, then pinning him to the floor. A voice breathed into his right ear, breathless and rasping. It was Yuri Volkov.

"We have you now, Emil. And it will not pass quickly."

Emil felt himself being lifted to his feet as easily as if he were a sack of beets, and saw his pistol go skittering across the floor as Volkov kicked it away. A gun barrel poked into the nape of his neck, while Volkov wrapped his other arm around Emil's chest. On the floor of the closet, the first man had passed out in a pool of his own blood.

Then Claire and another of Volkov's men appeared in the bedroom doorway, standing side by side. He held a pistol. She was empty-handed.

Emil's mind offered him a fresh calculation, whether he wanted it or not. Two of them held guns, and both were fit and free to act. Claire was momentarily free as well, but unarmed, and Emil might as well have been a goat, trussed for slaughter. There was no sign of Ron Kent, nor any noise of his approach. Even if he arrived, he was unarmed.

Obviously, this wasn't going to work out, and, as Volkov had just said, it probably wouldn't pass quickly. Maybe they would at least leave Karola alive.

57

As Claire came into view of the bedroom, she saw a living, breathing Emil Grimm, and, briefly, was thrilled. She then noted the gun barrel at Emil's neck, and the muscular man who gripped him from behind, and reassessed.

Moving alongside her was the Russian who had come in through the door. He, too, was taking stock of the scene as they approached the bedroom doorway in tandem. He had released her at the sound of the gunshot, but still held his gun. Not an advantageous position for her or for Emil. The dropped lamp was well out of reach.

She now recognized the man holding Emil as Yuri Volkov. He shoved Emil through the doorway and spoke as they advanced.

"We are taking Herr Grimm with us, plus whatever he brought with him. Step aside or be shot. Your choice."

She stepped aside, and in doing so spotted the body of the third man on the floor of the open closet, which explained the gunshot. In the middle of the bedroom floor lay Emil's Pistol-M, but in her current position she'd never reach it without drawing fire from at least one of the two remaining Russians.

Volkov spoke.

"Maxim, check the living room closet."

The Russian to her right did so, and immediately found the pilot's case and the folder propped next to it. He flipped the latches on the case, checked inside, then returned to her side.

"Looks like it's here, all of it."

Claire realized belatedly that, by watching, she had missed her best opportunity to rush into the bedroom. And where the fuck was Ron? She listened in vain for the sound of footsteps from downstairs. He should have returned by now. Had the Russians dealt with him already?

All four of them now stood near the middle of the living room. She caught Emil's eye. He blinked, seeming resigned. But after everything he'd told them about the fates of Lothar Fischer and Andreas Plotz at the hands of Yuri Volkov, there was no way she was going to let Volkov take Emil out of here, not if she could help it.

She wondered why they would even bother now that they had all of his goods. Out of cruelty and malice, for having made them work so hard? Or was their reasoning more pragmatic—to find out from Emil whether he had any further allies who needed to be erased? Karola, for one.

Claire slid marginally to her left. She was now the closest of the four of them to the bedroom door, and they were arrayed so that once she got through the doorway, she would momentarily be out of the line of fire. She was poised to bolt when the bigger Russian, who must have realized the same thing, grabbed her right forearm and dragged her toward him.

"Nyet," he muttered, shaking his head. "Don't move again."

He raised the barrel of his gun to her temple just as footsteps pounded heavily up the stairs. Then he released her to redirect his aim toward the doorway. Claire swung her elbow in a blow to his chin, which knocked him off balance long enough for her to level him with a swing of her fist to the bridge of his nose. He dropped to his knees with a roar of pain, the gun falling. She kicked it away and it spun beneath the couch.

Volkov twisted Emil to one side and took aim at the door over Emil's shoulder as the door opened. Emil thrust his right elbow into Volkov's stomach, jolting him enough to make the shot go high. It blew a shower of plaster from the ceiling that pelted them all.

Volkov shouted angrily and threw Emil to the floor as he turned his gun on Claire, who crouched instinctively, watching the man's eyes. She was deciding whether to dive left or right when another gunshot resounded from across the room in more of a cough than a blast.

The side of Volkov's head erupted, throwing a spray of blood, bone, and viscera onto Claire atop the white dust that had already coated her from the ceiling. She shuddered like a wet animal, then came up out of her crouch to see Clark Baucom in the open doorway, breathing deeply, face sweating, a look of primal rage in his eyes. His blue wool overcoat was as powdered and spattered as Claire, but all three of them were still standing.

In his right hand was the vintage High Standard HD 22. Steam was drifting from the suppressor at the end of its long and slender barrel.

Then, more footsteps, rising from below. Baucom turned, Emil pivoted, and Claire picked up the fallen lamp for the possibility of more action when all of them saw it was Ron Kent, a late arrival to the party.

"About goddamn time," Baucom said. "What the hell were you even doing down there?"

"I fucked up," he said, panting, then looking at the floor. "I was looking for more of them, but, well . . ."

Then, seeing Claire and the mess she was in, he tentatively came forward.

"You okay?"

"Yeah," she said, her voice emerging in a croak. The fallen Russian to her right groaned and wobbled as he tried to stand. Claire swung the lamp against the base of his skull with a crack. He moaned and collapsed back onto the floor.

Only then did she notice that she was covered with gore—on her arms, her chest, and no doubt her face. She swallowed hard and tried not to shake.

The only one of them who hadn't yet spoken was Emil. Claire looked in his direction to make sure he had come through everything in one piece. He said nothing, but nodded stoically, as if to acknowledge her concern.

And for that one moment, at least, the four of them were comrades in arms, comrades in secrecy; comrades in everything that this profession of theirs had ever compelled them to do on behalf of duty or country.

58

Surprisingly—or perhaps not, considering where they were—Emil Grimm was the one who seized control in the aftermath. Even as one man lay dead, a second lay prone in a closet, and a third moaned and twitched on the bloodied floor, Emil strolled briskly downstairs to address a small crowd of neighbors who had come out into the night to see what all the noisy fuss was about in the apartment that had been empty for so long.

An older woman wearing a nightdress beneath a moth-eaten overcoat accosted him immediately.

"Were those gunshots?"

"No, no. A nail gun. Some workers. There was an accident, a few broken windows, but order has been restored, and now I must use your telephone to call for medical help."

Without hesitation, he showed her his Stasi ID. She eyed him carefully for a second or two and invited him inside. Emil reached Dorn right away. He gave a brief description of what had happened and asked him to bring at least three men. After hanging up, Emil vowed to never show his ID again. If he had been able, he would have burned it on the spot.

Kent and Baucom were initially appalled by his decision to call the detective. But Claire, having already glimpsed the dynamic between Emil and Dorn, surmised that it was just the right move, although she was still a little unsteady from all that had just occurred.

Emil went back downstairs to continue placating the neighbors.

The three Americans decided it was best if they remained out of sight for the moment, so they waited for Dorn in the kitchen, where they wouldn't have to keep looking at the bodies. Baucom had trussed up the two living Russians with butcher's twine from a kitchen drawer. The biggest one, in the living room, was still groaning, only woozily conscious.

Kent was extra solicitous with Claire. He wetted a dishtowel at the sink and approached her with a look of concern.

"Here. I'll clean you up."

She nodded and held still. His motions were tender, caring. The coolness of the wet towel was calming. Baucom, sensing he was intruding on something, retreated into the living room for a smoke. Kent spoke to her in a low, soothing voice.

"She'll still do business with him, you know."

"Ward, you mean? With Kolkachev?"

He nodded as he wiped her forehead.

"She's decided he's a worthy asset. Having Volkov out of the picture only makes him more desirable. Less baggage for down the road."

"She's that cynical?"

"I thought we all were. Oh, and another thing I should tell you. Ward's had me working under a cover name."

"I figured that was the case, but didn't want to make an issue of it. Do I ever get to know the real you?"

"Paul Bridger."

"Yes. You're definitely more of a Paul than a Ron. I've also noticed you've stopped calling her Lindsey."

He reddened, then smiled.

"I hope you don't think my loyalties are always so easily swayed."

"Only when truth and honor demand it. Not that we talk very much about them in this business."

Dorn arrived soon afterward. Baucom retreated back into the kitchen, and the three of them listened while Emil, out in the living room, calmly offered a blow-by-blow of the events of the past hour as the men paced between the living room and the bedroom. The detective's responses were probing, but only to a point. Partly, she supposed, because he was already familiar with Volkov's doings, but also because he already seemed intent on negotiating the rapids of change, a nimble paddler who was quickly finding his way. She noted that each man seemed to hold leverage over the other, although it was difficult to judge which of them held the upper hand.

Then their voices went silent. Footsteps thumped toward the kitchen, and Dorn loomed in the doorway, hands on his hips as he eyed the three Americans and a new arrival.

"You're multiplying in number. Not good. I also see that you ignored my request to leave by midday, but for the sake of consistency I will continue to refer to you in my reports as Herr Grimm's 'friends'— although only if, this time, you depart as soon as I'm done with you."

"Gladly," Claire said. Kent and Baucom nodded in assent.

"Very well. I now need to hear your versions. Propriety calls for separate interviews, but the need to have you on your way has persuaded me to let you do this as a group, out in the room where it happened. So, if you please . . ."

He gestured them through the door.

Ron Kent—or Paul Bridger, as Claire now knew him—asserted himself to offer his version first, seemingly out of a need to confess that he had failed his colleagues.

He'd been returning from the Turkish takeout with a bag of food, his distress call completed, when from a few blocks away he saw a man enter the downstairs door. Being unarmed, he paused to assess his next move, racking his brain to figure out how he might procure any sort of weapon, or what might be the best course of action.

"I guess I froze," he said. "Brain-locked, or whatever you want to call it. Not for long, but long enough."

Not until he heard a gunshot, and then saw Baucom come into view from the other end of the street, had he concluded that his wavering indecision might be fatal, so he then broke into a sprint, and arrived too late to do anything but watch. In his belated urgency, he had somehow never dropped the bag of food, which now sat on the floor in a corner of the room emanating a vague aroma of onions, yogurt sauce, and greasy shaved meat. Forever afterward Claire would associate the smell of a doner kebab with this moment.

Baucom, in his account, said he had initially followed Claire from her hotel room in Berlin, but later set off after the Russians after crossing their paths near the dacha. They'd eventually led him here. Claire then told her version. As Dorn questioned her, it became clear that he had settled on a characterization of Yuri Volkov as "a Russian with mob ties and a history of violent acts." She was fine with that.

All the while, Volkov's body lay among them, his mouth wrenched open by his final gasp of agony, showing his teeth like those of a felled predator of the forest. Claire studiously avoided looking in his direction.

Grimm stood on the far side of the room as everyone else talked. He gazed out a window and smoked an unfiltered cigarette that he kept having to relight. His face was unreadable.

When Dorn was finished, he summoned the members of the ambulance crew, who had already removed the wounded man in the closet, to take away Volkov. The next time Claire looked at where he had fallen, there was only a dark, sticky blotch upon the floor to account for his presence.

A few feet away, the third Russian, still on his stomach with his hands tied snugly behind his back, finally opened his eyes. Claire, not caring if it was proper or not, bent down and whispered in his ear.

"Enjoying me yet, comrade?"

The ambulance crew then returned to take him away as well.

Shortly afterward, an American in his late twenties, wearing khakis and a puffy down jacket, came briskly up the stairs to announce that he had come to retrieve the three of them.

"I brought my own car," Baucom said.

"We've already taken possession of it. I'm also supposed to tell you that you've been reassigned to Prague, effective retroactive to last Tuesday."

"Reassigned? Hell, I'm retired."

Claire immediately saw the move for what it was, a lifeline for Baucom to avoid any punishment, and a means of saving face for Ward.

"Don't look a gift horse in the mouth, Clark."

He shook his head, trying unconvincingly to look upset, when instead he was probably now the happiest man in the room.

"What about our car?" Bridger asked.

"We've taken possession of that as well."

Then, with unmistakable smugness, the young man made it known that all of them would be facing hours—perhaps days—of debriefing, which would be presided over by a gray eminence of counterintelligence from the highest corridors of Langley.

Claire would have found this more daunting if she hadn't already known this was a reference to the recent arrival who had bumped Lindsey Ward from the VIP suite at Harnack House, and that his main reason for coming here was Markus Wolf, not them.

She shared that with Bridger, who seemed relieved to hear it. It felt like another brick in the wall they had begun building between themselves and Ward. If Bridger had failed them in a moment of hesitation, she felt sure he would be steadfast in the coming battle to define this op. They also had the valuable items in the pilot case on their side of the ledger, and the information in Emil's folder, which in the long run might count for even more.

What none of them could have yet known was that, four years later, a fifty-two-year-old CIA officer based in Langley, Aldrich Ames, would be arrested and unveiled as the most destructive mole in Agency history, and that a key piece of evidence against him would be his use of a dead drop under a pedestrian bridge in a park near Little Falls Parkway. Also by that time, Operation Rosenholz, as this near fiasco would come to be known, would have earned a status as one of the CIA's top achievements of the Cold War, for its retrieval of the complete set of East Germany's agent files for all of its operatives in the West. Meanwhile, a Russian source known as "Leonid" would still be active, run by Lindsey Ward, who by then would be serving only two seats below the director's chair.

Dorn returned to the room just as the young CIA man excused himself to wait outside.

"Four of you now." He shook his head, then turned toward Emil. "Grimm, if you wish, I will give you a ride to pick up your car. Frau Weber has regained full consciousness, and she's been asking for you."

Emil nodded, brightening for the first time in hours. Then he turned, and his eyes sought out Claire, who crossed the room to meet him.

"I am going to do everything I can to assure safe passage for both of you," she said.

"I think we both know that's not your decision to make."

"But I'll have an influence. We all will."

"I trust you. I'm just not sure I believe you."

"I understand."

He nodded again and bowed slightly, almost courtly in his gestures. Then he put on his wool flat cap and followed Dorn down the stairs. Claire moved to the window and watched them emerge into the street, where they climbed into a green-and-white police car. Another Wartburg, which made her smile.

As it drove out of sight, Grimm's wool cap was a dark smudge behind the window.

She felt certain that she would never see him again.

59

Emil took Karola home from the hospital later that night. They slept at her house to avoid the lingering smokiness of the dacha.

Dorn had treated him remarkably well. Now that the lieutenant's murder case was effectively closed—with one of the chief suspects in the Bernau morgue, and the other two in custody—he no longer seemed interested in badgering Emil to return the strips of microfilm. Or, maybe, having met the Americans, he had already concluded who Emil must have given them to. Being a realist, he also knew that Kolkachev would almost certainly remain beyond his reach.

"What will you do about Krauss?" Emil had asked him.

"I've been in touch with the new interior minister, Herr Diestel. He assures me they are eager to receive any and all evidence with regard to Krauss's role in these matters. He was also quite interested to hear of Krauss's unauthorized new offices."

Emil had smiled in admiration.

"I have a feeling you won't be driving a Trabi much longer, Lieutenant Dorn."

Dorn had smiled back but said nothing further.

In the morning, Karola looked nearly like her old self, although her voice was still raspy. Emil brought her coffee in bed and showed her the passport the Americans had made for her.

"My very own escape and evasion kit. Isn't that what we used to call this?"

"We still do. Even those of us with only one more paycheck coming. But I must ask you something important."

She put aside her mug of coffee and folded her hands on top of the sheets. She looked a little nervous.

"All right, go ahead."

"Are you prepared to leave this place behind forever?"

She smiled, seemingly relieved.

"My God. I was worried you were about do something silly and inappropriate, like proposing marriage. Already I was imagining how I would explain it all to Bettina. But, yes, I am prepared for that, as long as you're coming with me."

He leaned lower to kiss her.

"I am. First, we will say farewell to Bettina. Tomorrow. A private ceremony."

"Yes. She'd want it that way."

They took a rowboat out into the Bauersee to scatter his wife's ashes, although Emil kept a small vial for himself. It was one of several things they did over the next few days, setting their affairs in order for travel, even though their destination wasn't yet clear. Karola contacted her eldest son, who would take over the house in Prenden and its farmland—as long as the new government didn't confiscate them first.

On the fourth day, a young and cheerful man from the U.S. embassy arrived in an official car, asked a few questions, and snapped a photo of Emil against a pale backdrop. He returned the following morning with yet another passport. Like Bettina's, it was West German.

"We think this one will work better for you than that other, older one you had. Plus, it's good for another ten years."

The man called himself Carl Adams. It was almost certainly a fake name.

"Thank you, Carl. I'm sure you're correct."

"I was also told to tell you that, while recent actions appear to have bought you some time, no one believes you should wait more than a week before putting this item to good use."

"I quite agree."

Emil wasn't particularly fond of the new name they had chosen for him, but he was pleased with the cash balance of the account they had established under that name at a bank in Barcelona, so he supposed he could learn to live with it. Karola promised to come up with a more acceptable nickname. Eventually they decided she would just keep calling him Emil.

That night, they spent a few hours perusing maps and routes. Then they packed the Wartburg for the drive the following morning to West Berlin's Tegel Airport, where a pair of tickets to a warm destination near a Mediterranean shoreline would be waiting at the Lufthansa counter.

At dawn they made a final stop at the dacha. Movers would soon arrive to clear out the place. Items ruined by smoke would be tossed. The rest was salvage, although Emil had already donated his books to a library.

He couldn't bear to step back inside, so he waited while Karola did instead. She emerged a few minutes later with a snow globe from Bettina's closet. Emil remembered it as a gag gift for his wife from a long-ago weekend in the hilly Sächsische Schweiz region, near Dresden. The sight of it brought a tear to his eye.

"Why that, of all things?"

"Well, look at it, Emil. The trees, the little cabin, the snowflakes. To remind us of these woods, of course."

"Yes, these woods."

It was now early March. The snowfall of the previous days had melted, and in a few weeks the forest floor would begin sprouting with green. Trees would bud and bloom, and the contours of the hills would disappear into a verdant lushness, dense enough to make you wonder if winter had ever even existed.

Emil restarted his weary old car, and they drove away on the gravel lane, the Wartburg exhaling a final contribution of blue exhaust into the mist of the beeches and pines.

No one followed, and no one watched.

They reached the border in twenty minutes, and crossed without incident.

Acknowledgments

"Rosenholz," the CIA operation which features so prominently in this book, is historical fact. It did, indeed, result in the secret acquisition of the identities of more than a thousand foreign agents of the HVA, the East German intelligence service run by the Ministry for State Security, or Stasi. As this book also describes, those identities were contained in bits and pieces of interlocking information, like those of a jigsaw puzzle, that existed in three different files. You needed all of them to see the total picture.

The details and timetable of Rosenholz remain cloaked in secrecy. That's fine by me, because it leaves plenty of room for a writer's imagination to roam free. No one outside the CIA is yet even sure who sold, stole or handed over the records, or at what price, although theories abound:

Perhaps a KGB officer sold them for $1 million, after initiating the deal in Berlin and consummating it in Moscow. (Someone like Gregor Kolkachev, in other words.) Or, no, others say, the price was actually a measly $65,000, and the KGB man was in Warsaw. Still others maintain the seller was someone—or several someones—from inside the HVA, high officials who peddled the files in exchange for cash and protection from prosecution. (People like Emil Grimm and Lothar Fischer, in other words.) This latter version was supposedly favored by spymaster Markus Wolf, although his death in 2006 means he's no longer available for follow-up questions.

It's possible that both versions contain grains of truth, meaning there could have been competing bids involving sellers from the KGB and HVA. If so, it doesn't take much effort to see how that could have evolved into something dangerous, or even deadly.

Whatever the case, Rosenholz was an intelligence coup for the CIA, one that even the German government didn't find out about until 1998. The files then became a point of contention between the two countries until 2003, when the CIA finally turned them over to Germany—after making its own copies, of course. *The Washington Post*, which has written only sketchily of the op, later quoted a former intelligence official as saying, "When the complete history of the closing days of the Cold War is written, this will be one of CIA's greatest triumphs."

The most exhaustive published exploration of Rosenholz is a lengthy article in the January 2012 issue of the scholarly journal *Baltic Worlds* by Helmut Müller-Enbergs, a German political scientist, and Thomas Wegener Friis, associate professor at the Cold War Center of the University of Southern Denmark. But they, too, reach no firm conclusions.

A few other items worth noting:

In the months after the Wall came down, the CIA really did try to recruit HVA spies by cold-calling them from pay phones, like boiler room salesmen in a Florida real estate scam. When that tactic predictably yielded scant results, they began visiting HVA targets door to door—"like the goddamn Fuller Brush man," as Clark Baucom says in chapter 3. And, yes, one of the prime motivators for those approaches was an offhand comment by President (and former CIA Director) George H. W. Bush, who said, "I hope we're getting some of that," as he watched TV coverage of East German protesters throwing documents out the window of Stasi headquarters. *The Main Enemy*, a wonderful account of the CIA's Cold War endgame by Milt Bearden and James Risen, was invaluable in educating me about this strange and turbulent period in Agency history. The personal recollections of fellow author Bill Rapp, who worked for the CIA in Berlin at that time, were also quite helpful.

Markus Wolf really did have an A-frame dacha in the woods along the Bauersee, near the village of Prenden, where there was also a well-appointed HVA safe house. Wolf did indeed meet secretly with emissaries of the CIA as he was trying to negotiate his future in the chaotic months after the fall of the Berlin Wall, and he did so with his third wife, Andrea, at his side. The most prominent of those emissaries, dispatched personally by the CIA director, asked Wolf for help in identifying a KGB mole who had penetrated CIA headquarters. Wolf, in his 1997 memoir, *Man Without a Face*, says he politely declined, mostly because he had no information to offer. Of course, that's what you'd expect him to say.

To my knowledge, Wolf never actually bumped into a CIA operative in Czechoslovakia during a Warsaw Pact military exercise in 1978, as described in Chapter 19. But the colorful story that Clark Baucom tells in that chapter—of a pair of Western military attachés being waylaid by an irritated Soviet officer who then shows them his maps—is drawn from the real-life experiences of former military attaché Otto Chaney, an Army colonel, who later told his tale to a U.S. Congressional Committee. I learned about it thanks to former Army colonel William S. Gross, who passed it along after coming to one of my book events in Dallas.

Oh, and Stasi chief Erich Mielke really did keep the Berlin police files for the 1931 Bülowplatz murders—files which incriminated him as one of the killers. They were locked in a safe at his villa at Wannsiedlung Wandlitz. Go figure.

My research into what it must have been like to work for the HVA in those frantic months of early 1990 is indebted to many sources. Dagmar Hovestädt, spokesperson for Germany's Federal Commission for Stasi Records, provided helpful information on topics ranging from the date of the HVA's final paychecks to the level of ostracism Stasi employees soon began receiving from neighbors and friends.

Thanks also to the fantastic Stasi Museum, which is based in the agency's old headquarters on Normanenstrasse. It is a treasure chest of material, not least of which is Erich Mielke's office, perfectly preserved, along with several conference rooms, corridors and paternosters once used by him and other top ministry officials. Also helpful were my visits to gloomy Hohenschönhausen Prison, the DDR Museum, the Plattenbau Museum, the German-Russian Museum in Karslhorst (next door to the former KGB headquarters), and the following books: *The East German Handbook*, a compendium of items from the collection of the Wende Museum, produced by Benedikt Taschen; *The Firm: The Inside Story of the Stasi* by Gary Bruce; *The History of the Stasi* by Jens Gieseke; *East German Foreign Intelligence: Myth, Reality and Controversy*, edited by Thomas Wegener Friis, Kristie Macrakis, and Helmut Müller-Enbergs; *Seduced by Secrets: Inside the Stasi's Spy-Tech World* by Kristie Macrakis; *Battleground Berlin: CIA and KGB in the Cold War* by David E. Murphy, Sergei A. Kondrashev, and George Bailey; and *Betrayal: The Story of Aldrich Ames, an American Spy* by Tim Weiner, David Johnston, and Neil A. Lewis.

My own visit to Prenden and the wooded trails of the Bauersee in February 2020, just before the Covid-19 pandemic shut down travel around the world, were invaluable in helping me shape the book's plot and atmospherics, as was my visit to the former housing compound of East German leadership, at nearby Wannsiedlung Wandlitz, an eerily quiet sylvan refuge which still looks much as it did when Mielke, Erich Honecker, and all the others lived there.

I wouldn't have been nearly as comfortable with all this material if I hadn't lived and worked in Berlin from 1993 to 1996, only a few years after this novel is set. My first year there was particularly instructive because my office was initially in a battered old *Hinterhaus* just off Oranienburger Strasse, only a few blocks from Tacheles, the colony of squatting artists which is the setting for chapters 41 and 42. In those pre-gentrified days, the whole neighborhood was still something of a bohemian paradise, even though nearly every raffish block looked and smelled much as it had throughout the Cold War. I now realize I was privileged to have witnessed a brief, free-wheeling golden age, during which neither East nor West seemed to hold sway. At that moment, at least, the heart of the city seemed to truly belong to its inhabitants, and they honored that status with their joy and their creative energy. I also owe thanks to the 2017 book, *Berlin Calling* by Paul Hockenos, for its memories of the earlier years of that fleeting era.

As always, thanks also to the peerless editor, Edward Kastenmeier, and to all of the other wonderful people at Knopf, whose support, hard work, and good cheer improved and illuminated these pages; and to the incomparable agent Ann Rittenberg, for those same indispensable qualities.

A Note on the Type

This book was set in Janson, a typeface named for the Dutchman Anton Janson, but is actually the work of Nicholas Kis (1650–1702). The type is an excellent example of the influential and sturdy Dutch types that prevailed in England up to the time William Caslon (1692–1766) developed his own incomparable designs from them.